Unmistakably Yours

THANKSGIVING
BOOKS & BLESSINGS

COLLECTION ONE

UNMISTAKABLY YOURS

A Sweet Western Historical Romance (Rated PG)

Thanksgiving Books and Blessings Collection One, Book 7
and
Holidays in Mountain Home, Book 8

USA TODAY Bestselling Author
KRISTIN HOLT

Sweet Romances
Appropriate for All Audiences

The books in both series are loosely connected and may be read in any order.

To hear about New Releases, Special Sales, and *receive a FREE novella*, Sign up for Kristin Holt's Newsletter:

www.KristinHolt.com/newsletter

(note: Kristin is spelled with two i's, and is "e-free")

Unmistakably Yours

One Prize.
Two Contestants.
Three Miracles.

Mountain Home, Colorado
August 1887

Expanding T.A. Murphy's Grocery Emporium into the adjacent store should be easy, as he and the landlord already shook hands. Yet his clueless neighbor, Miss Jane Vancoller, intends to enlarge her silly tea room into the not-so-vacant premises. The Tea Room is plenty large, but the Grocery Emporium must stockpile adequate winter supplies before winter's blizzards close off the high mountain valley.

Negotiations should be simple, but the landlord delights in pitting Hank and Jane against one another and foolishly involves the community— and the annual harvest celebration— in the business decision. The festive atmosphere tempts matchmakers to unite the disparate Tea Room and Grocery Emporium, along with incompatible Hank and Jane.

Discovering a solution...
Warding off misguided matchmakers...
Uniting two hearts ravaged by the past...
... will take a Thanksgiving miracle!

All Stories in the Thanksgiving Books & Blessings Collection

(beginning with earliest time setting)

GONE TO TEXAS
Book One, *by Caryl McAdoo*

GATEWAY TO THE WEST
Book Two, *by Susette Williams*

TRAIL TO CLEAR CREEK
Book Three, *by Kit Morgan*

HEART AND HOME
Book Four, *by P. Creeden*

NO TURNING BACK
Book Five, *by Lynette Sowell*

DAUGHTER OF DEFIANCE
Book Six, *by Heather Blanton*

UNMISTAKABLY YOURS
Book Eight, *by Kristin Holt*

ESTHER'S TEMPTATION
Book Nine, *by Lena Nelson Dooley*

Dedication

And to Rocky V. Palmer: Friend, Reader, Hero, and Copy Editor extraordinaire.
Naming a hero (if only his middle name) after you seemed highly appropriate. Again.

Copyright

eBook and Paperback Cover Art © 2018 by Carpe Librum Book
Design: www.carpelibrumbookdesign.com
eBook and Paperback interior design template © 2018 Caryl
McAdoo.
Copy editor- RVP The Man Editing:
rvpthemanediting.weebly.com/

Unmistakably Yours

Historical Note

Throughout the nineteenth century, the term "lovers" was <u>G-rated</u> and was a common word used for a couple in love. The term "making love" was also <u>G-rated</u> and widely used for the process of falling in love or nurturing the bonds of love. Both terms were widely used in delicate and mixed company, by preachers, newspapermen, and the general public. (See *A Note from the Author* at the end of this book for links to citations.)

Social clubs increased in popularity throughout the latter nineteenth century. One reason was the invention of and increasing availability of labor-saving devices. Social clubs sprang up in small towns, rural areas, and in cities of all sizes. Many clubs were specific to young men or young women of courtship age and designed for culturally acceptable purposes (like arranging for chaperoned dances). The wide variety of social clubs was significantly different from the "gentleman's club" model of the aristocracy in eighteenth- and nineteenth-century London, in that the social clubs were not both a physical location and a membership-only connection. Ladies' social clubs in the Victorian-era United States included everything from Ladies' Library clubs to Bachelors' Clubs for Defense during leap years to the more casual sewing circles and quilting circles in American folklore.

Let our
LIVES
be Full
OF BOTH
Thanks &
GIVING

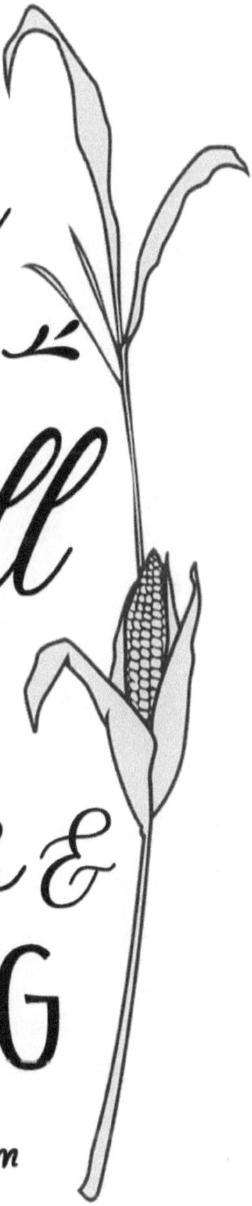

www.KristinHolt.com

"Where there is great love, there are always miracles."

Attributed to Willa Sibert Cather (1873-1947)
American Novelist

Chapter One

Mountain Home, Colorado
August 1887

"Oh, no. No, no, no. This will *never* do." Mrs. Ann Abbott waved her fan at the blinding pace of a hummingbird's wings. "The heat is stifling. You should open the rear door."

Jane Vancoller, proprietress of the only tea room in Mountain Home, pasted on a pleasant smile— a skill she'd perfected. "Both doors are open to catch a breeze, if there were one. The striped awning arrived in a timely manner and saves us from direct sunlight."

The late summer heat tried the patience of all. The temperatures were uncomfortable but brought in a steady stream of visitors seeking shade, an icy beverage, and a rest. Behind the subtle fragrance of flowers, perfumes, tea, and pastries, the industrial odors of fresh paint and furniture oil smelled *new*. And remarkably like a dream come true.

"I told Mayor Abbott this morning," Ann said,

speaking of her husband, "this August heat has been dreadful. Mercury this high belongs to July, not temperate August. And certainly not so near September."

"Yes."

A crash reverberated through the wall. Jane flinched in her seat at one of the tables for two.

The pesky Murphy boys played marshals and train robbers in the vacant store between their father's grocery and the Tea Room. Why didn't the little varmints play in the meadow a half-block away?

One boy whooped and hollered, and Jane resisted the urge to massage her temples.

"I suppose we can't blame you for the heat or the uncommon noise next door." Mrs. Abbott, thin to the point bony prominences showed in her small hands and wrists, was given to sour expressions. How a thin, pinched woman possessed a full-bodied voice, Jane would never understand. "I must say it's stuffy in this little room, much more than in my rose garden."

Fortunately, Jane also had tremendous practice keeping retorts to herself. She held silent and watched as Ann perused the Tea Room's parlor— and tried to see the decor through the other woman's narrowed eyes.

Would Ann see past the heat, past the thud of little feet against bare floorboards, to the peaceful and serene setting? Would she appreciate the delicate rosebud-painted teacups? Or the quality of the china service?

Wallpaper and matching draperies brought a sense of home to the feminine retreat.

At the height of beauty, lacy tablecloths and fresh flowers graced each of nine circular tables. Half of the small tables seated two; half seated three or four. The arrangement was ideal for intimate conversations, quiet reflection, or the gathering of friends. A place for women.

Another thump sounded through the wall, immediately chased by the rapid pounding of running feet. What were those boys up to?

Inside two weeks, the demon horde of Murphy boys would be enrolled in school, and days in the Tea Room would be peaceful.

Rather than explain all that, Jane allowed Ann's perusal. At the moment, guests were seated at two of the nine tables. Harriet, Jane's only employee, rolled the new teacart from kitchen to dining room and their guests. Chilled dessert dishes held dainty scoops of rapidly melting lemon snow.

Ann took a delicate sip of tea. She carefully lined up the decorative handle of the demitasse spoon with her saucer.

"You haven't many chairs." As usual, Ann ignored the finer points and spoke plainly. "What? Twenty, maximum?"

"Twenty-four." Jane held her pleasant expression, though she wanted nothing more than to terminate the interview. Yes, she needed the money the meeting would bring but desperation would give away Jane's secret.

Ann took up the rapid beat of her fan once more. "I can't picture this small room, crowded with thirty men and women."

Seating that many in mixed company would require removing the tables and bringing in chairs.

"We'll manage."

"I cannot picture men here, can you?" Ann seemed to smile behind her teacup.

"Neither can I, Mrs. Abbott."

Ann sighed. "I'd wanted this to work. Truly, I did. Now that I've seen your lovely little tea room, I believe I've no choice but to host the committee meeting in my rose garden."

The entire community knew how Ann Abbott took pride in her rose garden and her wealthy husband's place at the top of Mountain Home society, such as it were. She took immense pride in her role at the head of the annual harvest festival committee, as well as many other clubs and organizations, including Jane's beloved Ladies' Library Association.

Jane took pride in her tea room. She wouldn't change it to accommodate men.

"Darling—" Ann pinned her dark eyes on Jane. "Why on earth did you make your ladies' tea room so small?"

"I didn't—"

"You do understand," Ann said, as if Jane hadn't spoken, "we can't afford to lose a single contributing member of our committee. The festival is in six weeks. *Six weeks.*"

"Of course." Jane understood; she couldn't afford the loss of a single customer.

"It's not too late, you know. You ought to speak to my husband. Mayor Abbott still hasn't rented that real estate."

She'd thought about leasing both— and now wished she'd found the means. She had no trouble conjuring the clatter of twenty-dollar gold pieces falling into the mayor's coffers.

"Remove that wall," Ann continued her grand vision, raising both hands to sweep the vista. "Expansion will give the front wall another set of windows. Move the library shelves to that wall and banish those naughty children to the great outdoors."

Jane would have smiled at that, had she been able. The paint had barely dried. Ann's orders for renovation sounded like money. *Lots* of money.

"I—" Jane's throat dried to the point of pain. She liked her tea room just as it was. If she must expand to meet the demands of her clientele, merely to pay the lease...

"Good." Ann patted her lips with a white linen napkin and set it beside her plate. "I knew you'd want to please us."

"Yes." Renovating would decimate her savings. "Of course."

"I suppose the Ladies' Library Association could attempt to meet here— *once*. Before construction begins. We have the ticket supper to organize and six short weeks to accomplish it."

Why did Jane feel grateful for that scrap?

"If you begin now, you'll have the construction out of the way before the harvest festival. We'll hold our completion meeting here. By then October's cold will be upon us."

Jane nodded, fighting to hold her tongue and retain her false smile. What choice did she have but to keep her most important customers happy?

Burdened with a tray of carefully stacked china cups and saucers, Jane backed through the swinging doors into the Tea Room's kitchen. A steady stream of guests, one and two at a time, had kept them busy. She and Harriet had a short two hours to wash dishes, clean the dining room, and prepare for a bridal tea to be held at five o'clock.

She turned, heading for the sink, and drew up short.

One filthy Murphy boy, wrist-deep in *wedding cake.*

"*Stop.*" Horror clutched her throat.

The wedding cake round had been in the ice box. Perfectly frosted. Ready.

Now, the ice box door hung open letting out all the cold.

The largest of three cakes, was toppled upside down on the floor where the terror had dropped it.

The expensive china nearly slipped from her tray. "What are you doing?"

Icing clung to the boy's chin, lips, and cheeks. Had he bitten into the cake, a pig at a trough? He broke off an enormous lump of cake and with a smirk, stuffed it into his mouth.

"Oh, no you don't." Jane settled the dishes, then grabbed for the urchin's arm.

He ducked beneath the table.

Fingertips brushed the dirty linen shirt but missed boy.

"Harriet," Jane yelled. "Help!"

The imp bolted for the door. Jane caught him by the upper arm just as he cleared the threshold. Instantly, the kid dropped. He plunked his little body onto the alleyway dirt and squirmed for freedom. Bare, dirty heels struck her shins.

"Oh, no you don't, young man. On your feet." She clutched him by both arms and wrested him to stand. He resisted, curling his legs beneath him.

Had no one taught the youngster proper behavior?

Harriet's footfalls sounded her approach. "What has he done?"

"Destroyed the wedding cake." Icing clung to her overskirt where the varmint had wiped his hands. "Fetch Mr. Murphy, will you?"

Odd, but the ragamuffin said not a word. If Mr. Murphy *ever* disciplined this son, or any of his brood, perhaps the boy would show a scrap of fear.

Male laughter and conversation came from the adjacent store— adult men, this time.

"I believe," Harriet said, tipping her head toward the voices, "he's next door."

Jane hefted the lad high enough to carry about his ribs and suffered bruising blows to her shins for the effort.

As her mother had done before her, Jane pinched the boy's arm to command his attention. "Cease this instant. Your behavior is deplorable."

Harriet opened the rear door of the vacant store. The brat plastered the door frame with two icing-smeared hands and two filthy feet. Icing was made with butter, and butter made for a poor hold.

Jane had won that singular battle.

Now, to win the war.

Hank Murphy had his landlord right where he wanted him: smiling, nodding, and ready to shake hands.

"Given the past many winters," Hank told Mayor Abbott, "people should be storing additional foodstuffs, planning for the worst, but they're not." Rationally, he knew that wasn't entirely true. Ranchers and farmers put up food for winter. Even in town, ladies tended kitchen gardens and bottled the excess.

He'd talked to several who'd taken the last decade seriously, had enough for themselves, and had excess to share. "What about the townsfolk who don't prepare? 'We have a store in town,' they say. 'We'll buy what we need, or put it on credit.'"

"These are modern times." Abbott's heavy, thick mustache was stylish, but that didn't make it attractive. "Might you be irrational?"

Irrational? "I'm responsible to bring supplies into the valley, where they can be purchased." The burden kept him awake some nights.

The mayor's gaze roamed the sacks, barrels, and crates. Plenty more would be delivered in the weeks and months to come. As long as the trains kept running, he'd squirrel away more.

"You realize folks say this winter will be mild." Abbott's prominent brow puckered. "Not that I'm one of them, Hank, but you must know folks around here wonder if you're cracked."

"Let them talk." Come winter, all they'd wonder about was the cache he'd set aside, and if they'd be able to buy what they needed.

The mayor's gaze narrowed. "I've let you use this vacant real estate for months. It's time for me to collect on our agreement."

"I'm ready." Hank needed the space more than ever. "Let's shake on it."

Abbott grinned, supremely satisfied. "Four dollars a month, additional."

Four dollars! "Capital for winter supplies has to come from somewhere. How about a discount for leasing two stores?"

"Four bucks *is* my cut rate. I'd ask triple if leasing to someone other than a current tenant. Don't you think this prime real estate is worth my price?" The mayor's wide smile and the steadiness of his gaze underscored his lack of pretense. He believed this yet-to-be-rented real estate was worth that much.

Maybe, in another time, it would be.

The all-brick block that bore Abbott's name had been completed last spring, and most of the rental spaces snapped up quickly by merchants and professionals. Still, nobody had signed for this shop. Hank had been in the business long enough to know that if merchandise was overpriced, it wouldn't move. A man had to lower his price until the thing sold, value notwithstanding.

Some money was always better than none.

"You'll be doing a lot of good, helping secure grain

and beans. You'll be a hero, come winter, when the mountain passes are choked with snow and trains quit running."

"Hero, huh?"

"Yes, sir." Hank had no trouble sharing the responsibility or the glory. "I should've rented both spaces from the start."

Abbott's grin deepened. "I knew loaning you this place as a make-shift warehouse would help you see the light."

The landlord-mayor had more to say. At least another sentence. But the clatter of shoes upon floorboards and the hiss of angry female dragging a recalcitrant four-year-old at her side obliterated everything else.

Miss Vancoller. High color pinked her cheeks. Spirit sparked in her eyes. Her ramrod-straight posture and set of her jaw, like a barometer, announced what he already sensed deep in his bones.

A storm was brewing.

The overdressed, lace-and-china proprietress stomped her boot for emphasis as she halted. She swept young Clyde to her side, her clutch on his arm effective. *The duchess* consistently dressed all fancy, like she attended a wedding. Or funeral.

Mayor Abbott bowed slightly, lifting his hat to reveal a retreating hairline and dark curls about his ears. "Good day, Miss Vancoller."

The woman spared their landlord a glance. "Mayor." She spoke through clenched teeth.

His boy peeked around her voluminous skirts. The kid's eyes were the most expressive he'd ever known—

told a father everything.

Icing ringed the boy's mouth and clung to his chin. His hands were covered in cake and icing. As was the front— and now the side— of the lady's expensive overskirt. Washing couldn't save the pastel cotton.

She shook with indignation. Any moment, she'd open her mouth and peace would evaporate. So like a woman, wasn't it? Sweet as pie to her friends and a deadly viper to men. And active little boys.

He'd learned his lesson— no matter how lovely, a beautiful woman's nasty temper killed his interest in her right quick.

"*Mister* Murphy."

She sounded like a strict schoolmarm with a ruler in her fist and a penchant for smacking little boys' knuckles. Come to think of it, she sounded like every teacher he'd ever had. And his own mother.

He shouldn't needle her. Really, he shouldn't. Yet he lifted his flat cap and gave her a slight bow. "Miss Vancoller."

The woman pursed her lips. Impossibly, her posture straightened further. "I caught your son *in* the cake I'm to serve to paying guests in less than two hours."

His gaze slid to his son's for confirmation. Sure enough, the boy was guilty. If the icing hadn't given him away, the truthfulness in those expressive eyes admitted everything.

Hank had no trouble imagining the allure of cake and icing.

"He trespassed on my business property, *opened* the ice box, and pulled the cake out." She shivered, swinging her gold eardrops into motion. "He ate it *off the floor*."

The kid fought to free himself. "Release my son." He gestured to Clyde to come. "I'll pay for the cake."

"Oh, no you don't, Mr. Murphy. Your sons run wild, terrorizing our town and these premises." Her voice rose in pitch and volume. "I would think the landlord expects you to leave those children too young to work at home. Perhaps under the care of a nanny."

He'd tried to set aside his original opinion of her, but this put the icing on the cake.

"Why are you smiling?" The woman was a shrew. Demanding, bossy, and *impossible* to please. "Answer me. Why is this child running wild? I heard you'd hired a nanny."

Three or four questions asked, but he'd give a single answer. "He's four. Four-year-olds go where they please."

"Unacceptable. Four-year-olds obey their nannies, their parents, and adults."

"Like you?"

She gasped. "Yes, like me. Any obedient, reasonable child would respect an adult and her property. They need a nanny to teach them how to behave."

"No, they don't."

"They most certainly do." Miss Vancoller's lips firmed. "You *did* hire a nanny, didn't you?"

"I did. And my sons fired her."

Miss Vancoller blinked.

"You, madam, understand nothing about children."

This time, when he gestured to Clyde, he didn't allow the duchess to prevent his son's obedience.

She made a sound halfway between frustration and fury. "He destroyed my wedding cake."

"As I said, I'll talk to him. He won't do it again."

"That's not enough. The wedding cake your son ruined was purchased by Mrs. Cresswell for a bridal tea that begins in less than two hours."

Not much could be done about that now. "Did Clyde eat it all?"

She sputtered. "No, but—"

"Slice it, present pretty little pieces of cake on your pretty little plates." Contempt thickened his voice.

"Have you seen the cake? It's ruined." Fury climbed in the paleness of her freckled cheeks. "The bride's mother-in-law wanted the cake displayed. The bride is to cut the cake and serve her guests."

"Tell Mrs. Cresswell that's not possible. Or see if Whipple's has another. I said I'd pay for it."

She tossed both arms open wide. "I made that cake. *I* did. Not the bakery." She rolled her gaze heavenward. "Have you any idea how many hours' work went into that cake?"

He didn't want to know.

As if she finally noticed sacks of flour and jugs of molasses, she demanded, "Why are your stores here? Mrs. Abbott said, not five minutes ago, that this space is available."

"It is." Abbott sounded gleeful.

"It's not." Hank glared at the mayor. "As the mayor and I were discussing when you interrupted, I will rent this space. It's my storage room."

"No, Mr. Murphy. *You* are mistaken. Mrs. Abbott told me I must increase the Tea Room into this shop."

"Must?" He chuffed.

"My tea room serves a *vital purpose* in Mountain Home."

If silly lacy curtains and tiny chairs, little china teacups served a purpose, he couldn't find one. Except to tempt women to avoid work, ignore their children, and indulge in gossip. Oh, and find fault with their husbands. And stoke the fires of jealousy when women made comparisons.

That was a subject he wouldn't argue with her. Not now, not ever.

At his side, Clyde squeezed his daddy's hand and snuggled in close. The boy had always been sensitive to contention. When home had become a battlefield, he'd been inconsolable.

Miss Vancoller paused and pressed a palm over the lacy yoke of her pale green dress. Something was under there... a lump. Jewelry? An ugly wart?

"Miss Vancoller, you do realize the owner's wife is not authorized to enter into a contract."

"I know that." The venom had left her voice. "So now, Mr. Abbott, I'll speak to you about renting this store."

Hank propped his free hand on his hip. "As I said, Mr. Abbott and I came to an agreement."

They both looked to the mayor who lifted his shoulders with indifference.

"Abbott?" Hank nearly snarled.

"I don't have the lease agreement with me. Nothing is official without signatures."

"We shook hands."

"Actually, Murphy," the mayor replied, "we didn't."

"Nearly."

"We discussed the rent," Abbott mused. "At four dollars, fifty cents a month."

"*Four* dollars—"

"It's been entertaining and instructive, but I must be on my way." Abbott lifted his hat and without offering to shake Hank's icing-covered hand or risk dirtying his trousers from incidental contact with a four-year-old or the icing-smeared woman, gave them all a wide berth.

Hank called to the mayor's retreating back. "We'll finish this conversation. Tonight."

First and foremost, Archibald Abbott was a businessman. He'd named his price, and the fact that two storekeepers now vied for the space shouldn't raise the price... much. Maybe no more than that half-dollar. The expense couldn't be avoided, and Hank would make the money back when emergency supplies sold after the season's first blizzard.

"Good day." Abbott waved a casual goodbye.

Miss Vancoller folded her arms tightly. She inched up her chin. "Just so you know, Mr. Murphy, I intend to rent this space. I urge you to find a storeroom elsewhere." She strode with purpose to the back door. "I'd best not find your sons in my kitchen. Do try and teach them."

Hank wished he could say no woman had been this furious with him, but that'd be a lie.

Chapter Two

Hank carried Clyde through the back door into T.A. Murphy's Grocery Emporium and straight to the sink. Though a couple waited for service, Hank couldn't greet them in his present temper.

Oscar Harris, the pharmacist Hank had taken as a partner, wrapped a purchase. In seconds, he'd be free to see to the couple.

Hank balanced Clyde on his knee, boosting the boy's belly onto the porcelain sink. He turned the tap. Clyde plunged his hands into the stream.

At moments like this, Hank believed the expensive lease— with all the advances a new building offered, like hot and cold running water— to be money well-spent.

He savored the comfort of his sturdy son in the circle of his arms and forced the hitch in his shoulders to relax. He worked soap into a lather from Clyde's little hands to the elbows. Dirt and icing swirled down the drain. Much more followed when Hank took his soapy palm to the boy's face. Clyde needed a full bath, but that would have to wait.

Excitable Spinster Vancoller had been right about *one* thing— Clyde had no right to trespass and help himself to her baking.

Once their hands were dry, he sat on one heel to look his son in the eyes. "We've talked about this, Clyde. You must not go in Miss Vancoller's shop."

He didn't expect words, but regret filled the boy's luminous eyes. He'd learned. Love for this child swelled in Hank's chest. He'd suffered more than any of them. "Promise?"

Clyde nodded.

"That's my good boy."

"Yoo-hoo."

Hank's shoulders bunched, startled by the far-too-recognizable Ina Dimond. The flirty woman paid daily visits to the Emporium.

"I said, yoo-hoo, Mr. Murphy. Good afternoon to you." She stood at the glass counter, settling in for a lengthy chat.

After the catastrophe involving Clyde, wedding cake, and Miss Vancoller, he hadn't the patience. But a grocer must be every person's friend. That meant warm greetings and remembering names and details, so he set Clyde loose and greeted the lady.

"Thank you, Miss Dimond. A good afternoon to you."

"What are you doing, hiding behind the counter?"

The boy was long gone, but she'd witnessed the hand washing and likely the mud and frosting.

Hank detested meaningless chatter. Three days this week, she'd snared him into a twenty-minute conversation yammering on and on about nothing.

He cast about for a pressing task, any way to free himself from the woman's clutches.

"Miss Dimond." Oscar, apparently, could read minds. "We received a new carnation-scented soap, direct from New York City."

And just like that, Oscar saved Hank. True, Miss Dimond would be in the Emporium another half hour at least, but she'd leave with a fragrant bar of soap and a smile on her face.

One smile from well-dressed Oscar Harris, and she'd buy anything the man was selling.

But Oscar was so much more than twinkling blue eyes and overlong hair of dark blond. His charisma drew women to him. Most tripped over themselves to be near him.

Moments after Miss Dimond paid for her purchases and exited, Hank whispered to Oscar low enough so no one would overhear. "Thanks for distracting her."

"It's easy to show her a bit of attention. If kindness removes the target she pinned to your chest, so much the better."

"Thanks, friend. I'm not interested in romance, and I've told her in every way I know how."

Oscar assessed Hank. "She's lonely."

The man's speculation rang true— and that made Hank uncomfortable. Yes, he wanted her business, but that was it. One marriage had been more than enough for him, and Ina Dimond evidently had marriage on the mind.

The store was empty of customers at the

moment— not a desirable realization for any storekeeper, especially one who'd spent his savings to open and stock a fancy grocery emporium in the new, most stylish block in town.

Oscar reclaimed his stool behind the counter, rubbed his left knee, and grimaced. "How did the talk with the mayor go? Did he sign?"

"No."

"No?"

"I had the mayor seeing things my way when Miss Vancoller dragged Clyde in, covered in icing and cake, staking her claim on the vacant real estate at the top of her lungs. If Abbott's half the businessman I know him to be, he'll double his asking price. He knows one of us will pay it."

He ached to punch something. Or someone. He'd been so close!

From his stool, Oscar dusted the display shelves of patent medicines. The man always kept busy, cleaning, dusting, tracking inventory. "I recommend you tell Miss Vancoller why you need that space. Winter survival is far more important than her library."

Library? "It's a tea room."

"And a lending library."

The woman's purposes were far from life-or-death. "Books won't fill empty stomachs."

"I know that. I suggest you tell her this."

"Women cannot be reasoned with. Especially *that* woman."

"Most women I know are reasonable creatures."

"Not in my experience, but you're not required to agree with me." Hank opened the newfangled brass cash register and removed four dollars— more than enough to pay for the fanciest wedding cake ever baked or sold in Mountain Home. "I believe I'd best avoid Miss Vancoller for the near future. Take this to her, will you? For the cake." He'd record the expense in his ledger, though he doubted he'd forget.

Oscar accepted the money with a nod. "I will, as long as she doesn't shoot the messenger." He straightened the last bottle he'd dusted, then tucked the feather duster out of sight. "The way I see it, the only other option is to push forward with the mayor and get that contract signed."

"I like that idea better."

Jane met Mrs. Cresswell— mother of the bridegroom— at the Tea Room's door.

"Thank you for coming early, Mrs. Cresswell." Jane wiped her damp palms on her apron and drew a breath to calm herself.

"Your note didn't say what the trouble is." Maggie Cresswell, with more silver than dark brown in her hair, had a reputation for fairness. "Tell me, please. I'll help."

"I made the cake rounds this morning. They turned out beautifully, iced, finished..."

"What's done is done." Maggie put her arms around Jane as if they were mother and daughter. Or sisters.

Jane's heart squeezed in pain. Oh, how well she remembered embraces like this from Mother. How much she'd needed this, at the darkest point in her life. How much she needed the kindness, especially tonight.

The dear woman had paid well for the cake and for the evening's event to take place here. It would've been so lovely, if not for the naughty little brat—

"And?" Maggie prodded, slipping her arm through Jane's.

"One of the Murphy boys opened the lower latch on the ice box door and pulled the largest cake onto my floor. He ate it with his dirty hands. Where it lay."

"Oh, my. The poor mite needs a mother, doesn't he?"

Maggie sounded far from irate. Sympathetic, even.

"I have no wedding cake to display. It's not possible for the bride to cut the cake— I feared, given the unusually small pieces, that in her happiness she'd cut them too large and half her guests would go without. I shouldn't have— forgive me— I cut the small cake the boy didn't get to, only to realize I'd made the problem worse."

"I am disappointed." The sweet lady's lined face pinched but not in anger.

"I'm heartbroken, Mrs. Cresswell. I'll refund your money, of course. You paid for a wedding cake for the bride to cut. I can't meet that agreement."

"I believe that won't be necessary."

No one could be so generous... not even kindhearted Mrs. Cresswell. "You'll want to see it before you're so good."

Jane walked arm in arm with Mrs. Cresswell to the display table, draped with the Tea Room's best table cloth, displaying carefully cut slices of cake arranged upon pedestal cake plates.

Not a wedding cake, but if no one knew that had been the intention...

"You set a pretty table." Mrs. Cresswell smiled at Jane— a real, genuine smile. "Which Murphy boy, did you say?"

Had Mr. Murphy called the little monster by name? She couldn't recall.

She'd not asked— that much she knew. There were simply so *many* of them. And they all moved so quickly. "I don't know. One of the youngest?"

"Ah." Margaret patted Jane's back and eased away. "My Ray was a little boy, not so long ago. Among the naughtiest this town ever saw. And now? He's to be a husband."

Yes. Ray's bride would honor her bridesmaids tonight, here. Celebrating friendship and the newness of romantic love. With cake that had been lovely prior to a varmint invading her ice box—

"I'm not so old I don't remember the messes he made." Maggie squeezed Jane's hand. "Nor so old I don't recall how easily my boy made a mess of things while I wasn't looking."

Jane's chest throbbed with heartache. Which was worse? Loving, maternal replies to this fix, or a strong talking to?

Mrs. Cresswell smiled. "It's a good thing Ray's bride is a girl of good sense. She'll need it."

"She'll be upset when she sees the cake?"

"No. I meant that Ray remains rough around the edges," his mother whispered. "And, lovely lady that she is, I promise she won't care one whit that the cake is already cut."

True to the elder Mrs. Cresswell's word, the young, soon-to-be Mrs. Cresswell complimented the display table, thanked Jane and Harriet for their kindness, and dished the cake slices much as she would have, had she enjoyed cutting the cake.

If anyone noticed the miniature cake servings had been supplemented with heart-shaped lemon cookies from Whipple's Bakery, they said not a word.

At the earliest hour acceptable, Jane turned Mayor Abbott's doorbell key.

Mr. Murphy had spoken to Mr. Abbott about his intention to rent the empty real estate, and she'd do the same. He'd heard her express interest, but that wasn't enough.

Jane followed a stately, silver-haired man bearing a distinguished English accent through the home's vestibule and toward the in-home office the mayor favored above his city-provided room.

Who was this Englishman? She'd believed she'd known nearly everyone in Mountain Home.

The mansion's opulence was resplendent in the tasteful blend of summer draperies that kept the heat outside, thick carpets beneath her shoes, and the delicious scent of quality furniture oil.

The staircase and banister shone with a recent polish.

Evidently Mrs. Abbott paid her housekeepers well.

All acquainted with Ann Abbott knew she did not keep her own house.

The scent of roses hung in the air, melding deliciously with the lingering aroma of the mayor's cigars. Definitely Diamond brand. He'd purchased the costly cigars from Father's tobacco shop and, by all appearances, continued to favor them. More likely, he favored Diamond cigars *because* of the expense.

Nothing but the best for Mr. and Mrs. Archibald Abbott.

The English butler— *who* in Mountain Home employed a butler?— knocked on the office door, paused for a precise interval of two seconds, and opened the door. "Mayor Abbott, Miss Jane Vancoller to see you, sir."

"Thank you, Wells. Do come in, Miss Vancoller."

"Thank you," she said softly to the butler, then smiled warmly at Archibald Abbott as he rose to greet her. "Thank you for seeing me, Mayor Abbott." She'd done the right thing, it seemed, in waiting for the socially appointed hour.

How tempted she'd been to arrive at first light.

"Yes, of course." The mayor indicated a chair across from his desk.

Jane caught sight of the mayor's wife, Ann, seated in an upholstered wingback chair to the side of the desk.

"I'm so glad," Ann said with emphasis, "to see you're making the effort, Miss Vancoller."

"Thank you, Mrs. Abbott. I recall our conversation." She'd thought of little else.

Ann sipped from her teacup. "And your promise."

Ladies never held others to thin promises.

The statement stung, more than the breach of etiquette. Guests must be served tea before the hostess partook. The tea ritual always observed before conversation ensued— whether a social call or business, it mattered not.

Jane accepted the chair Mr. Abbott indicated and turned her attention fully to him. "I see you understand my purpose."

"Indeed, I do." He sat, eying her too closely, for a bit too long. "After my visit with Hank Murphy this morning, I'm pleased you'd pay a call."

That man! Her stomach sank to the vicinity of her knees. Already? Hank Murphy paid a call before a decent hour, intentionally undermining her efforts.

Dryness invaded her mouth. "Yes, sir."

"Oh, goodness. Where are my manners?" At the expensive tea service, Mrs. Abbott poured a fresh cup. With a knowing smile, she added cream and sugar. "I do know how you take your tea, do I not?"

Not. Jane enjoyed sugar but not milk; quality tea didn't need milk to offset bitterness.

"Thank you." She accepted the cup and saucer, relieved when her hands didn't shake. The bone china, so thin as to be opaque, easily cost four times that at the Tea Room.

Mrs. Abbott *did* enjoy the best things in life.

Jane took a sip to moisten her mouth and wet her voice. All that remained was to learn what their landlords intended. To whom would they lease the contested space?

She sipped again and nodded in appreciation of

the fine Indian tea— despite the flavor muddied with cream. No China tealeaves for Mrs. Abbott.

Mayor Abbott leaned back in his chair. The polished marble surface of his desktop reflected a bit of north-facing daylight allowed through lace curtains. "We've had a fortuitous conversation, Mrs. Abbott and I, after Mr. Murphy's call this morning. We've come to a decision."

Jane's heart rate spiked. So quickly? Without hearing her argument?

She'd never been a day late with her lease payments and never would be.

Mrs. Abbott had been adamant that the Tea Room expand. She must have spoken with her husband, in the Tea Room's favor.

Had Mr. Abbott chosen Mr. Murphy, anyway?

Mr. Abbott looked to his wife, so Jane did, too. Communication she couldn't understand passed between them, wordless, in the way of long-married couples.

She missed Law the most at moments like these. He'd smiled at her like this, across a crowded room, and she'd known the most delicious rush of awareness. He'd known her so well a mere expression would inform him of so much.

She came to herself, her fingertips upon the keepsake she wore about her neck, with memories threatening her ability to smile.

She pushed away topics she couldn't think about in public. Instead, she focused on her posture, on one more sip of tea with too much cream, and awaited the verdict.

Something told her she wouldn't like their decision. But what could she do? She was female with a mere five months' lease history, and she knew the way of things. Men preferred to rent to men.

Men who were undoubtedly flawed.

Enormous flaws, like irresponsible fatherhood. His band of sons ran wild. The brat who'd ruined her cake had been positively feral.

"As mayor," Mr. Abbott said from behind the massive desk, "I'm most concerned about the wellbeing of our town's citizens."

Translation: concerned how the decision would reflect upon him.

"We've determined to involve the citizens of Mountain Home."

Jane's mouth fell slack. The Abbotts were eccentric... but to include unaffected parties in a business decision?

She needed information but couldn't find the words to ask.

Mrs. Abbott bubbled over with self-important satisfaction. "Our little contest will work all sorts of wonders, Miss Vancoller. And bring additional business to the Tea Room, I assure you. We anticipate greater attendance at the Harvest Festival than ever before, because of our intention to involve each and every citizen in determining which of you wins the building."

"Wins?" Her question came out as a croak. They made the building sound like a prize.

She sipped tea, wishing the brew's restorative powers had taken hold.

"Indeed. You see, that desirable real estate isn't

about the money." The mayor's smile shone brighter than the gold stickpin in his necktie.

The Abbots had worked hard to secure their place near the top of Mountain Home's Society. Evidently, they aimed to reign as king and queen.

Mrs. Abbott set her teacup and saucer on the cart. "You'll hear a bit more at Tuesday's Town Council meeting."

A clear dismissal.

A dismissal that left her prepared argument useless.

With trembling fingers, Jane placed the delicate teacup on its saucer and set both upon the table at her elbow. She stood, thanked the Abbotts for their hospitality, and followed a uniformed maid to the door.

The maid bid her a good day and shut the door just as Jane realized she'd failed to ask the most important question: *Did Mr. Murphy conceive of this scheme?*

Chapter Three

On Tuesday, the town council met in Mrs. Abbott's rose garden. If the massive Queen Anne made a statement about the Abbotts, the garden served as an exclamation point.

Hank arrived at the appointed hour but not a moment early. With Oscar busy mixing prescriptions for Dr. Cheney, Hank had left Elias in charge of everything else. At thirteen, Elias was half-man, half-boy, and reliable as could be. Elias with Austin, age eight, could handle the shop for an hour.

Hank stood at the back with the latecomers. Every chair the Abbotts had brought out was occupied.

The duchess, in her typical finery, was seated beside Mrs. Abbott. Sunlight spilled through the leafy trees and dappled her brunette hair with dancing polka dots of gold. She looked deceptively lovely in her pale green dress.

She must've found a way to remove the icing stains on her overskirt. He'd heard more than one housewife promise nothing worked like buckwheat flour for greasy spots on fabrics.

"Welcome, one and all." In a fine suit, his new bowler at a jaunty angle, Archibald Abbott addressed the town council and guests. "Over the past four years our city's Founders' Day events have been well-attended, but the soon-to-follow Harvest Festivals have not. We have considered the timing of various harvests to ensure the date is right. We've looked at the average day of the first appreciable snowstorm."

The mayor, in his fancy three-story home, could not comprehend true want. He'd never known a moment's hunger in his entitled life. Since their interrupted negotiations last Monday, the man had offered nothing but fluff and platitudes— and promised this meeting would answer Hank's questions.

"It's time to act." Abbott smiled through a carefully timed pause. "Let us make this year's events better attended than ever."

Polite applause lasted mere seconds, but Abbott seemed pleased.

"In so doing," he continued, "we secure two necessary goals— a more unified community as winter closes in *and* a lucrative week for our merchants. With one comes the other."

A bee visited a rose somewhere behind Hank. Maybe several bees. The droning buzz fluttered on the warm breeze, the honeybee steadily going about its work.

"How will your city council ensure this year boasts the best attendance of the decade?" The mayor paused. "We have devised a plan. Already, people are talking about the competition. That talk includes far more speculation and interest in the competition than in traditional festival events."

Hank didn't bother to raise his hand. "Competition? *What* competition?"

"Why, to see who wins the real estate you and Miss Vancoller are both determined to secure. What could be more democratic than to settle the dispute with the assistance of those who will be affected by the lease?"

Abbott had led Hank to believe the agreement was all sewn up. They'd talked about this, Abbott and him. *Twice.* Abbott had insisted on waiting. *No need to sign the lease today,* and *Your storage is safe, right where it is.* He might not have lied outright, but he sure as shooting hadn't told the whole truth.

Hank's gaze snagged Miss Vancoller's. She inched up her chin. How much had she known, prior? Was this "contest" *her* idea, her way to secure the square footage?

"You do realize," Abbott continued, addressing Hank directly, "a larger attendance boosts the economy— and in doing so, the people purchase the supplies you're so insistent they have on hand for the greatest blizzard of the century."

Hank wasn't so sure one led to the other. "How do you suppose attendance will guarantee preparedness?"

Some would, sure. But what percentage? Ten percent? Twenty?

Hank narrowed his gaze, watching Abbott's every movement. Something wasn't right about the man's story. He had personal reasons for the public involvement and the most likely? That new block of upscale construction couldn't pay for itself if stores continued to gather dust. At least four— some on the second level, some large, some small— had never had a tenant.

A man who dressed like Abbott, with an expensive wife like Mrs. Abbott— and what, three children? Four?— could not afford to let property sit. So, what did he do with his role as mayor? He drew attention to *his* new block, attempting to locate renters.

Abbott tossed an arm wide. "We will involve the citizenry. Curiosity is a powerful thing, Mr. Murphy. Curiosity is free advertisement."

Hank's fists clenched.

"Mayor," the stationer called, "you talk like it's election year. That's not 'til '92."

Everyone laughed.

Everyone but Hank.

Another bee buzzed in a drunken arc, heading for a luscious bloom. The bee knew what to do while summer declined.

"Election year or not," Hank said loudly enough for all to hear, "I want to know why, as a town council, you're not helping our community prepare for winter. Have you forgotten the winter of 1880 when trains stopped moving? People *died*. Hundreds more suffered for months." His voice broke. He clenched his fists harder, fighting the tide of emotion. "Have you forgotten six long months of winter in '82? How 'bout the beef lost on the hoof in '84 and '85? Or how we lost our spring planting because winter ripped May from our grasp?"

His voice broke, again, and he sucked in a great lungful of air. Was he doomed? Like a prophet no one believed?

Councilmen, one by one, glanced from Hank to the mayor. One spun his hat between his knees and refused to look up.

"Murphy?" Thaddeus Whipple of Whipple's Bakery stood, his expression direct and kind. "The Western Almanac claims the coming winter of 1887 to 1888 will be the mildest of the decade. The worst is behind us."

Murmurs of agreement rumbled through the small gathering and Hank's heart grew heavier. Would no one take him seriously?

"Hank Murphy." Mayor Abbott released a breath through pursed lips. "You're beginning to sound like Chicken Little, with your talk of the sky falling."

That demanded a response. He jabbed a finger at Abbott, though the man stood more than ten feet away. "And you, sir, remind me of the squirrel who lazed away the days of summer and refused to prepare for *winter's... inevitable... appearance.*" He emphasized the last words with jabs.

A dozen faces registered surprise.

Mrs. Abbott fanned herself with dizzying speed.

The duchess choked and popped her fan open to mask her face. Was she *laughing*?

Thaddeus Whipple grinned. Then he chuckled without making a sound.

Pettingill, the tailor at the end of the way, *did* chuckle aloud and within seconds, nearly all in the garden laughed with genuine mirth.

Rocky Gideon, made wealthy by way of The Peerless Mine, clapped his hand on Hank's shoulder. "I love your spirit, Hank Murphy. You're likely cracked in the head, but so far, you're harmless."

In the face of Rocky's gentle cajoling, Hank couldn't hold onto his indignation. Like water flowing around a logjam, tight emotions swept away.

A smile of his own came quickly, and another clap of Rocky's hand upon his back had him laughing along with his neighbors.

Hank chuckled alongside everybody else. He did sound cracked, didn't he?

"In case you're right?" Rocky squeezed Hank's shoulder and played to the audience. "We'll all be merrier for your hard work."

"Good afternoon, Miss Dimond." Oscar Harris put on his warmest of smiles for the lonely woman. He understood the necessity of showing gracious appreciation to patrons.

Every pharmacist and store owner knew ladies opened their purses when they found items that made them happy. Last time she was in, she'd loosened her purse strings to buy a new toilet soap with the lightest scent of carnation and the accompanying hand lotion. She'd left happy, and his shop had benefited from the sale.

T.A. Murphy's Grocery Emporium wasn't *his* shop, *per se*, but he and Hank Murphy had shaken hands on the deal, making him a full partner.

The druggist position was his. Permanently.

Nothing else mattered.

With only matronly spinster Ina Dimond in the shop, he could afford to lavish her with attention. "You're looking well. A bright spot of sunshine."

She smiled— now that was a nice improvement. Last he'd engaged her in conversation, the woman's unhappiness had made it difficult for her to smile.

An old bachelor knew a thing or two about loneliness.

"Blue looks well on you," Oscar heard himself say. Where had *that* come from?

Young Elias Murphy swept the floor with surprisingly good care. Oscar coughed, relieved the boy was occupied and unaware of Oscar's discomfort.

He'd long been gracious and friendly with customers. He did *not* flirt with customers. Especially when that customer was lovely and several years younger than he.

She was *quite* lovely.

Even lovelier for the pink glow in her high cheekbones. As usual, she'd wound her braided hair about her head. The fashionable style suited her and showed off the length and fullness of her tresses.

The woman was statuesque. And sturdy— though he instinctively knew she wouldn't like that compliment.

"My list." She'd rapidly returned to business. "And basket." She left both on the counter and took a few steps toward the door. "I'll be at the Tea Room for a short while. I'll return for my order in an hour?"

"Absolutely, Miss Dimond. Enjoy yourself."

She stayed put. "I heard Mr. Murphy's trying to rent the empty store between here and the Tea Room."

"Is that so?" If Hank wanted Miss Dimond to know, he'd tell her.

"Indeed, yes. The catch is Miss Vancoller wants that same real estate."

"Hmmm." Was Miss Dimond genuinely interested? Curious? Or digging for gossip?

"Personally, I think the Emporium should have it. The space, I mean."

Hadn't she intended to patronize the Tea Room? He straightened his left leg slowly, trying not to draw attention. He wanted to squirm. That blamed, aching leg. "Is that so?"

"Yes." She seemed to think it over, even as she wandered closer to the counter. "I'm thinking the smaller that tea room, the better. I suppose you're also on the side of your employer. You'd like to see the Emporium win that space."

Win? "Hank Murphy isn't my employer. We're business partners." Perhaps she'd missed the announcement in the local paper. Why did it matter if she believed him an employee, or an owner?

"Naturally, you'd want to win."

"I wouldn't mind winning. In general, winning is a mite more enjoyable."

He enjoyed making Miss Dimond smile.

At a natural lull in their back-and-forth, she paused. "I've enjoyed your company, Mr. Harris. I'd be most delighted..." Her hesitant smile told him far too much. "So delighted, Mr. Harris, if you would come to call."

How had such a lovely woman, somewhere in her thirties, retained so much innocence? Were he deprived of sight, restricted to his senses of scent and sound, he'd place the lady in her early twenties. So innocent was she.

"Thank you." The invitation honored him.

Innocence was a quality to be adored and respected. An admirable trait.

But the quality had a dark side. She couldn't be expected to see he was not the kind of man for her. Truly, he was not a man any woman would want.

A decent man, a good man, would protect her in her innocence.

He wanted to be that better man. The man worthy of her trust.

She'd understand, someday, far in the future. And when she understood why he never called, he hoped she'd remember him with fondness.

Hank ruminated six long days after the town council meeting.

On Monday morning, a brilliant idea was born as he persuaded his sons to go to school. He'd listed reason after reason by way of explanation.

Miss Vancoller couldn't be much different.

He needed to explain why he needed the storeroom. Once she understood, she'd step aside. Once she withdrew, the impediments to his lease would disappear.

"Miss Vancoller?" He tapped on her shop's kitchen door frame. At this early hour on a Monday morning, her saloon would be closed.

Through the screen door, he heard splashing water and dimly followed movement.

"Yes?" Her voice, feminine and sweet, raised his hopes.

He opened the screen door enough to see her well. She turned from the sink, her sleeves pushed up to her elbows. Suds clung to bare, pale forearms. She wore an apron to spare the choice fabric of her heliotrope-colored costume.

At the moment, her store was dark and silent. Her assistant, Miss Harriet McCormick, seemed to be absent.

He ought to begin with niceties, so he wished her a good-morning. "You received the money? For the cake?"

She dried her hands on a dishtowel and hung it to dry on the back of a kitchen chair. "Yes. That was good of you."

Maybe not good, but certainly the right thing to do. "Step next door for a moment, will you? I want to show you something."

"Why?"

"I want a civil conversation regarding the real estate we both want."

She nodded, her posture stiff. He held the doors for her as she preceded him into his storeroom.

He watched her take in the neatly organized barrels, sacks, crates, and cardboard boxes. She held herself straight, her arms folded snugly. A few dark curls had worked free of their pins... or maybe she'd styled it that way on purpose.

Women. He'd never understand them.

She paused in the aisle and turned to him. "Have you no other storeroom?"

The question he'd been dreading. "No."

"Why not?"

Her wares were nothing like his. How could he help her understand? "You've seen the display shelves and drawers behind my counter?"

"Yes."

"My new emporium, with new architectural design—" He'd been a nearsighted fool. *Again.* "The design was supposed to allow for behind-the-counter storage. We could conduct inventory between customers. We'd shelve everything on hand in the same room, with drawers, bins—all of it organized."

Her lips firmed.

"Go ahead," he told her. "Say it."

She shook her head, even as a smile formed. She laughed. A lovely, feminine sound that walloped him in the middle.

"I apologize, Mr. Murphy. I'm not laughing at you."

"I find that hard to believe." As had her expression, hidden behind her hand fan in the mayor's rose garden. Did she see him as utterly ridiculous?

"I know. I'm sorry." She folded her arms over her middle, apparently relaxed and at ease for the first time since he'd known her as a businesswoman on Main. The simple loss of all the starch in her corset made her far more approachable, more appealing. More feminine.

She'd left the sleeves of her summer-weight heliotrope bodice at her elbows. Her full skirt, adorned with lace at the edge of the draping, had been hemmed an inch or two shorter than a standard gown, evidently to allow her brisk movement between kitchen and dining room.

That raised hem afforded him a peek at her brown leather boots. Low heels, fashionable pointy toes, and buttons that marched up the scalloped edge. Pretty boots... and surprisingly practical.

He became aware, suddenly, of her attention to his person. She took him in from his flat cap to the toes of his boots. From his too-long hair to the absence of a collar to denim coveralls. As long as folks trusted Hank as a businessman, it didn't much matter if they preferred he dress in a proper suit of clothes.

He did a great deal of lifting, bending, loading and unloading freight, tending to the horses, wrangling dirty little boys— and all of those daily tasks were hard on clothing. He'd destroyed two suits of clothes before he'd opted for a working man's wardrobe. He fit in with the millers, miners, farmers, ranchers, and loggers.

Real soon, though, Miss Vancoller's assessment lasted too long. Past the decent into the overly personal.

"Are you done?" he asked, attempting to speak in a neutral tone. He'd been looking at her booted ankles— no worse than what she'd done. He saw no reason to embarrass the lady.

She cleared her throat and stood a little straighter. "Why didn't you rent a larger space from Abbott at first? I know you thought to try a different arrangement in your shop, and that's all well and good... but where did you intend to store this?"

He massaged his jaw, rasping callused fingers and palm over two-day stubble. "I didn't need a place. At first, the store's newfangled design worked well, until I needed to think about winter and the potential of weeks or months without a train. Abbott agreed to let me keep my wares here. He gave me the keys."

"Mr. Murphy..."

"Call me Hank." He removed his flat cap, swept his shirtsleeve over his brow, and resettled the hat upon his head. "Everyone calls me Hank."

"Mr. Murphy, one obvious solution is to store your wares elsewhere."

The woman thought she knew everything. "Have you hauled freight in winter?"

"Not yet, but I will."

"Tea? A few replacement teacups?" His frustration doubled. No, tripled. "Your tea chests weigh how much? Five pounds? Have you lifted a barrel of pickles or sack of flour?"

To his surprise she searched his face for a long moment, evidently thinking about all he'd said. "No. I haven't."

"Miss Vancoller." He folded his arms and settled in his boots. "I've considered every option." She opened her mouth to argue, so he continued. "If I build a warehouse on the nearest available property, I'll lose hours of daylight to the hauling of merchandise. Through snowdrifts." Not to mention the strangling expense of constructing a building.

"The station is close. Rent a warehouse."

Did she think him daft? He'd looked and found nothing suitable. Cramped, leaky roofs, vermin infested, or north-facing doors that would be ice-locked by December.

"Winter brings ice and snow. An abundance of it. Do you comprehend the risk involved with moving barrels, crates, and sacks from warehouse to store?"

She folded her arms, calling attention to her shapely figure. How was it, with blood pounding in his ears, he heard her dress rustle? "You fret over the possibility of a smashed crate?"

"I fret over injury to the only two horses I own. I see risk to my freight wagon, and likely injury to my brother and sons. Moving merchandise in icy weather is dangerous."

Her posture reached a pinnacle of stiffness. She set her jaw and closed her eyes for a long moment. Reining in her temper? Squashing a paroxysm? Fighting for patience with his argument?

"Why," he demanded, "would I risk all that on ice, when I have a viable option, right here?"

She held her ground but turned her face to the side. Pearl buttons marched in tight formation up the front of her bodice. Like vigilant soldiers. As inflexible and as unforgiving as she.

He pushed away the dark thoughts. "Why do you want to expand? I read you wanted small, cozy, and restful." The weekly *Times and Seasons* had interviewed her when she'd opened her doors back in April.

"I misjudged the space required."

More honesty than he'd expected. "That so?"

"I need more floor space to serve larger clubs."

"Stack the tables against the wall and set the chairs in rows. You'll seat more that way." He grinned at the ease of solving her problem. "Issue resolved."

"It's a tea room, Mr. Murphy. I make my living from beverages, luncheon, cake, and puddings. On *dishes*."

Why did that matter? "So...?"

"Have you tried to sip tea and nibble a cookie, without benefit of a table?"

"Yes."

"Naturally, you have." She managed to sound both resigned and indignant. "My guests require tables. And tea service, water goblets, silverware, and napkins. My parlor was designed for a maximum of twenty-four, and that's all it will accommodate."

He snapped his fingers, proud of his inventive solution. "Spread out your guests. Offer different tea at different hours. Discount as much as you can afford at your slow hours. Bring people in when you want them."

"You don't understand."

Why did he try to help this woman? Nothing pleased her. "Enlighten me."

"Spreading guests out defeats all I've set out to accomplish. I must seat forty-five, perhaps fifty souls. At tables. All at once."

His head spun. "I imagine you have a valid reason for all that—" he circled a hand— "*nonsense*."

"Nonsense! Nonsense? Social clubs pay well for exclusive use of my tea room, and they do so for the privilege of holding meetings."

Her voice tightened and rose in pitch. Her body

tightened up, too. Like the problem leached her patience dry.

Somehow, he'd forgotten. The duchess hadn't an iota of patience. "If your temperance saloon—"

"It's a *tea room*. A parlor if you must refer to it as something else. My business has nothing to do with temperance."

"Forgive me, *Duchess*. If your fancy parlor isn't large enough for double the people—" was the woman daft as well as cracked?— "Not your problem."

"It most certainly is!"

"Truthfully, no. Not your problem. Let them meet at the park or in somebody's garden. *Problem solved*."

Chapter Four

Uh-oh.

Hank held his breath, his attention riveted to Jane's face.

Dora would've started screaming by now.

"If you'd allow me to finish my thought, sir, you'd comprehend why I need to seat them simultaneously."

More talking. That's just what they needed. This woman sounded crazier and crazier the more she spoke. "Go ahead."

The duchess splayed a hand at her collarbones over that curious lump. "They come to me because *I* worry about the details so they don't have to." She'd worked herself up into a lather. "I offer a valuable service to Mountain Home residents. You imply they don't need my valued service, and I take umbrage to that foolishness."

Foolishness? He knew which of them owned that foolishness, and it wasn't him.

"Miss Vancoller." He'd tried to sound calm, but his

teeth were still clenched and he might have pointed at her with the same vigor he'd conversed with the mayor in his rose garden. He stuffed the offending index finger deep into the pocket of his coveralls. "Only one of us can have this room. And only one of our purposes has a chance of keeping a gnat alive through winter."

"A gnat?" In a fine tizzy, she advanced. "If I don't offer more comfort, more ease, they'll return to their rose gardens and parlors."

"Yes, a gnat. Choose your own variety of vermin if you want to, but my point's the same. Which will be a valuable service to the residents of Mountain Home, come a blizzard like in '80?" The woman chapped his hide. "Tea and biscuits? Or meat and beans?"

He had his dander up now. His blood pumped with vigor and he may have, marginally, raised his voice. He was not that kind of man, and he'd learned in another lifetime that yelling destroyed relationships. "This rigmarole is utter nonsense. Tell me why club meetings aren't at somebody's house?"

"Be *still*, and I'll tell you."

Hank wanted to roar. The duchess had to be the most infuriating woman he'd encountered. Given his history, that thought came as a surprise. Rather than open his mouth and risk the roar escaping, he merely nodded. She'd better start talking.

"I want the club members to come to my tea room." She spoke slowly and softly.

"And?"

She held up a finger, clearly chastising him for speaking. "I need them to come to my tea room. Do you comprehend?"

The roar he'd tried to suppress nearly escaped. He tumbled his hand in a hurry-it-along motion.

"I need the money clubs pay to meet in my tea room."

That made *no* sense. "You're saying you don't make a profit from your luncheon guests?" How was that possible? "I've seen the women, young and old, parading in and out."

"You'll degrade this conversation to that crass subject?"

"Money?" He fought to hold onto his temper. "If that's what this boils down to, yes."

"Do you know what I pay monthly for the privilege of this address?"

"I can guess." His rent had doubled when he'd removed from the old address to the new Abbott's Brick Block. The Tea Room was smaller than the Emporium, by less than half.

"Do you know the price of a cup of tea, Mr. Murphy?" Sass seasoned her tone.

At least he wasn't alone in losing his patience. "I know eight varieties by sight and scent. I can eyeball a precise tablespoon, even without that spoon for reference. I can scoop a perfect four ounces from the tin. The scale is a formality to appease the purchaser."

"How talented you are." She ladled on the sass with a heavy hand. "Does your talent extend to finances, Mr. Grocer? Do you know what my profit is, once I pay for expensive, imported teas and the fuel to boil water?"

"Uh..."

Sparks of something— Indignation? Superiority? Dignity?— glittered in her green, green eyes. Freckles scattered over the bridge of her nose and cheekbones, reminding him of a sprinkle of cinnamon sugar over the sweet cakes his step-mother had made.

He liked freckles.

"My profit is two cents per cup. If they take milk and sugar, I make three cents. Thus, I rely on pastries, sandwiches, soups in cold weather, and the likelihood that my guests will remain awhile and desire a refill."

"If your profit is too scant, charge more." The woman worked too hard to brew tea for guests who could brew their own. At home. Where normal women had work to do.

"You are an unendurable man."

He'd been called worse. "I'm certain you're correct."

Why had he thought an explanation would help? How had he thought, just once, a woman could be rational and persuaded to see what he tried to accomplish.

"Do you know," she asked, her voice shaking, "how much I invested in teacups and silver? Linens? A hotel-sized ice box? Tea tables and chairs? Flocked wallpaper? Carpeting? Draperies? Lamps? Teapots? Platters?"

He knew what a big ice box cost as he had one in the market. With no clue what china and silver and linens cost, he opted for silence.

"If ladies' clubs do not rent my tea room, I will not be able to remain in business."

Anxiety strangled her soft words and filled him with the kind of ache he didn't know what to do with.

"My lovely tea room opened five months ago, this

coming week," she whispered. "I operate at a loss, Mr. Murphy. If I fail to secure frequent situations with larger social clubs, I will be forced to close my doors."

Was that true? Her financial situation couldn't be that dire, could it?

If he didn't *need* this space, he'd give it to her. He would. He'd step aside like the gentleman he'd grown up to be, despite his mothers.

The thought of her closing her frilly little tea room and mourning its loss like the beloved friend it was made his chest burn.

He did not want to be the kind of man who stole a woman's dreams.

She trembled, pressing her lips together. She held her breath... withholding tears? She averted her gaze and at last drew a breath.

An odd sense of helplessness swamped Hank. He didn't know what to do. He couldn't forfeit his hold on the storeroom. What could he possibly say?

The woman didn't have the same kind of demands that he faced, with fatherhood and a young brother in his care.

Aww! How had he missed it? "You support your mother, eh?"

She cut him a glance. Good. Her eyes were dry. He could respect a strong woman.

"I do. And you support your children."

"You can't be in that bad of a way. You're dressed well. As is your mother."

Old Mrs. Vancoller was a widow, he knew, but... Mr. Vancoller had left his family in comfort. The man had owned the tobacco shop, Hank had learned, and left it to his wife and daughter upon his death a few years back.

She couldn't understand any of this, not unless she'd experienced the anxiety and panic of slowly starving through a deep, white winter. "Jane, do you know hunger?"

"It's Miss Vancoller, and yes, I know hunger. I am hungry at present."

"I mean so hungry you wonder if you'll ever feel satisfied again? So hungry you have dark thoughts about survival?"

She blinked, even as a hand lifted to cover her mouth.

Unbelievable! "You thought I referred to the Great Hunger. Just how old do you take me for?"

"You have seven or eight sons. Maybe nine. You could be two score years."

Forty? "I have four sons and one half-brother. And I'm thirty and two years of age."

She puffed her cheeks and blew it out. "I'd have guessed an even baker's dozen."

"Do stay on topic, Miss Vancoller." Remnants of the brogue laced his tone, now that he let it. "I'm a Murphy and proud of it. American-born and proud of it, also, I am. My parents fled Ireland, married aboard the vessel, and by the grace of God, reached America with body and soul together."

Seconds passed. He watched as every scrap of argument left her. "They must tell painful stories."

"They never talked of it. This," he emphasized with a sweep of his arm, taking in the room's contents, "is about difficult winters, right here."

She watched him. "The newspaper said to anticipate a mild winter. Not just our people but scientific opinions from New York and Washington. They say the worst is over."

"Not all written words are truth." Too many would believe the reports. They'd fail to prepare.

She leaned against a barrel of dried and salted beef. The fight seemed to leave her. "Folks call you Chicken Little."

"Yes, they do. And all creation will come here when their winter food supplies run lean. They'll expect January's shelves to be as full as September's."

"Consequences of living in modern times."

They shared a small smile over that observation. "Well said, Miss Vancoller. Well said. The railroad changed everything."

She perused his stores. "This room holds evidence of significant investment."

"I can't sell what I don't have."

"What if you can't sell out before spoilage decimates you?"

"That's not likely."

The pause in their discourse seemed natural. And powerful. As if her heart might be softened enough.

Her gaze searched his face. "Why is it you don't believe the meteorologists? Weather is their science."

"I don't need book learning to use my own two eyes. I don't need somebody to tell me something I can see for myself. I've learned to observe Mother Nature's many signs." Most important, the nagging feeling in his gut didn't lie. "Have you been in the other two groceries in town?"

She blinked.

"Have you?"

"Not of late."

"I have. Neither one has enough to see our residents properly fed 'til early summer." He'd caught her attention with that one. Good. "If the winter of eighty-seven to eighty-eight is as severe as its predecessors, we're in for a long one. You know wind fills the mountain passes with drifted snow. We've prime avalanche territory."

"Whoa." She shook her head, her loose curls bouncing in a most distracting manner. "I don't understand one thing. Why are *you* responsible for everybody's wellbeing? Aren't we all responsible for ourselves?"

Old pains awoke, burning his conscience. He'd pay for his foolishness for the rest of his life. "I'm no different than a lawman who keeps his ear to the ground." An adequate comparison, maybe. He struggled to find another way to explain himself... one that wouldn't rip the scab off serious wounds. "I'm no different than you— ensuring you have the popular tea variety in the kitchen."

"But—" questions lurked in her eyes, deepening their color— "why you? Why not a coalition of all three grocers? Why not the town council?"

"Because they're ostriches."

She chuckled, shaking her head.

"Maybe the best reason is I'm a father. I dread hearing my children cry with hunger pangs." Heartache increased such that he rubbed hard against his breastbone. Some things a father couldn't bear.

"They're innocent. I'm responsible."

"I agree. I feel the same way about my obligations to my mother, but I don't feel an urgency to care for the entire town."

"You're not a grocer. I am."

"A grocer who's preparing for Armageddon." She comprehended but not completely. Her tone held no sass, no disrespect.

"I can't sell what I don't have." Must he repeat himself? "What would you do if somebody you know comes to you for help? Pretend it's February and your own food supply is running out."

The question made her uncomfortable. She couldn't meet his eye. "I'd help. I think."

"What if you didn't know them? Never met them a day in your life?"

She shrugged, her gaze averted.

One more nail in the coffin: "What if they have children, emaciated with hunger? What then?"

She winced. Her previously proud posture seemed to curl in on herself. Long seconds passed.

She swallowed. "What happened?" Her eyes were wide, ghosts of imagined horrors skimming her expression.

He shrugged, unwilling to answer. Seconds stretched, becoming more and more ill at ease.

At last, she spoke. "If you're right, these beans, grains, rice, dried fruits, dried meats— your investment will save lives." She sounded sincere. Serious, too.

She gazed at him as if he'd done something remarkable. Or worthy of commendation. "You're a good man, Hank Murphy. A very good man."

He looked away, uncomfortable with her ill-informed compliment.

"If necessary," she whispered, "I think you'd give this food away."

He wasn't the saint she made him out to be. "I'd prefer to recoup my capital."

She watched him for another long, silent moment. "Is this why Mayor Abbott conceived of the competition? Because he knew you and I would be at a deadlock?"

Hank snorted. "Abbott does things for one reason and one reason only— business and self-interests."

"I believe you've stated two reasons."

Spoken like a woman. "All I wanted was for you to comprehend my reasons, Miss Vancoller."

"I understand you too well, Mr. Murphy."

He doubted that. His hackles rose. Women! Impossible to live with, aggravating as could be, and utterly incapable of viewing two sides of a disagreement.

The time had come to speak plainly. "I need this square footage."

"You need it. Therefore, I can't have it?" Her voice crackled with ire.

He held out both hands, though calming a hysterical woman had never been within his reach. "Abbott made his intention clear; he'll lease to only one of us."

She narrowed her eyes, as furious as the day Clyde helped himself to wedding cake. "Naturally, that person should be you."

Had she listened to a word he'd said? "You said all

this—" he gestured widely— "would save lives. You said—"

"I know what I said." Bright color shaded her cheeks.

"Good. Let me do what I need to do. Withdraw your lease request."

Her mouth opened and hung slack for a long second. "Did you not hear what I said?"

"Believe me, madam, I heard every word."

"If you believe I'll forfeit the survival of my business, you are terribly mistaken."

"Darling," Mother said with palpable irritation, "if you'd just *try* to make yourself appealing to men, you could find someone new and be happy again."

Jane set the hot breakfast skillet back on the stove top, clenched her jaw, and kept her back to her mother.

One, two, three...

She would not speak in anger. She would *not*.

"The right man," Mother said from her place at the kitchen table, "is out there, somewhere."

No, the right man was in heaven.

Gone, forever. But her love for him, her memories had not died. She loved him as much today as she had the day he'd been stolen from her.

How could Mother pretend that marriage was still possible?

Especially after the brouhaha with Mr. Murphy at the beginning of the week, she'd lost all faith in men. If he was a representation of her pool of potential husbands, then she held by her original decision. She would *never* marry.

Even if Jane wanted to wed— which she most certainly did not— who would want her?

How could she promise her life to anyone else?

Seven, eight, nine...

"You have so much to give," Mother insisted. "And you're still young."

How often must Mother bring up this subject? Once a week? Twice? She rolled her eyes to the ceiling, seeking patience.

"I think," Mother went on, evidently unaware— *still*— that her advice was not welcome, "you're punishing yourself, darling, choosing to remain single when that isn't at all what Law would want. You've grieved him long and hard, and it must cease."

Jane whirled on her mother. "You talk as though I'm wandering around in widow's weeds, sobbing in the cemetery." Mama had allowed her one year— one paltry year— of black. "I lost the man that would have been my husband."

Words spoken before God and witnesses could not have made her love Lawrence Riddle more.

"Yes, daughter. But he's been gone these five years."

"I am soon to be thirty years of age. I know my mind. I know my heart. I will not wed simply to make you happy. I won't."

"Then do it to make *you* happy. Allow a good man to take care of you."

Jane did not need a man for financial support.

She did *not* need a replacement for Law; *no one* could fill his shoes.

On the Wednesday morning of the Ladies' Library Association meeting, Ina Dimond had a very good feeling about things.

September had brought cooler temperatures— and the day had started with a kind of delicious chill in the air only those weary of summer's heat could fully appreciate. By late morning, the sun had chased away the crisp quality to the mountain air, leaving the outdoors splendidly perfect.

Optimism and excitement gilded the edges of everything. The sun shone a bit brighter and as she took in her figure in the long mirror in the corner of her bedroom, she liked what she saw.

That, in itself, was a momentous occasion.

Mature women, of an age where her own children should've been grown, wed, and providing grandchildren to rock-a-bye, typically did not like what they saw in the mirror.

She couldn't help smiling as she strolled the few blocks from the family home where she now resided alone, to Main Street. She'd arrive on time for the Ladies' Library Association meeting, enjoy luncheon with friends and associates, then— her belly tingled in a delicious manner— perhaps, she'd pay a visit to Mr. Oliver Harris. Such a nice man.

A full seven days had passed as she waited for him

to call (this exhilarating morning made eight). He'd not yet knocked on her door. Perhaps he needed encouragement.

What a challenge! She'd ordered herself to stay home this past week and out of the Emporium. When he called on her, what would they talk about, if she'd already visited him that day?

Today, as her reward for extremely fine behavior, she'd treat herself to a new bar of rose-scented toilet soap.

She nodded and smiled at those she knew, enjoying the swish and swirl of her cotton dress— the most fashionable summertime costume she owned. She'd restyled it several months back to match the images she studied in *Godey's*. The underskirt now had lacy ruffles. The back of her overskirt was now adorned with crisp knife pleats at the bustle.

As she approached Miss Vancoller's Tea Room, Ina noted the mostly-full seating area— not too full, thank goodness, but the meeting would be comfortably well-attended. How lovely!

There, near the door, were Mrs. Temperance Stuart and Mrs. Caroline Finlay, ladies she'd not visited with in too long. And there, one table to the right, her dearest friend and next-door-neighbor, Mrs. Maggie Cresswell. Oh good. Maggie's table had room that Ina might join her.

As she stepped into the shade of the awning, ready to cross the threshold—

That *witch*, Mrs. Zylphia Speare Hudson, who stole the love of Ina's life.

Ina's confidence imploded. Her heart seized. All

the glory in her day burned to ash.

As if Zylphia had slapped her across the face, Ina pulled in a great draught of air.

She couldn't breathe.

Her chest hurt... as if... as if...

As if no time had passed since the awful moment when her life ended; when Zylphia remained seated at George's elbow, in George's dining room, the room *Ina* had polished and dusted and served meals in for the five years since Mrs. Tilde Hudson, God rest her soul, took ill.

Ina blinked, forcing the terrible memories into submission.

Right there, in the middle of the lovely Tea Room, the woman tossed back her head and cackled. The woman's throaty laughter grated against Ina's eardrums.

And her last nerve.

She— Ina— was to have wed Mr. George Hudson. It would've been so perfect. Ina had already become a member of the family. George and his grown son, Morgan, couldn't do without her. She'd made them a comfortable home and met every need before they anticipated it.

Until the witch had arrived and ruined everything.

Just like today.

Her glorious day, at the Ladies' Library Association meeting, ruined, dashed, by the *witch*. She held court with her daughter (yet also her daughter-in-law) Mrs. Elizabeth Hudson. Adoring faces surrounded them. Fawning and smiling and nodding like imbeciles.

How Elizabeth turned out so well, with a mother

like Zylphia, Ina would never understand. Elizabeth had proven herself to be a sweet girl, and she had made Morgan Hudson a fine wife. Ina couldn't help but have strong motherly feelings for Morgan— because she, herself, should have been his stepmother.

"Hello, Miss Dimond." The baker's wife, Mrs. Whipple, held her daughter's hand. "Are you going in?"

Ina was in the way. Blocking the entire doorway. Heat flushed her cheeks and pulled her back to herself.

"Uh... just a moment. Please." She stepped out of the way to allow the young Adaline and her mother to enter.

Maybe Ina could walk in behind these ladies, blend in, sit on the other side of the room...

But in that moment, Zylphia looked up and waved to the Whipples. "There you are!" Zylphia called, to the young matron.

Never, certainly not after the way she'd thrown Ina out on her ear, would the witch invite Ina to be seated.

She'd likely gaze right through her, as if Ina were invisible.

Unimportant. Unnoticeable. *Unwelcome.*

Ina's breaths become too shallow, too rapid. Her vision dimmed and her heart pounded.

She couldn't face this. No matter how much she enjoyed the Tea Room, no matter how she'd happily anticipated this library meeting, no matter how beautifully the day had begun— she *couldn't.*

If she were stronger, if she were more confident, she would march right up to Mrs. Zylphia Hudson and upset the woman's digestion.

But her heart tripped ever faster. In her distress,

color must be high in her cheeks. Anyone who glanced at her would know she wasn't confident and wasn't strong.

She retreated a few steps, grateful to be caught up in the swell of pedestrians on the walk. Some peered into the empty shop between the Emporium and the Tea Room. A steady flow of shoppers entered the Emporium.

The beautiful, fresh, new, T.A. Murphy's Grocery Emporium.

Precisely where she wanted to be.

But *now*? How could she face Mr. Harris like this?

Did she dare?

Why would a handsome, well-educated man want to spend two minutes in her company? If he'd wanted to spend a moment with her, he would have called.

Had she mistaken Mr. Oscar Harris's interest in her? She wasn't invisible to him... was she?

Somehow, George hadn't seen her. In her invisibility, over five years of loyal service, he'd sent for a mail-order bride.

Ramifications being what they were, George had been shackled to the worst possible match. He'd married the witch, so blind he'd not seen what stood before him.

Ina turned away, her head down, twisting her reticule strings in her hands.

No, today was not the day to buy rose-scented soap.

Chapter Five

Circumstances being what they were, the delivery boy was still out on foot when an important prescription was ready, so Oscar found himself on the street instead of sequestered within the Grocery Emporium.

Main Street seemed busier than usual. More people strolled by, interested in viewing the new brick block the mayor had constructed.

The Grocery Emporium had seen far more people inside. Many familiar faces stood on the boardwalk outside, visiting.

A young boy cupped his hands about his face, leaned against the glass, and peered into the vacant— or not so vacant— shop between the Grocery and the Tea Room.

With all this traffic, he'd best hurry back to his post. When not compounding prescriptions, he assisted customers with sales, answered questions, unpacked crates of merchandise, and kept the lines moving. Nothing could substitute for prompt and courteous service.

He noted Ina Dimond, looking fresh and lovely in a pastel cotton dress coming his way. He lifted his hat— but she didn't seem to notice him. She twisted the cords of her reticule so tightly her fingers turned red. Her skirts swished in time to her rapid footsteps.

From behind, the slump of her shoulders seemed pronounced.

She carried not a single shopping bundle.

She walked alone. Not toward the shopping district, but away.

What had happened to upset her so?

Where was the friendly, vivacious, smiling woman? A week ago, she'd visited with him over the pharmacy counter and invited him to pay a call.

He'd done the right thing, staying away. But knowing that didn't ease his conscience.

He'd always thought her lovely, unusual, and striking with understated beauty. But now, to witness her abject sadness—

They were two of a kind, Ina and he. Loneliness, a mirror-image of hers, had, long ago, proved his undoing...

Desire to follow nagged him. As if she'd hooked her finger in the chain padlocked about his heart and beckoned he follow.

Passersby milled about. Many called their hellos, greeting him by name. He raised his hand in greeting, lifted his hat to a lady or two, but kept his attention mostly on Ina Dimond's retreating back.

Was he the *only* one to notice her state?

He glanced back at the Emporium. Had she been

inside, looking for him? More and more folks entered the building. From here, he couldn't tell how many people were inside, but the pull to follow Miss Dimond tugged on him like a living thing.

Three running steps in her direction brought Miss Dimond into view once more. She'd halted and searched her reticule for something. Clusters of people parted and streamed around her. She didn't seem to notice when an elderly man lifted his hat and wished her a good day.

Instead, she pulled out her hankie and blew her nose.

Was she crying?

Her shoulders trembled on a rise, then fell. Like bread dough that had risen too long and deflated.

As if *she'd* been left waiting.

Waiting...

Oh, no. She'd stopped by the pharmacy counter, hadn't she? Expecting to see him?

She shouldn't do that...

He'd never be the right type of man for a nice lady like her. Never.

She'd understand that, someday. Likely, someday soon.

The realization forced his decision. "Excuse me, sir, ma'am." He lifted his hat to the couple he'd bumbled into. He settled the bowler and quickened his pace to Miss Dimond's side.

The least he could do was escort her home.

"Current registered members of the Ladies' Library Association; sixty-three." Tiny Mrs. Carrie Gilbert, wife of Pastor Gilbert, presently served her fifth consecutive term as secretary to the Ladies' Library Association. She took the club statistics seriously. "Our rise in numbers constitutes an increase of six members."

Library club members, filling perhaps three-quarters of the Tea Room's capacity, expressed pleasure at their growing numbers. Monthly meetings were attended mostly by matrons with grown children and women not yet wed. Many more, too busy to attend regularly, kept their club memberships current, paid annual subscriptions, and checked out books to read with their families.

"In the past month," Mrs. Gilbert continued, "we have added two annual subscriptions. We retired one book from the collection."

Jane's heart seized. "What book?" She dodged right, trying to see around too many flowerpot hats upon the ladies' heads to the library shelves situated, unfortunately, also behind Mrs. Gilbert.

Too many faces swiveled toward Jane. They must think her mad.

This wasn't the time or place, and yet, she couldn't hold her tongue. "Which book?"

Mrs. Gilbert scanned her note pad. "I apologize. I don't rightly recall..."

"Does anyone know?" Jane searched the surprised faces of her club members. She was one of them, a paid member of the library. And she needed to know.

Even if the book had come unglued, suffered death by fire, or been chewed to bits by a dog, she *must* have it back. What had she been thinking, giving her precious inheritance away?

But she did remember. She'd donated most of Lawrence's books because he'd want them to be read. The library owned them now.

Heat stained Jane's cheeks. "I'm sorry. Do continue." She busied herself refilling water tumblers.

A true pastor's wife, Mrs. Gilbert had already calmed. "I apologize, Jane, for my failure to note the title. I'll call on you with the information. Please expect me shortly after the meeting concludes."

Conversation hummed once more, and Mrs. Gilbert was forced to recapture attention. "Next scheduled subject. We are in receipt of three new books, purchased as scheduled for our library. Our new titles are *The Adventures of Huckleberry Finn* by Mark Twain, *The Adventures of Tom Sawyer* by Mark Twain, and *The Strange Case of Dr. Jekyll and Mr. Hyde* by Robert Louis Stevenson."

Jane retreated to the kitchen for a fresh teakettle and another platter of cookies. She'd created the iced lemon cookie receipt on her own. The delightful result had earned many compliments.

From the kitchen, Jane overheard Mrs. Gilbert call on Mrs. Zylphia Hudson for a report on the costs of printing an updated directory of library contents.

While Jane prepared the fresh pot, she missed the introduction and much of the original statement, but she had no difficulty overhearing Mrs. Hudson's emphatic and defensive voice. "Having visited the stationer across the way, I can say his price is a sliver better than the job office. Our pamphlets, with a plain card cover, stapled at the spine, will cost us thirty dollars per one hundred and fifty."

"*Thirty dollars?*" Someone asked, surprised by the expense.

Jane might've been alarmed by the total, had she not recently outfitted this parlor with multiples of everything and a few expensive individual items— a fashionable tea cart, a stove for her baking, and one of nearly every kitchen implement she'd require.

She wheeled the prepared tea cart back into the parlor. Fragrant tea made her wish she could sit and sip... perhaps once everyone else had gone.

"If I may?" Harriet McCormick, Tea Room employee, had been elected Ladies' Library Association Treasurer. "I'm hearing whispers we cannot afford the library listing booklets before our ticket supper at the Harvest Festival brings in money. That's simply not true." Harriet had given the financial report at the beginning of the meeting, but it seemed the complainers had been tardy and missed that part.

Harriet held up a hand to ward off complaints from the late arrivals. "We have more than enough to meet our scheduled purchases and the outlay required to prepare for the annual ticket supper. In truth, we have enough to cover those expenses, twice."

With that, everyone settled down. Fewer whispers occurred behind hand fans.

"Time for refills," Jane whispered at Harriet's ear. "I'll pour. Serve cookies?" She pushed the platter into Harriet's hands. "Perhaps a cookie will sweeten a disposition or two."

Harriet smiled and picked up silver-plated tongs and cookies from the cart.

"Yes." Mrs. Hudson spoke loudly enough to be heard over the hubbub, apparently in reply to a question. "That comes to twenty cents per pamphlet."

Discussion erupted behind hand fans, the buzz and rumble of conversation most unladylike. Had anyone listened?

"I have a marvelous idea that will solve this concern over expenses." Mrs. Hudson spoke more loudly, determined to be heard. "I suggest we sell advertisement space, by the page, half-page, or quarter-page. Suppose we extend the length of our directory by four pages; the advertisement income alone might pay one-half of the expense."

"That's a lovely idea," Mrs. Ann Abbott, the Ladies' Library President said, "I second the motion."

"Wait a moment." Mrs. Maggie Cresswell raised her hand. "Advertisements don't sell themselves. Who will take responsibility? Who will go door-to-door?"

"Door-to-door?" Mrs. Howard Bayliss, née Arrah Cresswell, sprang to her feet. The young matron might be family by marriage to angelic Maggie Cresswell, but one wouldn't know it, considering the contrast in behavior. "How vulgar. Are we men? Are we *drummers*?"

Zylphia Hudson took umbrage. Her offense might have something to do with the fact that Arrah had given Zylphia's beloved son-in-law (and stepson) the mitten and wed a wealthy mine owner instead. Obviously, Zylphia liked things the way they were, with her daughter married to her stepson, but Zee could nurse a grudge for decades.

"I never suggested," Zylphia fairly yelled over the noise, "we go door-to-door like a common drummer peddling wares."

Leave it to Ann Abbott to leap into any dispute with both feet. She stood and rang the silver bell she used to call their meetings to order. The tinkling bell eventually cut through the din. Most of the hubbub faded.

"No one need go door-to-door." Ann's smile suggested triumph. "I say we mail a letter to every business in Mountain Home."

"That would work." Mrs. Gilbert clasped her tiny hands at her tiny waist. "I like it. I volunteer to address the envelopes."

Harriet looked up from serving cookies. "We have adequate funds to cover postage."

"Thank you, ladies." Zylphia calmed. "We offer a valuable bit of real estate within our library pamphlets. Once business owners learn about this opportunity, they'll come to us. Don't you think so, Miss Vancoller?"

Jane had no good answer. All of her potential customers already knew about her establishment, and she hadn't the funds necessary to buy a quarter page, much less a half or whole. "I imagine many will want to pay for an advertisement."

"If the association pays thirty dollars for these pamphlets," Ann Abbott told every woman by way of sweeping her gaze through the parlor, "we must have a guarantee that the money will be replaced."

"Annual fees should cover a listing of all library

titles." This from the organization's vice-president, Temperance Stuart. "The balance will be recouped by paid advertisements. If that fails to cover expenses, we'll sell the remainder to new library members at a slight discount."

"Perfect!" Ann rang her little silver bell at a mad tempo. "Did you hear Mrs. Stuart's solution?" Ann waited until she gained full attention. "Temperance, say that once more."

Temperance Stuart and Ann Abbott had one of the oddest friendships Jane had ever witnessed. When mining tycoon Rocky Gideon had been engaged to wed Temperance, the previous minister's daughter, he'd begun building the stately Queen Anne mansion now owned and occupied by the Abbott family. Temperance had wed attorney W.W. Stuart, for love, a coup that ended what would've been a less-than-ideal union between Temperance and Mr. Gideon and eventually led to the marriage of Mr. Rocky Gideon and Felicity Cartwright— Temperance's half-sister. *That* had been awkward.

But that barely scratched the oddness of the Ann-Temperance friendship.

The greatest oddity came in Ann's proclivity for inviting Mr. and Mrs. Stuart, in for holiday meals. Probably to show off her grand dining room that might once have been Temperance's.

Thank goodness Jane hadn't been invited to dine at the Abbotts'. How would she tolerate the ostentatious show of wealth?

Back when Rocky had asked Felicity to be his bride, he'd built her another mansion on the rise above town with an exquisite view of the river and mountainous scenery. They'd nearly filled that big house with children.

The fulfillment of a lifetime of dreams, according to Felicity.

Jane had fully expected to wed. By now, she'd have easily borne children. At least two. She'd have filled her days with seeing to the comfort and happiness of her family. She'd be reading to her children instead of alone.

"The Harvest Festival," Harriet announced, grabbing Jane from her thoughts, "is our last, best opportunity to increase awareness of our library. Last week, a lady from the Erickson ranch came in for tea. She's in town only once a month, yet, until she saw the bookshelves here, hadn't known we'd begun a library. She asked a dozen questions. She is one of our new subscribers."

"This lack of awareness is precisely what we must change." Mrs. Abbott's posture was that of an army general, preparing to attack. "We *need* that space next door. Miss Vancoller, I want you to speak to Mr. Murphy and arrange to move our library into that storeroom of his. Right before the front window."

Jane ceased pouring in the nick of time. Tea hovered at the too-full brim of Mrs. Cresswell's cup. "Sorry," she whispered.

Jane's gut twinged. She would *not* ask that man for anything. Especially after their *discussion*.

Mrs. Abbott's dark eyes lit with enthusiasm. "It's perfect. We want the library to be there permanently, so to house it there during the festival will help. Possession is half the battle, or so they say."

Panic seized Jane, rendering her speechless.

Leave their precious books next door, where the Murphy brood played? They'd destroy their treasured collection within a day. No, within an hour.

Temperance Stuart, who Jane usually liked, jumped on Mrs. Abbott's soapbox. "Do you know how many people peer through the glass into that store, to see what the talk is about? Folks need to see the library through that window."

Harriet raised her hand. "We can't tend the library unless it's inside the Tea Room. We'll be unusually busy during the festival."

"Precisely." Temperance made a gesture of reassurance. "We'll take turns staffing the library."

"Harriet and I can handle the library here," Jane insisted. "We always do."

"You'll be busy. I don't see how you can give the library adequate attention, especially now. How will you answer questions, sell subscriptions, complete registration forms, and sell surplus directories? No." Temperance sounded adamant. "I second the motion of moving the books next door. At least for the festival."

If the loss of one title— maybe Lawrence's and maybe not— had disrupted her equilibrium, what would the entire library at risk do? "Who will safeguard the library from the Murphy children? They run wild, roughhouse constantly—"

"You're not listening." Frustration tinged Temperance's tone. "The books will not be your responsibility if they're next door. The association will schedule one of us to be there."

But not at all hours.

Stung, Jane fought to swallow the snide retort perched on her tongue. Temperance wasn't listening to her, or the real danger from the Murphy demons.

Temperance sighed heavily. "If our motion is overruled and the books remain here, you *must* open the lace curtains so the books can be seen. And the books must be moved to display at the window."

Must the club force her into an impossible situation?

If she insisted upon keeping the library inside the Tea Room, she could well imagine Library Association ladies, like Temperance, talking well above a whisper to would-be library patrons... or worse, accosting tea room guests to pay annual library membership fees.

This would *not* go well. Not well at all.

With a dozen pairs of eyes censuring her, Jane chose the least-offensive argument. "I want the curtains to remain closed. To maintain the Tea Room's serene atmosphere."

More than one lady blinked, as if surprised that atmosphere had anything to do with the Tea Room. Those few hadn't been in on a normal day, when ladies sat one or two per table and relished peace and quiet. Normal days were a beauty to behold.

"Atmosphere?" Mrs. Zylphia Hudson stood. "Curtains?"

Jane fought to maintain self-possession. She curled her hands into fists, though her short nails bit into her palms.

"Forgive me." Mrs. Hudson spoke slow and easy, but Jane sensed the coiling viper within. "I'm among the newcomers in Mountain Home, I know that." She scanned the room, her stately gaze flitting from woman to woman, at last resting on Ann Abbott. "I didn't think our library was a permanent fixture of the Tea Room."

Ann chuckled. "It's not. Jane and Harriet, longtime club members, offered a temporary solution. Excellent location here on Main in the new Abbott Brick Block and all."

"Well, then." Mrs. Hudson smoothed the awful purple of her costume. Someone ought to tell her that shade of vivid purple reduced her to a gray pallor. "The simplest solution is obvious. We'll remove contention about retired books—" she speared Jane with a venomous glare— "and end arguments governing the state of lace curtains. I propose we remove the library to another location. Permanently."

"May I have a second?" Temperance asked.

"Second."

"Second."

"Second."

Too many voices, all at once, to discern who wanted to take the library away from Jane. Her chest constricted. Hot tears burned behind her eyes. She swallowed, hard. Miss Jane Mary Vancoller did *not* cry. At least not in public.

"With a nomination and a second," Ann Abbott declared with the tinkle of her bell, "we have need for a vote. Per Ladies' Library Association rules, we have one week to spread the word of the vote to all members. Ballots will be cast two weeks from today at our next scheduled meeting."

Chapter Six

"When, exactly," Harriet asked Jane once they were alone in the Tea Room, "did you make an enemy of Zylphia Hudson?"

"I've no idea." Exhausted, Jane sat in the parlor. She needed to put the place to rights, but that would have to wait.

"I thought the woman neither liked nor disliked me. We've visited when she's come in with her daughter or friends, but..."

"She's an odd one. Might not have noticed she upset you."

Jane drummed her fingers on the lacy cloth. "I suspect you're right."

She'd nearly decided to stand and begin clearing the china to the kitchen, when in the unnatural quiet, she heard the clattering run of little feet...

... and the quiet snap of her screen door against its frame.

The Murphy Gang, *again*?

She sprinted for the kitchen. Sure enough, a platter of cookies waiting on the work table had been disturbed. Crumbs of various sizes were scattered upon the plate, table, and floor.

"Why, those rotten miscreants!" Jane picked up a cookie that had landed icing-down on the floor. "Does their father ever tend them?"

Harriet took up the broom and began sweeping. The icing glaze had dried to the cookies, mostly. The floor would require mopping.

More work.

More sweets, stolen by greedy little boys.

She'd had more than enough. "Perhaps I'll catch the little varmints red-handed, eating the stolen cookies." She'd haul them to their father, again, and this time, she'd demand he discipline his children.

"I'll stay and clean up." Harriet swept crumbs into the dustpan.

Jane crept through the alleyway and, peering through the screen door into the vacant shop, found the heavy wooden door standing open and a voice— a child's— wafting out.

Without a sound, she opened the screen door and slipped inside.

There, amid the crates, barrels, sacks and cardboard cartons, her ruthless neighbor knelt on one knee, his arms around two little boys. Both brats had one cookie in each hand, bites gone from each.

Boys two and three? Numbers two and four? Murphy had said he had four sons and one brother, but she still couldn't tell the kids apart.

"Russell, you know better than to steal." To her

surprise, Mr. Murphy's tone remained level, filled with kindness and disappointment but no anger. "Whether cookies or money, stealing is not right. Stealing is not the behavior of honorable men."

"Yes, Pa." Russell's chin nearly touched his chest. His words were low and soft and barely carried.

Murphy had been short-tempered and demanding with her, but with his children, he seemed to have an abundance of patience. He also seemed to have a handle on disciplining his sons.

"I want you to grow up to be honorable men," he told them.

Both boys examined the cookies in their hands. Sunlight winked upon their wet faces.

"Yes, Pa."

"You, too, Clyde."

Clyde must've been the younger one, who clung to his father and the cookies with the same intensity.

Sunlight streamed through the window at their backs, illuminating dust motes filtering upon them like dew distilling from heaven. Mr. Murphy kissed the little one's hair, even as he embraced him more surely. He hugged and kissed the bigger boy.

The image of this father's gentle discipline reminded her, too well, of the time she'd given Mr. Herschstein the wrong change, shorting him ten cents. That dime had made her heart beat fast and evoked within her a wicked kind of excitement... until Mr. Herschstein left the premises and Father taught her a lesson she'd never forget. Every word had been uttered with love and kindness, in a low voice that no one else had heard.

Just Father, herself, and God.

Her conscience had been pricked that day. From then on, she'd taken extreme care when making change. Every customer received precisely what he'd purchased and paid properly, to the penny.

In the many years she'd worked alongside her father, he'd taught her many valuable lessons. Much more than how to keep a clean store, or the importance of treating customers like dear friends.

She'd learned to work hard. She'd discovered the joy of a job well done.

Homesickness, excruciating and more acute than it had been in years, welled within her until she feared she'd sob aloud. She missed him still. Every day.

How could Mr. Murphy, of all people, renew that pain, that poignant and persistent ache in her chest?

Why must he be the one to remind her of tender moments with her own dad?

Regret tasted bitter on her tongue. She'd misjudged Hank Murphy. She'd believed he made no effort to teach his children right from wrong.

This man was *not* clueless about fatherhood.

She'd been woefully mistaken about him.

Yes, she respected her opponent, but that didn't mean she had to *like* the man. Because she didn't. She *couldn't*.

Even if he evoked a dozen memories of her own father.

Even if he were like her dad, just a little.

"Miss Vancoller," Murphy told his sons, "is busy with a big party in the Tea Room. When it's over, you must bring the pennies from your piggy banks—"

"No, Papa." The bigger boy wailed in distress.

"—and pay Miss Vancoller for her cookies."

The bigger boy shook his head with unmistakable denial. "No. I don't have enough pennies."

"I think you do have enough. You've been saving for a good while."

What was the child saving for? Her conscience pinched. How could she accept this child's money? Worse, how could she not?

The little one buried his sticky face in his father's chest.

The larger boy, called Russell by his pa, dashed tears from his cheek with his sleeve. "I—" *hiccup—* "I'll put it back." *Hiccup.*

"Do those cookies look like they did when you picked them up?" Hank remained calm, his arms about his sons.

"No." The bigger kid held one up, showing the missing bites. "I eated one."

"Miss Vancoller can't sell those cookies to anyone. They don't look new."

"But... Papa!" Russell's sobs grew louder.

"You two go straight home. You get your money, and you come right back. We'll wash your hands and faces, and I'll go with you to apologize to Miss Vancoller. You'll tell her you're sorry, and you'll pay her for the cookies."

From now on, Jane would see to it the cookie platters would not be a temptation to little boys. She'd buy another table to use as a sideboard. She couldn't help it if a cake or puddings had to be on ice, but she would no longer leave treats unattended on the kitchen table.

"She's mean, Papa."

Russell didn't think much of her, did he?

"I'll go with you, son."

He kissed both boys again, and as he moved to stand, to probably shoo them out the back door, she slipped outside.

They hadn't seen her, but they'd opened her eyes.

Though she'd been a wretched example two weeks ago, when one of his brood destroyed the wedding cake, she would be in control today. She'd be kind, and she'd be proper.

She'd take Mr. Murphy's approach as her recipe for success.

If only the Tea Room owner were a man.

Despite years of lessons about proper behavior and honesty and despite the fact he owned a store of his own, Hank had faced this same embarrassing moment with another shopkeeper. Back in Dakota Territory, when Austin had been small, he'd taken a spade, of all things, from the feed store.

He'd helped himself, and when Hank had accompanied his son to apologize, to make restitution, and to teach his boy consequences to his behavior, the transaction had been perfunctory. He'd known what the shopkeeper would do when a child returned the stolen property and apologized.

But the Tea Room's owner, Miss Jane Vancoller,

had proven herself highly excitable. Mercurial. Hysterical.

No wonder his boys were scared to address her.

Truth be told, Hank wasn't looking forward to approaching the woman either. Who knew how she'd react? What she'd scream, what she'd demand?

How many nights would he wrestle his boys into bed, only to have the pair suffer nightmares about Miss Vancoller?

He hated the tightness in his gut, the echoes of yesteryear and the pain his boys had suffered long after Dora's death. If she'd once looked at the lads with love in her eyes, he'd missed it.

Some mother she'd turned out to be.

With one son's shoulder under each hand, he steered them through the front door of the Tea Room. The heavy door had been propped open to enjoy the temperate early September day.

Inside, Miss Jane Vancoller and Miss Harriet McCormick bustled about, sweeping and mopping. The tables had already been cleared, the linens and dishes out of sight.

Jane Vancoller halted, her broom and dust pan in her hands. She took in the two boys at first, then her eyes trailed to Hank's face. A long moment passed. He knew, just knew, any moment she'd burst into accusations, demanding to know what they'd done *now*.

Instead, she offered a kind smile. "Mr. Murphy and sons." She smiled at the boys.

Clyde tried to duck behind Hank's leg. With a firm hand, he insisted the boy remain put. He'd learn, soon enough, that he couldn't take things without paying. If the lesson weren't so important, he might have let it pass.

"Welcome to the Tea Room." A question seemed to linger in her expression.

Hank hesitated to reply. He'd helped Russ practice what to say. The boys needed to do this, as much as they could, on their own.

"Would you men like a seat?"

Hank nudged Russell a few inches closer to Miss Vancoller. "We're not here to dine. Go ahead, son."

Both boys clung to Hank. And both remained silent.

Miss Harriet claimed the broom and dustpan from Jane and retreated with the cleaning implements to the back of the shop.

Alone now with Jane, Hank couldn't help but notice she'd approached. Just two steps but close enough now that his boys clung to him more tightly. Just like they had when their mother had been at her worst.

Not fond memories.

The soft gray of Miss Vancoller's summer dress, trimmed with lace and ruffles, swags and tucks, and an eye-catching bustle... was it new? He'd not seen her wear it before.

The gown reminded him even more of Dora. The kind of gown meant for show and less for motherhood. Perhaps a woman with servants could wear such a thing, but not a woman with diapers to change and wash and a meal to prepare.

But the duchess wore it to sweep and mop.

Slowly, Jane Vancoller lowered to sit on her heels,

surprising him. But then she opened her arms to the boys— a totally unexpected behavior. "Come here, boys. I might be better able to hear you."

The motion was so feminine, so utterly female... he caught his breath.

Why must he see the duchess as a woman? A lovely woman, whose expression softened, who treated his naughty sons with kindness.

He was *not* interested.

No matter how lovely.

Once this apology was through, he'd take his recalcitrant sons home, put them to work where they couldn't get in trouble, and with luck, be done with conversation. Maybe he wouldn't have to talk to her again until the contest had concluded, and he'd won the lease contract. After that, what could they possibly have to talk about?

She'd be angry. With him and with Mayor Abbott.

Her anger and bluster would be a blessing. Hank would have the space he needed, while Jane Vancoller went about managing her tea room.

That would be that.

He might not be interested in Jane Vancoller's offer... but his sons were.

As sober as a condemned man headed for the gallows, Russell walked to Jane. He halted just beyond her reach. The kid had every right to be scared of the woman.

"I'm sorry Miss Van Collie real sorry I took your cookies and ate them and I shouldn't have I sorry." In one breath, Russ spat out his rehearsed apology and dove for cover behind Hank.

"Try again," Hank urged the child. "Slower this time." At least Miss Vancoller hadn't started screaming. "Remember your manners."

The boy grabbed his flat cap, pulled it off, and clutched it to his chest. Pale hair stuck up every-which way.

Hank noted the woman's smile. Not gleeful triumph, but the kind of smile a parent fights to hide when a boy's antics are sweet and ill-behaved.

"Ma'am, I'm sorry I eated your cookies." Nerves made the boy antsy.

The kid had learned to expect the worst— one of Hank's greatest failures as a father. But never again. He put a steadying hand on his son's shoulder. "What do you have for Miss Vancoller?"

With a heavy sigh, Russ dug into his pocket and pulled out a handful of pennies. One dropped and landed with the barest of sounds upon her expensive rug. He dropped to his knees and grabbed the coin in his too-full fist.

Once on his feet, Russ offered his fist with copper showing between a finger or two. "Stealing ain't right. I must pay for 'em."

The duchess looked to Hank, a question in her eyes. He nodded. Take the boy's money, he urged.

She offered a cupped hand, and he dropped his money inside. Seven or eight cents. Either the boy had held some of his savings back, he'd lost some along the way, or he'd sneaked money out of his bank and spent it on one of his many forays into the candy store.

Likely the candy store. The boy had a serious sweet tooth.

"Thank you, Russell, for your honesty."

This encounter was progressing far better than Hank had expected.

The duchess counted the pennies with a fingertip upon her palm, pinched together three, and returned the money to Russell. "Your change, sir."

What was this?

He'd expected her to complain about the mess the boys must've made, yelled that the boy's meager pennies would never cover the cost...

But she'd proved him wrong.

She'd kept her attention squarely on Russ, and her expression had softened, as if she liked the boy.

None of this played out like he'd imagined. He didn't know whether he liked this softer side to Miss Vancoller, but watching her with his boys made him uneasy. Might as well hurry this along.

He nudged Clyde out from behind him. Holding tightly to the boy's hand, he brought the four-year-old to face her. The boy's eyes pleaded for mercy.

"Clyde apologizes," Hank told Miss Vancoller. "He agreed to never go in your kitchen, or any part of your tea room, again."

She searched the boy's face, evidently seeing his contrite nature for herself. "Thank you, Clyde."

"You might doubt his word, given the wedding cake incident." He suspected she doubted a good many things about his sons and their collective or individual word of honor. Hank did, but he understood that boys had to grow into some of these things.

"Not at all." She gestured for Clyde to come to her. She knelt, such that the little one could meet her eye squarely.

She'd met the boys at their level. She'd spoken with kindness and showed affection. Hank found himself confused by the stark difference between the wedding cake and the cookies. If he were confused, the boys had to be, too.

Clyde tightened his grip on Hank's fingers.

"It's all right. Go to her, son." The boy communicated much by way of touch. Holding hands, hugging his papa tight, kicking and writhing when he'd tried to escape Miss Vancoller's capture the day of the cake incident...

"Please?" She seemed remarkably genuine.

Russ counted his pennies again and closed his fist. "She wants your pennies. She won't take 'em all."

For all of Clyde's silence, the boy was smart as a whip and had steady hands for one so young. He'd seen the amount Russell had been charged for the cookies. With care, he pulled pennies from his pocket one at a time. Barely four years of age, and the kid could count and manage basic figures.

With one last glance to his papa for support— and protection?— Clyde approached the duchess. He put the pennies in her hand, also one at a time.

Hank expected the woman to demand Clyde speak, but she did nothing of the sort. Instead, she put her arm around the boy and pulled him in. As easy as if she'd been his mother— no, make that aunt— his whole life, she curled her arm about him. She held the boy close, soothed his back, and still held out an arm for Russell.

That's all Russ needed to see. Half a second, and

he'd slipped into the curve of her arm.

Hank narrowed his eyes at Jane. What game was this? He squinted at the woman... as if that would allow him to see through her machinations.

What did she hope to gain by showing his sons kindness?

He willed her to look at him, so he might read the truth in her eyes. But her eyes remained stubbornly closed. And that lovely half-smile on her lips.

"Thank you for apologizing, boys. You're forgiven." She looked at him then, over his sons' heads. "Will you forgive me? For my short temper?"

Both little ones nodded. Why must children be so trusting?

Once, not all that long ago, he'd been like them. Too quick to forgive and forget. That mistake had cost his sons far too much.

He held Jane's gaze, his jaw tightening. He couldn't trust her to behave herself the next time something happened with his boys and her shop. No matter how hard he tried, there would be a next time.

What if she turned hysterical again? Time would certainly tell.

Two weeks back, she'd been a banshee. Furious at Clyde for ruining her wedding cake. True, these were single cookies, and apparently the guests had already been served, but today, she looked like she'd forgive them anything. And offer them cookies.

"Mr. Murphy?" she asked, a hopeful smile on her face.

She wanted forgiveness, absolution, and who knew what else.

But for the moment, she held his sons as if they were the dearest of friends.

Most of all, this lovely woman wasn't Dora. He'd have to remember that. He nodded a reply, not trusting his voice to hold steady.

"Thank you," she whispered, holding his gaze. Happiness fairly radiated from her expression, as if he'd given her something of immense value.

Her smile widened and her eyes twinkled with pleasure.

His innards tingled and his heart beat harder. All he'd done was bring his boys to do the right thing. And nodded in acknowledgment of her apology.

Instead of behaving like she should, the woman seemed... happy.

Maybe she wasn't impossible to please, after all.

Maybe.

Chapter Seven

At Ina's age, one of her greatest privileges was entertaining a gentleman caller without a chaperone, but she was no fool.

The front door stood open wide, with only the screen door between her home's interior and the street. The parlor draperies were open. Anyone passing by could easily see into the front parlor, and note the propriety between her guest and herself.

If only he'd happened upon her that morning, not in the late afternoon's abysmal heat, then this *tête-à-tête* could've been pleasant and cool. But then, she'd been in her house dress— a tired old thing at least a decade out of fashion.

"Allow me to refill your glass." With nerves that wouldn't abate, Ina poured icy lemonade for Mr. Harris. Advantages to waiting on him for days included plenty of lemonade in the ice box, a fresh order of ice, and gleaming parlor furniture.

"Thank you." His smile reached his eyes. The man

had the most intriguing dark ring about blue irises. His blond hair had grown longer. His full facial hair, thick in his maturity, was both darker and redder than the golden hair on his head.

She itched to touch both.

Mature men, she'd discovered, were undeniably attractive.

This mature man, in particular.

But for now, she simply must keep him entertained and comfortable so he'd stay. If he departed mere minutes after arriving, she'd die of embarrassment.

Or a broken heart.

Or both.

He sipped lemonade.

"Sweet enough?" She leaned in.

His grin did silly, immature, girlish things to her insides. She might swoon.

He saluted her with the glass. "You make delicious lemonade, Miss Dimond. Perfect for this warm day."

"Thank you."

His hair, wind-mussed and cut to emphasize his jaw, called to her. Maybe one day he'd allow her to comb her fingers through those locks.

The mantel clock ticked loudly.

"You're too good to walk me home." She'd said so. Twice now. If only she were talented with conversation. What did she know of conversing with men?

Mr. Harris scooted forward on Mama's sofa. He held his full glass of lemonade, condensation gathering on the cold glass, between his spread knees. He sat so like a... *man.* So virile, strong, and powerful. The seams of his suit of clothes pulled on the breadth of his shoulders and muscled thighs.

His presence, coupled with his size, made her feel... *feminine.* And *small.* Two words no one tied to Ina Dimond.

"You have a lovely home." He looked away, allowing her to breathe. His gaze traveled over the hearth, the trinkets and books upon the mantel, the book cases filling the walls on either side of the hearth. "And many books. Yours?"

Relief loosened her tongue. "Mostly my father's. I'm considering donating many of his books to the Ladies' Library Association." Her mood soured. She didn't want to think of Zylphia Speare.

"Is something wrong?" His gaze had resettled on her face. So attentive and remarkably kind. He almost persuaded her to disclose everything.

"I love the idea of sharing my father's books and his love for learning. He owned many volumes, about many subjects. The Ladies' Library Association welcomes donations, but as it is now, the books take too much space in the Tea Room, and the planned expansion—"

Oh, *no.* She closed her eyes, as if the pallid effort would erase her words.

Men did not like to be challenged. Her father had been adamant; peace would reign in his home. Heat washed through her. Mr. Oscar Harris would never call again if she challenged him about disagreeable subjects. "I misspoke. I— I didn't mean to speak of it."

Incompetent! Stupid! Ignorant!

The man spun his hat between his hands. Any

second, he'd stand and make his excuses. How mortifying to see him go so soon.

"I might disagree, Miss Dimond, but I assure you, that's no reason to ignore the subject. Some men might like their women silent and their daughters obedient. But I can't say I cotton to that kind of thinking."

"You are most unlike my father."

He held her gaze, a challenge sparking in those blue, blue eyes. "Your verdict, Miss Dimond? Is my dissimilarity to your departed father a good thing?"

"Oh, yes. A very good thing." Forty-year-old women did not swoon over a man's attentions. That silliness belonged to girls of seventeen.

"Excellent. I find," he said as he extended his long legs, "I rather like hearing your opinions and your reasons. I'd like to hear what *you* think, as I want to understand you."

He wanted to understand her? Whatever for? Every man of her acquaintance, since the day she'd first pinned up her hair and donned a long dress, had found her either invisible or objectionable.

"I want to know," his voice melted honey and dreams of white lace and orange blossoms, "and tell me true. What happened today on Main?"

"Tell me true. What happened today on Main?" Oscar asked Miss Ina, determined to understand, protect, and help. "You can tell me."

Immediately, he regretted prying. If he would

remain uninvolved, he couldn't put himself in the middle of all this. That meant no intimate questions.

"I'm sorry." He should not dawdle in Miss Dimond's parlor, and he most certainly should not have asked for details. "I should go."

"Please, don't. I'll answer your question. I *want* to answer."

She lowered her gaze, sadness sweeping in with gale force winds.

How could he leave, now? "Yes, ma'am."

"You may be aware I kept house for George prior to his marriage."

Not Mr. Hudson. Not the Hudson men. Not George and Morgan.

For George.

Ina met his gaze. "You asked what happened. What happened is this: I can't go to the Ladies' Library Association meeting anymore."

In true feminine style, the lady had completely changed subjects. First, housekeeping for George, then her inability to go to club meetings. "Why not?"

"Zylphia Hudson, George's new wife, was there. Holding court."

Interesting choice of words. "I see." But he didn't.

"I thought her presence wouldn't matter, but my reaction to Zylphia proved otherwise. Oh, how ever will I manage the Harvest Festival?"

Oscar managed unpleasant social occasions by choosing to not attend. "You like this Harvest Festival?"

"I always went. I enjoyed it."

That meant she had once attended but not in recent years? Why did she hold back?

"George hired me as a housekeeper and cook," her voice small and vulnerable, "through Tildie's illness. We were close friends, Tildie and me. My parents were both gone, I had no family, and thus, had time to spare. I cared for Tildie and her family until she drew her last breath."

Pain echoed in Ina's words, but she didn't seem to want a reply.

"Sometime," she whispered, "in the years between the funeral and Zylphia's arrival, I discovered I'd lost my heart to George."

She turned her gaze from her lap to the window, focused far beyond the street, beyond the mountains filling the window frame. Tears filled her eyes, shimmered there, and overflowed. She blinked, those haunted blue eyes witnessed that place in the past.

Ina's ongoing love for George Hudson would certainly explain her distaste for Zylphia— the woman who usurped her place.

"George sat there, mute, and allowed a woman he'd just met to throw me out." Barely a whisper, but he saw what the words cost. "Only Morgan cared."

Morgan Hudson, the gunsmith's son. Both were highly skilled men of good reputation. Now, he finally placed the new Mrs. Hudson.

Oh, yes. They'd met.

Flirtatious, friendly, and always visiting with someone. Mrs. George Hudson had been in the Emporium a time or five and always had plenty to say, none of it mean. Zylphia Hudson might be an irritant, but she wasn't poisonous... to anyone but Miss Ina.

Far more than understanding stirred in his breast.

This woman, alone in this house, past the age of home and family and children, had made George up like a husband, and his grown son, Morgan, her own. She'd wanted that dream of home and family and wanted it still.

"You know, he never mentioned a word to me, or to his son, about sending for a bride until the day before she arrived."

"Must've come as a shock."

Had Hudson no idea the gift within his reach? A devoted woman, a loving woman. How could he have lived, day after day, with Ina Dimond in his kitchen, preparing his meals, cleaning his home... and not noticed her?

George must've been blind. Ina was the original article. A woman whose heart had so much to give.

She'd make a wonderful wife.

How— *why?*— could he look at Ina as a would-be wife and criticize George Hudson for not wanting her?

He didn't want her, either.

He *didn't*...

Maybe he did.

But he didn't want to want her.

Panic seared through him. Hot and intense and terrible.

How had this happened?

A man like him had no business taking on a wife. He'd make a horrid husband.

No woman would take on the likes of him, with all his troubles. Lulu, his sweet girl, had fainted when she'd seen him on crutches. The next day, her brother had returned Oscar's ring. Lulu never had recovered from the shock.

He'd not thought of her in months.

His heart pounded, as if he'd run on his bad leg, all the way back to the pharmacy. With the galloping heart rate came his body's insistence that he breathe rapidly, too.

Sweat beaded on his forehead. He fished for his handkerchief and blotted his brow.

Ina finally looked at him. "I apologize. I shouldn't have burdened you with all of that." Her soft smile stole years from her features, softened lines, and gave him a glimpse of the young girl she'd been.

"You're no burden, Miss Ina."

He'd overheard once, some time ago, that Miss Dimond had never married. He didn't doubt that as the truth— he simply couldn't comprehend *why*.

At age forty-two, all he could see was the decade between them. What was she? Thirty-two? Thirty-three? Younger, appealing, and so sweet.

Lemonade burbled as she refilled his glass. She took her seat and leaned closer, with elbows upon her knees. "I need a certain favor of you, and I do hope you'll agree."

"If it's within my power to grant, I will."

"Please. Escort me to the Harvest Festival?"

In the pale blue of her eyes, he glimpsed a reflection of himself. Lacking confidence, uncertainty, and a hint of desperation.

How could he deny her anything?

If she wanted to enjoy the festival, maybe face George Hudson and his wife, he could give her an arm to learn on. "I'd be honored, Miss Dimond."

On Friday evening, quite by chance, Jane locked the Tea Room's back door as Hank closed the Grocery. Harriet had left early with a headache. Hank seemed to be alone, too.

In the alleyway behind the new brick block, dusk teased her senses. She recognized Hank, though the light was so low that color drained to that odd breath when vivid hues give way to ghostly shades of gray.

Was he smiling? Glad to notice her? Or was that a glower? If only he'd speak, she could infer much. "Good evening, Mr. Murphy."

"Evening to you, Miss Vancoller." He sounded pleased to see her. Good.

Mrs. Abbott had given Jane an assignment, and she must act before her tentative peace with Hank Murphy went up in smoke. "May I walk with you? I have a favor to ask."

"What have they done now?"

They walked side by side toward the street.

"Your boys?" She chuckled. "Nothing. They've been well-behaved." Not a single sweet had been stolen, but she'd ensured nothing tempting was visible... nor stored in the lower compartments in the ice box.

"Now you've piqued my curiosity. What else could you want with me?"

"Other than the not-so-vacant shop?"

He chuckled. How could he be so relaxed? She'd been tied in knots since this whole mess started.

Hank put his hand to her back and guided her across the street.

His touch, though appropriate in every way, evoked unwelcome awareness. The man was... *different*.

Taller and sparer in movement than Lawrence.

The music of his footfalls was in an altogether different register.

To walk together, as she'd done with Lawrence, daily, put this man, this *new* man, in that locus belonging to Law.

In that space, tucked in her heart, where Law yet lived.

How often had she closed her eyes— for just a moment— while walking home and sensed him beside her? The sensation was nothing more than a memory and a wish rolled together.

She tried not to listen to the cadence of Murphy's heels on the sidewalk, but something about this man called to her. She ignored her senses.

How *foolish*, this response to a man she didn't much like.

She loved Lawrence Riddle, still. She'd always love Lawrence.

She shook herself, determined to ask her question, complete the task given her, and hurry home to retire, where she would not recall Mr. Murphy. Not once.

As one, they stepped from the street to the boardwalk. Good. Two blocks and they'd part company. He lived one direction, and she the other.

"Tell me," he said, "about the favor you want."

"I've been tasked by Mrs. Abbott to borrow your storeroom's window."

His head whipped around. "What does Mrs. Abbott want with my window? It's more hers than mine, at least 'til the contest concludes."

"A common courtesy, that's all. Mrs. Abbott is president of the Ladies' Library Association."

He slowed, grasping her elbow and turning her to face him. Enough light spilled through windows and from the twilit sky to mostly read confusion in his expression.

"We want to set up the library before your storage room's street-side windows. We need to draw attention to the library and seek new subscribers. We'll put a sign on the walk outside and use the door. But only during the festival."

"I understood the library and your tea shop were connected."

She winced. "Only in the loosest of terms."

"And...?" he prompted, digging for more.

"And I've learned that one does not slight Mrs. Abbott. She asked me to seek your permission, so I'm asking."

"Permission granted. I'll move my wares away from the window so you have space for bookshelves. A chair or two? A table?"

How was this solicitous man one and the same as the T.A. Murphy she'd argued with, over the same bit of real estate? "Yes. Thank you, though it won't be me. The library will staff someone. They won't let anyone rob you."

"I doubt anyone will roll away a barrel. That's not my concern." He paused. "I heard a vote will be held at the next library meeting, in a couple of weeks."

"Who told you that?"

He ignored the question. "Why remove the library?"

Just as she'd suspected, the man hadn't heard a word she'd said during their *discussion.* "Because I haven't room to properly display the books *and* enough tables for my patrons."

"You never mentioned this."

"I recall the conversation perfectly. I explained the necessity of seating large social groups—"

"I remember that part. Well. You did not mention the books."

Hadn't she? "I might be mistaken. I honestly don't recall."

Hank stilled. They must've slowed their pace over the last block, for Hank simply... halted. "Did you just admit you might be mistaken?"

His arms hung at his sides. If only the moon would rise! She'd dearly love to see what was going on in T.A. Murphy's thoughts.

"Yes," she told him, "I believe I did."

"I'm astonished. I met a woman with a streak of decency." His tone was buoyant, lighthearted, and filled with funning.

Who knew this foul-tempered man, beneath the crust, truly wasn't foul-tempered? Who knew he'd grant permission so easily?

"Thank you," she told him again. "The Ladies' Library Association thanks you. We'll move the books in the night before the festival? Maybe a day or two earlier. I'll ask Mrs. Abbott."

"You're welcome." He pushed his hands into his

overall's pockets. "Which way will you vote? To move the library or keep it?"

How would she vote? To keep the books! ... though she hadn't a chance. Several times, she'd stood at the bookshelf, running her fingers over the spines. She'd opened several volumes that had been Law's, leafing through the pages.

She folded her arms to hold herself together. "If sentiment remains the same as this past week, the library will be gone before the meeting concludes."

He must've heard sadness in her tone because he stepped nearer, and his big hand grasped her elbow. The simple way he showed support heated her insides.

His presence— large, warm, and near— pressed upon her. The emotion could not be fear, yet it weighed as much. Maybe more.

To find his touch exciting and new... and unfamiliar gave her a queasy stomach. She couldn't enjoy his nearness... could she?

No— she couldn't.

Not when she'd made vows to remain faithful to Lawrence.

"Goodnight, Mr. Murphy." She pulled away and nearly ran toward home. She forced herself to take measured strides.

"Goodnight," he called after her.

Chapter Eight

"Harris?" Hank glanced up from the ledger he held a pencil over, his eyes refusing to focus. "You married?"

"Me?" Blond, heavily muscled, Oscar looked up from his medicine chest. "No. Never."

One quick glance reassured Hank that he and his business partner were still alone. "I was. Obviously."

"Uh-huh." Oscar continued counting small vials of something or another. He jotted a quantity on the inventory form.

"Children?" Hank pressed.

"No."

Interesting. Oscar was at an age where his oldest children might be grown and on their own. "My boys are a blessing. A gift I cherish every single day, but that marriage? An unmitigated disaster."

Oscar abandoned his counting. He sat on his high stool and watched Hank with interest.

How could Hank explain what had happened with Jane Vancoller last week, both when the boys had paid for lemon cookies and when he'd walked her toward home? The grocery had been busy as a beehive on Saturday, so now, on Monday morning, he finally had a chance to voice the concerns that had nagged him ever since.

"I know the love of a father— that's something I understand. There's not a thing under creation I wouldn't do for my boys." *Boys* accounted for his brother and his sons, so he'd taken to using the term.

Hank tossed the pencil on the ledger and let it roll until it toppled to the floor. "But there's one thing I'll never understand. How is it a woman can be indifferent about her child?"

The question had dogged him for a nearly a decade. No way would Oscar Harris have something new to offer in the problem-solving department, so why bring him into family matters?

Oscar grunted and massaged his left leg like he tended to do. "I figure the world is full of people without a heart."

Hank hadn't asked, but he could add two and two and come up with four.

That leg had been injured. Could've happened on a farm or in a city. But something about Oscar's bearing made Hank think he'd damaged that leg in the war between the States.

The idea made sense. Oscar had been of an age to take up arms to defend the Union. Maybe he'd fought for the Confederacy. There were some crates a man didn't pry the lid off of, and a man's war stories were one of 'em.

War always brought out the worst and the best in

human beings. Oscar had probably seen a good deal of heartless men. "Heartless women? You ever come across one of those?"

Oscar leaned back and folded thick arms over his chest. "Any specific woman you have in mind? You're not talking about Miss Vancoller." He managed to make his supposition a statement rather than a question.

"No." Hank pushed off the counter and took to polishing the glass. "Though I'd have said yes, before last week."

"You took your sons to pay for lemon cookies."

Hank had left Oscar at the counter alone. Austin had skedaddled to find Jimmy, since Russ had been home with Clyde to pocket their pennies, and the youngest hadn't been napping on the pallet in their room.

"She took the boys' apology with the grace of a queen—" no, like a loving mother, but that didn't sound right. "How can a childless woman hug my boy better than his own mama ever did?"

Emotion stole his breath. Images of her flitted through his mind. Jane, kneeling at Clyde's level, her arm about him and welcoming Russ. She'd seemed right, somehow. Warm and genuine and affectionate.

Everything his boys had missed out on in their lives.

Everything the kids needed, though they didn't know it.

She'd allowed dirty little hands on her new, pale-gray skirts. She'd noticed. Had she cared? No! The woman had hugged the boy closer.

How, exactly, was he supposed to forget all he'd

seen?

Worse, how would he rid himself of a maelstrom of emotions? He kept circling 'round and 'round, caught in the eddy.

"I don't know." Harris fiddled with his case of medicines, the drawers fanned open, revealing a dizzying array of vials, bottles, boxes, and cubbyholes. His eyes might be fixed on the contents, but the vision he saw was long ago and far away. "I don't understand much about women."

Hank grunted in agreement. "My boys were born, and I loved them instantly, every last one." Why did he speak of this? The words poured out with the speed of a runaway train. Where was the brakeman? "For the first time, a woman shows my boys motherly affection, and I—"

What was he supposed to do with the hitch in his heart?

Worse, he feared he knew why he'd taken her elbow in his hand last Friday night, why he'd been eager to step in, solve the library problem... And why he'd been eager to touch her, to be near her.

The big question remained. Why had she fled for home?

He sucked in a deep breath, forced himself to calm. What was *wrong* with him? "Oscar, have you a patent medicine on that shelf to cure what ails me?"

The druggist's straight, light eyebrows scrunched together. "What's that?"

"I need something to knock some sense into a fellow."

Oscar chuckled. The warm kind that said *I can*

relate. "We have bottles that claim to cure anything, even stupidity." His too-handsome smile slowly faded. "I think," he said, "you don't need a potion."

"I don't?"

"When a remarkable woman happens along, a man ought to look twice."

Oscar might've stuck to his guns, but Hank's probing conversation about women and black-hearted mothers and love had made him think.

And think he had, 'til closing time, and through procurement of ingredients and the churning of ice cream.

Unable to restrain himself, he acted on Miss Dimond's invitation and called on her at home. If pressed, he'd acknowledge he'd come calling for two specific reasons. First, he wanted to. Second, *he was wanted—* and that, he discovered, could be mighty difficult to ignore.

He climbed the steps to Ina's front porch, and upon finding the door standing open, the lighter-weight screen door dimming his view inside, he knocked upon the frame.

"Coming," she called from the back of the house. Her footfalls upon the floorboards and then the carpet of the vestibule— perhaps too fancy of a name for the simple, small home Ina's father had built.

She opened the screen, a dish towel in her hand and an apron over her dress.

Not expecting him, then. He couldn't help but smile as her eyes lit up. Brilliantly blue.

"Good evening, Mr. Harris." She untied her apron, lifted it over her hair, pinned up in its usual braided coil upon her head. She clutched the apron and towel behind her back.

Such an endearing image.

He couldn't come courting without a little gift. Somehow, her favorite scented soap didn't seem right. And flowers were in abundance at this season. Every man brought flowers.

So, he lifted a tin pail, filled with ice cream, and dripping water droplets of condensation. "Might you have two spoons, Miss Dimond?"

Her laughter lifted his spirits. "I believe I do." She held the screen door open wider, inviting him to enter. "On second thought, shall we sit outside?" She tipped her head toward the bench beneath a shade tree on the front lawn. "There?"

In a matter of moments, Ina had joined him on the bench. He held the pail of melting ice cream between them.

She'd brought out more than spoons. She'd laid a napkin over her lap and offered him one as well. His napkin, draped over the thigh nearest to her, was well-pressed and spotless.

She dipped a spoonful of delectable cream with a diced bit of peach. With a hand cupped beneath her spoon, she lifted it to her mouth.

Where had his manners gone? A gentleman did not stare at a woman's mouth— especially while she ate.

Her eyes closed as she seemed to roll the bite over

her tongue, allowing the confection to melt. "Delicious."

"Thank you."

She chuckled. "Taking credit for Whipple's Bakery's recipe, are you?"

He pointed at her with his spoon. "Who said anything about Whipple's?"

"If not the bakery, then who?"

"You think I bought this from your friend, Mrs. Cresswell? She has a churn, you know."

"Yes, I do know Maggie's churn. I've turned that handle every summer for years. Everyone has a churn these days." Her laughter came easily, a lovely companion to her ready smile.

Miss Dimond's expression glowed with her smile.

So did her eyes. He held her gaze, enchanted by the blue so much like the September Colorado sky.

He cleared his throat. "You also don't seem to know that I can do a great deal with a university degree in Chemistry."

"You made this?" Her surprise and pleasure pleased him.

"I did. It's a simple thing to read a receipt, measure ingredients correctly. Oh, and to bring about a mild chemical reaction. Salt and ice. You know."

"Yes, I believe I do know." She spooned another mouthful, this time with a prominent bit of tangy peach.

With cream and sugar melting on his tongue, Oscar watched Ina's simple pleasure in savoring his concoction. He swallowed hard when she looked at him, an eyebrow raised.

He blinked.

She nudged him with her shoulder. "What? You clearly have something to say."

He swallowed, hard. "I..." Truth was, he hadn't been thinking. He'd been lost in her.

Absurd!

Men like him did not lose their minds in the company of lovely women. He'd had decades of practice, but this one did strange things to his equilibrium.

"Have you other amazing talents with chemistry?"

"Beyond my work in the pharmacy?"

She nodded, her attention fixed on him, as if she truly wanted his answer.

"Plenty." He leaned a bit nearer to whisper. "I can write a secret message with nothing other than juice of a lemon and reveal it with nothing more than a candle."

Her smile was contagious. She shook her head, chuckling with him. "Parlor games?"

"If you prefer."

She leaned nearer, teasing him with the scent of carnation soap, clean woman, and peach ice cream. "Can you pull a rabbit from a top hat?"

"Not with chemistry as the means."

"Ah. Now that's a disappointment."

He shook off the twinge of inevitability— yes, he would disappoint her— and dived back in to the teasing conversation. Right now, she enjoyed his company.

"If not a rabbit, how might you entertain me with chemistry?"

"I can make an eggshell melt away, leaving its contents undisturbed."

She narrowed her eyes. "That does sound like

magic."

He enjoyed another bite of melting ice cream. "Pure chemistry, I assure you."

Chemistry, he understood. Elements remained constant, reacting the same way, every single time. So unlike people.

"How, then?" She searched his eyes, as attuned to him as he was to her.

"If I give away my secrets..."

"You claim you're a chemist and not a magician. I trust you can reveal your secrets. The answer is probably in a chemistry book, somewhere."

"Vinegar." He enjoyed the sparkle in her eyes, this ease of conversation, the complete absence of others vying for his attention. Conversing with her at her home was so much more enjoyable than stealing a minute or two at the emporium.

"Vinegar?" Curiosity infused her entire being.

"Yes."

"Everyday household vinegar? The kind I buy at the Grocery Emporium?"

"Yes. Normal vinegar."

"Show me."

"Now?" He chuckled, blindsided by her almost childlike enthusiasm. Such a little request, to demonstrate the simple chemical reaction. "Well, I suppose..." Her reputation was far safer here, on the bench in her front garden. "... in the Emporium?" Others would enjoy the display, too. Ina might enjoy sharing the experience with neighbors.

She took the pail from his fingers and spooned up the last taste of peaches and cream. He found himself pinned to her, watching with fascination.

But she didn't bring the melted cream to her lips. She lifted it between them and met his gaze. "You should have this."

To accept a morsel from a woman's utensil felt like a flirtation.

Yet her expression was far from indecent. Just sweet, gentle Ina, gracious with the last drops of the dessert he'd made for her.

Her image, spoon raised in offering, and he hesitant to accept, etched itself deep in his memory. That told their story, didn't it? An innocent, hopeful offer to a jaded, hesitant old man.

Before he could think too much, add too much to their growing story, he accepted the cream. A drop must've trickled over his lip and into his beard because she was quick with her napkin.

He would've eased away, assured her he'd wash his face with soap before bed— and behind his ears, too— but risked glancing into her eyes.

This woman was something special, indeed. That talk with Hank had made him see that more clearly. Combined with talk he'd heard between women as they completed their purchases, he'd learned more about Ina Dimond's nature in this one day than he'd pieced together up to now.

She slowly lowered the napkin to her lap.

Their gazes remained intertwined.

How could he express all he wanted to say? He had to start somewhere. "I hear you've offered a considerable number of volumes to the library."

"Who told you this?" she asked, three parts playful

to one part insistent.

"A person who purchased a patent medicine."

"You won't say?"

He had the oddest urge to touch the tip of her nose with his fingertip. This close, he could see the fine lines at the corners of her eyes. Whispers of lines— laugh lines, he hoped, for she deserved laughter— at the edges of her mouth. But the finest of character lines on her forehead troubled him the most.

What did Ina Dimond have to fret over? What caused her worry?

What did she dread?

What did she fear?

She raised that same napkin to blot her mouth, her chin. She covered her nose. "Do I have... a problem?"

He'd been staring. "No, you silly goose." The old endearment slipped out. Where had *that* come from?

"Silly?" Her eyes opened a bit wider. "Goose?"

"Words of endearment, I assure you."

Turning her face a bit away, she assessed him with narrowed eyes. "If you say so."

"I say so." A question had plagued him since he'd heard of Ina's generous donation. "Why did you donate so many titles to the library?" He'd been so hopeful, electrified, really, by the hopeful sign.

If she gave so many books to the library, that must mean she intended to participate... that insecure Mrs. Hudson hadn't as much power over her.

"They were my father's. I've not opened more than one or two in all these years he's been gone. Someone should enjoy them."

"I accept your answer. But I'll bet there's something more."

She narrowed her eyes. The Cupid's-bow of her lips compressed into a line. Her effort to remain mum dissolved as her smile lit her features. "After our talk last week, I decided I'll go to the Ladies' Library Association meeting, despite Mrs. Hudson's presence or absence. It's my club, too."

Happiness and pleasure made the years fall away. The woman was radiant, an absolute beauty— and she hadn't the vaguest notion.

"What's more," she continued, "I'd determined to donate enough books to make that library every bit as much mine as it is hers."

Much later, when Oscar strolled toward his rented room, he looked at his buoyant happiness with cynicism.

He'd enjoyed Miss Ina's company far too much. Evidently, she'd enjoyed their time together as well. Lovely Ina Dimond deserved far more than him. He knew that to be true. Eventually, she'd want to leave him, so he'd do the only honorable thing and make that eventuality easy for her.

If she fancied the idea of marriage, she'd tie herself to him, and that would be an unmitigated calamity. She couldn't commit to the right man, the much better man, if she were hampered by him. The gentleman he wanted to be, the gentleman she *believed* him to be, would end their association.

He'd keep his commitment, by accompanying her to as little of the autumn social event as possible. In the meanwhile, he would not call.

Chapter Nine

"Jane, darling." Mrs. Abbott's patented tone was two parts condescension to one part impatience. "Coffee pairs perfectly with apple dumplings. Tea, no matter the variety, does not."

Jane bit her tongue. Did she dare tell one of her most frequent patrons that a tea room wasn't meant to serve coffee? Her patience had worn thin. "Mrs. Abbott, if coffee were on the menu, the Tea Room would be a coffeehouse. Or a café."

"Oh, that's silly." Ann tipped her head back and laughed. "Fresh apples are in season. I saw the beauties you carried in just now. Do tell me you're making apple dumplings. I bet you are. My mouth is watering already."

Yes, she'd intended apple dumplings. But not coffee.

"I've scheduled a small, intimate meeting at two o'clock. Here. Three ladies, including myself, so save my favorite table for three, won't you?"

"Yes, Mrs. Abbott." The table, she could do. But if the woman made a habit of coming in before the Tea Room opened to issue her imperial orders, Jane would—

Well, she didn't know what she'd do, given the amount of money Mrs. Abbott spent here, but she'd think of something.

"All three of us will take coffee. Hot, rich, with cream and sugar. And two apple dumplings each."

Jane's threadbare patience nearly snapped. "Am I the proprietor?"

"Yes, Jane, and you know I'm your best supporter. I want to see the Tea Room succeed."

Jane doubted that. If Mrs. Abbott felt strongly about the Tea Room over the Grocery Emporium, she could have persuaded her husband to lease the adjacent space to Jane. She'd seen a dozen poignant examples of the influence Mother had exerted. In Father's eagerness to please her, he'd yielded to her wishes as often as possible.

But Mother had a much more congenial nature— or had, at least, *before*.

"You realize, don't you, that if you and your mother would consent to share the receipt for your mother's blue-ribbon apple dumplings, I could offer them to my friends at home."

Why hadn't she noticed the lengths Ann went to, in order to have things her way?

Yes, she could give away Mother's receipt... but she'd lose more than a family heirloom. She'd lose Ann's business. At least today.

Perhaps the receipt was a small price to be rid of

the woman.

"No?" Ann asked, but she failed to pause and wasn't interested in a reply. "Ah, well. I'll be in at two with my friends. I'm looking forward to coffee with my dumplings."

The moment Ann left the Tea Room parlor, Jane walked as calmly as she could manage to the back. It seemed she had an errand to procure coffee beans and a mill. The Tea Room had received its orders.

Harriet looked up from the drawer where they kept demitasse spoons. "Have you seen the paring knife?"

In this well-organized kitchen, everything had its place. "No. I've not used it since..." She'd trimmed a fine ribbon of lemon rind to flavor the cookies. "Last week." She'd sliced the lemons in half and juiced them to thin the icing.

"Those naughty boys..." Harriet began.

"They've not sneaked in here, for nearly a week." Jane met her employee's eye.

That we know of. The thought hung between them.

"You're sure the paring knife is missing?" Jane glanced from the basket of beautiful apples to the tall cabinet housing the china service and utensils.

"I've searched for it since you carried in the apples. It's gone."

"Very well." Jane took her reticule from its place in the bottom drawer.

"What will you do?" Harriet's expression said she'd confront Mr. Murphy if Jane didn't.

"I'll purchase a knife and coffee and return

promptly." She had no trouble confronting a thief but couldn't make accusations without proof.

Hank *needed* to talk to Jane.

She'd been on his mind since Monday's awkward discussion with Oscar Harris... the moment he'd realized the older man was right. Very few women deserved a second look. In this instance, the duchess had earned his cooperation.

He'd hoped to speak to her at the Tea Room, but his free moments coincided with her busiest hours. All day, he'd hoped to walk her home, but she'd closed before he could lock up for the night. He broke away from his family once the boys were fed and headed toward bed. Despite the fading daylight, he knocked on Jane's front door shortly after seven o'clock.

"Mr. Murphy." Jane seemed surprised to see him. The inside of her home, lit and warm, carried the aroma of supper.

She'd changed into a lightweight at-home dress. Calico, plain, serviceable, and different in every way from the fancy attire she wore to work. No bustle, no ruffles, and no pleats.

He shuffled his boots. "Am I interrupting your supper?"

"No. We've eaten." She opened the door wider, revealing a tidy and well-appointed parlor. The two-story frame structure, an upright-and-wing construction, was common in town. The eaves dripped with gingerbread carvings. White paint peeled in places, showing the lack of a man in the house. "Come in, please. Mother is in the parlor."

"Might we visit on the porch instead?" The fewer ears to overhear this topic of conversation, the better.

"If you'd like."

He waited for her cue. Would they sit on the porch swing or stairs? Did she prefer they remain standing? Given her awkward and rapid departure the night they'd walked toward home together, he'd determined to avoid the same conclusion to tonight's conversation. He'd waited too long to talk with her to have her bolt into the house prematurely.

She pulled the door shut and joined him. He watched her glance to the swinging bench, built for two, then discard the notion as quickly. But she did offer him a smile. "Is something on your mind?"

Receding daylight kissed her golden locket, upon its sturdy chain. "This is what I've seen you wearing—" poor choice of words— "I've noted its presence, beneath your bodices." He grimaced at the ever-worsening comments.

Gentlemen did not comment about a lady's bodice, nor anything she wore beneath it. He opened his mouth to apologize, but she didn't seem upset by his inappropriate comments. She caressed the surface with fingertips, the gold probably warm from the heat of her skin. If anything, she'd turned inward, remembering a time when she'd been happy and deeply in love.

Lockets were intended for keepsake photographs. Whose likeness did she carry?

A dozen different people knew Jane well and had

been in town most of her life. He'd considered asking those folks who Jane mourned, as she must've had someone. A woman like her wouldn't have remained single without a reason. But he'd refrained from asking. If he ever heard the tale, he wanted *her* story.

He wasn't ready to ask. Given her hesitancy to speak of the locket, he doubted she would divulge her secrets about the man she'd loved.

A jolt of— no, this was *not* jealousy. *Couldn't be.* Jealousy had no place in their... friendship.

Yes, *friendship.*

What else? A competitor? Like shoes pinching his son's toes, the category no longer fit.

Instead of speaking, she strolled to the porch railing, effectively turning her back.

He might not be ready to ask for details about the man, but curiosity about the woman overrode good sense. "Why do you hide a lovely piece of jewelry?"

Women clung to physical memories of loved ones. He'd seen more than one widow wearing mourning jewelry— one, a glass vial containing tears spilled in grief. The whole point of wearing the pieces was to bring remembrance of loved ones forever lost.

He wasn't sentimental. But somewhere— in Dora's Bible?— was a lock of her hair. The women who'd washed and dressed her in preparation for burial had snipped a curl. Hank had tucked it away. Eventually, their sons might want the memento.

"I wear it out of sight," she said too low for anyone else to overhear, "because Mother detests it."

Bad memories for her mother? Not what he'd thought to hear. He joined her at the rail overlooking her front lawn. He wanted to ask, but she closed the topic of conversation by slipping the locket inside the neck of her summer work dress.

Maybe, one day, she'd say more. But probably not.

The sharing of that story would be an intimacy of startling depths, one reserved for a new love. And that, no matter how intriguing, would never happen for him.

"You aren't here to ask about my locket. Why did you come?"

"Something has occurred to me, and it bears discussing."

He'd snagged her complete attention.

"You and I," he said, "are not required to go along with this contest."

He'd expected an argument. Instead, she searched his face. "What do you have in mind?"

"I suggest we work together. With effort, we can turn this contest rigmarole to our advantage."

"You're not serious."

He huffed. "Why wouldn't I be?"

"Because Mayor Abbott owns the building and can rent to whomever he pleases— not necessarily you or me. And because the Abbotts, both Mr. and Mrs., enjoy nothing more than attention. All the talk in the Tea Room these past weeks is a mere sliver of the town's interest in the matter. Everyone is curious. They're waging bets—" her voice rose, as if the idea horrified her— "on the outcome, as well as what challenges he will present."

"Yes, I've heard all of that and more. Folks talk of little else." People came in to ask questions and learn the latest on the only subject anyone wanted to discuss.

He'd grown weary of the gossip. "Don't folks have something better to do than jaw about this mysterious competition? Like harvest their fields? Carry their grain to the mill?"

"I believe the people of Mountain Home continue to tend to their work."

In the settling dusk, crickets sang their autumn ballad. Even the insects knew summer was gone and harvest season had come.

She stepped to the porch swing and settled into one side of it, leaving room for him, but did not extend an offer. "Mr. and Mrs. Abbott are over the moon with the attention. If we disrupt their glory by refusing to play along, he'll take away your storage room."

A twinge struck, hot and sharp. "The outcome is far from decided. I'm aware I might be required to move everything out of that store and put it someplace else."

She watched him closely, evidently weighing her options. The green of her eyes seemed brighter, more vivid in tonight's waning light. "That's what distresses me most."

"Aw, don't worry about me. I'll be fine."

"My apologies, Mr. Murphy, but you misunderstood. How can I prepare, when I haven't a clue what to prepare for?" Her volume and confidence shrank over the course of that single question. "I suspect this year's festival will be unlike anything Mountain Home has known."

"I think you're right." Hank found the admission easy to make. "I've heard Abbott himself doesn't know what he'll present come opening day."

"You believe that?"

"No, I think it's his way of deflecting unwanted questions."

She glanced left, then right, as if assessing whether neighbors might be out in the cool of the evening. She patted the empty seat beside her.

She didn't have to ask twice. The chains supporting the swinging bench jangled. The wooden slats protested his weight but held fast.

The seating arrangement was cozy, with little room to spare. Her warm figure nearly touched him. Her heat breached the minuscule distance, making him acutely aware of how close she sat. He'd scoot further away, but the wooden arm already bit into his ribs. Knowing the duchess, she hugged her side of the bench, too.

Had her father built this porch swing with courting in mind?

Maybe she wasn't at all troubled by the proximity, for she dived back into conversation. "I think it's claptrap, and he *does* know. If he is to succeed in bringing the most people into town for the festival, he must increase the talk and shroud the whole thing in mystery. Thus, he's not saying."

Behind her words, filled with discomfort, lay far more than that. "You'd be more comfortable knowing what's coming." She'd as much as said so. "And the thought of being on display, forced to compete, feels—"

"Terrifying. Yes. Exactly!"

"No ax throwing for you?" He chuckled, relieved when she joined him with a wide grin with a flash of white teeth in the fading daylight.

"No ax throwing."

"Pie eating?" He pushed the swing into motion, his boots grazing the porch floorboards. His attention snagged on the lift of little curls at her ears and nape. The stray locks bounced with the motion and temperate breeze.

"Perhaps one slice. You'll win that one for sure."

"Greased pig?"

"Now you're delusional." She chuckled.

Somehow, he couldn't take offense to her choice of words. He'd been called delusional by many. Every effort to see winter met with preparation had brought on teasing that had turned mean a time or two.

But Miss Jane Vancoller, lady that she was, hadn't a mean bone in her body. "If you think I'm chasing a greased pig, you're wrong."

"Nah. I doubt you'd play a game meant for men and boys. I like that about you, Miss Vancoller."

Her fingertips returned to caress the locket, and her gaze focused well beyond the street. He must've brought up another memory. "I apologize, I didn't mean—"

"No need to apologize." She drew a breath, the kind that brushed the calico of her sleeve against his. "I should forfeit the contest. If I make a big announcement and ensure everyone knows, that would take the power away from Abbott."

Her words and the wealth of emotion behind them filled him with an ache— but not heartache. Just aggravation with Abbott and his games. "You don't want to do that."

One little shrug. Her movement brushed against

him. He sensed the resignation in her tone and her posture. This would never do. He'd not come here to add to her troubles but to ease them. "We have additional options."

"Such as?"

He spread his hands in a gesture of myriad possibilities. "Contrive a draw so neither of us is a clear winner."

"Your idea has merit— if our intention is to frustrate Mr. Abbott. But you require a storage room. Given my experience in your crowded store this week, I imagine you'd like to divide that available real estate to both enlarge your store and provide the much-needed space for storage."

The woman was correct, of course, but he didn't like her giving up on her own requirements simply to avoid contention. "I'll remind you that your reasons for wanting the lease haven't changed. You were filled with fire and determination when you confronted Abbott and me."

She'd pinned her attention to her hands, clasped in her lap, but now, looked directly at him. "That was before."

Before what? "Stay and fight."

"Why?"

The cinnamon-sugar freckles strewn over her creamy skin decorated the bridge of her nose and cheekbones. He couldn't have painted a more idyllic balance of life and vitality if he'd tried. Potions to erase freckles sold briskly at the Emporium. Why fools found freckles unbecoming, he'd never understand. "Your freckles—" he swallowed, his heart somehow crowding his windpipe— "are beautiful."

He'd spoken aloud, hadn't he? He palmed his face, bracing his elbow on the bench's arm. He truly was cracked, as mad as some claimed. He fisted the other hand and tapped it on his thigh in frustration.

Blame the propinquity— and his lonely heart.

He should go. Immediately. Before his tongue spoke more tomfoolery.

"Thank you." With the lightness of a butterfly alighting upon a flower, she rested her hand over his fist— the one on his thigh.

He nearly flinched clean out of his skin, but she didn't let go.

He peered between the digits at the shocking image of the duchess's hand situated lightly over his fist.

Her touch— hesitant and light— brought an immediate rush of pleasure. She offered comfort in this simple way, and he liked it. He liked it immensely. And that brought its own harvest of problems.

What to do now?

Tease about a game of rock, paper, scissors?

Paper did indeed cover rock... for the win.

All he could do was unbutton a little... and try not to enjoy the warmth of her touch too much.

She toed the swing into motion again. The crickets continued their serenade. Degree by degree, the evening air cooled about them. Light from a lamp indoors spilled over their shoulders. Woodsmoke scented the air and contentment germinated in his chest.

But all that mattered was the duchess's hand on his.

How he wanted to open that balled fist and turn it over. He'd not held a woman's hand in a coon's age, not like this. Oh, all right— he wasn't holding her hand. She held his... sort of. Dare he attempt to correct the matter?

Moments passed without conversation, and he felt her relax beside him. Gradually, the tension eased from his muscles, too, and his thoughts returned to the purpose for his visit. "We can play this any way you'd like, including flat refuse to participate, unless he announces the contests ahead of time. Even then, we might unite forces against him."

"I never thought I'd say this, but I think Abbott's on to something. Curiosity brings people in, and people in my tea room order a cup and a pastry. My chairs have been filled. You've seen an increase in sales, haven't you?"

"I have. Many want the gossip, but they also open their pocketbooks. Business is brisk."

Without too much thought— heaven forbid he mess this up, too— he shifted, clasping Jane's hand between his own. "So, what's it going to be? Do we play along with Abbott, for the good of business, or do we both refuse to participate?"

"You'd do that? Refuse to participate, with me?"

She sounded so hopeful, his heart twisted. "I would." He swallowed hard. "For you, I most certainly would."

Chapter Ten

"I would. For you."

Hank's words echoed in Jane's mind, flooding her with tender emotion. Nothing so simple as happiness or contentment. Hope stirred. And something much like appreciation and respect clouded more delicate, harder to recognize sentiments...

She *liked* Hank Murphy. How could she not? One by one, he'd pulled every single stake holding down her argument. She couldn't dislike an affable man. Nor could she find the strength to pull her hand from his.

How many hours had she spent in this swing, side by side with Lawrence? They'd wiled away far too many enjoyable hours to count. Law had held her hand here, too. He'd read aloud to her. Sometimes, she'd read to him.

And now, as if she'd never sworn fidelity to the man she'd loved— *still loved!*— she waited for guilt to sweep in and spoil the pleasure of a warm man beside her. Why hadn't she noticed the breadth of his shoulders before?

The moments stretched, and the echo of his words weighed upon her like a promise. *"I would. For you."*

She held his gaze and witnessed the truth. He would sacrifice his own ease, comfort, and safety...

... for *her*.

Lamplight shone through the lace curtains, casting shifting patterns on his skin. The man was so near, so warm. If she lingered another second on the man's sincerity, she might do something foolish.

"You asked which course I wanted."

"That I did."

He sat too close. Heat from his body made her far too aware. And made her yearn for companionship. She'd missed having a particular someone to spend time with.

Law would want her to be happy. He'd been one of the most giving, unselfish people in her acquaintance. He might not want to see her in love with someone else, and maybe not married, but if Law looked down upon her from heaven, he would be pleased to see her happy, wouldn't he?

Yes. Law would want her happiness. And her stability.

She'd worked hard to ensure that stability for herself and her mother. Hank Murphy had worked every bit as hard, perhaps more, to care for his sons and brother. She couldn't take that away from him. No intangible fear outweighed a man's need to provide for his family.

"I say we follow through." Anxiety twisted in her middle.

"You're certain?"

She nodded. The twist in her insides made speaking questionable.

"There is a but, Duchess. I see it in your eyes."

Law had never given her a nickname. Neither had her parents. She'd always been plain old Jane. When Mother was most beside herself, she'd use Jane's full Christian name. *Jane Mary Vancoller, are you listening?*

She owed Hank an explanation. "I'm scared of what fantastical contests the Abbotts will devise. The contests, I suspect, will be as grandiose and amusing as possible."

"Like tightrope walking?" He winked. "How are you with your balance, Miss Vancoller?"

She couldn't help but chuckle. The man could be endearing when he tried.

"No, not tightropes. But I expect many somethings, each one more ridiculous than the next."

He searched her expression, as if he not only hoped to discern her secrets but wanted to understand.

She'd missed *this*... friendship and association with another person.

But that wasn't the whole truth, and her conscience knew it. She'd missed the depth of connection she'd enjoyed with Law. Sheltered in the isolation of the moment, in the deepening twilight, in close proximity, she thought she enjoyed the same magical experience with Hank Murphy.

But that was absurd. She'd see that in the light of day. One of his marauding brood would pull the watermelon cake she'd just finished off the kitchen table at the Tea Room, and then she'd recall tonight's lapse in judgment.

"Jane?"

She blinked. Her given name sounded right— so right she couldn't object. How could she? They held hands, and she'd been fancying herself in the same wondrous association that she'd had with Law.

If only the anniversary of his death weren't weeks away. This time of year always brought melancholy and increased difficulty with Mother.

Hank lifted one hand to cup her jaw in the crook of his forefinger. The brush of his callused finger raised gooseflesh. "Where are you? You're a hundred miles away."

She couldn't think with this man so near. Thinking, near men, was far too important to leave to chance. She smiled, squeezed his hand, and disengaged herself. "I foresee laughter at my expense."

"That's not going to happen." He cut her off, speaking with masculine confidence.

"You can't stop everyone from sniggering at my misfortune." Especially when he won contest after contest. "You know Mayor Abbott. And you're familiar with his inclinations."

"Yes. But I have an idea that will work." The wooden swing squeaked as he shifted a little. "I say we form teams of people willing to step in and take our places. Picture this: Abbott announces a pie-eating contest. You don't want to eat yourself sick, but I don't mind. So, you tap your 'second', put that hollow-legged youngster in your seat, and that kid eats twice as much pie as I do. You win."

Her own laughter took her by surprise. Where had the anxiety gone? His plan intrigued her and might work. "Why would you want to help me? I'm your competition."

"Maybe, maybe not." Something curious flickered in Hank's eyes.

"Abbott says I am. He's pitted us against each other." And caused an awkward situation. She didn't like being at odds with Hank Murphy. Friendship would be much easier.

As would having a team to pick and choose from so she wouldn't have to chase greased pigs. Or climb a pole. Or hit the bullseye from fifty paces.

"I like your idea."

"I knew you would."

The man could make her smile, that was for certain. Quite a gift, given her state of mind. "Now, only two questions remain. How do I convince people to sign up for my team?" She had loyal friends, all of them women. Women every bit as devoid of ax-throwing talents as she. "And how do we convince Abbott and the whole county to accept alternates?"

"Leave that to me." He stood, making the swing rock.

The autumn breeze immediately stole his heat. She'd rather enjoyed sitting beside him. "What will you do?" She'd also enjoyed the way he included her in his plans and ideas.

Heavy footfalls sounded on the porch as he strode to the stairs. "You'll see. But I promise you, Miss Vancoller, everything will work out splendidly."

She remained put, listening to his footfalls on the

walk, with the echo of his promise reverberating in her heart. He'd persuaded her to trust him.

That surprised her, but not as much as the stirrings of hope.

Could it be the man was no longer the enemy? And no longer the competition?

Then what, precisely, had Hank Murphy become?

On Monday morning, Jane had the immense pleasure of sleeping until dawn. Without a single special occasion on the Tea Room's calendar, she would open at ten o'clock. She'd placed an order for bakery sweets, so other than tea, she hadn't a thing to prepare.

What a lovely, delicious feeling.

Until, of course, Mother had awoken. Truly, she should've left home before daylight and without conversing.

She tipped her face up to the sunshine at the corner, a block from home, and forced the tension and anxiety and tightness in her body to unwind.

Mother had been unbearable that morning. Demanding, critical, harsh. Loneliness had to have been speaking. *"Why don't you ever stay home with me? I'm here alone, all day. I'd think you'd have more respect for your widowed mother."*

As if Mama's mind were riddled with holes, some things no longer made sense. Like earning a living so they could afford to eat. And pay property taxes.

Jane took a deep breath, enjoying the crispness to

the air. Mama had returned to bed for a nap. Before the day was through, Jane would visit the minister's wife and ask her to find someone to visit Mama during Jane's longest days.

Or, better yet, wouldn't Miss Ina Dimond be a wonderful boon? She'd proved herself reliable and loving time and time again with ailing citizens, working as a nurse, companion, and housekeeper more than once. Yes, she'd definitely speak to Ina.

September's cooler temperatures made for a glorious morning. She strolled slowly, glimpsing the first change of autumnal color on the mountainside. How lovely! Within two or three weeks, the mountain would be a conflagration of brilliant shades of red, orange, and gold. Browns and greens would hold their own, providing a color palette worthy of a master.

Childish giggles shared Jane's attention. She'd not seen little ones out and about. Hadn't she heard the schoolhouse bell clang an hour ago?

More laughter, followed by hissing whispers.

Where were they? Behind Mr. Terrell's barn? *In* the barn?

"No. Not like that. Like this." The child's voice came from nearby. Too near to be the barn or another structure.

Large shade trees lined the particular property. Tall, full, and still shrouded in full green leaves. That one, with a trunk not ten feet onto the lawn, had branches low enough for a boy to reach...

A little foot— bare and dirty— swung beneath the fringe of summertime's leaves.

If the child weren't careful, he'd tumble and break

his neck. Jane crept closer, determined to prevent startling the kid.

"See?" the little voice, more familiar by the moment, ended with a shriek. The little foot stilled then jerked. The thump of fist upon flesh sounded clearly, because she stood close enough.

Jane parted the leafy screen. "Why did you hit your brother?"

Two little faces whipped toward her. Russell and Clyde Murphy. Both had the same expression she imagined belonged on the faces of any gang who'd been caught in their hideaway.

"He ruined my carving." Russell made to shove Clyde, who perched on a branch several inches higher than himself. "See? R. M. That's me. Russell Murphy."

The boy's words had lost some crispness. He'd lost his two front teeth since she'd seen him last.

Jane slipped under a branch and came closer. Sure enough, carved into the bark of the branch before Russell, two clumsily formed initials. The *R* faced left, rather than right. "Very good. Aren't you due in school today, Russell?"

"Nope. Don't gotta go to school."

"That's slang, Russell. In school, children learn to speak our language properly and learn their letters and numbers." In her youth, Jane had learned a good deal about respect for adults and respect for the property of others. It seemed Russell Murphy had skipped class when such subjects were addressed.

"I know all my letters." Russ glared at her. He returned to his carving, enlarging the period after his R. "I don't want to go to school."

Russell was apparently unaware that defacing a tree with his initials might well lead back to him. Ah, the blunders of a six-year-old gang leader.

Playing hooky, apparently, with his too-young-to-attend brother.

The knife handle in his fist caught her eye. "That's a nice knife you have. Where did you get it?"

Russell's hand stilled. "I found it."

"Oh?" Maybe mentioning the fact that his father made him pay for things he took would awaken the boy's conscience.

"Finders," the s lisped, "keepers."

Or, maybe not. Did Russell own a conscience?

After all Hank Murphy's hard work to teach his sons honesty, he'd be disappointed to see this. She certainly was.

"May I see your fancy knife?"

"You'll give it back?" He eyed her with wariness borne of living with elder and younger brothers.

"I will."

Both pairs of young eyes tracked her as she accepted the knife from Russell's dirty fingers. Yes. Either this was her favorite missing paring knife— now hopelessly dulled by hours of whittling by a young boy— or one just like it. "It's a handsome knife. I used to have one."

Clyde, who'd watched every movement and tracked every word, leaned his cheek against the trunk.

"It's a fine knife," Jane repeated, turning over the familiar grip in her hand. Muddy fingerprints had dried, leaving a dry grit on the bone handle. "Where did you find it?"

"Nowheres. It ain't yours. It's mine." Russell's attitude confirmed what she'd expected.

"*Isn't*. It isn't yours." Jane watched the guilt deepen in the boy's countenance— and she'd bet that discomfort had nothing to do with his misuse of the English language.

A vivid memory swept in, a day much like today, a temperate September day as she and Law had worked together in her father's tobacco shop. A boy had grabbed a tin of cigars and bolted for freedom.

Law had caught the boy. She'd expected him to give the thief a talking to, or present the kid and the evidence to the boy's father. Or the sheriff.

But Law had met the boy on his own level, eye to eye. The mix of no-nonsense and kindness in Law's expression had taught her a powerful thing.

Beneath the grime and dirt and poor manners, Russell Murphy somehow managed to tug on her childless heart. He needed the love and care of a mother. Or grandmother. Or loving nanny.

In the absence of all three, a neighbor would do.

Lord knew they needed her. Any one of them could cause a heap of trouble, all by themselves. Austin worked in the store, or had gone to school, but the youngest? "Where's Jimmy?"

Russell held out a hand, palm open, demanding his treasure. She set the handle in his palm, careful to protect his fingers from the hopelessly dull blade. With the knife safely in his fist, he raised a thin shoulder in a halfhearted shrug. "He's too little to climb trees. We told him to go away."

"Does *no one* watch the baby?"

Russ cast her a sideways glance. "He's not a baby. He's two whole years old."

Just two and running wild. He could fall in the river, tumble down a well, slip through corral fencing and under the hooves of a jittery horse. Her heart pounded. Familiar terror reminded her how easily and quickly life ended.

"We must find him. Come down and help me find him."

Clyde stuck out his tongue and blew a raspberry. *Little brat.*

"Nuh-uh. I'm busy." Russell fisted his knife and thrust the abused blade into the branch.

"You are *not* busy. You should be in school."

"I don't gots to go to school."

Her temper simmered, and she wanted to paddle both boys. Obviously, she didn't have what it took to mother the motherless. "I'll tattle to your father, tell him where you are and what you're doing, unless you come with me, right now. We must find Jimmy."

Clyde bawled. Argument and aggravation, rolled into one. For a kid who had nothing to say, he cried awfully loud.

Russell skewered her with a glare. "He's scared of you."

"I'm no danger to you. I'm your neighbor."

Clyde's wail increased. Tears ran down his cheeks.

Had she frightened the child with her urgency to find the baby? "What's wrong now?"

"He's hungry. So am I."

She glanced between two little faces, one streaked with tears. Hungry? That would not do. Every bit as heart-bruising as the thought of a two-year-old wandering town, entertaining himself, in continual danger. If his older brothers were hungry, what of the barely two-year-old?

Had their father fed them before he'd opened the store that morning? How many hours had passed? Why had Hank Murphy allowed his sons to fire their nanny? The man needed to assert his authority as their father.

"First things first. We find Jimmy, then we eat." She reached for Clyde, and miracle of miracles, he held out his arms and allowed her to lift him down.

Her muscles protested at the kid's surprising weight. He'd not missed many meals.

Russell leapt to the ground, his knife in his fist.

Jane flinched, certain he'd poke an eye out on that dull, filthy blade. "Looks like you need a sheath for your fancy knife, young man." One more thing she could do to help.

"Breakfast, right after we find Jimmy?" Russell asked, obviously bargaining.

"Immediately after."

"And don't tell Papa." His folded arms and weight upon his left hip put her instantly in mind of Hank Murphy. A chip off the old block.

"Don't tell your father what, exactly?" Already, this sounded like a bad idea.

"Don't tell about my knife. Don't tell him you saw us in our favorite tree." He raised his chin. "Or we won't help find Jimmy."

At the moment, finding the toddler seemed far more important than a matter Hank likely knew all about. No boy could hide a favorite knife from his father. "I won't tell."

"You swear?" Russ demanded.

Clyde mimicked his older brother, folding his arms the best he could, weight on his left leg.

If only Russ knew the influence he had on the younger ones, he might behave himself. "I promise."

The boys watched her, apparently assessing her vow.

She crouched, balancing on the balls of her feet. She offered Russ the most binding handshake she could remember from childhood. "Pinkie promise?"

"Pinkie promise." Russ locked his pinkie with hers, raised and lowered with all the seriousness of a notarized signature.

Jane walked with two Murphy boys in search of young Jimmy, who, despite Russell's insistence, was still a baby.

She learned several important bits of information in the following five minutes:

One: Russell knew a great deal, including Jimmy's favorite places to play.

Two: Hank Murphy considered his children. The home was unlocked, and he'd packed his son's lunch pails for school. He'd left Jimmy's jam sandwich under a towel on the kitchen table.

Three: Jimmy had eaten that sandwich (except for the crust).

Four: Hank was a surprisingly adequate housekeeper— or the widower had hired help.

Five: Apparently, Jimmy's inability to climb trees extended to his inability to climb into the high bed without help. The baby had the uncommon brilliance to

nap when he grew tired, for they found him sprawled on
his little mattress in the corner of the bedroom shared
with his brothers.

Dark hair at his crown, recently combed with
pomade, now stuck out at an odd angle. In sleep,
Jimmy displayed the kind of trust only children knew,
with all four limbs cast wide. A freshly laundered
shirttail had pulled lose from his short pants. If he'd
worn stockings and shoes, they were long gone.

Jane tiptoed in and pulled the quilt to the boy's
middle.

Relief left her heart aching with gratitude. They'd
found Jimmy so easily and safe. But next time?

How long did she have until these boys, one or all,
would be taken from her?

On the front step Clyde and Russ resumed the
folded arms and shifted weight posture. "You promised
to feed us," Russell stated.

"I honor my promises." Jane turned back to the
house. "I'll fetch your lunch pails."

"No."

"No?"

"We want cake."

Clyde nodded.

"Cake?" Sweets did nothing to compensate
hunger. But the boys' lunch pails confirmed they'd
eaten breakfast *and* lunch.

"Or cookies." Russell's crooked, flirtatious smile
stole another corner of her heart. "You promised."

Chapter Eleven

"No more argument," Hank informed the five young faces around his table. "School has been in session for three weeks. You're going."

Actually, only Russ would attend full time. Austin worked the busy afternoons and evenings, but he would spend the mornings in school.

Weariness weighed heavily on Hank, and he wanted nothing more than to retire early. Not a chance of that, not with young boys who wouldn't finish their supper of canned peaches, Whipple's Bakery bread, and thick slices of cheese. This song-and-dance of refusing to finish eating was only one delay tactic in their arsenals of refusing bedtime.

He must've walked an extra five miles, hurrying home to see to the boys every hour. Elias took the twenty-minutes-past jaunts, while Austin, when working the store, took the twenty-minutes-to turn. The kids knew what was expected, and they did it.

"You mean the boys," Elias stated, no hint of a

question in his tone. "I'm needed at the Grocery. You've seen the numbers of people coming in."

At thirteen, Elias had finished school and had proven to be trustworthy at the store alone when Hank had to track down a missing boy or two. Never knew where a two-year-old could wander off to.

"And you need me." Austin stood and planted his palms on the tabletop, on either side of his dish. For a growing boy, he didn't have much of an appetite. "Pa, I need to work. The store is busy. You need me, just like the boys my age work with their fathers to bring in the harvests. It's no different. Besides, I'm too old for school. No one my age goes anymore."

"Doesn't matter what anybody else does. You're going to school, until noon. Every day." The argument trod a well-worn path. "You're eight."

"I'm nine."

"Don't sass me." His son wouldn't see his ninth birthday for months. "I know your birth date. You *need* an education. Shopkeepers have no choice but to read, write, and figure arithmetic. What's more, I'm your father, and you'll do as I say."

"Yes, sir." Austin set his jaw, as contrary as ever.

One would think, given his reaction to the constant tension in his childhood home, he'd be more agreeable.

Though his eyes had filled with grit, Hank rubbed them with the heels of his hands.

More often than not, Russ and Austin slipped away somewhere between home and the schoolhouse and stayed gone 'til the bell rang or until Austin could arrive at the store. The argument seemed impossible to win.

Much like the "contest" for the storeroom next door to the Grocery Emporium...

... which brought his attention back 'round to Miss Jane...

... and something awfully important that wouldn't gel in his tired brain. Something about Jane. He'd not seen her since their conversation on her porch, when he'd promised to gather folks to their teams. He'd already found a dozen willing subscribers.

So why did he feel like he'd left something important undone?

He'd finished his meal, barely tasting it as it went down. He rose and carried his own plate to the dry sink. "Finish your supper. All of you. Don't waste that food."

A quiet rap sounded on the door.

"Miss Vancoller." She stood on his stoop, her hair freshly brushed and rewound in a bun at the nape of her neck. A shawl covered her shoulders and she clutched a leather-bound volume to her chest. He couldn't help the happiness that blossomed within at the sight of her.

"I've brought a gift. To you and your sons."

He glanced at the family, still gathered around the table. The youngest children had fallen motionless, staring at him, or maybe Miss Vancoller, with round eyes. "You do realize Elias is my brother." The little ones gaped, in silence. Surely they weren't afraid of her, not after the kindness she'd shown Russ and Clyde after the lemon cookie incident.

She blinked. "I... Yes, I do believe I heard that."

He motioned at the boys. "Finish your supper.

Elias, see to the boys, then the horses. I'll meet you in the barn in a minute."

"Yes, sir."

Hank shut the door behind him and joined Jane on the walk. The little house hadn't much of a porch, and the stoop hadn't room for two adults to stand comfortably. "What did he do?"

She blinked, surprised. "Elias? Nothing."

"And my sons? Have they trespassed once more?"

"No." She seemed inordinately interested in the toes of her boots. "I've not seen them in my kitchen."

"Now that's a pleasant surprise. Given the visit we had from the schoolteacher, I'm amazed."

"Oh?"

"It seems Russell has emancipated himself from the classroom. He's angry that both Elias and Austin work in the store. And frustrated that Clyde and Jimmy are too small to enroll."

"I see."

Jane, evidently, wasn't interested in that subject of conversation. Time to move along. "You've brought a gift? Mind if I ask why?"

"Yes. *The Adventures of Tom Sawyer* by Mark Twain."

"I hear it's good."

"Yes. It's wonderful." She smoothed the cover, her fingertips caressing the papers' edges. "With your permission, I'd like to give it to your eldest boys."

"You mean Elias and Austin."

"Yes."

"Books are a mighty fancy gift for boys you don't know."

She held perfectly still and assessed his face, apparently making up her mind. "Austin waited on me in the Emporium yesterday. He reminded me of someone very dear to me, a man who was much like him in his youth. This book belonged to him."

Thoughtful... but— "Neither Elias nor Austin read much. We work long hours."

"Precisely."

What could a father say to that?

"This book is filled with adventure, excitement, a haunted house, great escapes, buried treasure. Fascinating to a young man's mind. I'd hoped Austin might find the story stimulating and want to read in the evenings when he's done at the Grocery." She offered the book.

He opened the cover, quickly locating the owner's name, inked with awkward, youthful penmanship. *Lawrence Riddle.*

"This title changed the course of his life." She nodded at the book in Hank's hands.

He knew a thing or two about the "adventures" of Tom Sawyer, his runaway antics, and the trouble he'd stirred up. "Turned him from a life of crime?"

His smile, quick to begin, melted from his face at her pained expression.

"No." She cleared her throat, folding her arms tightly over her middle. "Law struggled to read. He never had a single day of formal education. But this title so captured his mind that he read and reread it and taught himself the words he didn't know." Pride echoed in her voice. Pride and love. And a longing so intense, he felt her pain from a distance.

Maybe this book could capture Austin's mind and teach him something in those winter evenings when his brothers fought their way through school work. He leafed through the pages. Not a single marking. The pages were pristine, yet fell open easily as if the book had been read over and over again.

"This one, of his entire personal library, was his favorite." She smiled, but no happiness reached her eyes.

He offered it back to her. "We can't accept this."

"Please." She held up a single hand, warding off his gesture. "I kept it back, when I donated the majority of his library, because of the sentimental value."

"Precisely why you should keep it." Who was Lawrence, exactly? A cousin? A dear friend?

"I've made up my mind. I've read the book many times, and now it's yours. May it bring much pleasure to you and your family."

"Thank you."

The conversation lagged. Two seconds passed, then three. He tapped the precious book against his palm, wondering if anything remained to be said. He still had five boys to wrestle into bed and a short night ahead before he'd fight half of them to go to school. He fought a yawn.

If only he had someone— *anyone*— to help with the load five dependents generated. He hired out the laundry, managed the housework a bit here and a bit there, yet everything important seemed to fall through the giant cracks in the family's foundation.

Miss Vancoller took a step or two toward the gate. "Thank you, Mr. Murphy."

"I should thank you, Miss Vancoller."

"Might I suggest—?" She met his gaze, something significant lurking there.

He waited. Even he knew better than to rush a woman.

"Perhaps," she said at last, "you might read aloud to the boys, until the story captures Austin's attention."

He'd planned to give the book to Elias once they'd finished in the barn. "You doubt the others will want to hear the end of the story?"

She returned to worrying the gold locket beneath her bodice. "How much schooling has Austin received?"

"As many weeks as I could insist upon." He'd moved the family to Mountain Home after Dora's passing, and since, he'd not had a moment's success keeping Austin in school. "He went every day school was in session, before—" *his mother died.* He cleared the thickness from his voice. "Before we pulled up stakes and moved here."

"I watched him add my purchases together with ease."

The compliment came easily and sounded sincere... so why did it dredge up nagging concern?

Sunset approached, casting long shadows over his lawn and hiding more of the woman's expression. The worst of the day's heat had fled, leaving a crispness to the air that would make sleeping comfortable.

If he could sleep.

"Seems like there's more you'd like to say." He waited. "Care to tell me what's on your mind?"

Jane Vancoller was the oddest woman he'd had the fortune to meet. As recalcitrant to speak her mind as any female he'd crossed paths with. Customers generally told him precisely what they needed and what they wanted. Some went so far as to haggle prices. Unlike Dora, who'd never hesitated to rant and rave and tell him precisely what she thought, Miss Jane Vancoller seemed to take care to avoid hurting his feelings.

Ha. That ship had long since sailed.

"Does Austin read, Mr. Murphy?"

"Yes, he reads—" He stilled, every piece of the puzzle finally aligning and bringing everything she'd said and her reasons behind parting with a special book into focus.

When had he last *seen* Austin read?

Memories, one right after the other, zipped past. Austin arguing he didn't need school, that he was of necessary help at the store. Austin, willing to listen while Hank or Elias read aloud from the paper or Bible but never taking the newsprint into his own hands. He'd thought the boy simply hadn't the interest...

He stared at the cover of the book, the title swimming before his eyes.

How much had Austin— all of the boys, Elias included— gone without because Hank had been stretched so thin? Both father and mother, operating a business, rushing through mornings and evenings at home with his boys...

Why did a stranger notice in one transaction what he'd never seen?

Besides, did it matter? Lots of people couldn't read or write. But Austin talked about remaining a shopkeeper in the family business well into adulthood.

He had no wild imaginings, no intention to do something else.

Shopkeepers needed to read. Invoices, statements, account books, labels...

He held Jane's gaze. "Are you sure?"

"I thought you might discover that for yourself."

"I believe I'll do just that."

"Might I suggest one more thing?"

Why was Jane so hesitant to speak her mind? "Please do."

"You might subscribe to the library. I know the library owns many titles that would please your boys."

Library. That nagging something, just beyond reach, banished exhaustion and pronounced him a fool. He'd promised to help Jane prepare for the coming festival, to let her use the coveted space for the library—

The library...

Aww, shoot. That was the glimmering something that lingered beyond his reach. He'd forgotten Jane.

"The library ladies voted today, didn't they?" He swallowed hard.

She whirled to face the gate, a hand over her mouth.

"I'm sorry, Jane." Shoot! He'd not meant to upset her. He took two steps closer, then three. "I meant to check on you earlier. How did the meeting proceed? What happened with the voting?"

She shook her head. Her frame trembled.

He couldn't stand knowing he'd hurt her. They'd reached a truce late last week, on her porch swing. When she'd held his hand, and he'd held hers.

Placing his hands on her shoulders seemed the

most natural thing in the world— and the tremors in her little frame told him plenty. If she were mad at him, she'd have no trouble saying everything on her mind. She'd proved that in the storeroom between their businesses.

The ladies' club had voted to take the library someplace else. Nothing else made a lick of sense. "Aww, shoot. I'm sorry, Jane."

Jane Vancoller did not cry in public. She did not cry because a library she loved had been taken from her. Most of all, she did not cry because a man showed unexpected kindness.

The warm, anchoring hold of Hank's hands upon her shoulders soothed and comforted. She liked the closeness, but she'd rather look him in the eye. Slowly, she turned about. Hank stood close enough to be a dance partner. She wished he'd take her in his arms— she needed a hug. But good women didn't stand on the street, embracing men they weren't related to.

She needed the conversation to continue. "Walk with me?"

Hank paused, as if waiting for something more. "You're not angry with me?"

"Certainly not. Should I be?"

"No, ma'am." He pocketed *The Adventures of Tom Sawyer* away, then offered her his arm. She tucked her hand into the crook of his elbow and let the warmth of his body chase away the evening chill. Nights had become nearly cold during the past week.

And, to her dismay, Hank Murphy had become her stalwart anchor in the storm. *How* had that happened?

She'd intended to keep to herself, to focus on her business, to ensure the Tea Room's success. Instead, she'd become swept up in the current of contested real estate and a man whose need for that space outweighed her own.

If she weren't careful, this... friendship... would come apart at the seams. Hadn't she learned that everything she loved would be taken from her, sooner or later? The library had proved her fears to be true, yet again.

At the corner, Hank paused. "Shall I walk you home?"

She should say yes. Leaning on this man, even more than she did now, would not be wise. Tonight, she couldn't be wise. Not with her heart in shreds. "Let's walk a while."

They passed by homes with glowing lamps behind windowpanes. The crickets sang their nightly melody. A dog barked in the distance, and somewhere nearby, a woman called her children inside. Jane's conscience pinched. "I shouldn't take you away from your boys. It's bedtime."

"They've bathed and had supper. I have time for you."

Magical, wondrous words that made tears gather. She would *not* cry. How long had it been since she'd had a kind, listening ear? Since Papa's passing? He'd been present and loving, as had Mama, after the accident that had taken Law. How she missed them both.

Tears twisted her throat, the delicate tissues burning. She missed her mother. The wonderful, loving woman that had been, before widowhood had stolen her sweet nature.

Hank covered her hand in the crook of his arm. "Are you well?"

She couldn't speak without betraying her emotion, so she shook her head.

They strolled past the tree his boys had hidden in, where R.M. was carved on a branch. She'd kept that little boy's secret— though she doubted he believed in her. The way he'd eyed her from the kitchen table, ripe with distrust, had hurt her heart.

He clasped his hand over hers, warm and secure. "Will you tell me what happened today? With the ladies' vote?"

She needed to speak of it, and his request seemed sincere. "I knew from the moment the ladies called for a vote that the library's safety, with me, was in danger. I suppose I hoped they'd choose to leave the library with me."

"Aw, Jane. I'm sorry." He squeezed her hand, conveying more compassion and kindness in that solitary act than she'd had from anyone else in years. "Where will they remove the library to?"

"First, to the window in your storage room." She drew a deep breath, hating the tremulous, ragged edges that announced her fragile state. "After the festival, Mrs. Abbott spoke about using one of the smaller, available shops in Abbott's Brick Block to house the library permanently."

"Who will operate the place? How will the association afford to pay a librarian?"

She shrugged. "It's out of my hands. The association voted."

Emotion rioted, tearing her first this way and then that. She hated how well acquainted she'd become with disappointment. Loss and grief had been constant companions for far too long.

But tonight, betrayal seemed the greatest of all.

Chapter Twelve

Darkness deepened as they walked, and Jane tugged her shawl more tightly about herself. A breeze teased her hair, and in the faint light from the house on the corner, she noted Hank's locks tossed in the wind. He'd answered the door without his flat cap, without his jacket. "Are you cold?"

"No, ma'am."

She preferred it when he called her Jane. But to say so seemed too forward, too presumptuous. He'd called her by her given name a time or two but to ask him to do so might cause trouble. Who knew if the man had grown as fond of her as she had of him?

"I've wondered why the library is so important to you." He chose their direction at the intersection, taking them further from home rather than starting to turn back. "I could guess, but I'd rather hear your reasons."

Could she tell him about Lawrence? He could easily ask someone else about her connection to the library, and he'd hear a distorted version. She might as well start slow and discover if she could speak of Law without tears. "I inherited a large personal library some years ago, and though I loved the titles and reread many, I determined that their former owner would want his books to be read frequently and enjoyed."

"Lawrence Riddle?"

Hank had been asking questions of those about town.

"I saw his signature inside the cover of *The Adventures of Tom Sawyer*." Even now, he carried that beloved title in his pocket.

"Yes."

"I gather your connection to Mr. Riddle is your reason for loving the library."

"You're most perceptive." Not a trait she'd have believed Hank Murphy capable of before.

"Who was he?"

At the coming intersection, they could turn left or right, but the road did not continue straight. She opted to take the left-hand option, so she might point out the tobacco shop that had been Father's. "Let me begin with my father's former business. I may find it easier to speak of, if I ease into this."

"I hear," Hank said once they'd reached the corner, "your father owned a successful tobacco shop, and you worked it with him."

"Yes." She pointed across the way, to where the same store still stood, with only the sign painted fresh to reflect the new owners. "There it is."

"Why do I sense so much more to this story?"

"Because there is much more."

"You can tell me. I'm not the enemy."

That made her laugh. If not her enemy, then what was he?

"Tell me?"

She hesitated, moved by his sincerity. Why not share that small part of herself? Nearly all the old timers in Mountain Home knew. He could easily discover answers from any of them. "As evident by my mother's age, I came along late in life. As my parents' only child, my father and mother treasured me. Mother wanted me at home, working at her side. Father wanted the same thing."

"You chose the store?"

"You're a perceptive man."

He chuckled. He possessed the finest set of teeth. White, straight, and so handsome. Especially when he smiled. Law's teeth had been crowded, overlapping in an endearing way.

"I loved working beside my father. I loved the social nature, the coming and going of men who visited with Papa. And the fragrance of the place. Earthy aromas, sweet, spicy, and delicious."

"Why don't you still run the store? Forgive me. I know I'm forward, but you talk as if you were well suited to it."

"I did want to, and I'd have been content to continue with the family business, in the same building." The choice had been taken from her.

"But...?"

"How much have you heard about my father's passing?"

"Nothing."

She wished he'd already heard. The more he knew,

the less she'd have to reveal. At the moment, she doubted her ability to relate the story without breaking down.

"Lawrence worked alongside my father and me in that shop. Papa was nearly sixty-five, and at his age, he was anxious to relax and enjoy his final years. He'd long planned to give the shop to me as a wedding gift. As his only child, he wanted his legacy to be my inheritance. Law and I would marry, and as husband and wife, run the store together. We'd continue to see my parents' needs and care for them."

The familiar pain resurfaced, constricting her throat and burning with an intensity she couldn't push down. Yet she took solace in the fact that if anyone could understand her loss, that someone would be Hank Murphy. Hadn't he lost his wife, the mother of his children, two years ago?

All she knew was he'd moved his family, sans wife, to Mountain Home and opened a grocery, his four children and brother in tow. Jimmy had been an infant then, so he'd hired a nursemaid. And, supposedly, the children had fired that nanny.

"What happened?" Hank asked quietly, calmly, as if he wanted to know... not for the sake of gossip, but because she mattered to him.

That thought proved delicious. And tempting. Even if it wasn't true.

Where to begin?

To her surprise, she wanted to share the story and her pain. "Lawrence and I were deliciously happy and so in love. We'd planned a Christmas wedding." She'd enjoyed a magical kind of love with Law... the kind that only came once in a lifetime.

"I'm terribly sorry." Coming from Hank, the words meant something. He understood the depths of her sorrows. He knew how much she'd lost.

She nodded, unable to speak. She fought her emotions, wrestled with the pain that clung to her after all these years.

Finally, she continued. "My dad believed the tobacco shop was no place for a lady without a husband or father. Yes, it was my legacy, but as I'd determined to never wed—" she choked up again, embarrassed for Hank to see her this way.

He waited, patient. *So patient.*

Perhaps one minute passed. Maybe two. Finally, she managed to whisper, "Papa sold the store. Neither of us could bear the memories."

Hank allowed her to take her time.

"Losing Law was hard on my father. He'd been the one to assign Law to unload the wagon. He'd—" *been consumed by guilt.*

She couldn't speak of the accident. She *couldn't.*

Her throat constricted even more tightly. Tears burned behind her eyes. Two losses, so close together. She and Mother had been devastated.

"An accident?" he asked, when she'd been silent too long.

She nodded, riding the wave of hot emotion until it finally released her. "After father's heart gave out, Mother and I walked in a haze for months." They'd barely survived. Mama had emerged from that darkest time a shadow of her former self.

Truth be told, Jane wasn't the same woman either.

Some days she doubted she'd find her way through the gloom, through the vast ocean of grief, and to the other side.

Hank listened without interruption. She couldn't help but respect and admire this part of his nature.

"Finally," she said, "I realized the money from the sale of the business wouldn't last forever. Either I would have to invest it in something that would turn a profit, or we'd be forced to diminish our living." Honestly, did Mama need *another* black bonnet? They hadn't a spare dime to spend on frivolous things. Mother didn't seem to comprehend and spent more than they had.

"So you invested in a business highly suitable to women."

She blinked, surprise stealing her ability to speak. How, out of an entire town that had known her the majority of her life, could Hank Murphy— a stranger among them— be *first* to comprehend her reasons? "Exactly." Others believed she'd chosen a tea room for love of tea, or because she enjoyed surrounding herself with dainty, ladylike things.

Her justification for a tea room had been precisely as Hank surmised; she'd required the opposite of her life with Lawrence and Papa. The opposite of cigars and chewing tobacco, with aromas earthy and rich. She'd chosen the most feminine option.

How surprising and wonderful to feel understood.

She'd known that she and Hank had commonalities, from shopkeeping to the obvious loss of a spouse. He comprehended the terrible weight of the too-expensive Abbott Brick Block.

They passed by the tobacco shop and its

neighbors, turning toward the lumber mills on the riverside.

"Why," she asked, "do you own a grocery? Why not an ice company? Why not repair shoes?"

He chuckled.

"I'm serious. Why aren't you a farmer? I genuinely want to know."

"The day my pa died, my stepmother sent me to find work. I preferred working in a store over tending a rancher's stock."

"When did you own your first store?"

"I saved my money, lived lean, worked several extra jobs— freight wagon teamster, mucked stalls for the farrier, assisted the blacksmith. By the time I was first marr—."

He'd nearly said *married*. Remembering his wife, evidently, caused him the kind of searing pain she understood.

"By the time I was first a father, I'd almost saved enough to begin. With financial backing from friends, I set up a small grocery in Dakota Territory. I had to go somewhere without an established mercantile."

All the light had gone out of his voice. How she wished she could see his expression. Had he removed his family to Colorado after her death, to escape every reminder?

"I wasn't in a position to carry much extra," he said, his voice low. "Takes a while to build up an inventory and longer to afford to let it sit."

How well she comprehended the limitations that constrained a person new to business. Yet hesitancy shaded Hank's voice. Something significant had happened.

"Winter came in October that year. Early and hard. Lasted seven long months."

She stilled, understanding coming all at once. "The Snow Winter."

The winter of 1880 to 1881 had been difficult in Mountain Home, but the newspapers and telegraph reports had made it clear that the Great Lakes region had it far worse. The Rocky Mountains, despite the deluge of snowfall, had been spared.

Jane had lived that winter, safe within her cozy family circle. Lawrence had moved into town by then and worked for her father. That winter had been almost magical, with Law welcomed into their family home. All over town, families had doubled-up to conserve fuel for light, heat, and cooking.

By the end of the interminable winter, Lawrence had gained Papa's blessing, and they'd begun courting, officially.

Unofficially, they had a full season of courtship under her parents' watchful eyes. Lawrence had confessed he'd fallen in love. She'd never known that depth of contentment. Nor had she known romantic love could be so brilliant and so abiding.

Hank's gaze settled somewhere in the far distance, likely on that terrible hard time. Painful memories scored his expression, illuminated now by the rising moon. If he'd had responsibility for Elias then, his brother would've been little— six years of age? His first child, Austin, would've been a baby. Jimmy's size. Just two.

She felt Hank's muscles tighten further. His

shoulders bunched and his posture so rigid it seemed he'd snap.

Still, they strolled the streets, aimless.

"Can you tell me about it?" She spoke softly, half expecting he wouldn't hear.

"I sold out— everything— in fifteen minutes. A terrible storm of ice and snow had descended. I kept back what I dared, but it wasn't enough. My family went hungry alongside our neighbors."

Understanding descended, all at once. No wonder the man harbored a desperation to ensure that awful experience never happened again. Not to his children and not to anyone else's.

"Some blamed me outright. Others spoke ill behind my back. I butchered the milk cow in December, and shared the meat as far and as wide as possible. My wife was livid. Indignant, she was, that I'd take milk out of her baby's mouth."

The pain and damage to this good man's conscience had been overwhelming. "I'm sorry."

He didn't seem to hear. "Crews worked to clear the tracks, but the snow continued to fall and the wind blew and trains couldn't get through. Out of desperation, two young men, weakened by months of privation, attempted a rescue on snowshoes. They trudged twenty miles and pulled back sixty bushels—" he swallowed audibly— "of grain. On a sled."

Hank looked at her then, the pain in his eyes a living thing. "Those men did more to help the community than I. They saved numerous lives."

"You're not responsible for the weather—"

"They believed I had two hundred pounds of

wheat, two hundred pounds of potatoes, one hundred pounds of coffee."

She blinked. What? Why would the people believe he'd squirreled away stores of that proportion?

"I lied." He gestured vaguely. "I didn't have the stores yet, but I'd sent for them. I told folks the month before that I had all that, and more, in the storehouse."

"Why?" Her voice failed. How he must have hurt, so deep, so vivid...

"I needed them to do business with me. If they took their money to De Smet, I wouldn't have the funds to invest in winter supplies to then sell."

"Hank—" His given name slipped from her lips, and she allowed it to remain. "I'm so sorry for your pain, for your losses."

"I was a fool."

Yes, lies, generally, proved foolish. But she couldn't blame him. He'd found himself in an impossible fix and done the best he'd known how. She doubted this changed man would lie to today's townspeople.

"I've regretted my foolishness and my lies from the moment I spoke them."

"I know." No wonder he'd diligently taught his boys to be honest. Throughout their lives, Hank would be a fine example to his sons and brother— an example Jane respected.

"By spring, we had nothing left. No friends, no desire to stay." He sighed, his tone heavy. "I moved the family on, but the mistakes in Dakota Territory followed me. Can you understand my craziness?"

"I can. I do." Everything made sense, now.

"You don't think I'm behaving like Chicken Little?"

"The gossipers have been unkind. They don't know you, Hank Murphy. You're a good man. A good man with a heart of gold." She meant it. Every single word.

"No, Jane. I'm not. That's where you're mistaken."

"I disagree." She halted, there on the walk, and faced him. "If you want me to think ill of you, you must confess to much worse than this."

"You want worse?" His temper sparked, and the way his voice rose made her recall that first argument in the disputed territory between their stores. "I'll give you worse."

His chest worked like a bellows, but she wasn't afraid. This man would never hurt her.

"My wife died of diphtheria, weeks after she gave birth to Jimmy. The only thing that saved the children was Dora's inability to nurse the baby. We'd sent the children away."

Jane tried to see things through Hank's eyes, truly. But to carry guilt over diphtheria? No one could prevent one from catching the contagion, and no one could prevent deaths from the disease. "You're not responsible. You know that, don't you?"

He shrugged, and as the moon slipped behind a veil of clouds, she wished, again, that she could read his expressions. How much he must be hurting inside, still, after two years.

"You misunderstand me." His voice sounded strangled, as if emotion had climbed his throat. "I'm not a good man— not worthy of happiness— and I haven't a heart of gold. My wife died a horrible, strangulating death..."

Diphtheria did that. Membranes cut off air. The illness was so devastating, doctors could do little to save patients. Why would Hank believe he had the power to save a woman on death's door?

"She died, Jane. She died, and I couldn't bring myself to feel an iota of grief."

She blinked, certain she'd misheard.

"All I knew at that horrible, dark time..."

Jane waited, holding her breath. She needed to understand this, needed to understand *him*.

"My wife, the mother of my children, passed from this world, and *all* I felt was monumental relief. Now you know the worst of it. I'm not what you think me to be. I'm not a good man, and this heart," he smacked his chest with an open palm, "is not worthy."

Jane saw the chance to impress her much-different opinion upon the thick-headed man and took it.

She encircled her arms about Hank's neck and, without a moment's hesitation, pulled him in for her kiss.

This first kiss was far from tender. She kissed him with all of the emotion in her heart, all of her conviction that this man, Hank Murphy, was *good*.

If he'd not grieved his wife, there must have been a valid reason, and he could tell her all about it. Later.

A heavy moment stretched, and all the while, Hank stood rigid.

Could she have embarrassed herself worse than this? Had she misread this man? Had he no affection for her?

For a split second, she considered pulling away, then running.

But then his arms came about her, his embrace different from Law's in every way. His touch, his stature, his height, the scent that clung to his skin and clothing— everything about him was unfamiliar.

He wasn't Lawrence Riddle.

Hank softened and returned her kiss, forcing her to slow and to calm.

How delicious, how wonderful, to be held and kissed... and yet so *wrong*. She'd sworn to love Law forever, to be true, forever.

Hank broke that interminable kiss, his breath hot against her cheek. "*Jane*. What are you up to?" The stubble of his beard scraped her cheek, the sensation welcome after all this time.

Her heart pounded, hard and determined. "Convincing you that you're wrong."

He kissed her cheek, slowly, with reverence. "I'm not wrong."

"You believe I'd toss aside vows made when my beloved died, to kiss a black-hearted man?"

"I don't know." He released her and gripped her arms to disentangle himself.

"Do not push me away, Hank Murphy."

He stilled.

"I stood in the rain at the funeral while men shoveled muddy clods onto his coffin..." She could do this, she could. "And promised myself that if I couldn't have Lawrence Riddle, then I'd have no one."

"See? You're a good-hearted woman. I don't deserve this, or you." He nearly succeeded in pulling away.

"Be still." She pushed up on her toes and touched her forehead and nose to his. "I know you. I've witnessed your tenderness and compassion with your sons. I've seen your relations with the townspeople." She kissed him once, swiftly. "I've seen the food you've squirreled away, in preparation for helping those folks. Most of all, I've felt, in my heart, the goodness in yours."

Their breaths mingled. The cool night air cocooned them, as if no one else existed. They could've been anywhere, or nowhere.

"Jane—"

"If you think I'd discard my vows to remain faithful to a man who's passed on, for a man of questionable integrity, you are sorely mistaken."

He pressed a kiss to her forehead.

Finally! She'd broken through his thick skull. Now, for the exclamation point, a final truth he could not argue. "I think I'm falling for you, Hank Murphy, in fact I know it. You'd best resign yourself to that fact. I love you for reasons neither of us can deny."

Chapter Thirteen

In the hours and days since Oscar Harris called with peach ice cream and a smile, Ina had floated from one cloud of happiness to another.

She caught herself grinning, humming a pleasant tune, and daydreaming— whether mopping her kitchen floor on her hands and knees or visiting grumpy old Mrs. Vancoller, Ina had been giddy and happy.

Until days and days and days passed.

Fourteen very long days.

Oscar had enjoyed himself with her, sharing his peach ice cream.

He should've returned to call by now.

Evening after evening after evening she'd waited long after the Grocery Emporium had closed for the night, but he never called.

He never sent a letter.

She hadn't lived to age forty to lose the first and best beau she'd ever had.

"Enough waiting." Ina dressed in her Sunday-best

chestnut-brown costume, styled her hair, took extra time to put a bit of color on her cheeks and lips. Once confident she looked her best, she gathered her reticule and locked the front door.

She needed groceries, including a loaf of Whipple's Bakery bread. And she'd heard fresh apples were in. Perhaps a few more things, too, should she discover a golden opportunity and invite him to come for supper.

She wouldn't overstay her welcome. After all, the man was at work.

She needed to see him.

When he smiled, took a moment to greet her, stole a moment to take her hand and give a secret squeeze... then she'd be content to wait. After all, she had the Harvest Festival to look forward to— and a perfect ensemble to wear for the occasion. She'd spent many hours on a smart new costume of woolen navy-and-gray plaid that was practical, warm, and stylish. With only one week until the social event, she hadn't time to waste.

By the time she reached the corner of Main and glimpsed the T.A. Murphy's Grocery Emporium— when would they change the sign to reflect Oscar Harris's half-ownership?— she felt positively invigorated.

And thrilled by her prospects.

How lonely she'd been without him.

So many people crowded inside the Emporium, that the back of the line was at the door. She visited happily with ladies in front and behind her in the queue, until she could finally see past the hats and bonnets, and beheld her golden-haired fellow.

Dressed as smartly as ever, his longer-than-stylish hair mussed a bit, as if he'd gone out without his hat and the Colorado wind had tousled the locks. Lamplight gilded his pale hair with gold. He assumed a pose: one elbow leaned upon the glass display case, braced by the other palm.

He tossed back his head and laughed. Ina's belly flashed hot. Such a beautiful man. Solid, sturdy, and strong. The breadth of those shoulders, the width of those arms. She wasn't too old to appreciate a fine male specimen when she saw one.

Especially when he was hers.

All around her, ladies and gents chatted about the soon-to-come social event, various contests, and which team they'd joined.

Teams?

"Oh, yes." A woman Ina did not know explained. "The personal competition events, such as horse races and foot races, are still on the program. But this year, teams will compete in events like ax throwing and tug-of-war to see if this emporium or the Tea Room claims the disputed territory."

Ax throwing? Tug of war? Oh, my. My, my.

A few steps closer, a few more guests bustling out with their purchases in their arms and baskets, and at last Ina was near enough to catch bits and pieces of Oscar's conversation with patrons.

"You know the Emporium will win the tug of war event," a man in front of her said with unusual volume, effectively denying her the pleasure of Oscar's voice. "Did you see the sign-up sheet on the clipboard? Fifty-four men registered. Some of them, no doubt, simply to prove a point to the teetotaler next door."

Plenty of Coloradans, with numerous states and territories, fought for temperance. Ina didn't know what she thought about all of that. Folks who liked a drink weren't going to give it up quietly. Maybe Jane Vancoller was a teetotaler. What did Ina know about such things?

At his counter, Oscar continued talking with a pair of young ladies, one wed, one not. His smile grew wider, warmer, more genuine.

Must he assume familiarity?

A spear pierced Ina's chest, striking her heart.

Her breaths came far too quickly. Sparks blurred her vision... or maybe that was simple fury. Oscar lifted the young, unwed girl's hand to his lips. He lingered, his kiss to her knuckles, his remarkable blue eyes affixed to the girl's face.

How *dare* he?

Jealousy ignited her dangerously short fuse. She rushed the counter.

"Oscar?" She searched his face, watching for the instant he recognized her. *Her*, his girl. Here.

His smile drooped.

No. *No!* He should smile warmly. He should greet her at least as well as the others. Ina glared at the flirtatious fools. Shame on them. And shame on Oscar for falling for their coquetry.

She couldn't breathe, not with a heavy and pungent knot of jealousy in her chest. This was much worse— *infinitely worse*— than when George had brought that wretched Zylphia into their home.

"Ina— Miss Dimond." Oscar pushed off the

counter, standing to his full height. Had he been *sitting*? So casually braced on the counter, leaning closer to those women?

"What are you doing?" Her voice quaked. She *hated* showing weakness.

The chatter behind her escalated, swelled, as the stupid women related to those who'd failed to witness— that Ina Dimond, the spinster, the old maid, the unwanted, passed over and passed-by woman, whom no one wanted—

"I'm working, assisting customers." Oscar's jaw flexed. No overly handsome, golden-haired smiles. Not for her.

Dowdy.

She couldn't believe this was happening— not again. Horror squeezed in, shoving jealousy aside.

Plump.

Old.

Foolishly dressed in a costume designed for a much younger, much thinner woman.

As if all at once, conversation in the store ceased... but whispers persisted. All eyes were pinned on her, and found her lacking.

Must Oscar remind her of her myriad flaws?

"I trusted you, Oscar. I trusted you and I loved you and you—" she gasped, the horror and the enormity of the loss, *in public*, trampled her broken heart.

His jaw locked.

I loved you, she'd said. Humiliation swept in, hot and brash and vivid. She should've known she'd bumble this. *Why* had she come?

She'd never find love. *Never.*

She spun, tears spoiling her vision, and fled toward the blurry square of light that marked the open doors.

She ran.

"Ina!" Oscar followed as quick as his damaged leg allowed. If Ina believed she could misinterpret a thin moment of time, misunderstand all she saw, and flee in a panic— she had a bit of truth to reckon with.

People stepped aside, making way. He caught a few looks of disappointment as he abandoned his post.

What choice did he have? Hank, Elias, and Austin could see to customers. "Forgive me, folks. Seems I have domestic trouble." "Domestic" wasn't quite right— but no other label fit Ina.

The lady whose hand he'd kissed cheered him on. "Go after her!"

A fellow or two shook his head. "Run the other way. That one's addled."

None of those fellows knew Ina Dimond like he did.

Apparently, he had a good deal to learn about her, still.

"Ina!" He searched the street, with no sign of her brown costume. No hint of her luxurious light brown hair beneath a straw bonnet topped with autumn's colors.

Where had she gone? Home?

With so many people on the street, coming and

going? No. She'd avoid them, one and all.

"Mr. Harris." A little woman, no taller than a child and every bit as slim, tugged on his jacket hem. "Excuse me, Mr. Harris."

"What?" He tried for a smile but couldn't manage.

"I saw Miss Dimond run that way." The woman pointed in the opposite direction of Ina's home. "I recommend you hurry."

"Thank you, ma'am." Pain seared through his bad leg as he half-skipped, half-ran. A charley horse seized his left thigh. *Ouch!*

He lost precious time leaning against the building, massaging the muscle. The moment the cramp released, he limped as fast as he could go.

At last he found her, her back to him, her head down. She must've been headed toward the park, for there it lay, not another half-block ahead. Or perhaps she'd run blindly, away from the crowd. For here, the street was quiet with no one else about.

He caught up to her, his bad leg screaming for relief. Without a word, he touched her on the shoulder. The way he huffed and puffed, in poor fighting condition, she must've heard him coming.

She slowly turned to him.

He held her gaze, her eyes twice as blue as ever before. Maybe because of her jealous rage. Maybe because of the brown she wore. Two bright pink spots blazed on her cheeks. "I've never known a woman as crazy as you, Ina Dimond. *Never.*"

"Crazy?" She gaped, like a fish out of water. Crazy-jealous, too.

"Yes, ma'am. Isn't that what unfounded jealousy

is?"

"Unfounded?" She gasped, offended. "*Unfounded?* I saw you kiss that woman—"

"Her hand, Ina. I kissed her hand in congratulations. She's newly engaged to marry."

"Oh." Her bluster and indignation shrunk, all at once.

Everyone else in the store had seen his behavior for what it was— congratulatory. Desperation swelled within him, cracking open the parapet he'd erected in defense of his heart.

He took her face between his two hands, and searched her eyes. Hadn't she run from the painful scene in George Hudson's dining room, when his mail-order bride arrived? Today made the second time she'd let jealousy send her running through the streets of Mountain Home. "Envy will destroy you, if you let it. This craziness must stop, immediately."

"But—"

"*No buts.* I am not worth it."

She covered his hand with hers. "Do not disparage yourself to me." She meant it. Somehow, this batty woman, in her desperation to lavish affection upon someone, had chosen him. Was she *mad*?

If only he were worthy of her devotion.

"You are an honorable man." She pressed her other palm to his chest. "And your heart is good."

Yes, sir. Stark, raving mad.

Her gaze locked with his and she searched the depths of his heart. He fought to deny her access, but failed.

Just as he'd failed in his avoidance campaign. He'd

stayed away for weeks, and for what?

With the smoothness of her skin and the silkiness of her hair beneath his touch, the shattering truth presented itself.

He'd gone and tumbled over his old bachelor's heart.

Affection— undeniable, absolute, overwhelming, and unbelievably stupid— bubbled over with the force of a chemical reaction.

Inevitable as potassium's volatile explosion when in contact with water, he'd gone crazy for this woman.

The realization weighed nigh onto a thousand pounds, a load far too heavy to carry.

He offered an elbow, urging her to take his arm. "My leg is killing me. What do you say we find a place to sit, so we might talk?"

For a moment, he thought she'd refuse. She pinned him with a glare so defensive, his heart ached for the pain he'd caused her. He'd constructed the avoidance campaign to avoid hurting her. And now it was too late.

"Take my arm, you silly goose."

She'd calmed some, twisting and untwisting the strings of her reticule. "Is that still a term of endearment?"

"Yes, ma'am. It most certainly is."

He cared deeply for a woman who, despite her madness, was a mite too good for him. If she opened her eyes, and truly saw herself, she'd realize she could do so much better than an old bachelor with one leg shattered by a Johnny Reb. That limb burned like the dickens, though a military surgeon had amputated it more than twenty years ago.

"Please?" he asked once more. "Sit with me?"

"I will, but only because your leg pains you." Finally, she slipped her hand into the crook of his elbow.

He fought his limp as they walked together the last half block to the park. His stump chafed against his prosthesis, despite lambswool padding and enough lineament to smell like a horse. Now that he'd found her and calmed her terror, the pain made him wish for a bottle of coca wine.

He doubted he deserved relief from physical pain. He'd known better than to call on her, to make promises with his presence... promises he couldn't keep.

At last they sat, side by side on a park bench in the shade. He couldn't easily look her in the eye, but that might be best.

"Ina, darling." He straightened his aching leg. "You mustn't allow yourself to become so overwrought."

"Then you mustn't go days and days without calling on me, and spend them all flirting with every female in town."

"I explained myself. I feel nothing for the many women who buy goods at the Emporium."

"What do you feel for me?"

He cut a sideways glance. The woman was direct if naught else.

Admitting he'd failed in his quest to remain aloof and without entanglements would make things worse. Admitting his heart yearned for her would spark a fire of destruction.

Before anything else, he had to ensure she understood that her behavior put her at risk. Without husband, father, brother, or son to defend her, she might well lose her freedom. He couldn't allow that to happen.

"You know I studied chemistry at length, yes?"

"More vinegar and dissolving eggshells?" She slid him a sideways glance, clearly not following.

No matter. She would see his path clearly enough in a moment. "Our minds are a fragile thing. The slightest upset can cause irreversible damage."

"You have a point?"

"I do. You mustn't push yourself to the edge like this. Jealousy as you displayed— unfounded and unreasoning jealousy— is a disease. An early phase of insanity."

She bristled, but he took her hand, irrationally pleased she hadn't worn gloves in the way of many western women. The sensation of her palm against his was glorious.

"Insanity?" she demanded. "You imply I need a sanatorium, do you?"

"No. But I understand more than some. I've seen strong men, solid men, lose their minds." Battle had broken strong men, men whose minds had shattered under the horrors of war. "I can't bear to see that end for you. *I'm not worth it.*"

"Oscar Harris, if you say that to me one more time, why, I'll—"

He interrupted her, pressing a finger to her lips, shushing her. He'd turned so far on the bench that he could easily hold her eye. "You mustn't behave in so ridiculous a manner. Not ever again. I don't know everyone in Mountain Home, wouldn't wager a guess about their actions. Will they take you away? Will they consign you as an inmate at an asylum?"

If that eventuality occurred, he'd never be able to secure her freedom. The thought terrified him.

Her eyes widened, finally understanding the threat. Slowly, she shook her head. "They wouldn't dare. They know me."

He hoped so. How he hoped so.

"I need you to understand one more thing." He waited until she'd turned to meet his eye. "I make my living as a pharmacist in a new and popular grocery emporium. Because of the silly contest for the empty shop, people come in to buy a single packet of needles or a single can of peas. Why? Because they must know the most current gossip. I am obliged to be friendly, to smile and show a gracious thank you because they chose to spend their hard-earned coin in our establishment."

She narrowed her eyes in distrust.

Women. This one, fresh and vibrant, so appealing... and yet so insecure, might not comprehend his purposes.

She looked down, twisting her reticule strings again. He laid his hand over hers, stilling her nervous movement.

"I am simply carrying on business conversations and friendly chats with respectable women, as this is necessary to conduct business. I also speak in a friendly manner with men. That's all. But I see how you suffer, how your heart nearly broke when you heard their laughter."

She looked away, her shoulders sagging and her sadness overflowing with every movement. She sniffed. "Are you done?"

Could he ever be done ensuing she understood she must control dangerous impulses? What if he'd failed her with pallid explanations? "Done? If you insist."

"No." She shook her head. "Are you done with *me*?"

A stronger man would say yes. A stronger man would walk away, right now.

"I'm sorry, Oscar. I'm a mess and I know it. Loneliness fairly consumes me."

Loneliness had dogged his heels since the war, since his life had changed. He hardly remembered normalcy. His heart softened, magnifying his connection to this woman. How well he comprehended.

The more he glimpsed the girl inside the woman, the girl time forgot, he lost more of his heart.

"I understand loneliness," he whispered, "I do. We need other people. We need to matter."

She nodded with vigor.

But she still wouldn't look at him, her gaze far afield, far away.

Had she no idea how much she was worth? In her sweetness, her crazy and overflowing affection?

The man who owned her heart would be blessed tenfold.

He lifted her hand to his mouth, and pressed his kiss to her knuckles. He scented roses on her warm skin. Roses from the soap she'd bought at his counter. Or perhaps the lotion.

Roses suited her.

Feminine, soft, lovely. And layers upon layers in a bud newly opening to the sun.

He broke the kiss, meeting her eye as he pressed his lips to her hand anew.

She finally looked at him, pain raw in the blue depths. "You kissed that young woman's hand, just as you kiss mine. That means you want me to spend my coin in your establishment."

"This," he brushed another kiss to her warm skin, "is genuine affection." He'd regret every single kiss, but for now, he'd do all he could to help her comprehend. "You are a remarkable and wondrous woman, Miss Ina."

Awe and wonder and the first hints of something more sparkled in the depths of her eyes.

"You deserve a man who can give you the world, who will appreciate the abundance of love in your heart."

Long seconds passed, her focus wholly on him. As if he'd become the center of her world.

He.

A broken, ruined man. A fellow who'd never had a woman's heart... not for long, anyway.

Her affection filled him with wonder... while it lasted.

Vertigo struck, lifting his stomach into weightlessness. *Fear?*

Couldn't be. He was not scared of Ina Dimond. But he was afraid of the devastating loss when she left him.

She *would* leave him.

The day would come when his prosthetic leg—

rather, his ugly stump, and the million things he couldn't do— would be too much.

But for now, in this moment, she gazed at him as if he were the only man in the world. Love shone in her eyes, and that love was so perfect, so complete... he craved it, *wanted* it...

"Will you honor your promise and take me to the Harvest Festival?" She sounded calm, sweet, content. All the crazy had been tucked neatly away in a drawer somewhere, and the key turned.

She seemed whole. Not a glimmer of jealousy. No doubt. No fear.

For her, he'd do anything... *while it lasted.* "Absolutely, yes."

Chapter Fourteen

On Wednesday, October 5, the day before the Harvest Festival began, the streets of Mountain Home were choked with people. Wagon after wagon rolled down Main, and much of the traffic was focused, understandably, on Abbott's Brick Block.

"I'll tell you one thing," Hank told Elias and Oscar, "Abbott achieved his dream of making this year the best-attended autumn social. I've never seen so many people all at once."

Folks had taken to staying with friends in town, filled up every room for rent, and camped outside town, and even filled the meadow a half-block from Abbott's Brick Block.

He wasn't complaining... for the most part. Sales had been up, his profit each day better than the week before, and better than the week before that. The books showed the increase. Despite how many came in just to collect gossip, he'd turned over a good deal of supplies.

He'd not have trouble paying the high rent this month, or next.

He wasn't the only merchant to benefit from the influx of people.

Women flocked to Jane's Tea Room. Every time he poked his head outside the Emporium, women were clustered about her door, coming and going. No doubt, Jane found the income to be well worth it.

But Hank had *one* complaint.

He'd not seen Jane for more than a few passing moments in the full two weeks since he'd somehow told Jane everything, *everything*. If their store wasn't packed with people, Oscar was running off chasing his jealous woman, or Hank was late to pick up deliveries at the train. Right when he needed time to go courting— could he bear to think of his time with Jane like that?— he lost more and more sleep and hadn't five minutes to himself.

Two weeks was an awfully long time for a woman.

Would she have thought things through, and changed her mind? She'd been adamant he was worthy, and deserving of happiness. She'd insisted she'd fallen in love with him... but that was *before*. A million things could've changed by now.

What if she regretted their kisses?

She'd kissed him first— a shocking, glorious, view-altering kiss that had felt like a promise, even to his jaded heart. But that had been fourteen days ago.

With every day that passed without a chance to talk with Jane, he discovered he missed her. His thoughts kept returning to her, no matter how busily engaged with his work. He needed to know if all that missing was in vain. If she'd rethought things, he needed to know.

As the day wore on, he'd hurried down the alleyway and looked in her back door, maybe half a dozen times, each time finding her engaged with customers and her parlor filled. And the knot in his stomach seemed to double.

Elias glared at Hank every time he returned from his jaunts next door.

Oscar selected two bottles from among his patent medicines and carried them along their hallowed space behind the counter. "This one promises relief to all that ails your digestion."

The glass bottle was heavy and cool in Hank's hand.

"And this one," Oscar tapped the red-and-gold label with the pad of his forefinger, "this one cures that stupidity we talked about, once upon a time."

Hank's belly twisted. Again.

He'd been behaving the fool.

He pushed both bottles back into Oscar's hands. "Didn't know you were one to diagnose a man's troubles." He wanted to call Oscar on his harassment. Hadn't he been the one to chase a crazy-in-love woman out of the Emporium after she'd publicly declared her love for him?

Oscar had been the fool that day. Who was he to judge?

"Diagnoses go with the territory." Oscar set the bottles on the counter. "If your belly's bothering you, sending you to the outhouse every five minutes, you might want to try the elixir."

Hank cut a quick glance at his partner. Was he irritated? Or blithely helping? "I'm not ill. My digestion's just fine."

"Glad to hear it." Oscar nodded to Hank, then turned to greet more folks Hank hadn't met. Lots of ranchers had come in for the Harvest Festival, and many who typically did business with other grocers had stepped in to see Abbott's Brick Block, and the warring merchants who wanted to tear a single shop into two.

Hank shoved his irritation aside and helped another customer or two.

But the minute he caught another lull between the crush of folks coming in, Hank ducked out the back door and trotted straight to Jane's kitchen door.

Inside, ladylike commotion carried like music. Gentle conversation, the murmur and babble of silverware on china plates and the homey clatter of teacups on saucers.

Like he'd done a dozen times that day, he opened the screen door and peered inside. Screens weren't meant to be seen through, at least not from the sunlit outdoors.

All morning, her kitchen had seen much use. Towering dishes waited to be washed. The tempting, homey, mouth-watering fragrances of pumpkin and spices... and another note of fall hiding in the midst... apples?— had tormented him all day.

He loved baked apples, apple crisp, apple pie, apple sauce. He never said no to anything with apples in it.

Finally— there she was! Jane looked wonderful, her cheeks pink and a twinkle in her eyes. Her smile seemed genuine and real. She carried her teapot and strainer toward him— or more likely toward the kitchen.

With every step she took closer to him, her smile holding and her expression one of gladness, the ever-tightening anxiety within him evaporated. She strode with confidence and welcome.

She looked *beautiful.*

"Hello, neighbor." Her appropriate greeting sounded warm and genuine. "Step into the kitchen with me?"

Inside, she washed out the teapot and set it to warm in the oven. "Is your place as hectic as mine?"

"Yes."

She filled a basin in the sink with hot water— wasn't the ease of hot-and-cold running water in Abbott's Brick Block a significant benefit?— and shaved soap into the rising water. "I've heard folks are taking bets on the different contests we'll see between now and Saturday night." Her worry over the matter seemed to have melted completely. "One or two women are beside themselves at the money their husbands will lose on bad bets."

"I've heard much the same."

She lifted a stack of dirty dessert plates into the suds, and he followed with a stack of saucers.

"Thank you." She took the saucers from him, and looked up to meet his eye. "Have you seen Mr. or Mrs. Abbott?"

He loved her directness, the ease with which she talked to him today... as if the two long weeks between them hadn't spoiled her affection for him. Unless he was mistaken, she seemed genuinely glad to see him.

Now that he thought about it... "No. Not since Sunday."

"I think they're hiding." Jane chuckled. "They brought all this attention upon themselves, and now, they've taken refuge in their mansion and won't take callers."

"Serves them right." He couldn't take his eyes off her. Her smile, and the light dancing in her eyes drew him. The light from the window wasn't as vibrant as through the bay window into the dining room, but plenty to see the hint of red in her dark hair. Lovely. Absolutely lovely.

She turned away to stop the flow of water. "The talk all morning has included the teams you've gathered. Thank you for doing that for me, too."

Her trust astounded him. He'd not shown her the list. All she had was hearsay. And still, she trusted him. Completely.

If Dora had trusted him, really trusted him... how their lives would have been better.

Warmth unfurled in his chest, expanding and overflowing. "You're welcome," he managed.

Her smile seemed to kick him in the gut. Such a welcome thing, her happiness and appreciation.

"Here I am, chattering away." Jane waved a little hand, then dried them both on a kitchen towel. "You didn't come over here for the gossip. What do you need?"

You.

The answer came so swiftly, with such certainty, it knocked him off balance.

Missing her had been like a long dry season... and these spare minutes in her company, a desperately needed rain.

"I, uh..." Did he dare admit he'd missed her?

Why not? He'd confessed far more than that. She'd confided plenty in him. And still, she seemed happy with him. Happy to *be* with him.

"I missed you." He held her gaze so he'd be sure to see any reaction.

Her eyes widened a smidgen, followed by her smile. "I missed you too."

"Good." He couldn't help but return her smile, his own far too wide.

Who knew that hearing those few little words from her could feel so good?

"The festival starts tomorrow." She leaned back against the drainboard at the kitchen sink. "I'm thrilled to report Harriet will keep the Tea Room going, along with help from the rest of the Ladies' Library Association officers. That will free me to compete... or send my seconds into battle in my stead."

"That's good." Had she always been so lovely? "We've decided to close, 'til we see when we might be able to open for business. Oscar's committed to take Miss Dimond, and my boys all want to enjoy the holiday."

"That seems wise."

He ached to touch her. Two steps closer, and he could pull her into his arms. She fit so well there, as if they were made to be two parts of one whole.

"Are you ready for this?" she asked.

His stomach tumbled, until he gathered the

fragments of his thoughts. Oh, yes. *This.* The festival. "Three long days at the whim of Mayor Abbott? How could a man be ready for that?"

She chuckled with him. He couldn't look away from her face. Now that he was finally in her company again after the long drought, he realized how much he'd missed her. Somewhere, deep inside, he knew how dangerous that could be.

"I'm not afraid anymore. Not of Abbott, not of the contests. Not since you stepped in to help."

"It was nothing."

"To me," she whispered, "it was everything."

With that tone in her voice and sweetness in her expression, he wanted nothing more than to hold her. But one more worry crowded the others. "What will we do when Abbott declares a winner?"

Her smile faded.

What would he do, if in winning the right to that lease, he caused this woman's business to suffer? Worse— what about her personal disappointment? He swallowed, the dryness of his throat near painful. "I don't want to hurt you."

"You're a fine man, Hank Murphy. I *know* you. You'd never intentionally hurt me."

"Never. That's a promise."

She stepped closer, so near her skirts brushed his pant legs and the scent of her perfume carried.

His pulse leapt, even as his hands spanned her tiny waist. He rather liked the way she slid her palms over his chest and up to his neck. As if they'd been together for ages. As if she were already his bride, and this weren't brand spanking new.

"A kiss for luck?" She tipped her face up to his.

Not an offer he could turn down, so he lowered his mouth to hers.

The feather-light touch compounded the profound emotions at being so near her. Here was the one woman— of that, he'd become certain— the *one* woman who'd been able to show him that not all females were like Dora. In fact, most of them were decidedly different than the mother of his children.

Why had he been so certain he'd be better off alone?

This close to Jane, and claiming another kiss— this one lingering long after the first had ended, felt absolutely right.

Right and *perfect*.

She pulled away before he was ready to let her go. He rather liked kissing Miss Jane Vancoller.

"I'll see you tomorrow, at the opening ceremonies?" She sounded hopeful, encouraging, maybe even hoping for an invitation to accompany him there.

But he had the boys to see to... Did she want to attend with his family? "Would you like, if you don't have other plans, with your mother, perhaps..."

"Yes."

He laughed. "I said that badly, and you have no idea what I offered."

"Doesn't matter what you offer." That seemed to be too bold a statement, for her cheeks colored. "Yet I believe you asked me to accompany you to the festival tomorrow?"

His smile worked up on one side. "Uh, no." He

couldn't resist teasing, just a little.

Her smile faded. "Oh. Begging your pardon. I'm—"

His hands were still at her waist, so he held on when she would've turned away. "Actually, I'm asking if you'd attend with me all four days."

She chuckled, delight twinkling in those amazing summer-green eyes. "The event lasts only through Saturday."

"I'm including Sunday's sermon. Pastor Gilbert sees it as an important part of the festival."

"That he does." Her smile remained sincere and as bright as a newly minted penny.

This woman's smiles transformed her from lovely to gorgeous. He wanted to be the one to make her smile. Today, tomorrow, and *maybe* forever.

"Very well. Mother and I will accompany you and your family, Thursday through Sunday."

"Thank you." Two weeks without her had been terrible. If given his way, he'd make sure this woman was never far away. "That's precisely what I want."

With a spring in his step and a whistle on his lips, Hank left by the back door of the Tea Room to return to the Emporium. He couldn't wait for the festival to begin— because he'd have the pleasure of Jane's company. Let Abbott throw surprise contests at them. Hank had an inkling that he and Jane, standing together, could handle just about anything.

Elias leaned against the back wall, outside the

Emporium's screen door. The kid's narrowed eyes and firm-set mouth said he had plenty on his mind, and none of it good.

"What happened?" Hank glanced inside, but found the screen blocked much of his view of the interior. "Things were fine when I left here, two minutes ago."

"Ten." Elias's temper was on a short fuse. "*Ten* minutes."

"I'm back. Let's go to work."

"Not until I say something I've needed to say for a full week."

At the end of the alleyway, children's voices called to one another, as a herd of schoolboys ran past. Beyond them, a wagon rolled down the street.

Elias, a young man in his fourteenth year, rarely confronted Hank about anything. Supposedly this was normal when boys grew older, but Hank knew little about that, having had no father to butt heads with.

"I'm listening." He gave the kid his full attention.

"Two weeks ago, last Wednesday, you went outside with Miss Vancoller, for just a minute. You recall that conversation?"

Indeed, he did. That conversation had cost him a great deal by the way of secrets.

"You promised me you'd be in, to help me in the barn."

He had promised, hadn't he? Instead, he'd ended up walking and talking and kissing. He'd returned home long after the boys were asleep and the house was dark. Hank had looked in on each of the boys, then he'd washed up and dropped into bed, beyond exhausted.

He'd been asleep within seconds.

In the two weeks since, they'd completed the evening chores, side by side. The kid hadn't said a thing. Why wait until now?

"I apologize, Elias." Hank resettled his flat cap on his head. "You're right. I owe you better than that."

"Yes, Hank, you do."

Sass and vinegar, from his kid brother? This was new. And most disagreeable. "I won't do it again."

"I think you will." Elias's chest rose and fell as quick as if he'd run a mile. The boy held his ground, his arms folded and his feet braced. "I'd hoped, as two weeks passed and you kept your distance from the lady, that you'd thought better of your actions. But today? You've got a swarm of bees in your trousers, the way you run to see Miss Vancoller every five minutes. You didn't go there to tell her about the volunteers for her team."

Hank paused, made sure he had a firm grip on the reins of his temper. Elias had a point to make, and eventually he'd get there. He'd worked up a head of steam, and wasn't his usual affable self. Apparently, he'd eavesdropped on a private conversation. "I believe I did mention her team. The event starts tomorrow, and there are details she needs to know."

"Is that why—" the boy's voice rose in temper— "you're kissing her?"

"*Lower your voice.*" The Ladies' Library Association had moved the books into the front of his storage room that morning. One of them staffed the library at this moment. She'd left the heavy door open, with only the screen door in place.

"I saw you kissing her just now—"

Hank jabbed a finger in his brother's face. "*Lower your voice, Elias.*"

"— in her kitchen, and I saw you with her that night."

Hank's heart slammed against his ribs— the only thing the kid could've seen was an embrace, a chaste kiss, and another couple kisses upon Jane's cheek. But in the dark? With little light from the moon? Who knew what the boy thought he'd seen.

Just as frightening, who knew what others might have witnessed?

"Be careful what you say, little brother." Hank lowered that finger, regretting his sharp reaction— but not what he'd said. "People have ears, and tongues have a way of wagging. What you say in anger might become cruel gossip that causes a lot of pain."

"You ought to take care what you *do*, on a public street, where anybody can see what you're up to."

Elias had worked himself into a lather. Hank's stomach soured, knowing far too well his brother was right. His reputation wouldn't suffer much, but Jane's would. "You're right."

Those two, simple words seemed to set the boy's ire loose. He calmed, in the space of two breaths.

Hank stared at his brother, the weight of two enormous realizations compounding the other.

First, Hank had done Jane a serious disservice by walking with her that night. He never should've allowed one kiss much less a second. What had he been thinking?

Second, Elias, at thirteen years of age, was more

man than boy. In this instance, he'd seen what Hank couldn't. That his own behavior was asking for trouble.

Elias swallowed, his Adam's apple dipping in his throat. "I have one more thing to say, and I want you to think long and hard before you answer."

Oh, no. What else had the kid heard? Or worse, what did he think he'd witnessed?

"You and Dora were as miserable as ever two people were. Why do you believe you can be happy with Miss Vancoller?"

Chapter Fifteen

In her tea room kitchen, Jane leaned against the sink, her fingertips upon her lips. Her whole body seemed to hum from Hank's kisses.

Thanks to him, she happily anticipated the festival's opening day, and whatever the Abbotts had planned. She shut off the water.

The dishes could soak for a few minutes. It seemed right now would be her best chance to look in on the library. Before opening that morning, the association had moved every book from her parlor, shelves and all. True to his promise, Hank had moved his supplies toward the back of the space, and provided a table and chairs.

With all the commotion on the street, with ladies coming in and out of her establishment, she'd never hear if the Murphy boys played in their favorite storage room.

Jane dried her hands and slipped into the alleyway, determined to check on the library and see which lady protected the books.

Voices echoed off the exterior bricks. Familiar voices.

Hank and blond Elias faced off, a mere thirty feet down the alley. She drew up short, hearing her name— and Elias's accusations. Hank replied, but his lowered voice didn't carry.

"Is that why," Elias yelled, "you're kissing her?"

Jane froze, her hand at her throat. Anger and venom soaked the boy's words. He must've seen them through the kitchen window just now. Hank chastised his brother, but with his back turned and his lower volume, she couldn't catch his response.

A denial?

"I saw you kissing her just now in her kitchen, and I saw you with her that night." Elias disapproved, that much was evident, even as Hank countered with, "Lower your voice, Elias."

Panic seared through Jane— the kind that threatened to upend her stomach.

She couldn't let them see her. Nor did she want to hear another word— but with the volume of the boy's voice, she couldn't prevent hearing. "People have ears, and tongues have a way of wagging. What you say in anger might become cruel gossip—"

The breeze shifted, carrying Hank's words away.

Just as easily, he could shift his weight, move enough the smaller boy could see past Hank's width and height. She couldn't let the boy see her. In his anger, who knew what he'd say? With her heart pounding and acid riding high in her stomach, Jane opened the screen door into the storage room.

Inside, their words were muted further, and she couldn't make out anything more.

What more was there to hear? The boy, Elias, took exception to her. He'd apparently witnessed plenty, and hadn't liked what he'd seen.

She leaned against the wall, and would've thudded her head against its unrelenting surface if not for the mass of curls cushioning her skull. What good would a head-banging do?

Mrs. Zylphia Hudson, in all her talk of glorious second marriages, hadn't mentioned *this*.

What had she been thinking, kissing Hank Murphy as if they were both free to do as they wished? He had five small dependents. Children who would either accept her or wouldn't.

The little ones might, in time, but Elias had made his viewpoint clear.

"Jane?"

Startled, Jane opened her eyes and whirled toward the feminine voice inside. Her pulse spiked further. "Ina."

"I thought I heard the door open and close." Miss Ina Dimond gestured over her shoulder. "I'm on library duty, and I... Are you quite all right?"

"Yes, yes. Quite all right. I came to see how you're getting along in with the library." She could no longer hear Hank and Elias outside, but the thought of Ina overhearing something more pushed Jane further into the building. "Let me see the arrangement."

A cool breeze swept inside, as the door to the front walk stood open. Ina chatted happily, talking about the three new library subscriptions she'd secured during her shift. Ina pointed out an A-frame sign just outside the door, calling attention to the library and its solicitation of new members.

Outside, people milled about, strolled, carried packages and conversations. Laughter and loud voices of greeting, discussions about the opening of tomorrow's events— all of it came as a stark contrast to Jane's newfound dismay.

One important detail Jane noted immediately was the absence of all little Murphys. Given the state of her conscience, that was a good thing.

"Have you seen the new library listings?" Ina put a booklet in Jane's hands.

"Nice, aren't they?" Jane flipped through the small tome, noting the dozen or more advertisements in the back, just as the association had determined to offer. But with her heart breaking, she couldn't admire the listing adequately. What could she do but divert? "You must be thirsty. Would you like a cup of tea?"

"Oh, that would be lovely."

Jane forced a smile— a talent she needed to lean on. "I'll be back in a jiffy."

"Wait— Jane? As I haven't a soul to discuss the library with, might we discuss a matter of some importance?"

Jane couldn't help it. She glanced toward the alley door. She'd have patrons to see to.

"It's your mother." Ina slid a chair back from the table, the scrape of chair legs dull in the commotion from the street. "Please, sit, for just a minute."

Her feet ached, didn't they? She sat. "What about my mother?"

Ina took her own chair and leaned closer, as if to confide a secret. "I've visited, as you asked. She and I have had several lovely conversations, but there's one thing you should know."

Could she handle another disappointment?

"Mrs. Vancoller is determined to attend the festival, beginning tomorrow morning. I don't know what your intentions are, given the contests and all, and I wanted you to know I'll be attending with Mr. Harris." Ina's expression glowed with the kind of happiness attributable to only one thing. The woman, a decade Jane's senior, was in love.

"Mr. Harris, the pharmacist?" Jane had heard about the moment in the Emporium, when Ina, in her broken-hearted jealousy, had fled the scene, only to have Mr. Oscar Harris follow. The ladies who'd retold the tale had thought it romantic.

"Yes." Ina's smile had never been so broad or so sincere. "Your mother could come with us, if you'd like. She shouldn't attend alone."

"You're most kind to offer, Ina, and I thank you for thinking of us, but we can't impose." Just as she'd hoped to enjoy the festival with Hank, Ina would want time with her fellow. "You'll not want to divide your attention from Mr. Harris."

"I will, if you need us to. Your mother and I have become friendly."

"Thank you." Jane reached for Ina's hand, giving her a squeeze. "The festival has brought so many people to town, I've been needed here at all hours. Mother has been lonely."

"It's been my pleasure."

"I'm most grateful. I'll ensure Mama is cared for tomorrow. I'll walk with her." Disappointment stung, deep inside. Given the conversation she'd overheard, she doubted Hank would follow through with his invitation. If his boys didn't approve of their association, they'd not have a chance...

"Your mother and I thought you'd be busy, with the competition. And with your beau."

Jane blinked, surprised.

Ina chuckled. "Your mama told me all about it. How Mr. Murphy came to call, and you two spent an hour or more on the porch swing, sharing confidences and holding hands."

Mother knew about that?

"But don't worry, Jane." Ina's smile held a bit of conspiracy. And shared happiness, as if her own romance colored her glasses with a rosy hue. "Your mama doesn't know about the kisses, and I didn't tell her."

Kisses? Jane choked. How did Ina know about Jane and Hank? Had she peered through the kitchen window just now, with Elias? Panic clawed at her belly. Or had Hank mentioned something to Oscar Harris, who'd told Ina? "Who said anything about kisses?"

"Why, Mrs. Abbott, of course. She was here, ensuring I managed things the way she wanted with the library. She's over the moon with joy, seeing as the contest has brought you and Hank together. I happen to think your new romance is glorious news."

Ann? "How does Mrs. Abbott know anything? I haven't seen her in weeks... She seems to have been reclusive." Did she have spies in every corner? On every street, after dark?

Ina's laughter sounded young and carefree. Gloriously happy. The way Jane had felt, until Elias took a tack to that bubble with his harsh statements in the alley. "She didn't say. But you know Ann. The woman's always well-informed."

"Indeed." This revelation complicated *everything*, well beyond her strained relationship with her mother. Knowing what she did now, including Elias's stark objections, how could she allow the Murphys to accompany herself and Mama to the Harvest Festival's opening ceremonies?

"Don't worry, Jane. I doubt your mother has heard. If she mentions anything about a kiss," Ina whispered, "you can trust she didn't hear it from me."

A few minutes later, when Jane delivered a steaming cup of tea, sweetened and white, the way Ina liked it, Jane had decided to beg off. She and Mama would attend the festival on their own.

On Thursday morning, the city park had filled to capacity a full half-hour prior to the opening ceremonies of Mountain Home's Harvest Festival. A general consensus determined that the pleasant temperatures and clear skies had contributed to the far larger attendance than ever before. Hank heard their tongue-in-cheek humor, knowing they all attributed the attendance to Mayor and Mrs. Abbott.

Amid the excitement, vivid chatter among the

people, Hank could see what the mayor had envisioned. A bonding community, significantly improved attendance, and good, clean fun— the only element that remained to be seen.

But Hank couldn't think about any of that. Last evening, Jane had sent a note to the Emporium, stating her mother's needs prevented her from attending the festival with him. If she'd told him so, to his face, he might've been able to sniff out a lie.

But in a note? What did he know of her handwriting?

Oscar, in his newly acquired wisdom about females and romance, had cautioned Hank. "You must love the whole woman, even the crazy parts."

Jane hadn't a crumb of the kind of crazy that Miss Ina Dimond carried in spades.

What was this about love?

Hank hadn't mentioned a single word about his affections for Jane to Oscar.

More importantly, Hank had never said the words out loud. To anyone. Thus, no matter what Elias claimed to have overheard or witnessed, no one could say Hank was a man in love.

Now, *where* was Jane?

He'd searched the crowd since arriving, anxious to find her and her mother. But the press of people made that impossible. He'd shaken hundreds of hands, accepted best wishes, been pounded on the back—

"There you are." Oscar offered a handshake. "Today's the day. I'm pulling for you."

Hank shook firmly. "Thanks, partner."

On Oscar's arm, Ina Dimond looked radiant in a

plaid costume of gray and navy. Seeing them together like this, side-by-side they made a handsome pair.

Hank recalled his manners and lifted his cap. "Miss Dimond. You're looking well."

"I feel quite well. Thank you, Mr. Murphy. You won't mind if I root for the lady's team, will you?"

He chuckled with them, accepted a firm smack on the back, and then, finally, he caught a glimpse of Jane's mother, in her ever-present widow's black, sitting on a bench, another old woman in black beside her. But no Jane.

Hank pulled at his too-snug collar. He'd not worn his proper suit of clothes in ages, and today, despite the moderate weather, found the jacket too tight and the necktie torturous.

He scanned the crowd from street to street, from the evergreen trees marking yet another boundary, to the platform reassembled just that morning. He'd never locate his boys in this crowd. Given the children's difficulty in falling asleep last night, and their chatter about the mysterious events today, they'd stay nearby.

He couldn't let Jane face the opening announcement without him. He had every confidence he could call up anyone on their lists to step in, but she'd not seen the sheets, and he doubted she'd respond with as much certainty. He'd promised her protection from embarrassment, and he'd ensure her comfort.

Even if she'd cried off and refused to attend with him.

"Ladies and gentlemen!" Mayor Abbott's voice carried— barely— over the laughter and greetings and curious discussions.

Hank stretched, desperately scanning the platform for Jane. Was she up there with Abbott?

The mayor lifted his speaking trumpet to this mouth again. "Ladies and gentlemen, your attention, please."

The crowd settled, but Hank couldn't begin this without Jane. He searched the crowd, so many faces, a sea of hats and bonnets blocking his view. There! A straw hat, like Jane's—

A hand slipped into his. *Jane.* She wore no bonnet on her dark curls. He gathered a general view of her costume— a pinkish costume of wool, trimmed with lace at the throat and cuffs. He cared for one reason alone, and that was his ability to locate her again if they became separated.

Her smile and the twinkle in her eyes showed her ease and comfort. She'd found him, come to him. His anxiety faded under the warmth of her touch. "I missed you," he blurted. He squeezed her fingers and lifted them to his mouth for a kiss.

"I missed you." In full sunlight, her summer-green eyes were more vibrant than ever.

Applause erupted around them— Hank glanced away from Jane long enough to see that nearly everyone had turned toward the platform and paid attention to the mayor's ramblings.

Jane appeared to be listening, too. She smiled, ever so slightly, just as laughter and more applause rang through the park. Ladies waved handkerchiefs.

Hank shook his head, forced himself to listen to the mayor, to pay attention to what the man said. His singular purpose in closing the store and meeting Jane at the park was to learn about the competitions.

How could he battle this amazing woman who still held his hand?

Applause, punctuated with whistles, swelled around them.

Someone smacked Hank on the back.

Jane leaned near, smelling fresh and clean, and of flowers. "That's our cue, Mr. Murphy."

Before he could shake his head to clear the fog, she'd slipped her fingers from his and scampered toward the platform and the focus of everyone in the county.

He followed, reminding himself he must clear his mind. He had contests to play— and wise seconds to pull from the crowd to stand in for Jane.

One alarming question remained. Could he protect the girl, and still play to win?

Chapter Sixteen

Jane stood on the platform, trembling. Her pulse raced and she feared she'd be sick. She'd never been one to enjoy attention, especially in such large doses.

She clasped her hands at her waist and fought the shakes. Despite the temperature, pleasantly hovering near seventy degrees, perspiration soaked through Jane's combination, chemise, and corset cover. Thank goodness her woolen costume had dress shields to save her the embarrassment of sweat rings beneath her arms.

When had she ever, in the entirety of her life—including the funerals— had she ever had so many eyes trained on her? Her heart pounded as if she'd run to Denver and back again.

Somehow, she had to survive the introduction. She fought to slow her breathing, promising herself this was the only time she had to be on stage. Hank had promised he'd find appropriate stand-ins, and she trusted him to help, even though their short-lived romance had begun to degenerate.

At the moment, any possible contest seemed overwhelming. He'd said there were plenty of seconds. Maybe she'd be forced to sit out every competition, which might be altogether best. How could she sit opposite Hank, vying for a prize he needed more than she, with her heart breaking?

Pain sliced through her cracking heart, but she forced the fissures to hold.

Everything would be fine, she vowed.

Everything would be fine... if she could hold on.

Mayor Archibald Abbott raised his voice trumpet. "Citizens of the great State of Colorado, neighbors, friends." He articulated each word with precision. "Allow me to introduce Mr. Thankful M. Murphy, proprietor of the T.M. Murphy Grocery Emporium!"

Thankful M. Murphy?— Hank was short for *Thankful*? How had she never thought to ask him what the T. stood for? She knew this man deeply in some ways, and yet not at all.

She'd have to remember to ask what his middle initial stood for... but no, that wouldn't be wise. Like a falling star, they'd burned brightly in the night sky... and shriveled in a moment.

Applause, whistles, and cheers greeted Hank.

Jane clapped, because celebrating him drove away the angst and the painful soon-to-be memories. If only she could whistle!

Hank swept an arm across his middle and bowed with panache, then raised his arm in a friendly wave. Soon both hands were aloft. He called to men by name. The first three names shouted in greeting became five, then ten. For a newcomer in town, he'd sure made fast friends of nearly everybody. That's what happened when a man ran an honest business and tried to be friendly.

Like Mama used to say, "Friendly people have friends."

When the applause quieted adequately for the mayor to be heard again, he raised the brass speaking trumpet. "And now, Miss Jane Mary Vancoller, proprietress of the Tea Room."

Jane held her breath, never expecting more than a moderate and ladylike waving of handkerchiefs. To her surprise, men and women alike cheered for her cause. Equal, if not more support.

She glanced at Hank, finding him smiling at her with the kind of enthusiasm and support she'd always wanted. Vindication, in that moment, for her tea room, for the service she provided, pleased her far more than she could say.

She couldn't just stand there, dumb. Hank had responded to the crowd, and she should, too. She curtsied with the awkwardness of a girl who'd never curtsied in her life. She raised a hand— *please, please dress shields*— and waved, so overcome by the support and encouragement, she pressed a hand to her locket.

Her eyes burned with a suspicious warning. Now was *not* the time to become sentimental.

"And now, dear friends," the mayor said, "let us commence with our Harvest Festival for the year eighteen hundred and eighty-seven."

The applause and cheers seemed to double. Jane found herself laughing at the stunned surprise that nudged aside her fright. The sheer excitement at the event, veiled in secrecy, had surely reached its peak.

The mayor gestured for silence. "This year, the occasion of our Harvest Festival will be different than in years past."

With this statement, laughter and whistles flitted through the audience. Mayor Abbott, wholly in his element before the crowd, laughed along with them. "In order to most effectively inform all persons of the day's entertainments, our valley's newspaper will run a Daily, for the first time in the history of Mountain Home."

The mayor's statement caused quite a stir. The commotion from the audience swelled, and Abbott shook his head in mock distress, then turned to Hank. The men exchanged a dialogue Jane couldn't overhear for the racket.

Finally, when Abbott attempted a second, and then a third time to regain quiet, the audience stilled. Every pair of eyes, except for the littlest of children's, were pinned on Mayor Abbott.

"Now, I'm certain you're anxious to see what contest will come first. Am I correct?"

More cheers, longer this time. The noise grated against Jane's nerves, and a headache started at the base of her skull.

"At precisely one o'clock"— thirty minutes from now, if she guessed correctly— "today's edition of the Mountain Home *Times and Seasons* will be available for distribution at the cost of two cents, in front of the newspaper office. Friday's and Saturday's editions will be on sale at said location at nine o'clock both mornings."

The crowd received the news with excitement. Men popped open pocket watches. Women consulted watches pinned to their bodices or dangling from chains about their necks.

Disappointment sliced through Jane and the shakes returned. She had to wait thirty minutes, and fight the crowds toward the newspaper office, all to discover what contest she'd face? How would she find Mother in this crowd? From where she stood upon the elevated platform, Mother's place was blocked from view. Mama had insisted upon sitting on her folding chair beside the park bench occupied by a friend of hers.

In the excitable crowd, Mama wasn't steady enough on her feet to walk as far as the Tea Room, much less their home.

Hank leaned near, close enough for the warmth of his breath to brush her cheek. A craving for his closeness, protection, and help washed through her, stronger than she'd believed possible. She needed this man, especially now.

"If I'd have known about the dailies," he said, close to her ear, "I'd have paid for advertisements."

She tried to smile. Truly, she did. But anxieties mounted. The audience thrived on the mystery, but the combination threatened to destroy her composure. Still, the confrontation in the alleyway, less than twenty-four hours ago, rang in her memory. She'd done the right thing by stepping back, and finding her own way to the park.

Which meant she had no claim on Hank's help to find her mother in the crowd.

"Now, ladies and gentlemen," Abbott turned, gesturing broadly to Hank and Jane. "Let us begin with the toss of a coin." He set the trumpet on its bell at his feet, withdrew a shiny coin from his pocket and placed it on the crooked thumb of his fist. He looked to Hank, then spoke with a politician's elocution and volume. "Call it in the air."

Abbott flipped the coin. The silver caught the midday sunlight, turning over and over as it rose.

"Heads!" Hank folded his arms and rocked back on his heels.

Flashes of sunlight reflected on precious metal as the coin spun and dropped...

Abbott caught the coin in his palm and slapped it to the back of his opposite hand. With the result hidden, he looked to the audience. "Ready?"

"Yes!" the audience roared in near unison.

Jane's pulse tripped, running far too fast. She detested the mayor's theatrical performance. But the crowd enjoyed themselves, with the little ones remaining interested.

Abbott lifted his hand to reveal the coin. "Tails wins! Miss Vancoller, you are our first contestant."

Heat flashed through her, followed by an icy wash of nerves. She blinked, fighting a lightheaded state. Maybe she'd learn immediately what she'd face. Maybe she wouldn't be forced to wait.

More whistles sparkled through more cheers. Everyone quieted quickly and some hushed others, as if the contest were the most critical news of the decade and folks desired Jane's fate.

None could want to know as badly as she.

Abbott reclaimed his trumpet and with fanfaronade, raised the device and repeated himself— and Hank's call of heads— for those beyond the reach of his unaided voice.

"Miss Vancoller is up first," Mayor Abbott repeated. "The front page of *Times and Seasons* will clarify when and where the contestants and spectators are to meet."

A rush of hushing hissed through the crowd. Jane swayed to the left, then to the right. Her vision blackened about the edges and she nearly stumbled over her feet.

Please, no. She mustn't faint. Not here, not now.

Hank must've sensed her trouble, for his sturdy arm came around her back and pulled her into his side. Her head swam and her ears rang. She closed her eyes, fighting nausea.

The only thing worse than fainting before the entire county? Losing her breakfast. She breathed through her mouth. Bursts of light spangled her closed eyelids.

Hank's lips brushed her temple. "Jane? Breathe," he urged. "Breathe. I'm here with you. You're safe."

Her heart cracked a little more. How she wished that were true. But she knew better. Nothing wonderful lasted for long, not for her.

Before Mayor Abbott concluded his remarks, folks scattered. A trickle at first, from the edges, but soon everybody headed in a singular direction— toward Main, and the *Times and Seasons* building.

Hank held Jane close, his arm about her waist. Perspiration beaded her forehead, and from the way she leaned heavily upon him, he doubted she had the wherewithal to make it across the park to her mother.

He could pray she was merely faint, upset, or overwhelmed. But bottom line, he loved her. No way could he walk away from her now, when she needed him. If even a little.

Where were his boys? He searched the scattering crowd, masses of dark suits, women in bonnets and costumes in an array of colors. Children ducked and darted between adults.

With careful attention, he noted faces. "Sims!" The regular in the Emporium would be good help, but he'd not heard. "Sims!"

The man chuckled, carrying on an animated conversation with two men and their wives.

A knot of youthful boys cut between Hank and the familiar face.

"I'm all right," Jane insisted, pushing against him without real force.

"Forgive me for arguing, Jane, but I don't believe you." *There!* "Oscar Harris!" With her secure in his arms, he moved a few steps to the right, to better see around a crowd of women with their tall, flowerpot hats. "*Oscar Harris!*"

His business partner walked with Miss Dimond, their arms linked. Oscar's face glowed, almost angelic in happiness. The man was so lost in Ina, he'd not come close to hearing Hank's shout.

"Hank, please. Find your boys. They need you, and I'll be fine. I'll sit here, wait until the crowd disperses a bit, and then I'll find Mother. She'll move slowly, if at all, so I won't have trouble locating her."

"You're not well." He didn't want to fight with her, but he would, if necessary.

"Hank!"

Elias. Thank God.

Elias pushed through the throng, concern marring his features. In his youthful strength, he leaped onto the platform, sparing no time for stairs. The boy glanced at Jane, his expression stringent.

No doubt he'd witnessed Hank steadying Jane the last minutes of the opening ceremonies. "Miss Vancoller is ill. She nearly fainted."

Jane and Elias eyed one another in a manner that made the fine hairs rise on the back of Hank's neck.

Wary.

Like two starved dogs circling a single meaty bone. As if they'd pounce, and with slight provocation, fight to the death.

Oh, no.

Why hadn't he turned about in the alley, to make certain nobody from Jane's place overheard the words he'd had with his brother?

She'd heard at least part. What other explanation was there?

That explained why she'd changed her mind, and refused to allow him to accompany her to the park this morning. And now, her reasons for pushing him away, though she needed him.

"Elias, we've a short order and no time." He'd treat

this like business to appease his brother. Later, he'd ensure Jane knew this was business of the heart.

"Yes, sir." The boy glanced at Jane with the kind of venom reserved for the enemy. Later, he'd ensure the boy knew his deportment required improvement.

"Round up the boys, quick as you can." He dug in the pocket of his suit, and tossed a nickel to his brother. "Send Austin for two papers. I need you to get the little ones, and go to that bench—" he pointed in the right direction— "and collect elderly Mrs. Vancoller. She needs your steady arm and a man to carry her chair. Walk as slow as she requires."

"Yes, Hank."

"Thank you." Emotion jumped into his throat, pleased to see the good man Elias would become.

"Where do I take them?"

Good question. The store was closest, but Main would be choked with people. He included Jane in the decision. "Are you well enough to walk to our home?"

"I'm *fine*, I assure you. Mother and I will be fine."

Egad, the woman could be contrary. "I'll see to it. You and your mother require neighborly assistance."

Elias would obey, but Hank knew his word choice would stoke Jane's ire. She'd be mad as a wet hen, but he'd deal with that later. He squeezed her as a sign of reassurance. "Take everyone to our house."

Elias jumped off the platform. "Yes, sir."

Thanks to Austin, fleet of foot and still young

enough to have no qualms about cutting in line, the Murphys were among the first to purchase today's daily edition of *Times and Seasons.*

Bless Elias's obedient efforts, he'd managed to wrangle everybody home safely, while Hank walked with Jane and steadied her the entire way.

Now, gathered around the dining table with his older boys, Jane and her mama, Hank needed to discover when and where to present themselves— and formulate a plan to ensure Jane's comfort and safety.

If she'd allow him to.

Blast Abbott's circus act for causing her distress. She sat at his left, a glass of cold well water before her. She'd consumed half of it, and her color had improved. She and her mother perused one copy of the newspaper, while he and Elias skimmed the other.

Seven people sat around his dining table, waiting with anticipation— okay, except for the littlest boys who didn't understand— and a bit of distress.

He skimmed the front page and located today's schedule of events.

Austin slapped his palm on the tabletop. "No fair reading ahead. We want to know, too."

Hank gave his eldest son the eye.

Austin returned to fiddling with their copy of *The Adventures of Tom Sawyer* and the scrap of paper they'd tucked between the pages perhaps one-quarter of the way through. They kept the book upon the table, and Hank read aloud to the boys as they ate breakfast and supper. As Jane had anticipated, the boys loved the story.

"Look!" Austin pointed to the paper in Hank's

hands. "On the back. A big advertisement with engravings. It's our emporium."

Sure enough, a half-page advertisement for T.A. Murphy's Grocery Emporium, citing the freshest of groceries and everything a family needs for comfort during long winter months to come. "I didn't pay for that."

The wording was right and the images appealing. Whoever designed it had done a fair job. He'd stop by the newspaper at first opportunity, maybe at the conclusion of the festival, and learn what he owed. A half-page might cost him every cent of profit he'd made in the past weeks, a definite problem, as he'd already reinvested most of it in one more large order from his distributors.

"Pa!" Austin had lost patience. "Read the schedule."

"Recall your manners, son."

He folded the paper, and tipping it toward the light from the window, read aloud. "Thursday, October 6, 1887, Schedule of Events: twelve o'clock noon, introduction of competitors at the platform and flipping of the coin, city park.

"One-thirty, competition between our two competitors, a pie-eating contest."

"Pie-eating contest?" Elias's jaw hung loose. "That's it? That's what this excitement is all about?"

Everyone stared at him, surprised— and not in a pleasant way. Except for young Jimmy who'd claimed elderly Mrs. Vancoller's lap and talked to himself as he fiddled with the jet buttons on her mourning costume.

Visions of men stuffing their faces with pie, barely

tasting the custard as they swallowed obscene quantities of pastry and pumpkin— "I suppose so."

"Is that all?" Mrs. Vancoller carefully disengaged Jimmy's grasp from her dangling earbob. "No further contests?"

Hank reread the schedule. "After the pie contest, another event at the park, on the platform, with Team Vancoller and Team Murphy—" He scanned further. "Miss Vancoller and I are to select six adults to participate on each of our teams."

Jane laid her paper on the table and tapped a column on the right-hand side. "An article about each of the scheduled items appears here. We are to gather our teams to assist us in a timed oral examination."

"What for?" Austin's attitude remained sour.

"To ascertain our knowledge of subjects from the harvest to the history of Mountain Home to mathematics."

Austin grunted. "I'd rather eat pie."

"Me, too, son. Me, too." This match could end badly. Who should he call on from their lists of volunteers? How would he ensure Jane had a good team, without dominating the competition?

"What is the time now?" Jane's locket must not contain a timepiece.

Hank opened his pocket watch. "Twenty past one."

Jane stood and slid her chair beneath the table. "We'd best hurry. A scant ten minutes remain." She straightened her skirt as if preparing for battle.

Skirts and battle *did not* belong in the same sentence.

"I won that coin toss." Her expression of

bewilderment charmed him. "How does one go first at a pie eating contest?"

"I've no idea."

Women shouldn't be compelled to participate in a pie eating contest. Such events were for men and their dubious table manners.

"Who will you choose as your second?" Hank tucked the newspaper beneath his arm and donned his flat cap.

Elias offered elderly Mrs. Vancoller his arm, and Austin carried her folding chair. Clyde took Jimmy's hand. The sight pleased him. He'd managed to do something right when training his boys to be attentive men.

"I don't know that I will defer. I might participate."

He wanted to ask if she were well enough to entertain the notion. She'd been ill on that platform, exposed to full sun. Clammy skin and perspiration on her forehead pointed to nausea. She'd nearly fainted. No fewer eyes would be upon her during the pie-eating contest. But to ask, again, would only put him in the line of fire. He'd asked after her health a few times on the walk home, and Jane had denied illness with increasing ferocity.

Consuming pie in large quantities, as quick as she could, seemed utterly foolish.

"You might?" If she stayed in, then so would he. No way would he stand her against someone determined to win. Or worse, someone bent on humiliating her.

"I might."

"Have you a parasol? Or a hat?"

"Are you my mother?"

Hank ground his molars. He didn't know whether to steal a kiss or chastise her cantankerous mood. "I'm not your mother, but I care about you and your wellbeing." Remarks like this had yielded poor results from Dora, who'd been driven to win the verbal battles, notwithstanding costs to herself.

Jane surprised him. "I'm more comfortable without a bonnet. Besides, I noticed the city councilmen carrying poles and a canopy into the park as we left. I believe they intend to shade the stage."

With everyone else on their way, thus no one to observe, he pulled Jane close. He didn't dare risk more than an embrace. "I want to protect you."

She surprised him with a kiss to his jaw. "I know."

Chapter Seventeen

Though the party wasn't likely to begin without them, Jane walked as quickly as Clyde's little legs and Mama's aged frame would allow. Hank carried Jimmy on his arm, and insisted on offering Jane the other.

His chivalry was merely one of the reasons she loved him.

They arrived in the city park to find an audience nearly as large as the crowd gathered at the opening ceremonies. The city council members ushered their group through the crowd and had gone so far as to save a front-row space for Jane's mother and the boys.

Austin set up Mama's folding chair, and Elias, who'd escorted her, helped her be seated. Baby Jimmy raised his arms, inviting Mother to pick him up.

By the look on her mother's face, Jane could only surmise that the little boy had won her heart. Clyde stood at her side, clung to the chair's wooden bar, and rested his head against Mother's shoulder. Quick as could be, she swept her arm about the boy and snuggled him close.

Jane took Hank's offered hand as he helped her up the stairs onto the shaded platform. Sure enough, a canopy covered the platform, suspended from poles at the four corners.

A table and two chairs faced one another, in a parody of the well-laid tables in Jane's Tea Room. Set with linens, two wooden crates had been turned upside down and draped with another tablecloth, effectively hiding whatever stacks of pies might be hidden beneath. The setup ensured those present could view both contestants and their progress.

The audience cheered as Hank bowed. He presented Jane with a sweep of his arm. This man had more panache than she'd realized. He pulled back the closest chair and seated her. He bent and put his mouth close to her ear.

She shivered at the delicious contact of his cheek against hers. Stubble of his beard brushed her skin.

"Did you see the half-dozen or more men— and a woman or two— who signaled us? They'll take your place. All you need do is say the word."

If several hundred pairs of eyes weren't fastened to them, she'd have cupped Hank's cheek and held him closer. Her heart brimmed with an immense gratitude to her town, and to this kind man. So many friends and neighbors who'd help her in any way possible.

His concern for her felt good. Protective. If this ended up the kind of contest that would threaten her wellbeing, no doubt he'd stand in her defense.

Like her daddy had done, only different.

Like a beau, or a suitor. Much the way Law had.

He traced his thumb over her back, where his hand rested upon her shoulder. The sweet and gentle touch, coupled with his deference, emphasized how much a suitor Hank had become.

Despite Elias's disapproval.

"Thank you." She turned her face toward him. "You're too good to the competition."

"I know," he murmured, and brushed his lips against her cheek.

Heat flushed up her neck and into her face as he rounded the table, his eyes affixed to hers. His expression added to the heat... like the big, bad wolf and Little Red Riding Hood, he'd gobble her all up.

Jane's stomach turned inside out at the realization... somehow, in the space of a pair of months, Hank Murphy had filled the vacancy in her heart, and brought happiness to the darkest, loneliest corners of her soul. How could she not love a man who obviously loved her in return?

She loved this man. She'd told him so, that late night they'd walked the city streets. She still meant every word.

Hank's smile, on this platform, on the most crowded and busy day of the year, seemed to be for her alone.

Slowly, he pulled back his chair and sat, and turned his attention to the crates. He lifted the corner of the tablecloth.

"No peeking!" Mayor Abbott made a made a show of playing to the audience.

"I'm not peeking." Hank dropped the cloth.

"See that you don't."

Laughter erupted as the crowd enjoyed the byplay.

Through his lifted mouth trumpet, Mayor Abbott pronounced, "Are we ready?"

Applause, punctuated with whistles, made Jane shiver with anxiety-tinged anticipation.

"On your mark," the mayor called.

Jane searched for a fork, but saw none. Would they be subjected to eating with their fingers?

Two city councilmen, in response to Abbott's words, lifted the tablecloth from atop the crates.

Jane peeked between the crates slats, startled to see one little pumpkin pie, perhaps four inches in diameter. A delicate golden crust surrounded seasoned custard, topped with three golden leaf shapes cut of pastry. What a beauty!

And yes, a fork and napkin.

Was Hank's pie so small? She peered over her crate to his, attempting to see between the slats. She couldn't see much, but Hank's scowl told her plenty.

"Get set!" Abbott bellowed through his trumpet.

"Wait a minute." Jane turned about in her chair to face Abbott. "Did I not win the coin toss? Am I to go first?"

Abbott chuckled. "Why indeed, yes." Then, through the trumpet, "The lady won the coin toss. She's first to attempt the competition. How much of a lead shall we give her?"

Immediate answers swarmed from the crowd. Shouts of one minute, five minutes, thirty seconds, and numerous others, blended together in a cacophony.

Abbott waved an arm high above his head, as if that would silence the crowd. "Those for a one-minute lead time, be heard."

A loud cheer erupted in approval.

When those quieted, he added, "Those in favor of a longer lead?"

Another group answered, loudly, but markedly less so than the first.

"One minute, it is!" The mayor announced, then nodded at his assistants.

Jane kept her attention on the crate— and what lay beneath it. The councilman at her side lifted the crate to reveal her tiny, patty pan pumpkin pie. Golden, perfect, and precisely right for one.

Jane's laughter dispelled the tension that had tightened her muscles all day. This, she could do!

The audience roared with laughter and whispers and more and more of those watching became aware of the pie allotted to Jane.

The mayor raised his speaking trumpet. "Is that a pie, Miss Vancoller?"

"Yes, I suppose so."

"Hold it up, will you?"

Jane displayed her pie, extended high above her head. Laughter and enjoyment banished the tension she'd battled all day. "I doubt I need a minute's head start... unless Mr. Murphy's pie is half this size. Then I'll accept my privilege."

"Very well." Mayor Abbott nodded to his man, who lifted the crate covering Hank's pie— so enormous, it barely fit beneath the crate. Why, the rectangle tin must measure sixteen by twenty-four inches. The thick pumpkin custard must be nearly four inches in depth.

Jane's laughter joined the enchanted crowd.

Applause and whistles expressed their enjoyment of the dissimilar pies.

She met Hank's eye, witnessed his confusion... and resignation. But rather than behave the spoil-sport, he shook his head almost playfully.

How had this happened? Had Hank been in on the jest, and known which seat would be hers? He'd led her to this one, after all.

Hank rubbed his stomach, to more laughter from their audience.

"It's not too late to call in a second." She couldn't help but jest with her man.

"Nah." Hank picked up his fork. "I like pumpkin pie."

Jane glanced over her shoulder at the mayor whose smile couldn't have been broader. He pointed a starter pistol at the sky. "Ready, Miss Vancoller?"

Jane faced her pie, and met Hank's eye.

A frisson sizzled through her at the heat she saw there.

"Go!" Abbott bellowed. The bang of the pistol made her flinch, though she'd anticipated it.

As if the event had as much action as a horse race, folks cheered. Fathers lifted children onto their shoulders to better see.

Hank scooped up an enormous forkful of pie and stuffed it into his mouth. He'd barely swallowed— without chewing!— before scooping up another massive hunk.

Jane would have to remember to send the baker a letter, thanking him for his kindness. She opened the provided napkin on her lap, and with ladylike decorum, forked a dainty bit of pumpkin to her lips.

"Papa?" Russell lay in bed, bathed, in a clean nightshirt, and in a neat row with his brothers in the bed. Lamplight shone on his freshly washed cheeks.

"Go to sleep, Russ." The day's excitement had wound the boys tight as could be.

"Papa. This is important."

"You've had two drinks of water. You've been to the outhouse. Go to sleep." Hank extinguished the lamp.

"I want to know something." Russ grew impatient.

Good. That made two of them. "What, son?"

"Are you mad Miss Van Collie won today, two times?"

He smiled at the child's interpretation of Jane's surname, and he'd taken her wins in stride— or so he'd thought. The crowds had enjoyed the entertainment, more than ever before. Once or twice, Hank had forgotten the contest had only one prize to be won... and he *needed* that prize. "No, Russ. I'm not mad. Now go to sleep."

He pulled the door halfway closed.

"I'd be mad," Russell whispered, "if a girl whipped me."

The following morning, Oscar joined the line growing on Main, and waited to purchase the Friday Daily.

He took another limping step forward, fire throbbing as his prosthesis abraded his stump. A lot of good the lineament he'd slathered on his bruised and broken skin had done. The pungent stuff stank, and hadn't offered an iota of relief.

If he hadn't promised Ina he'd purchase two copies of the paper prior to calling this morning, he'd move as slow as he had to, across the street to the pharmacy within the Emporium, and put away a half a bottle of coca wine.

One more fire-encompassed step, he nearly lost his resolve.

If Ina didn't want two copies, one to use, and one to save in her memorabilia, he'd find a used copy. Or send one of Hank's boys to buy him one later and hope they weren't sold out.

He leaned on his good leg to see what had caused the line's movement to halt, but couldn't see past all the people, spread out on the sidewalk two and three abreast. How long had folks been waiting before the appointed hour of nine?

Soon, men filed past, perusing the newspapers purchased. From the number of men and women eagerly reading the first page above the fold, it seemed today's schedule had been printed there.

But several men had already opened the paper to pages two and three. The line started moving well, and Oscar made his way past two or three business doors.

"Oscar Harris, our esteemed druggist." A fellow stopped, one Oscar had seen in the Emporium, and with a genial smile, offered a handshake.

"Good morning, friend." He shook firmly, and, banishing the pain to some far-away drawer in his head, locked it away. With a smile, he asked, "Good news in today's paper?"

"That depends, I suppose, on what you'd say is good news." He puffed his cigar, the fragrance too sweet for Oscar's taste in tobacco. The fellow held the cigar with his teeth, center-front, and puffed. He turned the page.

"As long as I'm not listed in the bereavement notices, I'd say that's good news." He winced as raw skin reminded him it bled.

He blew a smoke ring, as if that part of the routine were by rote. Finally, "This is good news, I'd say. Are congratulations in order?"

Oscar hurt too much for riddles and he wasn't in the mood for games. Fire had a way of doing that to a man. "I don't know. I've not bought my paper yet."

"Says here you're courting Miss Ina Diamond."

"It's Dimond. Emphasis on the second syllable." Why on earth would *Times and Seasons* report such a thing? Wasn't the Daily supposed to cover festival events? Maybe another advertisement for the Emporium?

Two men walked past, newspapers in hand. One lifted his hat. "Congratulations, Harris!"

Oh, no. He clutched his thigh, willing the nerves to stop screaming.

Evidently, something about himself and Ina, one

part truth to ninety-nine parts fabrication, ended up in the Personals. Why must small town papers act like the big cities'? If a place didn't have a Mrs. Vanderbilt or a Mrs. Astor to talk about, they included anybody's comings and goings.

He'd never cared for the Personals. Until today.

"You two attended the opening ceremonies together, and she wore a stylish new plaid suit. You're not only courting, you're engaged to be married."

"Uh-huh." Ina would love that, now, wouldn't she? At least that segment contained one part truth to one part fiction.

"I hadn't heard you were a Yankee officer."

Oscar grabbed the newspaper out of the fellow's hands.

"Hey!"

He opened the wrinkled paper, scanning for his name. "Where?"

"Page three." The familiar-looking fellow took a casual step back from Oscar. "An inch or so above the fold."

There, in fresh ink, a sentence that would forever change his life in Mountain Home, and not for the better.

Mountain Home's esteemed druggist, Oscar Harris, a graduate of the University of Michigan, was also a graduate of West Point. He skimmed. *... relieved of duty in the spring of sixty-four. Since, he's earned his livelihood as a druggist in Chicago, and more recently, in Denver, where his penchant for drink cost him a profitable situation with White and White Pharmacy."*

No one could rely on a man who drank too much.

Nobody cared how long he'd been sober.

No one noticed he'd not missed a day of work in years.

One bad prescription...

He glanced up, finding he'd crept forward with the line, and now stood two paces from the clerks who sold papers. With his jaw set, he pulled out a nickel, collected two papers and his penny, thrust the crumpled newspaper into the chest of the man who'd delivered the news, and limped toward Ina's home.

He was no prize, and she'd know that soon enough.

What had he been thinking, to go along with her request for an escort? He wasn't a man any woman should associate with. He sucked in a breath of air as the nerves in his stump burned hotter than Hades. He halted, fighting the urge to fist both pristine newspapers and toss them in a puddle.

If he wouldn't cause women and children to run, screaming in terror, he'd sit in the dust and remove his false leg, on the edge of the street, to ensure the battered flesh wasn't literally aflame.

But that time in Chicago had seared itself into his brain. He'd fallen on that blasted prosthetic leg, it came loose and pulled awkwardly in his trousers, as if he'd busted his leg clean through. Humiliation flushed through him, hot and wild, though the incident had occurred more than fifteen years ago.

Men he'd not known had stopped on the busy Chicago street, pulled him to his *foot*, and ensured he made it inside a shoe shop, of all places, and into the back room where he'd have enough privacy to put himself together again.

Humpty Dumpty. That's who he was. The man that all the king's horses, and all the king's men, couldn't set up again.

When he found out who told the local newspaper about him, he'd...

No, he wouldn't.

Because it was true.

If he couldn't look a man in the face here, in Mountain Home, sober as ever, and fill a doctor's prescription accurately, then he hadn't a thing to say.

He aimed to keep the fine reputation he'd built here. He'd secured himself a partnership with a good man, a man who understood a person's faults didn't make the man. They'd worked together for months, and he wasn't concerned what Hank would do. Besides, the partnership had secured his place.

He stood on Ina's front walk, taking in the whole house. A small, square, well-built home her father had constructed with his own two hands. He'd been among the first settlers here, made some money mining, and never left.

Weary as he'd ever been, Oscar sucked in a deep breath and let it go, debating how to approach Ina.

No sense hiding any of this. She'd be devastated, whether she heard about his drunkenness from him or somebody else. Nearly everyone would believe the statement, because it was in black-and-white, and the gossipers would grab hold of it like a terrier, and gnash him about until dead.

Ina's home stood with perfect symmetry, the front

door in the precise center, one window on the left, and its twin on the right.

A good man would inform Ina he'd been broken, inside where it counted. He was no match for her, and she should know that. All he need do was march to the door, make the pronouncement, deliver her newspapers, and depart.

He shouldn't be on his "feet" all day. To do so would take a bad problem and make it horrid. But to beg off? That'd be like pouring salt on the fresh wound of Ina's disappointment.

If she'd have him.

But there he went, putting the cart ahead of the horse.

Most likely, she wouldn't want him to escort her today. He'd proved a disappointment, and her disappointment would worsen when she read the paper.

Their time together was short.

She'd read the paper, and they'd be through.

He assumed military bearing, and knocked on her door.

Chapter Eighteen

"Mother, please. Do hold still." Jane managed to anchor mother's long, white, and thinning braid in a coil around the crown of her head. She reached for another hair pin.

"We have a full and exciting day ahead of us." Mother had read the day's schedule aloud, twice. Her folding chair waited in its place by the front door. Mama had been up since dawn, hardly willing to wait until the schoolboy across the street brought their newspaper, as arranged. She'd read it from top to bottom at least twice.

The opening day of the annual Harvest Festival had been both stressful and delightful. Given the enjoyment that encompassed most of the day, today carried a sense of promise, like the aroma of baking bread lingered long after the loaves cooled.

Brilliant morning sunlight filled Mother's east-facing bedroom, and in this warm and golden illumination, Mother's coloring seemed improved. If she'd only wear a spot of color, instead of severe black.

"You're quite the local celebrity." Seated before her dressing table, Mother turned to the Personals on page three.

Jane set three more hair pins. If she were in fashion, the Abbotts were to credit. She'd prefer a day in her Tea Room, enjoying the company of women, who in turn enjoyed the festival.

"The *Times* writers watch all you do, and take pride in sharing those details with the entire county."

She'd imagined as such. "Did they report our clever answers during the oral examination?"

"One or two. But they did mention that you arrived to the pie-eating contest on the arm of Mr. Hank Murphy. And, they waxed eloquent about the strong and certain affection between the two of you."

What had they done to give themselves away? Treat one another with courtesy?

The observation, though accurate, left Jane uncomfortable. Another glance in the mirror— at her dove-gray ensemble with white linen and lace at the throat and wrists— made her doubt her selection. What would the Personals reveal tomorrow?

"They also wrote, at some detail, that the two of you are engaged to be married, which marginally justifies your late-night walk through the streets."

"Late night? It wasn't long after eight."

"And had he been here, in our parlor with your mother present, nothing would be amiss."

Jane wanted to growl in aggravation. Mother, at age seventy, was as old-fashioned and prim as anyone's mother, anywhere. "Modern times aren't so constrictive. It's eighteen eighty-seven. Women walk out with their beaus, and no one sees it as inappropriate."

"Is that who he is? Your beau?"

She weighed her words, considering with care. "Yes, I suppose he is my beau."

"I'd hoped the paper was correct, and you two were engaged to be married. Once he spoke to your mother, naturally."

"You can't believe everything you read. No one verified the information with me, so it can't be accurate."

"What is there to verify? I hear you kissed him, too. I taught you better than this."

"Mother—"

"Mind your manners and respect your mother. What else is the newspaper to think? Only an engaged woman would behave this way. I see you do not recall the talk we had about propriety and the dangers for young, innocent girls around men."

"I do remember, Mama. Very well." She'd been seventeen, and mortified.

"Your behavior suggests otherwise."

Jane finished pinning a curl, and counted to ten. When that amount of time did nothing to soothe her temper, she counted to twenty.

Mama met Jane's eye in the mirror. "Have you nothing to say for yourself?"

"You were angry with me for showing no interest in men, no interest in courtship, and now that I'm spending a few minutes with Mr. Murphy—"

"I wasn't angry with you, Jane."

No sense arguing with Mary Vancoller. The woman was always right. "You wanted me to set aside my grief, to try to find a man who would make a good husband."

"Yes, I did, and I do."

"Did you not care for Mr. Murphy yesterday, when he and his family accompanied us from the opening ceremonies to his home, and then to the pie-eating contest?"

"I admire his cordial manners. His new grocery emporium seems to be doing very well. It's evident he needs a mother for his children, as those youngest ones run wild."

Who had Mother been talking to? Jane worked long days, and Mama had abundant time to visit with whomever she pleased, and to gossip about Jane, Hank, and the children. That thought chafed. "You seemed to enjoy Jimmy."

"He's a fine boy, and he needs a mother."

What about love? Shouldn't Jane want the best of romances with a husband, even if he'd been wed before, even with sons to raise? Must she settle for a loveless relationship because of her age, and her status as a not-quite-widow?

"At your age, Hank Murphy might well be your only opportunity."

Jane clamped her jaw, and put her long-practiced smile and contented expression to good use.

"You'll be thirty next month. *Thirty*, Jane."

Yes, she was aware.

"Men want their names associated with good women. Women who honor and respect themselves and others. What will your Mr. Murphy think when he reads the Personals?" Mother tossed the Daily onto her dressing table. "When he reads about your escapades, will he feel proud? Or embarrassed that the woman his name is tied to is free with her favors?"

Jane tossed the comb onto the dressing table, but the newspaper muffled what would have been a satisfying clatter. "Mother. Stop. I am not free with my favors."

"If your own mama can't bring these matters to your attention, then I don't know who will."

"Hank does not doubt my reputation."

"If you parade around town with one fellow, you'll do so with another."

"I will not." Mother had never been so ridiculous with Law.

Mama shrugged.

Jane wanted to purge the mounting aggravation with a scream. Or a growl. Or by unpinning Mother's hair all at once and whipping the mass into a froth with her fingers. In other words, she wanted to behave like the impetuous child Mother believed her to be.

"It seems you're determined to believe the worst of me, Mother, and that is a disappointment. You should know me better than this, and you should trust me, at nearly thirty years of age, to conduct myself in a ladylike manner."

Mother harrumphed.

"And," Jane added, rather pleased with herself for maintaining a moderate and respectful tone, "I'll thank you to show enough respect for Mr. Murphy's intelligence that you will refrain from pointing at our joint behavior with criticism."

"I'd never do such a thing."

Thank you seemed the wrong reply, as did *See that you do.*

"When I see your Mr. Murphy today at the tug-of-war event, I believe I'll ask him what his intentions toward you are."

"Don't."

"It's my place. With your father gone, it's my responsibility to secure your safety and future."

"At the tug-of-war? You can't conceive of a more appropriate time and place?"

"When would that be, Jane? Across the counter at his grocery, with others waiting in line to buy nutmegs?"

"Mr. Harris." Standing on her doorstep, Oscar didn't look well. Not well at all.

Perspiration beaded his forehead, and he held himself stiffly, as if he bore terrible news. "Come in, please. Come in."

She stepped back and ushered him inside. He limped more than usual— which was surely saying something.

He stepped into the parlor and presented her with two of today's newspapers. "For you."

"Thank you."

Where had the gracious, charming man gone? He'd never failed to greet her by name, compliment her

appearance or her smile, ask after her health...
something.

"Please, sit." She indicated the closest chair. Soft,
comfortable, and with a footstool, should he like to raise
his left leg.

He hesitated. He glanced at the upholstered chair,
then back to her. "I won't be here long enough to sit."

"Whatever is the matter? We'd planned to spend
the day together, you and I." Panic clutched her heart
and for a moment, she feared she'd raise her voice, and
that would never do. "You're to escort me to the day's
festivities."

He gestured helplessly to the newsprint in her
hands.

Oscar Harris and *helpless* did not belong in the
same sentence. Of all the men she'd ever had the
pleasure to meet, he'd proved the *least* helpless of all.

Ina took the papers to her chair, opposite, and sat.
"I'm seated, Mr. Harris. Now, you will sit, while I read
the Daily, and attempt to ascertain what it is you're
unwilling to voice."

She sounded just like her mother. She'd been a
strong woman, one to take control when someone had
to.

Instead of waiting for him to obey her, she set one
copy of the paper aside, the one she'd keep forever as a
memento of this glorious Harvest Festival when she had
a beau to call her own, and opened the working copy for
today's use.

They *would* use it.

She read the listing of the day's entertainments.
Finding nothing deserving of Oscar's mood, she

scanned the columns detailing yesterday's contests, winners, and comments. Folks speculated over who was favored to win today's competitions. Nothing there, either.

The back was filled with advertisements for various establishments and local professional services. Pages two and three were filled with residents' statements about the competition, and the fable of two squirrels— one who diligently prepared for winter, and the foolish one who lazed away the sunny summer days.

Ina finally looked up to find Oscar standing as stiff as if he faced the noose.

This would *never* do.

"Mr. Harris." She stood, remaining at her chair, though she wanted nothing more than to approach him. "Are you so offended by Miss Vancoller's dual wins yesterday, that you are unwilling to enjoy today?"

"No, ma'am." He clasped his hands behind his back and stared at a spot over her shoulder.

No, this would never, *never* do.

"I am an intelligent woman." She refused to let the emotional girl inside her take part in this conversation. "I am quite able to comprehend what is written or said. I suggest you explain yourself."

"Page three. Above the fold."

Where had this formal, distant, cantankerous man come from? Why, she'd grab his lapels and shake him until he smiled, until he teased and his eyes sparkled, and then she'd kiss him until he understood precisely how things were going to be... if she weren't terrified he'd push her away.

If she were to initiate their first kiss, she'd do so at

a time when he'd not be so eager to reject her.

"Page three," she repeated. "Very well."

She skimmed across each narrow column, landing, at last, on mention of Oscar's name— and mentions of herself, with him. Warmth pooled in her belly, the kind of pleasing happiness that only women in her situation could comprehend. He stood, as rigid as ever, while she carefully read full paragraphs. Though she kept her gaze fastened on the newsprint, she maintained vigil on her man in the periphery.

When she'd satisfied herself that she'd located and thoroughly digested any possible crumb that had knotted his tail feathers, she put the paper to rights, and neatly folded it. She clasped her hands before her, the paper between them.

Poor Oscar.

She wanted to banish the haunted expression in his eyes, forever.

If she'd learned one important thing from watching her parents, and by observing the little she knew of others' marital relationships, that was that a man needed to trust that his woman respected him, and accepted him, flaws and all.

Slowly, as to not cause him to bolt, she set the paper on the table beside her chair and approached him. She held his gaze, marveling that he cared what *she* thought of him. She. His temporary associate. After all, she'd asked him to accompany her to the festival. Truthfully, she wanted much more.

"I see," she said softly, as she took another step nearer, "the Personals have made a spectacle of you, and of me."

Sadness scored deep grooves about his mouth. He nodded.

"I also see that the words printed there have dealt a heavy blow to your pride."

He blinked, held her gaze, and then reverted to what must be a Union officer's behavior around a superior officer— his gaze pinned over her shoulder and far away.

Words would never measure up to all she had to say. Two steps, and she stood indecently near this man she loved. Trembling, she pressed her palm over his heart. He gasped, and she fancied she could feel his pulse racing through myriad layers of clothing.

He closed his eyes, as if in pain.

Not at all what she'd intended.

Either she act, now, and put things to rights, or she risked losing this beloved man. Acting embodied a tremendous risk as well.

Now, or never.

She slipped both arms about his middle and stepped so close she could lay her head in the perfect hollow of his shoulder. Ah, perfect. His heart beat strong and true in her ear. Her forehead pressed to the flesh of his throat. The contact, intensely personal, intimate in the way of lovers, thrilled her.

She held him, in no rush to put an end to this embrace. Let him make of it what he would. She hoped he'd recognize acceptance, affection, and admiration. She'd tell him so, later, when words held meaning.

If only he'd put his arms around her, then everything would be perfect. "Hold me, will you?"

A pause the size of Colorado coincided with the

stagnant breath of air he held in his lungs. At long last, Oscar put his arms about her.

Emotion rushed through her, sweeping aside decades of doubt and discouragement. Gaining momentum and intensity, that shockingly beautiful awareness of this man, this wonderful, tremendously good man, filled her eyes with tears.

Tears of happiness.

When had she been this happy? *When?*

Though she wanted to look him in the eye, to witness his reaction to tender words, that must come later. No way would she forfeit this embrace.

"I read every word." She held him tighter, smoothing the palms of her hands over his strong, solid back. "My dear, dear man." She swallowed the tears that thickened her voice. "My respect and admiration for you have only grown."

"Respect?" His voice sounded strangled and flooded with disbelief.

"Respect and admiration." Now, she did straighten, to show him the truth in her eyes. The dark rings of blue circled irises vivid and bright as the sky. How she loved this man who'd seen her when no one else had. "And love."

"No." He shook his head, but she'd glimpsed the pain and horror in his eyes.

"Yes." Clumsy, inexperienced, and hopelessly awkward, she took his face in her hands and made him look at her. "I know my own heart, Oscar Harris. I know how I feel. I know I love you."

Before he could speak, she kissed him.

A sweet, electrifying, joyful first kiss.

He mewled— a little sound of pleasure and surprise... and happiness.

Her heart pounded and nearly swept her away in a rush. Not that she knew these things, but it seemed he'd kissed her, too.

She eased away, fastened her gaze to his once more. "Nothing anyone says or prints will change the respect and admiration I hold for you."

He'd heard, but for reasons she could not discern, he didn't answer.

No problem. They had years and years to come to know one another in all those little ways.

"Now that we've settled that little matter, tell me, Oscar—" how she loved using his Christian name when they were alone!— "shall we attend the tug-of-war event at noon?"

"I..."

"And I'm so looking forward to the Ladies' Library Association's ticket supper tonight. I've already purchased our tickets. Say you'll go."

To her startled delight, the man she loved pulled her into his embrace and kissed her forehead. "Thank you, Ina. Yes, we'll go."

Chapter Nineteen

According to Friday's special edition, the tug-of-war contest would begin promptly at noon, with each contestant and his or her team to equal nine persons.

Her stomach tied in knots, and, grateful neither her mother nor any of the Murphys were with her, she scurried for home and a moment's peace.

The pie eating contest had been a farce. The crowd had loved it, and she'd been handed the victory.

Hank's sense of humor had lasted well into the oral exam, when her team's questions had been fair and reasonable— as had his, in her opinion. He'd benefited from long-time residents of Mountain Home who'd provided correct answers to the local history's questions.

In the end, the score had been painfully close. Miss Vancoller's Team, 20. Mr. Murphy's team, 19.

He'd been a good sport, shaking hands with every member of her team, and every member of his own.

The thought of a tug-of-war, on Main Street, with the great line being drawn from the door handle of the prize property at a perfect ninety-degree angle, made her ill.

No way would a man like Hank Murphy lose in a contest of physical strength, nor would he lose with good graces.

Mother folded the paper and set it on the table. "I suggest you wear your sturdiest boots."

"I suspect my only chance for winning is to allow the young men who usually compete in this event to play for me. If they will."

"What will Hank Murphy do?" Mother tapped her chin with a fingertip. "I bet he'll be in the mud with his team."

Mother actually wanted Jane to... to... "You can't mean for me to actually pull on the rope." Was her mother losing her mind?

"If the contest is as weighted as yesterday's, you might want to play along. Put on your sturdiest boots, Jane Mary."

Jane did as she was told.

She dressed in a simple skirt, hemmed at the ankle, and her sturdiest, least fashionable boots. If she'd find herself sitting in the dirt and mud (and worse) in the streets, she wouldn't do so in her best bustle.

At ten minutes to twelve, Jane stood at her mother's side on the boardwalk before her Tea Room. The neutral ground— or, rather, the contested ground— stood with its door open to library visitors. Mrs. Abbott chattered happily in that doorway, carrying on about new subscriptions and the donations of books from various families, as well as the large cash donation from the wealthy mine owner, Rocky Gideon. Her beloved library was growing.

Jane stood on her tiptoes and scanned the crowd for any hint of Hank. She would've gladly accepted his escort to the event, but he'd sent Russell with a message that he'd meet her on Main. His boys, in their excitement, hadn't slept a wink last night, and the little ones hadn't stopped bawling since Hank had woken them for breakfast.

At five to noon, the crowd choked the street. The long-used tug-of-war rope, a red handkerchief marking the middle, stretched through the competition arena. The noise and commotion grew, but still, no Hank.

City council members had erected sawhorses and planks as a barricade to keep onlookers back from the action. Conversation buzzed all around her, everyone discussing the potential outcome, yesterday's contests, and debating how one would rig a tug-of-war if they'd a mind to do so.

At two minutes to noon, Jane and two dozen volunteers stood inside the fenced area, waiting for her opponent to appear. Had this anything to do with the Personals in this morning's paper? Was he as put off with her as Mother had predicted?

Jane had been pleased to note not a single resident of Mountain Home had asked her about her nighttime walks or kissing in the dark. No one mentioned the comments in the Personals, one way or the other. Mother might be the only soul who cared.

"Anyone seen Hank Murphy?" Mayor Abbott

shook hands all around, asking his question again and again. Even Hank's partner, Druggist Oscar Harris, hadn't seen Hank nor his boys.

Oscar had paid careful attention to his dress, his suit of clothes neatly brushed and his hair clean and tied at the back of his neck. With Miss Ina Dimond on his arm, he must have decided to appear his best.

Jane grabbed the opportunity to greet Ina and squeeze her hand. Ina's smile, broad and genuine, told the whole story. She was thrilled to have Mr. Harris at her side— and the pair looked well together. Well, indeed.

But right now, she had a competition to face, and no one had seen hide nor hair of her opponent.

He didn't intend to forfeit, did he?

Every year, as long as Jane could recall, the tug-of-war competition at Mountain Home's Harvest Festival had been a casual event. They could count on an interested twenty or thirty people. Enough pairs of eyes to watch the red handkerchief, and to blow a whistle when the rope's center passed a finish line.

Today's finish lines were the seams where the contested storage room-turned-library abutted the Emporium on one end and the Tea Room on the other.

Today, Main Street was filled to the gills. Boys had climbed onto roofs for a better view of the street. Others had opened windows, removed screens, and leaned through.

The commotion and conversation grew. The mayor fired his starting pistol into the sky to call the audience to order.

Jane checked her watch, pinned to her bodice.

One minute after twelve.

Where was Hank?

"Miss Vancoller," last year's tug-of-war champion offered, for at least the fifth time, "We'll win this for you. No sense dirtying your pretty dress."

Not only did she have this eager leader, he'd brought twenty friends.

If Hank had been on the rope, leading his team, she'd half-planned to do the same. Now, she felt no such compunction. "Thank you, gentlemen."

One shook her hand. Others patted her on the back. Several in back raised their hats.

What seemed to be two dozen men ran for the ropes, picking up their favorite places— two on Hank's end fighting over the hind position. At last the dust settled, the rope with its red cloth lined up perfectly with the door handle of the coveted rental space between Hank's place and hers.

"Ladies and Gentlemen," Mayor Abbott said through his trumpet, enunciating even more clearly than yesterday, "Today's tug-of-war contest has more riding on it than our standard two-dollar prize for the winning team. Today's contest, together with all of the events, will determine which businessman will expand their business into that—" he pointed with an extended arm— "real estate."

Applause sprinkled through the gathering.

"If Murphy's team," Abbott indicated the nine men pulling toward Murphy's Grocery Emporium, "pulls the red cloth beyond the line of demarcation between his shop and the space under contest, he will win. Likewise, if Miss Vancoller's team—" he pointed to those in her stead— "moves the cloth beyond the wall between the empty shop and her Tea Room, she will win."

"Hey!" A fellow near the barricade yelled. "Doesn't Murphy need to be here? Does he forfeit his right?"

Abbott looked to Jane, and she quickly shook her head. She didn't want Hank penalized. Who knew what his boys had done that morning, or where they were? They could be up anyone's tree, carving with dull knives. The knife could've slipped and slashed young Russell's leg. Maybe Jimmy had run away in order to sleep in peace.

"I say we proceed." Jane spoke as loudly as she could manage.

The audience cheered in approval.

"Very well," Abbott said through the trumpet. "Miss Vancoller has determined that Mr. Murray, in his absence, did not forfeit."

Polite applause accompanied plenty of impatience. People were ready for a show.

Jane left the arena to stand beyond the sawhorses and planks. She found a sliver of space on the boardwalk, between Mother and Harriet McCormick. In the past few minutes, the library/storage room door had been shut up tight and everyone banished from the boardwalk before it, to ensure no one blocked the judges' views of finish lines.

"On your mark!" Abbott bellowed through the trumpet and raised his starter pistol to the sky.

The crowd shifted, restless and excited. Folks bobbed and weaved, trying to secure a better view. The men on the rope twisted their feet, setting their boots.

They flexed their hands, stretching muscle and tendon.

"Get set!" Abbott pulled back the hammer.

The rearmost man on each end leaned back, ever so slightly.

Jane tensed. Harriet squeezed Jane's hand and held on tight.

The crowd drew a single breath.

Abbott pulled the trigger.

Worry sent Jane straight to the Murphy home. Something must be amiss for them to miss out on the tug-of-war event.

The house Murphy rented seemed quiet as she climbed the porch steps. Windows stood open to welcome fresh air within. Ah, there, footfalls on floorboards inside. And little boys chattering away in the back of the house.

Jane rapped on the front door.

Heavy steps that could belong only to Hank came closer. He opened the door, surprise and a bit of happiness on his handsome features. "Jane."

She waited, anticipating his explanation. In the long blocks between their businesses and his home, she'd considered several possibilities. First and foremost, she remembered Hank mentioning that the boys had fired their nanny. Were they "firing" her?

"Come in," he said at last. "We're nearly ready to leave. We would have come for you." Impatience tinged his tone, as if he thought she'd given up on him and the boys.

"The event is over by now. It's nearly half-past noon."

He pulled his watch from his vest pocket and popped the lid open. Confusion drew his brows together. "I have fifteen minutes before twelve."

He turned the watch face to her, and sure enough, the softly ticking timepiece showed fifteen minutes 'til noon.

"Your watch is usually accurate, I gather." Something had gone wrong, all right. And that *something* involved at least one little boy.

Had the children read the Personals? Were they upset by the talk that their father and she were "a courting couple" and "engaged to be married"? Or had they read the gossip about their late-night walk? Something had triggered their childish retaliation.

Hank lifted the watch to his ear— unnecessary in the stillness. He wound the key all of one-half turn, all the timepiece required. Oh, yes, indeed. A naughty child had meddled with Papa's watch.

Movement inside the house caught her attention. Russell eased around his father to glimpse her face.

Jane wouldn't pretend to understand much about young males. She'd known her father and Law quite well, and she believed she'd become well-acquainted with Hank Murphy.

She might never understand small boys, but guilt, she comprehended. Guilt might appear quite different from one person to another, but in this case, Russ proved quite transparent.

Young Russ Murphy had called on her with the

news that his family would be late, so she should go on without them. He might have been persuaded by his older brother or young uncle, Elias, but Jane didn't think so.

Why would Russ go so far to keep his father from accompanying Jane to the event?

The brat deserved to feel guilty.

Her jaw ached from clenching her teeth. She narrowed her eyes at the kid. Hadn't she found him, mere weeks ago, in someone else's tree, carving into a limb with a stolen knife? So much for remaining silent and inviting the boy to trust her.

And so much for extending kindness when the child had helped himself to her cookies. How did he repay her kindness? With lies and subterfuge.

Hank watched her closely. He turned to glance over his shoulder, but caught no more than Russell's retreat as the boy ducked into the bedroom. Then to Jane, "Want to tell me what this is about?"

Mother had taught her a thing or two about conversing when upset. She knew better than to discuss this now, but she'd reached the limit of her patience. "Step outside with me, please?"

One quick nod and Hank joined her on the porch. He glanced inside, as if he, too, noted the silence within.

Could be that all five boys, his brother included, remained still as statues, straining to overhear their conversation. The Murphy Gang deserved to fret, at least for a few minutes, so she stepped off the porch and headed for the shade tree where the lawn met the street.

All around them, trees along the street had begun to shed their summer green and take on the robes of autumn. The mountains were ablaze in shocking reds and oranges, with splashes of yellow.

To tell, or not to tell? To this point, her decisions regarding his sons had proven poor.

In the cool shade of the tree, she met Hank's handsome eyes, feeling the tug of growing attraction mingling with aggravation with his meddling boys. "I understand, now, what you meant when you said the boys fired their nanny."

"They're just boys."

"Indeed." And old enough, every last one of them— except Jimmy— to know some pranks were not amusing. If they were hers, she'd have a thing or two to say about telling lies.

But they weren't hers.

"I'll talk to them."

Why didn't Hank's promise generate confidence?

She folded her arms, willing herself to calm. "Russ called on me this morning with a message, he said, he'd been told to relay. He said you were running late, that the children hadn't slept well last night and the little ones had been in tears all morning. And I should meet you on Main."

Hank rubbed his eyes with a thumb and forefinger.

"Why?" She needed answers. "Why would he go to great lengths to keep you from the tug-of-war challenge?"

His mouth lifted in a wry smile. "Last night Russ said he'd be mad if a girl whipped him."

"I see." Two heavily skewed contests yesterday, the humor of which had sailed over the child's head.

"Jane— please." He reached for her, the warmth and comfort of his palm on her shoulder welcome and yet patronizing. "Don't be angry."

She lifted her chin in defiance. This wasn't anger, or sadness, or anything of the sort. "I'm disappointed."

"I know." He squeezed, his touch far more welcome than it should be. "I'll talk to them. Each and every one."

She nodded, but only to acknowledge she'd heard. The boys were his responsibility. He was their father, and this, a family matter. "I should go."

"Jane?"

She turned back, the ache in her heart unwarranted. The naughty kids weren't hers. She knew better than to develop attachments and allow affection to rule her heart.

"I'm fine." She tried to smile. "I'll leave you to it."

Hank watched Jane retreat nearly to the corner, then turned to the house. She'd been correct about one thing: something troubled the boys.

That something troubled them enough that Russell— with or without his brothers' cooperation or knowledge— had acted in desperation.

He must discover why. Likely, the problem ran far deeper than Jane, a girl, "whipping him" in yesterday's matches. Something a lot bigger lay at the root, and he aimed to discover what. His family deserved the best of his love, patience, and help.

Elias met Hank at the front door. "Have you thought about that question I asked a couple days ago?"

You and Dora were as miserable as ever two people were. The kid had challenged Hank's delusions of finding happiness with Miss Vancoller. Though he'd had much on his mind, and enjoyed the crowd's pleasure at the contests, Elias's challenge had never been far. He'd carried the debate into dreamland after several sleepless hours.

"I have."

"You know I doubt Miss Vancoller will make you happier than you are right now."

Spoken by a thirteen-year-old who'd never kissed a girl. At least, not that Hank knew. The statement made him wonder if Elias had been behind Russ's message, and the changing of his pocket watch. He'd left his watch and chain on his chest of drawers. Any one of the boys had access to it, but it seemed unlikely that Clyde or Jimmy had the wherewithal to set back the time.

That left Russ, Austin, and Elias.

He held his brother's eye. "Did you change the hour on my pocket watch?"

"No, sir."

"Did you send Russ to Miss Vancoller's door this morning with a message?"

A pause, followed with a confident, "No, sir."

"Do you know who did?"

Elias shrugged. "The boys don't like her."

"Until today, they've been fair enough. Clyde hugged her. Russ, too."

"They love you more."

Hank opened his mouth to make a quick reply, like *a father could certainly hope so.* But something serious in his kid brother's eyes made him hesitate. "Disobedience is a poor way of showing affection."

"Is it?" Elias, on the cusp of manhood, pinned Hank with his blue, blue eyes. "Maybe the boys see what you can't."

The knot in his gut cinched ever tighter. He nodded, a silent invitation to continue.

"You forget, I was eleven when Dora passed." The kid's voice, earnest and serious, made him sound wise beyond his years. "I'd been with you six years by then. Long enough to see your misery with my own eyes. I heard it, too."

How could he deny that? Dora had voiced her dissatisfaction. Loud and bitter.

"Dora was awful unhappy, too. Marriage suited you two like a ball and chain."

The boy was right about that. But he'd been five at first— small, like Clyde and Russell. A child that young must have a distorted sense of *why* things were bad. Hadn't he? "I suppose it did."

Elias stared at Hank, his jaw slack. "Don't you recall the trouble that comes with a wife? You were surly and wretched. You're better off a widower."

Hank's heart stuttered against his ribs. "Hey, now wait a minute. I'm not intending to *wed* anybody. I'm simply being neighborly—" a lame excuse, and he knew it— "and cooperating with this foolish competition that's brought everyone to town. It's good advertisement for the store."

The boy folded his arms and did that thing with

his chin, settling his weight between his feet. The gesture felt achingly familiar 'cause he recognized himself in the kid. Or perhaps the boy watched Hank for everything. Learning the business. Learning to be a man.

Hank clapped his brother on the back. "You're right."

"Yes, I am."

Had he also taught the boy to be obnoxious?

Hank hung his head. "I'm not good at keeping a woman happy." Look how long he'd lasted with Jane Vancoller. What, a month? Two? Already, she took exception with everything he did... but regarding him as a father, she'd been furious with him from the beginning. Yet things had been better. They'd laughed. They'd enjoyed entertaining the crowd who'd come to watch them eat pumpkin pie.

And they'd kissed.

"Maybe. I think Dora was one of those people who like to be unhappy."

Hank couldn't help but nod. The boy was right once more.

"Dora wasn't good for you." Elias jerked his head toward the street. "And I say Miss Vancoller isn't good for you either."

He'd toyed with the idea of marrying, and evidently, Elias had realized it. That's what sharing secrets on a porch swing and strolling in the dark did to a man, especially when kisses came with the walking and talking. He thought about making things permanent.

Now, in the bright light of day, he saw he'd been

playing with fire. Reckless. Tempting fate. What had he been thinking? How dare he tempt fate to deal him another losing hand?— not to himself only, but to five boys who deserved far better lives.

"Thank you, Elias." He extended a hand to his brother, who shook it, solemnly.

He thumped his brother on the back. "Come with me to teach the boys a gentle lesson about honesty?"

"But you just said—"

"I know. Miss Vancoller and I aren't good for each other. Even if the boys acted out of a desire to protect me, they need to know honesty is best. They don't need to lie, and they don't need to change the time on my pocket watch."

Chapter Twenty

I want to know why you boys are mad at Miss Vancoller." He'd come inside and immediately gathered all five children around him in the parlor in a family council. He'd insisted everyone be seated properly in a chair. Some conversations required formality and dignity.

Austin folded his arms and pouted.

Russell glanced to Elias, almost as if he sought permission.

What did these two hide?

Clyde listened with care, but not a glimmer of guilt showed in his eyes. Only interest and curiosity.

Jimmy stood on his chair's seat and shook the ladder-back with the rocking of his whole body. Whether to attempt to knock the chair to the floor, or to destroy the piece, Hank couldn't guess.

Russ had distracted Jane at his doorway. She'd eyed the boy rather than meet Hank's eye. He'd turned in time to watch Russ slip into the bedroom rather than greet Miss Vancoller as he'd been taught.

Hank sighed with disappointment that had been building for months. "Russell, where do I keep my pocket watch?"

"On top of your big chest of drawers."

"Very good. That's where I keep it. How do I wind it?"

He kicked his legs, sliding to the front edge of his chair. "You twist the key." He pantomimed the action as he spoke. "And the big hand and the little hand move when you pull on the crown." More exaggerated actions detailing the work one might do to turn the time back on Papa's pocket watch.

Hank eyed all five boys.

Clyde sniffled and put his thumb in his mouth. He curled his feet under him and leaned his side against the chair's back.

Jimmy decided to follow Clyde's example and mimicked his brother.

Russell had discovered something awfully important to pick at with his fingernail on the sole of his shoe. Austin stared at the ceiling.

"Russ." Hank thumped his palms against his knees. "I thought, if moving the hands on my watch was an accident, you'd come tell me so we could fix it and go to the tug-of-war on time. You like the events."

"I would have!" The declaration came out as a single word. The boy sat so far forward on his chair he nearly tipped onto the floor. With his hands gripping the seat on either side of his hips, he struck the carpeting with the toes of his boots in rapid thumps.

"You would have, but what?"

Clyde covered his eyes with two fists. He sniffled. A tear rolled down his cheek and dampened his shirt.

Russ yelled, "He's mad at you."

"Why? Why is Clyde mad at me?"

This conversation wasn't proceeding well. He'd asked three questions, and so far, he'd gained utter certainty his son would grow up to be a confidence man. Whatever had happened this morning, the plan and execution had been Russell's. And he'd convinced the older boys to keep his secret.

"'Cause you went for a long walk with Jane." Russ bounced off his chair and onto his feet. He jumped up and down, moving mere inches forward. "You talk and talk and she told you that I had a knife, my favorite, my best knife ever."

What was this? A knife? "Russell, son—"

"She told you I took her knife from her kitchen, but she's wrong. It wasn't her knife, it was my knife. I know she told you." The boy's yelling had upset Clyde who's sobs deepened. Hank tried to pick the little one up, to hold him while he dealt with Russell, but his littlest son became milk toast, slipped through his arms, and scrambled into the corner.

His family was coming apart at the seams.

None of them could tolerate conflict or confrontation, no matter the kind. Each dealt with the scars differently.

How had they come to this, that he, their father, couldn't ask for an explanation?

"She told you I stole her knife," Russ continued. "She told you that night when you walked and walked and made Elias do the chores all by hisself 'cause my best-ever knife disappeared. It's gone!" he wailed as loud as any child ever had. "Miss Van Collie pinkie promised she wouldn't tell, but she did. She told! And you came home and you took the knife from under my pillow while I was sleeping."

Russ wailed louder, and with a dramatic spin on the ball of his foot, he dropped in an inelegant heap on the carpet.

Hank had been exhausted that night, and couldn't remember half of what they'd talked about— beyond his sordid past— but he'd remember hearing his six-year-old had stolen a knife. He knew one thing for certain. "Miss Vancoller did not tell me about your knife."

"She did!" Russ's wail was muted by the rug.

"Son, I understand your knife is gone, and I'm sorry about that. But Miss Vancoller did not tell your secrets. I did not take your knife as I didn't know you had one." This revelation made him wonder what else he didn't know.

He rubbed the back of his neck and turned to Elias. "What do you know of this?"

"Nothing, sir. I swear it."

"Don't swear."

"Yes, sir."

Hank turned to Austin, who'd not said a word since Hank called the family council. "What do you know about this?"

Austin glared at Russ. "Be quiet, Russell."

Austin, who'd been as kind as any boy could, must've shocked his little brother, because Russ fell instantly silent.

Clyde sat up, watching everything from the parlor

corner, completely silent himself. Even Jimmy ceased his attempts to fold his entire body beneath the chair, including limbs and head.

"Austin?" Hank waited. He imagined he wasn't going to like this, whatever *this* turned out to be.

"He had a knife, a nice one, with a bone handle." Austin fiddled with the lace of his boot, rolling the free end inches up into a tight coil before releasing it, to begin again. "Said it was his."

"It was mine!" Russell returned to jumping in place. "My bestest knife ever. Miss Van Collie told you—"

"It's Vancoller," Austin scolded, "not Van Collie."

"—I stole her stupid knife, but I didn't." Russell's screamed speech reached maximum volume.

Hank covered his ears with the flats of both palms.

"No more noise," he told his boys. "You will be silent, unless you whisper. Understood?"

Five pair of eyes, wide as could be, met his.

"Russell— Miss Vancoller said nothing about a knife, nothing about a knife she might have owned, and nothing about you and a knife. I don't know what happened, but I insist you cease the accusations."

Russ tucked his face into the crook of his elbow where he lay.

"Anything else, Austin?"

"No, sir."

"Russell, is there more to your story?"

The boy shook his head violently, left and right, left and right.

"You say Miss Vancoller pinkie promised she wouldn't tell me about your knife?"

"Yes, and she promised that she wouldn't tell you we climbed the tree in Mr. Terrell's yard, but she did tell you."

"No, she didn't. Not one mention of a tree or you climbing it." Hank folded his arms and, as he rocked back on his heels, his feet braced, realized he looked exactly as Elias had earlier that week.

Intentionally changing his stance, he stuffed his hands in his pockets and paced the parlor with slow, measured steps. He didn't know what to think about Jane. Who would make a bargain with a child, to withhold potentially dangerous information from his father? Especially, given the likelihood that the knife was Jane's to begin with? He knew his son. Chances were, the boy had taken it.

So, a knife in a tree on Mr. Terrell's yard. He could well imagine what a boy of six years would do in a climbing tree with a knife. Somehow, Jane must've come across his son, in his tree, clutching her knife.

And she'd not whispered one breath about it in all the days since.

Part of him wanted to take cheer, knowing she'd never tell a soul the secrets he'd confided in her.

But on the other hand, she'd not told him his young child had a *knife*. In a *tree*.

Old hurts nagged at him, like that last hour before Sunday supper, when hunger was as troublesome. He'd been stung by Dora, in more ways than one. He'd trusted her. She'd been his wife, after all. Trusting her had proved to be a colossal mistake. Her affection had proved fickle, along with her trustworthiness.

"Pa?" Austin sat in his chair like a little gentleman,

his feet still and his hands upon his knees.

"Yes?"

"Are you gonna take Miss Vancoller to the ticket supper tonight?"

Elias's head lifted, like an animal that scented danger. The boy had warned him off of Jane twice now.

"No," he answered with confidence. "Why? You boys want to go?" The food would be hot and freshly cooked. A treat they hadn't had at home in a month of Sundays.

Austin shook his head, but come suppertime, the boys would be more easily persuaded. Maybe a distraction would be the right thing to reward the boys with, once this was all ironed out. Maybe he'd take them to watch the ax-throwing contest and horseshoes contest, both of which would be held at the edge of town before the ticket supper.

All afternoon, between the tug-of-war and the other two competition games— both of which would be handled by their teams of seconds— (unless Russ delivered a message to somebody, calling them off) everybody had gathered in the meadow, a block from the store where farmers sold extra produce and autumn fruits.

"I just wanted to make sure." Austin's expression seemed as worried as any boy could be.

"Sure? 'Bout the ticket supper?"

"No. Sure that you're not taking Miss Vancoller to the supper."

"I need to understand one thing, boys. This whole problem with Miss Vancoller is because you say she told me about your knife, and about the tree, right?"

"She did!" Russell's volume rose. "She did tell you."

Hank raised a hand. "Russell— that's enough. She did not break her promise, and I won't have you saying she did."

The boy sniffled but remained silent.

Hank had one more question. "That's the whole story?"

Four boys looked to each other for answers, for support, and maybe for strength. Young Jimmy seemed to be the only one disinterested in the question or the answer.

Russell, who just might be their leader when the day came they were grown men, was first to speak. "Yeah. That's all."

"You boys are my family." Hank's throat tightened, but he didn't care if his sons and brother witnessed his emotions. They needed to know he loved them. "You're more important to me than anybody else, anywhere. I love you most, and I care about you."

"More than Miss Van Collie?" Russ needed more reassurance than anyone else.

"Yes, even more than Miss Vancoller." But somehow, his conscience had a problem with that one, which was absurd. No father could love a woman who wasn't married to him, and wasn't a relative, more than he loved his own boys.

Not possible.

Besides, he'd been through this, over and over again. He'd known that becoming involved, even superficially, with Miss Vancoller would be a bad idea— a terrible idea. Thank goodness things between them had been so poorly constructed that they rattled apart the first hard turn in the road.

Far better now than further along, when there might have been an irrevocable bond between them.

"Come here, fellows." He knelt and opened his arms. Jimmy came running. Clyde too. The little ones wrapped their arms around his neck, choking him. Russell barreled into Hank. Soon all five of them, even too-grown-up-to-allow-a-hug Elias joined the circle.

"I love you boys, every last one of you."

"I love you, too, Papa." Russell always had been a man of words.

Clyde gave Hank a sloppy kiss.

"Clyde loves you, too." Russ interpreted.

"Me, too." Jimmy's kiss was wet with tears and mucous. Ah, the joys of fatherhood.

Hank shook Austin's hand, then Elias's.

Moments like this were good. Real good.

"I'll work hard, every day of my life," he assured his family, "to make sure you're safe and feel loved."

"Good." Russell pulled out of the hug, apparently done. "Let's go to the ticket supper. I'm hungry."

On Saturday morning, Ina waited for Oscar.

Half-past nine came and went.

Ten o'clock.

She paced the front parlor, glancing out the window every few seconds.

Where was he?

Though his leg troubled him yesterday, he'd arrived with two copies of the Daily *Times* before ten o'clock.

Ten-fifteen.

Insecurities, buried in shallow graves, rose to haunt her. Images of Oscar, relieved to be alone, reclining on a divan somewhere unknown, smoking a cigar, a glass of whiskey in his hand...

Ten-twenty.

He knew how important this was to her, to have him by her side.

Ten-thirty.

This was absurd. Last night, they'd left the Ladies' Library ticket supper early, as his leg had been troubling him something awful. She'd assured him then that they didn't need to go out this morning.

He'd insisted they continue with their plans. He'd call for her, he'd said.

Had she misunderstood? Did he wait for her on Main? Or at the city park where the veterans' association held their annual pancake breakfast? She'd suggested that alternative in order to save him the many extra blocks. Maybe *he* had misunderstood.

She supposed any sort of emergency could have arisen. Maybe the doctor had sent for him, needing medicine prepared for a desperately ill or injured person. Or perhaps Oscar and Mr. Murphy had decided to open the store.

Quarter to eleven.

Or, maybe, he'd decided he didn't want to go out.

Or, he didn't want to go out with her.

Had he grown weary of her company? Was she too

old, too plain, too dumpy?

Thirty years' worth of insecurities were near impossible to banish... and at age forty, many were so ingrained in her nature, that nothing Mr. Harris said could make them go away.

At least he'd tried. He'd complimented her appearance. He'd laughed with her, held her hand, looked into her eyes as if he were mesmerized.

He'd kissed her back.

Still, the agonizing pain of invisibility struck her in the breastbone with enough force to drop her to her knees.

She'd been beyond invisible to her first love, George Hudson. Oh, how she'd loved him.

But now that Oscar had come along? Why, she discovered her affections for George had faded... now, if only the pain of his rejection would go, too.

She held a fist to the crushing pain in her breaking heart... and remembered the intense pain Oscar had suffered last night at the ticket supper.

Maybe that was the problem.

They'd left early, and she'd walked him to his rented room in Mrs. Ihnken's boardinghouse. He'd been embarrassed by his weakness, regretted his inability to walk her home. She'd assured him, hadn't she, that she'd walked herself home all of her life and she could do so again?

Eleven o'clock.

Was this because of the Personals?

Or her response to the Personals?

Eleven-oh-five.

Enough was enough. She tied her straw bonnet,

decorated with silk mums in autumnal shades, slipped her reticule over her wrist, and locked the front door. Her brown Sunday dress swished around her ankles as she strode with purpose toward Main.

No matter what it took, she would find Oscar in this town, no matter where he was. She'd learn, once and for all, where she stood.

Ina knocked on the Ihnken boardinghouse front door.

She fidgeted, twisting her reticule strings, willing old and grumpy Mrs. Ihnken to answer.

Maybe she'd gone to the festival.

No locked door would put Ina aside so easily. She needed to find Oscar. She'd already tried the Emporium, and despite the impropriety of the matter, she would locate his room and ensure he was not in bed, ill, before she turned the town inside out.

Why, he might have expired in his bed, and who would know?

Maybe next, she ought to find the stationmaster and ensure he'd not purchased a ticket out of town.

The kitchen doorknob turned. She let herself in. "Mrs. Ihnken?"

No one answered.

Meow. A tabby approached, but Ina wouldn't let it outside. That would give her presence away, so she pushed the cat back inside, only to have the sweet warm body wind its way through her boots. *Meow.*

With the door firmly shut behind her, Ina made her way to the staircase and hurried to the second floor. All the doors were shut. She could knock on each one, or try the more direct option. "Mr. Harris?"

She listened with care, and made her way further down the hall. "Mr. Harris?"

A groan, a decidedly male sound of pain and illness came from behind a closed door. She pressed her ear to the panel. "Oscar?" She tried the doorknob and it turned in her hand.

Oscar lay in a bed, pushed up against the wall. He'd thrown one arm over his eyes, apparently to shield the light.

Rumpled sheets covered him from chest to toes.

And oh, for goodness sakes, the odor! She'd known it, last night. The man was ill. Terribly ill.

He needed fresh air. Good, clean air, and a sponge bath. He needed broth and tea. He needed loving care.

His formerly tidy and neatly pressed suit of clothes lay in rumpled heaps on the rug. He wasn't the kind to throw his fine clothing on the floor. Why, right there, in the corner, waited a clothing rack he no doubt used to air out his clothing and prevent the need for more ironing.

She rushed to his side and touched the back of her hand to his forehead. Clammy and sticky.

He groaned and opened one eye the merest of slits.

"I'm here," she soothed.

"Go away. I don't want you here."

Because he was ill, she'd allow him his pride. No man wanted a woman to see him laid low. No one liked someone else to do for them what they might have been able to do for themselves, before illness took their independence.

She bumped something glass... and it rolled away from her beneath the bed. What...? She lifted the bedding to peer beneath the bed. Sure enough, a bottle.

She pulled it out, the yellow and red label striking a chord in her memory. *Vin Mariani.* A French wine, a tonic, medicinal. A coca wine, with cocaine in the red Bordeaux.

Mrs. Hudson, George's wife, had resorted to the elixir when the cancer had become too painful to withstand. The doctor had told her no more than two glassfuls a day, three at the most. Between the empty bottle in her hand, and the one on the table, two-thirds gone, the man she loved had consumed well beyond that limit.

Oscar glared at her with bloodshot eyes. "I'm drunk. Are you pleased? Just like the Personals said, I'm a worthless drunk. Leave me alone, I said. You're in my room, without an escort. You're in my room, and I'm drunk—" his speech slurred... intentionally?— "and beneath this sheet, I'm undressed. *You'd better run.*"

Chapter Twenty-One

"I'm not going anywhere. Not until you're comfortable." Ina held her ground. She had to. She loved this man.

"I'm not good for you, and I'm sure as shooting not good enough for you. Just go. Leave me in peace."

Ina propped her hands on her hips as if he were a recalcitrant child. "I won't go. You're ill, you're in pain, and you need me. I'll open the window and let in fresh air. I'll help you wash up, and we'll see to fresh linens."

Oscar snatched the empty bottle from her hands and threw it against the wall. The crash and rain of splintered glass made her shriek.

"See?" he screamed, sitting up suddenly in bed, the veins in his neck throbbing. "I don't want you!" Anger twisted his handsome face into ugliness. He thrust an arm at the door. "Get out!"

With tears forming in her eyes— unwelcome and unnecessary— she folded her arms. Anger frothed in his eyes, churning the usually beautiful blue to menacing ice. "You may not want me," she fought to hold her voice steady, "but you need—"

"I don't need you, I don't need anyone." He ripped the sheet off his legs and thrust his left foot off the bed—

A stump.

No foot. No ankle. No shin.

Red flesh, angry and chafed and... *bleeding?*

Suddenly, everything made sense. The stool behind the counter. His pain yesterday, his inability to walk...

How had she not known the man had lost a leg? The Personals had said... "Oh, dear heavens."

"That's right. I'm ruined. Now— get— out!" He screamed, loud enough to be heard outside the house, if anyone were nearby.

She took a step back, beyond his reach. He wouldn't hurt her... though with the influence of wine and cocaine in his system, a good deal of it, he might.

"You like that?" He gestured at his stump. "See? Take a good look. You'll have nightmares."

"I didn't know! I might be an innocent, but I know you fought to preserve the Union. You're a war hero. You're my hero. And I love you, more than yesterday."

"No, you don't." He flopped back onto the bed. The sheet covered everything essential, but the muscles in his shoulders flexed. He was so... male.

And so large.

"I do. I love you."

"No, you don't. And I'm no hero. Now *get out.* Go."

The pain in her rending heart doubled as it mingled with his. The man was in so much pain. Not only physical, but in his heart. And in his head, where the war still raged. She knew too much about everything soldiers lived with; Papa had come home from the war, but he'd brought the horror with him.

Her heart overflowed with compassion for this good, good man.

"Who will take care of you? Mrs. Ihnken isn't here. I know her, and she won't nurse you back to health. She's gone to the festival. She's not here."

"You know something, Miss Dimond? You're a nag. You pick and pick and pick at me, you stand in my room, uninvited and unwanted."

She folded her arms more tightly. This was the alcohol. And the cocaine talking. She'd seen it with Papa. And with the first Mrs. Hudson.

"And," he said, enough vitriol in his tone to fry her at fifty paces, "I don't love you. In fact, I don't like you, Ina. I don't, and I never will."

No words could slice to the bone... could they?

"You don't mean it." Her words came out as a whisper.

"Oh, yes, I do. I most certainly do."

"Let me stay. I'll bandage your leg. I'll air out your room, I'll go buy you another bottle—"

"*Get— Out—.*"

He honestly didn't want her, not even as someone to fetch a bottle of coca wine. Or someone to take out the soiled sheets.

He didn't want her.

She would not beg. She'd do nearly anything else.

With a hand clasped over her mouth, she bolted for the door, and leaving it open wide, clomped down the stairs like a lumbering bull.

He knew he'd slain her, but she wouldn't let him hear her cry.

No matter what, she wouldn't cry until she made it back within her own four walls.

"Jane! Oh, Jane!" Mrs. Ann Abbott, persistent as ever, cornered Jane on Saturday morning.

The annual horse race was more popular than the tug-of-war event. Two city blocks had been cordoned off, as usual, with members of the city council serving as judges stationed at key locations to discourage outright cheating or foul play. All vehicles and other obstacles had been removed, leaving rutted dirt roads, puddles, horse droppings, and an excited crowd milling beyond the barricades of sawhorses and planks.

As one of the chief competitors, Jane was allowed inside the "track." Apparently, Mrs. Abbott was allowed... because she was Mrs. Abbott.

"Good morning, Ann." Jane attempted a gracious smile.

"Where are you off to in such a hurry? I've been calling you, trailing you, for a block."

"The race will begin soon. I must join the others." She had no intention to ride, and with all probability, Ann knew that.

"We must discuss your participation in today's events."

"Perhaps later." Much, much later. "I need to

speak to Mr. Erickson before the whistle to mount up."

"You can't mean to defer."

"Yes, ma'am. I do." She'd been raised a city girl, traveling by buggy or wagon. Never in the saddle. People knew that.

"Now, Jane." Ann sighed, a long-suffering exhale that only irritated mothers seemed capable of producing. "It's possible you've not yet read the Daily, given your late arrival this morning, but you must be aware that the people are most disappointed that you didn't compete in any of yesterday's challenges."

Given the state of Jane's heart, and the messes she'd waded through, she couldn't muster the energy to care what people wanted. At the hitching posts, at least a dozen horses swished their tails. A few riders mingled on the boardwalk before Abbott's Brick Block.

Ann pulled Jane back into the conversation with a hand upon Jane's forearm. "You didn't participate in the tug-of-war, nor the hatchet-throwing, nor even the horseshoe game." Ann shook her head with a bit too much emphasis. "Nor did you attend the Ladies' Library Association ticket supper—"

"No, Mrs. Abbott, I didn't." She hadn't the patience to cope with this woman. "I'm a dues-paying member, yes, and I bought two tickets. I met my obligation to the association. As the library is no longer in my establishment, I did not feel it necessary to attend the function."

Ann folded her thin arms over her narrow chest. "What has happened? Why, just a few days ago, you were eager to participate."

Eager? No, she hadn't been.

When no answer was forthcoming, Ann pressed forward. "Don't you know how much everyone enjoyed watching you and Mr. Murphy battling for the building you both want? You should've seen how the attendance yesterday afternoon dwindled when observers learned you wouldn't compete. You two brought a special element of fun and entertainment that they missed in your absence."

"I need to go, Mrs. Abbott. I must speak to Mr. Erickson before the race."

"The town is relying on you, Jane Vancoller."

Now that was an empty platitude. Mountain Home relied on her? For what? Entertainment?

Jane took two steps backwards, determined to break free of the woman and her lecture. "Everyone loves the horse race, and the crowd is thick."

For every step Jane drew away from Ann, the other woman followed.

Ann huffed. "Do you realize, if you do not win the competition, the real estate will go to Hank Murphy?"

Jane closed her eyes and halted. If Ann didn't keep her threats to herself, Jane might say something unladylike and incur the woman's wrath. Without another word, she turned and strode with purpose toward the men and boys.

On the far side of the Tea Room, the fellows gathered in a circle, jawing about the race, and laughing.

Far closer, in front of the Grocery Emporium, horses swished their tails. Some whinnied. A big black stallion, tied to the closest end, tossed his head and danced a sidestep. The great beast was antsy and nervous, which made Jane anxious and nervous.

She'd ignore the stallion, and head for the boardwalk. Even she knew the danger in approaching a horse from the rear.

She caught a flash of movement—

A child, beneath the hooves of a roan.

Her heart leaped into her throat.

A child? Couldn't be—

But yes, there— dirty faces, dirty linen shirts. Two little boys.

Her endangered heart recognized each boy. Clyde and Jimmy, the littlest Murphys.

Beneath the barrels and hooves of nervous, agitated horses.

The life would be crushed out of them in a moment. All it would take...

She clutched her skirts and ran, straight for the great, terrible beasts.

Where was their father?

Did *no one* tend the children?

A scream clawed its way past her heart, lodged in her throat, and she nearly let it loose— and startle the horses? She swallowed the soul-wrenching pain.

The babies— *the little babies...*

Wretched, naughty, ill-behaved children that she loved with her whole heart, were in mortal peril.

She must do something, anything!

She'd lost too many loved ones.

Dear God in Heaven, she'd lost Lawrence to a panicked horse. She could not, *would not* lose anyone else. She must reach the children without startling or spooking the horses.

"Clyde!" she hissed, gesturing madly for the boys to come. "Jimmy!"

The baby blinked at her, and returned to amusing himself with a stick and dirt between his feet.

Clyde whisked his fingers through the dust in broad sweeps, as if he'd not seen nor heard.

She ran to the hitching post, intending to approach the boys from between two mounts, starting from their heads.

She'd reach the kids, somehow...

The black shied, backing up and pulling against the reins. He nickered and tossed his head.

She flinched. Her heart galloped away without her. Nausea rose and terror nearly rooted her to the spot.

Had no one else noticed the trouble?

Her shoes struck the boards with every running footstep.

Ahead, the men, locked in conversation, laughed and guffawed. They paid her no heed.

She gave the black a wide berth, and gained a better view of the remaining horses, many smaller. And calmer.

There— the boys crouched beneath a mare.

The image seared itself into Jane's memory. She'd never forget...

... and never forgive herself if the boys were maimed or killed—

The whites showed around the animal's brown irises.

Flesh quivered beneath her shiny coat.

Her ears flicked about, telegraphing her fright.

Jane approached with care. "Easy, girl."

The beast pinned her ears in warning.

Terror forced Jane's heart into a sprint. "Easy. Easy..."

"Clyde, Jimmy!" She eased between two fully saddled horses and ducked to call the children—

The babies scampered through dust and grime and droppings...

"No!"

... and beneath the barrel of a roan.

The mare shifted her hooves and whinnied a protest.

Jane rounded the frightened mare at her head and ducked beneath the hitching post once more.

A roan with a white blaze—

Her heart seized.

Recognition slammed into her as if she'd been kicked by the black stallion. No air moved in or out.

Her vision dimmed, spangles of light flashing before her eyes.

She knew this gelding from years of riding behind him in Papa's wagon. Knew his gait, temperament, and four socks.

Sold—

Why, then, was it here?

This horse, *this* gelding, had panicked and reared, struggling in its traces.

Within one minute, Lawrence lay bloodied, bruised, and trampled in a bed of snow.

And now, two tiny boys played beneath...

She must save the children.

Immediately.

Despite the urge to flee, she dove beneath the

barrel of the excitable horse and grabbed for any limb, any scrap of clothing. Her left hand closed around a baby's arm. Her right grappled in space.

Please, God, please...

Panic and tears and horror congealed in her belly. She prayed harder and held fast to the child, even as little teeth sank into her fingers in a bid for freedom.

"*Ouch!*" She sucked in breath, and shoving aside self-preservation, squatted and leaned beneath the hulking beast.

Finally! A glimpse of the elusive Jimmy. She snagged his arm and dragged both boys free.

With her chest heaving and tears ruining her vision, she half-dragged, half-carried the babies toward the sidewalk.

She'd nearly made it when the roan bobbed its head.

The bob morphed into a duck, and in a flash, the creature bucked. Hooves and white socks flashed.

She landed hard, bruising her ribs, elbow and cracking her temple against the boards.

In desperation, she dove for the boardwalk.

The little ones kicked and scrambled. Clyde sank his teeth into her hand, again.

"Ow, Clyde! Stop." She scooted back, pulling the little ones to safety.

Through a bit of a wrestling match, she managed to clutch both children tight, one safely within each arm. She held fast, their little heads nestled against her neck, and sobbed.

Fear and horror swirled and blended, calling to mind images of Law's bruised and broken body.

Blood staining the snow.

Blood poured from a gash on his skull, darkening his hair.

Steam clouded the animal's blowing breaths.

Little bodies thrashed in her arms.

Whether here or there, she couldn't say.

Ugly, heaving sobs shook her until her heart cracked wide.

Running footfalls pounded on the sidewalk. The boards vibrated as the riders ran closer.

Within a moment, a knot of men surrounded Jane and the babies.

Everyone spoke at once.

"Are you hurt?"

"What happened?"

"The children? Stepped on?"

She couldn't speak. Mortified, she hid her face in the children's sweet-smelling hair. How were the babes clean beneath the dirt?

Little Jimmy ceased squirming and snuggled closer, his tiny, warm body relaxing against her. One little hand closed around her curls that had fallen loose from their pins.

A wail escaped her throat. A high keening that belonged more to the wind than to a human.

"Miss Vancoller, can you stand?"

"Hand over the boys."

"Did anyone see what happened?"

Voices everywhere, male, harsh, and demanding.

"Are the boys injured?"

Strong male hands wrested Jimmy away. Then Clyde.

Jane curled in on herself, her knees to her chest and face in her skirt.

Apparently, Miss Jane Vancoller did cry in public.

"Mama!" a young voice hollered. "*Mama!*"

The men's incessant questions ceased.

Jane mopped her face on her skirt as one of them dangled a white handkerchief against her shaking hands.

She grabbed it, nodding when she couldn't speak, and hid her face.

Cracked.

She'd cracked wide open, exposing her raw nerves, broken heart, and tender underside.

She keened for Law, who'd lost his life far too young. She bawled for herself and all she'd lost.

Most of all, she sobbed for the gaping wound in her heart— for the little boys she loved and she detested, children so naughty and so full of life she couldn't bear to live without them.

An ineffable truth stared her down.

Love stripped her of defenses.

Love made her vulnerable.

Loving Law made her susceptible to destruction.

The Murphys had sneaked past sentries standing guard and wrought havoc one thousand times worse.

Loving Hank and his boys robbed her last vestiges of protection and left her one thousand times more impotent against the ravages of death.

How would she survive, if one of the trouble-seeking, tree-climbing, knife-stealing boys met with an accident?

A little body slammed into her, wrapped his thin

arms around her neck and squeezed until she couldn't breathe. "Mama. Don't cry."

She didn't care that she wasn't this child's mother... her heart didn't know any different. Clyde clung to her and she rocked him back and forth, back and forth.

More pounding footsteps. Hank's dear voice, yelling his son's names. "Jimmy?"

Worry squeezed his voice, rising in pitch and with the same fear she'd known.

"Thank God." Hank must've taken Jimmy into his arms, for she felt him drop to his heels beside her and the warmth of his big hand on her back was nearly her undoing. Jimmy patted her head with the finesse of a toddler.

"Hank," one of the men said, "your boy here spoke."

"Clyde?" He sounded hopeful and yet incredulous.

"Yeah, the one who won't let go of Miss Vancoller. Called her Mama."

Jane's sobs had quieted, but she couldn't catch her breath. She clung to Clyde as tightly as he clung to her, her face buried in the hankie and the boy's shoulder.

Hank sat on his heels and with murmured endearments, embraced Jane and Clyde.

The gaping hole in her soul filled... Hank and his children making up that deficit. Love flowed with such force— a river in springtime, gorged with snowmelt. That gushing, high-running current threatened to carry her away until she was miles and miles out to sea. So far gone, she'd never find herself again.

No. No. She couldn't do this. She *couldn't.* Never

again.

Love meant impending heartache, certain doom, and loss so great her soul rent in twain.

"I can't. I can't. I can't."

"*Jane.*" Hank soothed a palm over her hair. "Are you hurt?"

This man, this thief who'd stolen her heart, had become the village idiot. "Yes, I'm hurt! I can't, I shouldn't, I don't dare— I can't!"

"Get Doc Cheney," someone or another ordered.

"Sure thing." Somebody youthful answered, even as he ran, his boots thudding on the planks.

They think I'm crazy.

The diagnosis fit.

After Law, only one argument explained her stupidity.

She'd gone plum loco, to have believed, for even a moment, that loving again would be a good thing.

Why? *Why?* She'd known better. She'd known this would happen.

Of a sudden, Hank's nearness and the clutch of his little son suffocated and hemmed her in.

"Don't touch me. Don't touch me." She swatted at his hands.

Clyde loosened his grip and someone, probably Hank, picked him up.

She struggled to stand. More than one man offered a hand, but she refused the help.

Never again.

"No," she muttered in shaking breaths, shaking her head wildly from side to side. "No. No. No." She shoved through blurred shapes, indistinguishable one man from the next. Giving the killer roan and jittery black stallion a wide berth, she ran into the street.

"Jane, wait!" Real fear colored Hank's tone.

She couldn't see him, couldn't talk to him. Not now, and maybe not ever.

A man she didn't pause to identify approached across the vacant street, a threat coming for her. She veered sharply, and clutching her skirts above her boots, bolted down the middle of the street.

Fear and madness and grief flooded her veins with every heartbeat.

"Jane!" Hank again. This time, mere feet behind her.

In view of the entire town, Jane whirled and faced the man who'd stolen her heart, and proven her correct— love carried far too high a price to pay.

Her chest heaved, peppered with hiccups and sobs and the ugliest of sounds. Terror clawed its way from her gut and into the chaos in her head.

"Don't touch me," she warned. "*Don't* touch me."

Chapter Twenty-Two

On Monday morning, Oscar Harris was fresh out of options. He sat on the edge of his bed, stone-cold sober, and a headache the size of the Rockies pounding behind his eyes. Had he ever been this thirsty?

Since before dawn, he'd exhausted every possible method to arise and bathe. He'd kept trying, managing only to don his trousers and shut the bedroom door, as other boardinghouse residents arose, prepared for the day, and left for work.

Hank relied on Oscar, who'd never missed a day of work in Mountain Home. Since the Personals announced he'd been a drunkard, he must redouble his efforts to protect his reputation.

Four unpalatable facts stared him in the eye: he could not strap on his prosthesis until he'd further healed, he had no crutches, the water pitcher and bowl on his wash stand were dry, and he had no one to turn to.

Not even Ina.

She'd offered to do *anything...* she'd offered to help him wash, bring him another bottle of *Vin Mariani*, change his sheets.

He had no doubt she would've pumped water, lugged it inside, heated it, carried it upstairs, and washed his hair with her own two hands...

... and ask nothing in return.

Giving her up had nearly killed his selfish hide.

He'd done what must be done, despite the tremendous cost. He'd set her free.

So why did he drown in regret?

Why?

Because he was selfish. He wanted her laughter and her smiles. He wanted to bask in the warmth of her acceptance and love.

Only selfishness made him regret putting her needs above his own.

She deserved so much more than marriage to a cripple. A cripple who couldn't carry his own water, and without a borrowed crutch, couldn't make it down the stairs, much less the few blocks to the Emporium.

"Mrs. Ihnken!" He listened with care. With everyone else up and gone, he must act, or he'd die of hunger and thirst in this bed.

Below stairs, the range clanged as she shut the firebox door. She hadn't heard.

"Mrs. Ihnken!"

He resorted to pounding his one heel against the floorboards. Thud, thud, thud.

Heavy footsteps echoed in the big, quiet house.

She paused outside his closed bedroom door. "Mr. Harris? Are you abed at this late hour?"

"Come in, please."

The knob turned, and the door opened wide enough to see the cranky widow's face scrunch in disgust. "What is this? Your room stinks like a pigpen."

Though he sat in his trousers, his torso was bare. Still, she opened the door wide. She took in the rumpled clothing on the floor, the shards of glass, and the second empty wine bottle upon the floor.

"This is not who I rent to, Mr. Harris. I rent to a clean man, a druggist. You smash a bottle in my house? You lay in bed for days? You reek! You get up, now. You bathe. You clean this room."

"I want to, ma'am. I *need* to go to work." He clenched two fists in the bed covers. "I can't."

"You can!"

"I need help, Mrs. Ihnken. I need water, to drink and to bathe." Begging was humiliating.

"You pay for a roof over your head and two meals a day. You don't pay me to bring you water. You want water? You stand on your own two feet and you go downstairs to the pump."

"I haven't two feet!" As he'd done with Ina, he uncovered that ghastly left leg, and bared the ugly truth. He waited for her to gasp, to run for the door, to babble apologies and platitudes and scurry away only to return with warm water, soap, and soft cloths.

And a big glass of cool water from her well. His mouth was dry as sunbaked cotton and wouldn't moisten, no matter his efforts.

The blamed coca wine.

The old woman's eyes lifted to his, devoid of sympathy.

He dropped the trouser leg to cover his stump. "Please?"

She folded her arms in a huff.

"Will you send for Doc Cheney?" He tried for respectful. Charming was far beyond reach.

"Do you need a doctor, Mr. Harris, or do you need me to cut a willow switch?"

How *dare* she? An old war injury exacerbated beyond redemption. Yes, he needed a doctor.

"You suppose I've never seen a man without an arm or leg? My husband lost both legs for the cause. He remained a man, the head of the household, until he died."

Shame swept in. How he loathed his weakness, and the circumstances he'd brought on himself. If he'd never agreed to Ina's plan, never known of her sweet nature, never—

"Tell me, Mr. Harris. How would you escape this house, if it were on fire?"

What?

"How? Tell me."

"I'd hop to the staircase. Or crawl." At least he'd kept his knee.

"What of the stairs?"

"Sit, I suppose. Slide down on my seat."

The old woman smiled, for the first time in memory. "Go. Fetch water."

"And humiliate myself?"

"So, you won't save yourself, unless from death by fire."

"I never said—"

"Get up, Mr. Harris. Get up, and be a man."

Hank knew only one way to sweep difficult, nagging thoughts from his mind— and that was to throw himself into work.

Unfortunately, his usual good medicine didn't work. Everybody who came into the mercantile wanted to talk about the competition.

"What will you do, now that a woman schooled you, Hank?" one fellow asked.

Another chuckled and slapped his knee with glee. "Me and the Mrs. had a pool going, just a little one, with me siding with your competition. Not sure how you lost to a little woman, Murphy, but I thank you."

Before noon, a dozen similar comments had been made, and Hank had lost patience. He'd taken to answering every contest-related statement with something akin to "Have you come to buy your winter supplies?"

More than one fellow or lady left with a sour expression.

Let them go. Hank's attitude was as dark and brooding as the sky had turned. Where was the sunshine that had greeted the day? Thick, dark clouds rested on the mountains, like a lid on a pot. Fat raindrops splattered onto the windows.

Hank lit two more lamps to see by.

Shortly after, Oscar, who'd never been late, made his way through the front doors, leaning heavily on a single crutch. One pant leg had been pinned up to keep from dragging or flapping in the wind.

How had he not noticed, or at minimum, not been sure?

Hank drew up short, bit down on the sharp statement he'd been about to make about tardiness, and kept his gaze on his partner's face. "Morning, Harris."

"Good morning." Oscar made his way with care to the pass-through and behind the counter. "Looks like quite a storm is brewing."

"Yeah. I'm expecting a large delivery on the train. I need to leave by half-past three to hitch the team and meet the four o'clock."

Oscar, usually as bright and sunny as any man, merely nodded. He sat on his stool, and bracing himself with his one foot, leaned his crutch, too short by a several inches, against the wall.

The man probably didn't want to talk about it. Like deep pits on a man's face from smallpox, some things were plain as day for anybody to see. No sense talking about it.

"I lost my leg in sixty-four. That Johnny Reb's aim ended my life as I knew it."

Or, maybe the man did want to pry the lid of the crate of his wartime stories. Even though the war had ended more than twenty years ago.

Elias, who'd been occupied with the broom and dustpan, looked up. The boy had ignored every question raised about the competition by the curious, but this, he seemed interested in. "You don't need your leg to mix prescriptions."

Hank would've clamped a hand over the boy's mouth, had he been near enough.

Oscar chuckled. Then laughed outright. "You're right about that, boy."

"Where's your leg?"

"Elias—" Hank warned.

Oscar shushed Hank with a gesture. "I don't mind. The leg my mama gave me is buried somewhere in North Carolina, and my replacement, courtesy of the A.A. Marks company, is in my room."

"Why?" Elias put the broom away and came closer.

"I walked too much over the weekend. I can't wear my leg until my skin rests."

"Oh."

"More questions?" Oscar's sunny personality seemed to be returning. His eyes twinkled and his smile invited conversation.

"Are you going to marry Miss Dimond?"

A cloud blew across Oscar's sun. All animation doused, he shook his head. "No."

"But I saw you two together, I saw—"

"*Elias.*" Some things a man didn't say, but Elias hadn't learned that yet. "How 'bout you deliver the order to Mrs. Archibald? It's pulled, waiting to go."

"Do I have to? She comes in here, at least twice a week."

Hank nearly lost patience. He ran low on the commodity since the apple cart of his life had been overturned. "She likes delivery. Now go."

"Yes, sir." The boy turned to Oscar. "Sorry, sir."

Oscar nodded, forgiving the boy's overstep.

Within forty-five seconds, the boy had picked up the crate and exited through the back door.

"I don't mind answering the boy's questions." Oscar picked up his feather duster, dragged his stool a few feet, and leaning upon it, set to work on the bottles displayed on shelves.

"He'll learn not to ask questions that are too personal." At least the store had been empty when the boy decided to ask.

Hank hadn't been so lucky.

All evening on Saturday, and through Sunday, the kid had returned to the unwelcome subject of Miss Jane Vancoller.

Hank couldn't talk about it. The wounds were deep and severe.

"Tell me," Oscar said after a few quiet minutes passed, "Is a man better off on his own? I don't mean your brother and sons... I mean bachelors. Like me."

"Depends, I suppose." Hank looked up from the bill statements he'd organized. "Do you want to be a bachelor? No law says you must marry."

The hollowness in Oscar's eyes, in his expression struck Hank as new. He'd not been dissatisfied with bachelorhood before. In fact, he'd been happy, full of life and vitality.

But Miss Ina Dimond, with all her eccentricities, had brought more light, more sunshine, more joy into Oscar's life. What had happened? Unlike Elias, he wasn't willing to ask.

Oscar turned the handle of the duster 'round and 'round between his palms. "I used to think so. That a bachelor's life was for me. Freedom to do as I pleased, pull up stakes and move somewhere else if a business opportunity came my way."

He hung the duster on its hook beneath the counter, out of sight. He checked the door, and finding themselves still alone, used his stool like a crutch, alternately leaning on it while he hopped forward, and then dragging it back to his usual place. "But the festival days, escorting Miss Dimond, made me see things differently."

Hank could only nod. He could say the same.

Images of Jane, enjoying her lady-sized pumpkin pie, playing to the audience, while he made laborious work of a pumpkin pie large enough for the crowd. She'd sparkled with life and happiness.

She'd made *him* happy, too.

Darned if he knew what had gone wrong. Nearly forty-eight hours of spinning 'round and 'round, and he couldn't figure it out.

Silence stretched between them, like long, hot days of summer when daylight lasted nearly seventeen or eighteen hours.

"Miss Dimond might well purchase groceries at another establishment." Oscar sounded dejected. "The situation did not end well between us."

Hank nodded, comprehending far too well. He sensed regret in Oscar's tone, the way the clouds that dampened his happiness were connected to Miss Ina... Just like himself and Jane.

Since the horse race, when she'd chattered nearly incoherently about how she couldn't do this, couldn't, he'd been dumbfounded. Couldn't do what? Hold his babies? And why, exactly, had she been mad enough to order him to take his hands off her? All he'd done was pat her on the back to offer comfort. And embraced her because... well, because he couldn't *not*.

"I'd go to her." Oscar's attention was locked on his hands in his lap, as if he could see Miss Ina in his mind, and that's all he wanted. "I'd go and prostrate myself, beg her forgiveness..."

"Why not? You talk like she's sunrise and rain."

He'd best shut his mouth. Immediately. In his sleeplessness, he'd wrestled with the same question. He didn't know what he'd done to make Jane run from him, but he'd done something. He'd never know until he talked to her, until he asked her to forgive him, to explain, so he'd understand.

But she'd been so all-fired certain, insistent he stay away.

And then there was Elias, who'd pointed out every pitfall, every danger, and history repeating itself.

Jane seemed different than Dora... until she'd lost her marbles at the horse race. Until she'd raised her voice and yelled and shoved him away.

He didn't need another woman like that, and he sure as shooting didn't need another disastrous marriage.

"That's the crux, isn't it?" Oscar cleared his throat, squared those broad shoulders and looked Hank in the eye. "I don't beg, not out of pride because after the past several days, I have no pride left. I won't go to her because *she* deserves better than me. She deserves stability and wholeness and a man without demons on his tail."

Were he and his business partner so much alike? How had he not realized?

He nodded, understanding on a fundamental

level. Miss Jane Vancoller, who'd never married, who'd loved a perfect man in Lawrence Riddle, didn't need a fellow like him whose baggage would fill no fewer than three freight wagons, and weighed enough to break a steel axle.

"It's my doing," Oscar continued. "I realized that this morning. It's my doing. My fault. I let myself fall for her, think I could escort her to the competitions, do her that favor she requested. We'd stay friends, and no harm done."

Hank's heart pounded, picking up speed. In this, too, he mirrored Oscar Harris.

"I was a fool." Oscar drew a deep breath and slowly let it out. "A fool who will pay the greatest of prices, because I'm not the man she needs me to be."

Hank struggled to make heads or tails of the churning emotions roiling through him... storm clouds clashing within him, lightning strikes flashing in his brain. Every flicker of light another image, a moment in time of him, and Jane.

The truth emerged, whole and untarnished, from the swirling maelstrom. He'd held the most well-suited woman in his arms. He'd held her, and she'd told him his heart was made of gold, and she'd kissed him. Not only that, but she'd confessed she loved him.

What had he done? He'd allowed his kid brother, armed with the past, to warn him off. He'd backed away, and in so doing, had hurt the woman his heart yearned for... the woman who'd shown him kindness and respect and compassion...

And now, she didn't want to see him.

She'd told him they were through. She'd ordered

him to leave her alone.

"I must be," he muttered, speaking to Oscar, and to himself, "the greatest dunce in the history of all ignoramuses to walk the earth." Why— *why?*— had he tossed aside a chance for happiness? *Why* would he think loneliness and misery preferable?

"Mighty big words, for a dunce." Oscar's smile was forced and thin. "I believe, sir, I might deserve the title more than you."

Jane sat in a chair at her bedroom window and stared at the western horizon. Rainclouds had darkened the sky for the better part of the week, starving the brilliantly shaded autumn leaves of light. Everything seemed brown, dark, and dreary.

Most of all, her heart.

Mother knocked on Jane's door. "Harriet is here to see you."

Wind scuttled through the grove of quaking aspens. Leaves that had been brilliantly gold in their glory had faded to a dull yellow. Many had blown away in the winds.

Her eyes drifted shut and she drifted, nearly falling asleep again. Her head jerked as she woke. Tiredness surrounded her, day and night, never far away.

"Jane?" Mama's slippers whispered over the floor. Her touch was cool as she ran her fingers through Jane's unbound hair. "Did you hear me?"

She couldn't muster enough energy to do more than nod.

Hadn't Harriet been here, just yesterday? Or maybe the day before...

"Will you come downstairs to the parlor?" Mama always spoke so softly these days. Soft and sweet. Like a lullaby.

"I'm tired."

"I know, darling, but it's important you remember the Tea Room."

Oh, yes. The Tea Room.

"Harriet has brought excellent news. She wants to tell you all about it." Mama's hands lingered on Jane's shoulders, and for a long moment, she waited.

News? She yawned and her eyes drifted shut once more. News could wait. She'd hear, later. "I need a nap. Please give her my regards."

"Jane. Look at me." Mama came around to the front of the chair, beside the window.

In the wan light of the gray afternoon, Mama's pale skin had a gray cast against the stark black of her mourning costume.

So bleak.

"You've been inside this room for six days, and I understand you needed this time." Softness lingered in her pale, faded blue eyes. "It's time to come out. Harriet will be kind, I know it. You know it."

Mother was right, of course. Jane merely nodded.

"Good girl." Mother would've scooped Jane into her arms, had the clock turned back more than fifteen years. Jane had been much younger then, as had her mama... who now seemed... *old*.

Jane rose, and arm-in-arm with her mother, walked to the staircase. The house smelled good. Like apples and cinnamon. "Applesauce?"

"I thought you'd enjoy a warm dish."

"Yes, I believe I would." Hunger stirred in her belly.

Jane moved down the stairs with aching slowness. Maybe she'd fallen ill, and that's why she'd not been able to be up and about these past days. Or perhaps time had lied to her, and she was old.

Thirty was old, though, wasn't it? No, time hadn't lied.

Where had the years gone?

At the bottom of the stairs, Mama didn't allow Jane a moment to rest. She walked her into the parlor and straight to Harriet McCormick.

Anxiety and worry clouded Harriet's features, but upon taking in all of Jane, in a plain and simple house dress, her hair loose and long, lightened. "I'm thrilled to see you up and about. Come, sit with me. I have the most excellent news."

Chapter Twenty-Three

Harriet's hands were cool from the out-of-doors, and her cheeks pink and vibrant from the brisk air. The curls about her face had a wind-blown quality to them that made her seem both awake and thriving.

In the periphery, Mama walked toward the kitchen, probably to heat the teakettle. A lamp burned on the table beside Harriet, the flame turned up to banish the shadows. Jane winced and squinted; the light hurt her eyes.

"Oh, Jane. It's good to see you."

A few days had gone by, hadn't they? Days when she'd been so nearly swallowed whole by loneliness that she'd been unable to go out, particularly to Abbot's Brick Block. How would she bear to see Hank Murphy?

She wouldn't think of him. Not now, and not later. She'd focus on Harriet. "It's wonderful to see you, my dear friend."

"And employee." The gentle reminder carried affection.

She almost smiled. "I should ask after the Tea Room, shouldn't I?"

"I think so." Harriet folded her hands in her lap.

"Very well. How is the Tea Room?"

"Well, thank you. I confess I found myself in need of another pair of hands, so I took it upon myself to hire a girl."

Jane vaguely remembered Harriet calling earlier in the week, asking for a moment. Jane couldn't think, couldn't come downstairs, so Mama had relayed some sort of message, and Harriet had gone away and done the best she could. "Thank you. The Tea Room would've suffered without your care."

"You're welcome." Harriet's genial friendship, her constancy and dependability had been tremendous gifts. "Have you been well?"

"Yes, certainly."

"Has the Tea Room been as busy as during the festival?"

"Heavens, no, and thank goodness. Just yesterday, sweet Maggie Cresswell was in for a lingering hot cup and a slice of pumpkin cake, and complimented us. She favors the small, quiet crowd, she said, ever so much more than the large. By the end of the day, I think we had eighteen, all together."

Precisely what she'd hoped for when they'd opened. Small, peaceful, and comfortable. She missed those days...

"Are you ready for the news?" Harriet leaned close, whispering, almost as if she had the most delicious of secrets to share.

"Harriet, what is it? I've not seen you so...

talkative." Or happy... but *happy* wasn't quite right. *Energetic?*

"I do have much to say, and I apologize, but the news!" Her laughter, like the peal of bells, carried a jubilant air. "Business first? Or miracle first?"

What?

"Choose."

"Uh... business."

"I thought you might make that selection." She claimed a folded newspaper from the table beside the lamp, and opened it. "Business, business. Headline: Harvest Festival — The Least Expected Contender Wins."

Oh, yes. The contested real estate. If Harriet had determined to read business first and share the good news second, that meant Hank had won the lease. That was right. His plans and preparations would do much good for the wellbeing of the community.

"The city council," Harriet read, "deliberated for more than four hours on Monday, to arrive at a decision regarding the winner of the contests. As the *Times* reported in Daily issues, the Thursday contests of Pie-Eating and the Oral Exam were both won by the Tea Room team, under leadership by proprietress Miss Jane Vancoller. As Friday's contests were passed from team captains to volunteer teammates, with the same occurring on Saturday, the city council ultimately determined that only Thursday's tests would be counted in the final score. Thus, the win for the Harvest Festival in the year eighteen hundred and eighty-seven was officially awarded to Miss Jane Vancoller."

Harriet beamed. Lamplight reflected off her skin

and contributed to the sparkle in her eyes.

"Me?"

"They did say the winner came from behind."

"You're happy about this."

"Naturally. I'm with you, Jane. We need the business of large clubs to pay the lease, the expenses of operation, and to make room for the library. I witnessed your devastation the day the Association took the library out of the Tea Room. This is good news."

So, the business option had been good news, in addition to the good news option.

Why didn't she want to laugh, to jump up and down like a child would, happiness bubbling over? Why did guilt take her by the throat?

She knew why— of course she knew. She cared that Hank's plans, designed to help their town, had been thwarted.

Hank would be disappointed... No, given the heartache he'd divulged when they'd walked that night, long ago, he'd be devastated. He'd considered other options, and ultimately, needed the warehouse on site.

What if something happened to him, while he kept his warehouse elsewhere? He, alone, was responsible for five young boys. As Hank had rightly said, moving freight in winter, in ice and snow was dangerous. If an accident claimed Hank, Elias wasn't old enough to take care of the babies. Jane's conscience would never survive...

Let him have the contested space. She didn't want it anymore.

She recalled wanting it, she did... but why? Now, it seemed inconceivable that she'd *wanted* this.

"Don't move his wares. I don't want him to remove to another location."

"You don't?" Confusion dulled Harriet's enthusiasm.

"I'm not keen to force Mr. Murphy to move his winter stores. I believe he's shown uncommon foresight and kindness to our community. He's trying to help."

Harriet seemed to consider this. A moment passed, then two.

Steps sounded in the hall as Mama, moving slowly and a bit unsteady on her feet, carried the tea tray into the parlor.

Jane rose and met her mother. "Let me help, Mama. The tray is too heavy."

"Your arms are younger than mine."

Mama set about pouring, and Jane left that honor to her.

She watched Harriet's expression.

"It's your business," Harriet said at last. "If you've changed your mind, I will support your choice."

"Thank you."

"I do wonder what you intend to do about the library. Mrs. Abbott, a few days ago, came in to see you at the Tea Room. She talked at length about how you might best remove walls, plan a redesign of the floor plan, to include the library."

Mama handed a teacup to Harriet, who thanked her. She sweetened and stirred. Jane accepted her cup as well. Once all three of them were seated, Jane determined to answer Harriet's question.

"The library is in good hands with the Association's president and vice president. They'll locate a better place." Maybe she'd just needed time to acclimate to the idea. Though abhorrent to her when first introduced, now, she found the idea caused her no distress.

Harriet's smile blossomed and spread. Jane couldn't help but smile back.

Smiling felt *wonderful.*

Jane sipped, savoring the autumn flavors. Orange peel, cloves, mmmmm. "Delicious tea, Mother."

"Thank you, dear."

"Good news?" Harriet set her cup on her saucer. "Are you prepared to hear it?"

"Gladly."

Harriet read from below the fold on the front page. "Four-year-old child speaks first words."

Jane sipped, swallowed, listening. What was this? She'd not known of any four-year-old who'd not spoken at a natural time. Maybe this story had come out of Connecticut or North Carolina. Confidence and morale tales tended to be reprinted because readers desired something optimistic to read between bad news and worse.

"It's a miracle," Harriet read. "The four-year-old child of Mr. Thankful A. Murphy—"

Jane gasped. What was this about Hank's young Clyde?

"— spoke his first words on Saturday, last, as Mountain Home prepared for the annual horse race. Mr. Clyde Murphy, age four, has been vocal since birth, crying as babies will, but had never spoken, despite the tremendous efforts of his father and others."

Jane couldn't bear the wait. She had to know! She

set her teacup down on the tea table and nearly snatched the paper from her friend's hands. Instead, she clamped her hands over her mouth as emotion crested and threatened to overflow.

"Despite all attempts at bribery, Clyde Murphy remained mute. His father despaired that the child would ever speak."

Jane's mind whirled. She'd heard Clyde talk, hadn't she? She saw him in the tree in Mr. Terrell's yard. Holding her hand as they walked to find baby Jimmy. And then beneath the hooves of the red roan.

Tears burned her throat. Her windpipe constricted and a tide of feeling, so raw, so intense burned her nose even as her eyes filled.

Harriet adjusted her hold on the paper. "Prior to the opening of the races, young Clyde and his younger brother, James "Jimmy" Murphy, age two, were playing near their father, when they somehow slipped away, drawn to the horses as young boys often are. Upon discovery of the boys beneath the fastest and most powerful horses in the county, Miss Jane Vancoller risked her life to rescue Clyde and James from certain death."

Jane's tears spilled. She couldn't stop them, couldn't stop feeling so deeply. She'd been numb, numb and cold for days. Saturday's crying jag threatened to resume.

She pulled her handkerchief from her sleeve and pressed it to her face, fighting the tears. Miss Jane Vancoller did *not* cry.

"Upon rescue, multiple witnesses overheard Clyde Murphy clearly say 'Mama,' referring to Jane. Others added the boy's clearly stated sentence, 'Mama—'

Jane mouthed the baby's tender plea as Harriet continued to read aloud.

'— don't cry.'

Happy tears choked her laugh. She dried her eyes, grinning. "I didn't know."

"You didn't know Clyde refused to speak?"

"No. I'd no idea. None." She'd been caught up in her own world, shredded from the soul outward, so lost in the agony of the past she'd not been able to witness the present.

"One more editorial sentence, Jane. It's one you need to hear."

"I'm listening."

"Witnesses glimpsed something further that bears repeating. They noted the perfect romantic match in Mr. Thankful M. Murphy and our own heroine, Miss Jane Vancoller."

"Elias, strip the bed. Austin, fill the pail with half hot and half cold water— can you do that?" Hank had reached his limit on the dirt in his sons' room. Despite the lack of time at home, and no housekeeper besides himself, he'd managed to bathe the boys nightly before bed. But weeks had managed to pass since he'd cleaned their room.

Before bed, they'd do a quick job, as every little bit helped.

"Clyde," he continued, "broom and dustpan." The

little guy ran for the broom closet.

"Jimmy? Where's Jimmy?"

"Under the bed." Elias shook the quilt that had been on the boys' bed and draped it over a chair in the corner. He set about pulling off dirty pillowcases.

Hank dropped to his hands and knees. Shadows danced as his brother pulled off the linens.

Sure enough, there lay Jimmy on his stomach, busily working on something.

"Hey, kid. Drawing pictures in the dust?"

"Knife."

"Let me see that." He grabbed his youngest by the ankle and pulled him out. Sure enough, a bone-handled knife, caked with dried mud. "Is this Russ's knife?"

"Russ knife." Jimmy reached for it, and Hank lifted it out of reach. The boy wailed and dropped into a puddle on the floor.

Back through the doorway came Clyde, the dustpan in one hand, and the broom handle in the other. He'd dragged the business-end of the broom the whole way from the kitchen.

"Russell?" Hank called.

He listened, as did the rest of the crew.

"I'm trying." Russ must be still dipping water from the stove's reservoir.

Austin claimed the broom and began sweeping from the far corner, toward the door, just as he'd been taught.

The room had grown darker by half since they'd finished supper, so Hank lit a lamp upon a bracket, at a safe height upon the bedroom wall. Golden beams spilled over the dirty knife, and Hank wiped enough grime away to read the manufacturing company's name on the blade. He whistled softly. This knife had cost plenty when new. He tested the blade with his thumb. Dull as the edge of a spoon.

Russ lugged the bucket in and plunked it down. Water sloshed over the rim.

"My knife!" Russ jumped, swiping for the blade in Hank's hand.

"Hold on a minute."

Russ tried to capture the prize with two hands. "It's my bestest knife! I missed it for months and months."

Austin nudged the others aside and finished his sweeping. Not a pristine job, but adequate. Any bit of housework, even if done poorly, blessed his family. Hank wasn't one to go back and do it himself.

"Is this the knife you said I took?"

Russ's happiness shriveled and died on the stalk. "Sorry, Papa."

"Jimmy just found it under the bed."

"I put it under my pillow to keep it safe." Russ pantomimed the shoving of a knife. He could've put out his brother's eye. Even with a dull knife.

Hank suppressed a shudder. He sat on his heel and pulled his son in to the curve of his arm. Russ grabbed for the knife, but Hank didn't release it. "You remember you were mad at Miss Vancoller and said mean things, because you thought she told your secret?"

Russ's lower lip quivered. He nodded.

"I'll tell you once more. She didn't tell me. We just found the knife, where it fell."

"But we have my bestest knife back. Miss Jane didn't tell."

The lesson hadn't taken. "Next time, we need to look and make sure before we accuse somebody."

Russ nodded again. "I want my knife."

"Not 'til you tell me where you found this knife."

"It's mine." Russ squeezed harder, fighting for possession of the handle.

"So you've said. But knives like this cost money. More money than you had in your piggy bank."

"He took it." Clyde stood close.

Hank stared at the little one, stunned anew at his speech. Every time he offered a crumb, it felt like the heavens opened and a miracle blessed his family all over again.

"I did not!" Russ's temper flashed white-hot.

Hank held onto the boy, turning to put himself between Russ's flailing feet and Clyde. "Don't kick your brother."

"He's not supposed to tell." Russ's glare held venom.

Why the fury from a six-year-old? He'd need more of a lesson than a talking-to. This had to stop. "Russell, I want you to listen carefully to me."

The boy squirmed, fighting for freedom. He twisted back and forth, back and forth.

Hank dropped the knife and sat, holding Russ in a firm hold the boy hadn't a chance of breaking. He braced for the head bash sure to strike his breastbone—yeah, there it was.

"Hold still, son, or your punishment will be harsher."

"Pa!"

"Sit still, now." Hank looked to the others. "Elias, I need you to start the bathwater. Take turns, Jimmy first like always."

"Yes, sir." Elias left the bedroom.

"Austin, Clyde— take Jimmy and go with Elias."

Once they were alone, Hank held his boy, and prayed hard and fast for the wisdom to get through to his son. He'd let Russ be a boy, had disciplined with gentleness and love, and instead of becoming more obedient, he became more and more defiant. Not the worst of things at age six, but by ten? Twelve? Fifteen? What then?

Russ fought with all his strength, straightening into a board.

Hank had no desire to use his greater strength on his son. That seemed foolish. "Are you listening? I have something important to say."

"No. I won't listen."

"Not even to a story?"

The boy relaxed— a little.

"There once was a king in a land long ago and far away. This king was good and righteous."

"I want to hear about battles and wars."

"Maybe another night. Tonight, our story is about a king who had to fight a war with just his brain. He had to think stronger and faster than his opponent."

Ah, now he had the boy's attention.

He'd just begun to tell the tale of King Solomon, who, with a good deal of help from God, learned to discern lies from truth, when a visitor knocked on the front door.

"Coming!" Elias left the kitchen and opened the front door.

Mayor Abbott, of all people, calling at Hank's home, at this hour?

Interrupting a story that mattered a good deal. "We'll finish the story after your bath."

"I want to know about the king and his war."

"We'll finish," he said again, "when you're squeaky clean."

Chapter Twenty-Four

"Mayor Abbott." Hank offered his hand, and once the greeting was over, invited him to sit in the parlor.

Once Hank lit a lamp in the parlor and they were settled, and he overheard the nightly bathing routine in the kitchen— boys arguing, splashing of bathwater, the clatter of rocks from pockets clattering onto the floor— Hank turned his attention back to Abbott.

"At dark on a Saturday night. Something must be wrong for you to come by."

"No, nothing is wrong. But I have come with a purpose."

Mayor Abbott sat in the chair with his back to the window. Beyond the panes, as they'd not yet drawn the curtains for the night, evening wind whistled past the house, and the sun dipped toward the mountainous horizon. Despite the much colder air, the sun had been out in all its glory, from morning's first light. Autumn's robes had been brilliant, one last hurrah before everything turned brown.

"Go ahead." Hank had a little boy to get back to. The dirty bone-handled knife didn't make the best back-pocket material while sitting on a wooden chair, so Hank pulled it from his pocket and set it on the table at his elbow.

"It's possible you'd prefer the children not overhear what I'm about to say."

Hank glanced to the kitchen door and the commotion beyond. He usually remained in the room while Jimmy and Clyde bathed. Any amount of water could be dangerous to a toddler.

"Just a moment." Hank went to the kitchen door, charged Elias with tending the little ones, and shut the kitchen door.

"I need to put the boys to bed. Won't be more than ten minutes and Jimmy will run for his bedroom with wet feet."

"I'll be quick."

Hank nodded, gesturing for Abbott to state his business.

"After the race last Saturday morning, my dear wife brought to my attention that you probably don't know why Miss Vancoller reacted so... violently... to the circumstances."

He winced. He didn't want to talk about Jane. Every time he so much as thought of her, his conscience twisted in knots and he then thought of her more often, which wound him into a frenzy.

"Go on." The sooner Abbott started, the sooner he'd be done and the sooner Hank could do something else.

"Do you know how her fiancé died?"

"No." He hated admitting that. After everything Jane had disclosed, she'd not told him this, probably because the memories were too painful. If it were something average— consumption, for instance, or cramp colic— she would've said.

"Lawrence was unloading new stock for the tobacco shop in the alley in back. The horse spooked over something— we'll never know what. The animal reared, striking Law before he could put a safe distance between himself and the beast."

All at once, pain and heartache swept through Hank. No wonder...

"Inside the shop, Mr. Vancoller, his daughter, Jane, and a man or two heard the commotion, the horse's terrified screams, and for a brief moment, Lawrence's screams."

Too clearly, the picture formed in Hank's mind.

Armed with this knowledge, Jane's hysteria as she clutched Clyde, sobbing as if her heart were irrevocably broken, made sense.

He pulled off his flat cap, surprised he still wore the thing. He wiped his shirtsleeve over his brow, fighting his breathing, forcing it to slow.

Poor Jane.

How much had she witnessed?

"Law died on the second or third strike of the horse's hooves, but by the time the horse was under control, the body was bloodied and battered. The snow—" The mayor swallowed, as if reflexively.

Hank held up a hand. He couldn't hear any more.

No wonder Jane had been beside herself. No wonder she'd been determined to dive in and pull his sons to safety.

"One more thing." Abbott drew a thumb over his lips, as if gathering courage to say what must be said. "The red roan your boys played beneath? The animal she braved to get to your children?"

Dear Lord. Grief slammed into him with the power of a locomotive at full steam. Grief so hot and heavy, he held himself together by sheer force of will.

Abbott coughed. "Same horse."

"I'd have shot that horse through the heart."

Abbott nodded, placating with open palms and reassurances. "That's because you're a man in love."

Hank opened his mouth to argue, but lost his steam before he spoke one lying word.

He'd loved Jane for a long while. How could he help it?

Especially now, when he might well owe his sons' lives to her?

"How? How did this happen?" He had to know. If he'd do anything to make amends with Jane, he had to know.

"Mr. Vancoller sold the horse to a man headed through, on his way to Denver. Said he'd sell the horse for hide glue. Apparently, he claimed more money selling the young animal to somebody else. The current owner bought him off an impound lot in Denver."

Hank rubbed his eyes with his thumb and index finger.

"I want that animal gone from Mountain Home." How, he had no idea.

"Already done." Abbott rose, as if to leave.

"Why did you tell me this?" Hank stood, assessing

the man whose need for attention had pulled Jane and himself into the competition in the first place. "Why did you come here?"

"Because I happen to know you've not seen her since the race. A week ago."

"That's my private business." Emotion rode high. His heart pounded and the grief he carried grew heavier.

"I thought if you knew—"

"It's not your business, Archibald." He intentionally dropped Abbott's favorite title— mayor. This wasn't city business and the man didn't own Hank.

"Maybe. Maybe not."

Hank stared the man down, wrestling with hot, pungent emotions he didn't want to feel.

The kitchen door opened fast and banged against the wall. Jimmy ran, as naked as the day he was born, through the parlor and into the bedroom. Right behind him, Clyde followed, a towel around his shoulders. Two pairs of wet footprints marked their passage.

"I'll go." Abbott put on his bowler and headed for the door. "Now that you know the circumstances, I hope you'll do the right thing."

Hank bristled. How dare the man point the finger of blame at him? He'd tried to help, he'd shown Jane kindness and gone after her when she'd run. She'd ordered him away from her, commanded him not to touch her.

In the bedroom, the little ones made a cacophony of noise as they dressed.

None of this with Jane was Hank's fault. She didn't want him. She'd made that clear.

"What is the right thing?" he demanded of Abbott. "What, exactly?" His chest labored with breaths that came too quickly. "You're a fine one to point the finger of blame on me."

At the door, Abbott turned. "Who else would I turn to, Hank? You're the man who's courted her for months. You're the man she loves."

Abbott let himself out, the door clicking shut behind himself.

And, Hank's conscience added, *You're the man who loves her.*

Despite every honorable intention, he'd gone and fallen in love with Miss Jane Vancoller. How had he ever once thought he couldn't love his boys *and* Jane? How had he feared his heart wasn't big enough to hold all of them?

The miserable truth was he did love Jane. Wholly, and forever. She'd not crowded out his sons and his brother. She'd added to that capacity to love and to trust and to care, without an ounce subtracted.

He'd been a dolt.

He removed his cap and threw it to the floor with enough force to shatter glass. The soft cap struck and rolled.

Not satisfying enough.

He wanted to swear, to use every filthy word he'd ever heard— but Elias stood in the kitchen doorway, leaning against the jamb. He'd overheard some of the conversation. So, Hank thrust his fingers through his hair, knotted among the strands, and pulled. He paced to the front door and back again.

Even in his temper, Hank knew the undeniable

truth of one matter: he couldn't blame this problem—this gaping chasm between himself and the woman he'd come to love— on anyone but himself.

Not Elias. Not Abbott and his machinations with the Harvest Festival. Not even Jane.

Another truth tumbled hard and fast on the heels of the first. All week long, he'd grieved Jane's loss. That grief had haunted him for a full seven days and seven nights, and he'd mistaken it for any and every other malady... but mostly on his own defective heart.

He recognized the pain now as the same he'd suffered when he'd lost Dora to diphtheria. He'd believed himself numb, unable to grieve when Dora died... but this proved him wrong.

Maybe he wasn't as broken as he'd believed.

He'd grieved throughout his marriage, for things that should've been... for lost opportunities, elusive love, and the shocking absence of maternal love. They'd fallen short of their potential— and he'd grieved that loss.

Now, in arrears, he recognized he'd grieved her death, too.

So much for the lies he'd held onto as if they were truth.

Elias shifted his weight to the other foot. "What are you going to do?"

"I don't know." He halted his senseless pacing, not quite willing to look his brother in the eye.

"She risked her life to save Jimmy and Clyde." What was this? Elias arguing *for* Jane?

Hank nodded. His mind spun and spun. Jane, who feared that horse more than she feared anything else in this life, had acted with selflessness to ensure he never suffered the way she had suffered...

But she'd missed one critical point in logic.

If Hank had lost her, if she'd been struck by those hooves, if she'd died last Saturday, on Main, why, he'd—

Pain and grief and regrets and loss whirled and spun and tore him to bits. He sank onto the chair and dropped his head into his hands.

"I think," Elias said from his place in the doorway, "Miss Jane Vancoller is a much better woman than I'd thought."

Hank seconded the motion in his heart.

He'd made one bad decision after another. Why, exactly, hadn't he called on Jane, or at least talked with her mother, well before now?

Why hadn't he gone back to her door, every single day, until she'd been willing to see him?

Why hadn't he thanked her, again, for saving his sons?

And why hadn't he welcomed the truth that Clyde spoke?

"Mama," he'd said. Clyde had called Jane M*ama*.

Important enough to the four-year-old that he'd give voice to the feelings in his heart. He'd completed the sentence, his little heart aching because Mama cried.

"You're not mad at Miss Vancoller, are you, Hank?" Elias's tone sounded pinched, almost fearful.

"No. No, I'm not."

"I'm sorry I told you to stay away from her." The boy sounded as contrite as he'd ever heard him. "I shouldn't have done that."

Hank nodded. Who was he to judge, when his own behavior came under condemnation?

He stood and went to his brother, offered a hand. They shook, man to man. Hank pulled his young brother into his arms and hugged him tight.

When they parted, Elias raised troubled eyes to Hank's. "I think you ought to call on her, let her know how you feel."

Would she see him? Did she want to see him?

"You're right." He looked his brother in the eye, searching for answers. "What of you?"

Elias shrugged.

"Know this, brother. I'm a grown man. I will love whom my heart wishes— and that's Jane. She's a good woman, far better than I am. Tell me true. Will you give her a chance?"

"Yes, sir." A solemn oath.

Hank needn't doubt the boy's support. He wouldn't complain, wouldn't prevent Hank from bringing Jane into their lives. "I thought about what you said, about marriage suiting me and Dora like a ball and chain. You weren't wrong. We both looked at that the wrong way. It wasn't marriage that fit me all wrong— *Dora* fit me all wrong."

As the words came out of his mouth, he questioned every last one... maybe he'd been the one to fit Dora all wrong. While he'd raged about his inability to keep her happy for five minutes, he'd never stopped to ask if he'd done something to make her unhappy.

Chances were, in his youth and inexperience, he had.

If he married again— which he certainly hoped he

would— he'd try every single day to ensure he applied himself to Jane's happiness. He might need the wisdom of King Solomon to manage things right, but he could commit to do his best.

"Despite Dora and me," he told his brother, "that's independent of Jane and me. Entirely two different things."

The boy listened to every word. He nodded, understanding in his eyes.

"I don't know if Jane can forgive me for leaving her when she needed me the most, but I pray to God that she'll hear me out. If she'll have me, I'll ask her, soon enough, to marry me. Our family has enough love for all of us, don't you think?"

Elias's once hesitant smile bloomed. "I do think you're right. Go to her. Now. I'll put the boys to bed."

"Papa!" Russ bellowed from the bedroom. "Papa! Come finish the story. I need to know what happens to the king."

Chapter Twenty-Five

Perhaps because she'd slept too much over the past week, and perhaps because she saw the world through a different lens, Jane awoke before dawn.

The time had come to make a few necessary changes.

She covered her nightdress with a wrapper, and donned warm socks and slippers. Tiptoeing, in an effort to avoid waking Mother, she gathered a few things from her room, and went downstairs, skipping the squeaky tread second from the bottom.

She set her lamp on the kitchen table, started the stove and set the kettle to boil. She shivered in the cold, anticipating a hot cup of tea, and the warmth from the stove to chase the chill from her bones.

In four days' time, she'd turn thirty. *Thirty.* She grew old, alone, just like she'd determined to do when Law died. At the time, her decision felt loyal and just. Now, what she'd seen as a favorable trait— loyalty— she now saw as foolish and shortsighted.

So many foolish and shortsighted choices.

She could only hope she wasn't too late implementing a change or two.

She opened the clasp of the gold chain about her neck and removed the piece. The locket had represented her vows and a reminder of Law. She opened the clasp and held the contents to the light.

Three remembrances: a snip of Law's hair, a miniature photograph of him, and the engagement ring he'd given her. Mama had insisted she stop wearing the ring, so Jane had tucked the treasured piece into her locket, and worn the locket next to her heart.

As of that Sunday morning, four days shy of her thirtieth birthday, she determined she was through carrying the locket everywhere.

She picked up the ring, slipped it over her index finger, and examined it in the light. Never before had she considered selling the keepsake, valuing it far above the money it could bring.

As the morning sky hinted at dawn, she realized the desperation to hold onto this token of the past had melted away. Perhaps she would sell it, and use the money to offset the expenses incurred by her business.

With the water boiling, she set the tea to steep and opened her personal journal. She'd written at length through her courtship and engagement, taking weeks to document the tumult she'd faced when the accident had stolen her future. Teardrops had caused the ink to run in places. Testaments of another time, when she'd believed she'd never love again.

Now here she was, five short years later, romantically in love. She'd proved herself wrong— it was, indeed, possible to love again. How absurd she'd been, but her loyal heart didn't know any other way. Her "Loyal Heart" was both her greatest strength and her greatest weakness, and had caused her unnecessary pain.

The kitchen warmed, and the fragrance of the tea teased her senses. She poured through a strainer, sweetened her tea, and returned to the table.

She put pen to her journal, documenting the realizations.

As she wrote, another awareness struck... not only did she love Hank— with her whole heart— she loved him every bit as much, perhaps more, than she'd loved Law.

She held that truth in her heart and pondered it with care.

In this new light, what she'd seen as breaking her 'vows' to Law, wasn't that at all. Instead, she could see with new clarity, she added new loyalties, new vows, to her faithful heart.

She'd been faithful to Law, through their precious time together and long after he'd passed on. Now, she would be faithful to Hank. The thought seemed good and right.

Upstairs, floorboards squeaked as Mama moved about her bedroom, then slowly down the stairs.

Jane heated more water, preparing a pot for both of them, at least two cups each.

When Mama joined her, Jane had tea waiting, with thick slices of bread, toasted, with butter and berry preserves. Dawn lightened the sky in brilliant shades of pink and lavender. Wind tossed the colorful leaves on the branches, whisking many away on gusts of air.

"Good morning, Jane." Mama joined her at the table. "You're up early."

"I've had much thinking to do. I hope I didn't wake you."

"Not at all." Mama assessed the jewelry box, journal, pens, and Bible on the tabletop. "It's good to see you're more yourself."

"Thank you."

They ate in quiet companionship. Jane's thoughts strayed to the Jane who stubbornly made vows she'd been deprived of making with Law, before a minister, and the Jane of today, who could see her own mistakes.

"You're lost in thought." Mama sipped her tea.

An invitation to share her innermost secrets, if she dared.

As she hovered on the fence between divulging, or keeping her own counsel, she couldn't help but remember how things were when she'd been young. Before Lawrence, when family had meant herself and her parents.

Despite the strains on their relationship, the mother-daughter bond was valuable, and one Jane wanted to regain. If not now, then when?

How many more months did she have with her aging mother? At seventy, she'd outlived many of her friends.

"I've learned powerful lessons of late." Nervousness trembled in her middle as she stepped into the void between them. *Meet me halfway, Mother.*

"Oh?"

"I believed, with all my heart, that real love comes

once in every lifetime." The source of much contention between herself and her mother.

But now, Mama showed no hint of that contention. She waited, quietly listening.

"I can see now that I was wrong." Outside, the sky lightened further, bringing more clarity to the world, allowing her to see what she'd not been able to a mere fifteen minutes past.

Life had proved to be much like that sunrise. So many truths had hidden beyond her line of sight five years ago. Now, she saw them with startling and joyful clarity.

Mama extended a hand. "I'm pleased to see you smile."

Jane slipped her fingers into her mother's, a joyful sense of reunion filling the cracks in her heart. How she'd missed her mother's support, missed her listening ear.

"Jane, what did you decide you're wrong about?"

"I didn't realize my heart is big enough to love twice." She'd have never imagined that two men could win her heart and her love.

One then, and one now.

Five years ago, she'd never have believed that the end of Lawrence's life didn't mean the end of her own. She'd never have believed that she'd find love and happiness again.

True— she and Hank had a mountain of challenges to face, and their lives were far from perfect... but the circumstances of finding herself in love with him, and he in love with her, when she'd believed such a thing impossible...

"I think, Mother, that I've experienced a miracle."

Mother pulled her hand free to blot her eyes with her hankie. She wept and smiled and chuckled at her foolishness, and wept some more.

"Thank you, Mama."

"What for, darling? You found your own way."

"I'm grateful for your protection, your guidance, and your love through my lifetime. Every child should grow up with the kind of loving parent you were to me." Mama may not have been as present and as helpful after Law and Papa died, but one more thing Jane hadn't acknowledged at the time was Mama had been grieving the loss of her husband of nearly sixty years. Grief weighed on a person and darkened a person's view of the world and relationships.

Jane comprehended that now.

"Thank you," Mama whispered.

She seemed so frail this morning. Frail and elderly.

"Thank you for talking with me, Jane. I've missed you. I've missed you terribly."

"But—" She bit her tongue. She didn't want to argue, didn't want to fight with her mother.

But I've been here all along.

But you've been difficult.

But you've challenged my choices, expressed disappointment and dissatisfaction...

She'd learned, since Papa's death, how easy it could be to misunderstand someone she dearly loved, and who dearly loved her. If Mama said she'd been lonely, and had missed Jane— then that's how she felt, whether it made sense to Jane, or not.

Thank you for talking with me, Jane. I've missed you. I've missed you, terribly.

Had she pushed her mother away, too, just as she'd pushed Hank away? To protect herself in advance of inevitable loss? Mother, at seventy, couldn't live forever...

"I'm sorry, Mother." Jane reached for her mother's hand and held it between her own. Her hands, shaped so much like Jane's, were thin, knobby at the joints, and spotted with age. "I owe you an apology. I didn't mean to be distant. I didn't mean to leave you alone in your grief."

But she had, hadn't she?

The same ache and awareness of shortcomings swamped her as the day young Clyde Murphy had destroyed the wedding cake sweet Maggie Cresswell had ordered for the bridal tea... the day Maggie had shown her how sweet it was to receive forgiveness.

From that moment forward, Jane vowed, she would be eager to forgive, eager to reconcile, eager to build bridges instead of walls.

"My darling girl." Mama's eyes filled with tears again. "You suffer so deeply. You feel pain more acutely than most. How I've prayed to know how to help you, how to ease your burdens, how to help carry your load so you don't walk alone."

Jane's throat filled and tears spilled over her lids.

To hear her mother's tender confession, the depth of love in her mother's heart, Jane sensed the depth of a mother's love. She finally comprehended a mother's love for the amazing gift it was... for her own heart, in growing to make ample room for Hank and a new future with him— if only she'd not destroyed his affection for her— grew to encompass and include every one of Hank's boys. Even when they didn't like her.

"Thank you for loving me," Jane whispered.

Mama squeezed Jane's hand. "I've loved you from the moment I'd learned our own miracle had finally happened, and you were on the way." Mama's voice broke and she drew in a great lungful of air. "You, our greatest blessing, brought so much love with you, into our home, and into our lives."

How had she ever doubted her mother's love?

Had she been so foolish as to suppose a mother's love could fade in the face of loss and grief, because she'd not yet experienced the wonder of maternal love?

Maybe.

And maybe she'd simply been angry, blaming anyone who crossed her path.

And ensuring she held anyone who tried to love her at a distance, so when she lost them, too, the pain would be far less. "I'm sorry, Mother, that I didn't show you all the love in my heart for you. I'll do better, I promise."

"While we're apologizing, I beg your forgiveness for insisting you put aside your mourning black. I pushed you, and I shouldn't have."

The love and acceptance she'd felt from Maggie Cresswell came rushing back. Acceptance and love in response to an apology. Jane wanted to be more like Maggie.

"Mother— there's nothing to forgive. I apologize for bringing the matter up again and again. I shouldn't have." Looking back, there were many things she regretted saying.

Mama leaned closer and tucked a strand of hair behind Jane's ear. She'd not bothered to braid it, to keep it out of the way, not since the horse race when she'd been bombarded with one too many realizations and more truth than her heart could bear.

"You've suffered so much this past week," Mama said, stroking the curve of her forefinger along Jane's cheek— a sweet gesture from childhood she'd nearly forgotten.

How she wanted to remember these blessed things that had made her certain of her mother's love. Memories like those would last forever, and needed no physical reminders. No locket was needed.

"My heart nearly broke to watch you suffer in a world of darkness— this week, and even more so, after Law was called home."

Again, Mama's voice broke, and Jane squeezed her hand. As her mother had done, she remained quiet and gave her a chance to finish speaking.

Charity suffereth long, and is kind; charity envieth not; charity vaunteth not itself, is not puffed up, Doth not behave itself unseemly, seeketh not her own, is not easily provoked, thinketh no evil.

The scripture distilled upon her soul, and she understood.

She understood why her mother had insisted she set aside the black mourning clothes and return to living.

She comprehended why, now, Mama had been so hopeful Jane would find someone to love, and someone to love her in return.

"It's all right, Mama." She held her mother's eyes, so much like her own, and savored the sweetness in the moment. "I understand."

Chapter Twenty-Six

On any usual Sunday morning, Hank slept as late as possible. His choice of occupations afforded him this one morning of indulgence.

The morning after Mayor Abbott's enlightening visit, Hank awoke far earlier than normal.

He saw to the team, bathed, dressed, ate, washed dishes, saw to the children's needs...

... and *still*, the hour was far too early to call on a woman.

So, he read aloud to the children from the novel Jane had given them, extending two chapters further than he'd wanted to, if only to pass more time.

At last, nine o'clock. He donned his jacket, asked the boys to remain at home, and clean, so they might attend church together in a couple hours, and promised homemade cookies as a prize for obedience.

He knocked on Jane's front door at ten minutes after the hour.

Nervousness tugged at him.

What if she wouldn't see him? What would he say to her mother to persuade her?

After the longest of waits, Mrs. Vancoller answered the door. She clutched her wrapper closed at her throat. A long white braid swept over her shoulder and nearly to her waist.

He'd come too early.

"I'm sorry to disturb you, Mrs. Vancoller. It's most important I see Jane. May I come in."

"Jane isn't properly dressed, Mr. Murphy. This isn't the time for a social call."

No preliminaries, no pleasantries to soften the blow, no encouragement to call later.

His heart sank.

How determined had Jane been to avoid him?

Had she told her mother to send him away, no matter when he called?

He'd mustered the courage to come to her door now. But later? Would he convince himself the prize wasn't worth the challenge?

He decided to throw all of his chips in the middle of the table. "Please, Mrs. Vancoller. I need to talk to your daughter. I love her."

"I know." The old woman's smile, soft and sweet, said she *did* know.

What did she know of Jane?

"Mrs. Van— Mrs. Vancol-coller..." He stammered, nervousness stealing his poise and his courage.

"Bring your boys to Sunday supper, after church, here. I'll expect you all at half-past one." With a twinkle in her eye, she closed the door.

He stared at the closed door, her words echoing in his mind.

Bring the boys to Sunday supper. Half-past one.

He leaped off the porch, jubilant with the results. Not what he wanted, but it would do.

Hank approached Sunday dinner at the Vancoller home with trepidation.

A million things could go wrong, beginning with each of the boys— and ending with Jane's as of yet unstated feelings on the matter. All this time later, her hysterical *don't touch me* reverberated in his head.

But Mrs. Vancoller, and Jane, welcomed the Murphy family into their home and around their dining room table.

With each minute that passed, and each bit of conversation between Jane and his boys played out, most of his fears evaporated. Jane's smile put the rest of his fears to bed.

Her smile settled in his chest, right behind his breastbone, expelling the ache that had taken up residence the morning of the horse race.

He couldn't help but observe the interactions between aged Mrs. Vancoller and his boys. No matter how much he wanted to marry Jane, he wouldn't blindly wed a woman whose family would cause further pain and misery to his sons. The anxiety slowly left him as the boys were boys— spilled milk, swinging their feet beneath the table and occasionally kicking furniture or person, and talking with their mouths full.

Russell stabbed a bit of meat onto his knife and held it up to Mrs. Vancoller. "What kind of animal is this?"

"Russ—" Hank warned.

But Mrs. Vancoller didn't seem to mind. "It's a ham roast, Russell."

The boy sighed, as if his patience were sorely tried. He bobbed up and down in his seat from swinging his legs up and down, up and down. "What kind of an animal does ham come from?"

"Russell." Hank would've rounded the table and clamped a hand over his son's mouth, but imagined his own manners were on trial, just like his son's.

"I don't mind." Mrs. Vancoller possessed the patience of a saint. "Ham comes from a pig."

"Mmmm." Russell chewed, and without swallowing, exclaimed, "Pigs taste good."

When they returned home tonight, he'd remind the boys that table manners were not negotiable.

At long last, supper had finished, but Mrs. Vancoller had yet to excuse them from the table. Conversation continued as they dawdled over tea and dessert.

His boys, each possessed of a sweet tooth, had no difficulty remaining at the table and exclaiming over a cake that looked to be a slice of watermelon, green rind, white pith, and sweet red center. Raisins masqueraded as seeds.

"I want more." Russell announced.

"More, too." Jimmy said.

"Clyde wants more, too." Russ added, apparently

unconcerned that his brother often spoke for himself. Most of the time, Clyde had nothing to say and remained silent.

Hank considered packing up his ill-behaved boys and taking them home to stand in corners and think about all they'd done to offend Mrs. Vancoller.

"Mr. Murphy," the sweet old lady said, "don't you fret over any of this. Your little boys are children. They need a woman's guidance."

He opened his mouth to agree, and to apologize, but Mrs. Vancoller gave him no opportunity.

"The children and I," she continued, "will enjoy one another's company while you and Jane enjoy a walk together."

"It's cold outside." Russ said, too loudly for the dining room.

He did want to visit with Jane, alone. Russell could not embarrass his father worse than he had to that point, so Hank blotted his mouth with his napkin, set it beside his plate, and turned to Jane. She'd set her dessert fork down and now sipped tea.

"Will you walk with me?" Her eyes seemed very green today. Maybe because of the pink woolen dress she wore. The same one as that first day of the Harvest Festival, when they'd been competitors— and she'd made him laugh and smile and dream of good things to come.

"I'll collect my coat."

He held the heavy garment for her to slip into. She pulled on gloves, rather than a muff, which pleased him. No muff meant she'd take his hand. Or his arm.

How he'd missed her.

With his own coat buttoned to his chin, he turned to the boys who remained at the dining room table. "Elias, you're in charge. See to it the boys obey Mrs. Vancoller."

"Yes, sir."

Outside, the wind seemed to slice through his many layers— coat, a proper suit of clothes, and long woolen Union suit. Mid October, and already it felt like winter.

His breath puffed in a cloud of white as he offered his arm and Jane took it, as easily as if they'd never quarreled. As easily as if the horrible moments at the race hadn't occurred.

He didn't want to take his gaze from her face. "I missed you."

Her smile chased the chill away. "I missed you, too."

A very good sign, indeed.

"I figure the best place to start is with an apology." He'd been a poor husband, and had next to no experience with women, but he'd learn. And he'd try hard every single day to ease Jane's burdens, to smile with her, to chuckle at life's difficult moments.

"You've nothing to apologize for." She snuggled close to his arm.

"Ah, Duchess, I think I do."

"Are you calling me Duchess, still? After all we've been through?"

"Would you prefer darling? Or sweetheart?"

She playacted thinking his offer through. "I like Duchess best."

"Very well."

"As long as you promise to use it only when you're very sweet and very much in love with me."

His pulse skipped a beat or three, and his smile ran away from him. "I promise."

How had he thought he could stay away from this woman?

"I hesitate to risk the pleasant conversation, Duchess, but I have a bit of explaining to do."

She nodded, allowing him time to gather his thoughts. "I've told you my marriage was bad, that Dora hadn't been loving to the boys. I probably didn't explain enough..."

Recalling those times, the desperation in his boys' actions whenever he was around. They'd hugged him so tightly, had expressed affection over and over— in a plea for the same in return. Children should never doubt love from their parents.

"Dora was a deeply unhappy woman, and I've only come to understand, recently, that she chose that misery. Whatever it was she needed, she obtained from that unhappiness. She yelled, she screamed, and was impossible to please."

Rather than speak, Jane listened with her eyes, her ears, and her heart.

What had he done to deserve this woman?

"I'm often caught by old patterns. I'm often upset by the sense that I can't please you, that no matter what I do, it isn't good enough."

"Hank—"

"I know. Groundless. I'm nothing if not diligent. I'll not bring Dora into our marriage."

Jane sputtered— and laughed, the tinkling of

icicles or bells or the magic of a baby's chortle. Pure joy and happiness. "Was that a proposal of marriage?"

"Not yet. You'll know when I propose. Until then, know it's inevitable."

"I see. Have I any choice in the matter?"

"You do." He halted, facing her and grasping her waist with his gloved hands. "Would you deny me the privilege of committing my life to your wellbeing?"

"Phrased that way..."

Her teasing, the lightness of her tone, her genuine smile— all swirled together in the most buoyant sense of gratitude he'd ever known.

Gratitude for all of the good things in life.

Like Jane, who was nothing at all like Dora. He'd thrown it all in, every chip, every penny, and now, the deed to the farm. "I love you, Jane Vancoller. I love you more than I knew a man could love a woman."

Her expression softened. He fancied he glimpsed his own reflection in the depths of her green-as-summer eyes. Love swelled and stretched his heart. Again.

He imagined that phenomenon would continue, making room for more children and, someday, grandchildren.

With those soft eyes and a contented smile, she remained silent, but he didn't mind. She'd gone out on a limb, the first to declare love for him. If he had to wait a decade to hear those three words, he could, because she showed him, always, how much she loved him.

"I had an astounding experience this morning." She blinked and smiled even more broadly.

He held her waist, wanting to pull her closer,

maybe steal a kiss. "Oh?"

"I realized, among a dozen other things, that I'm glad you aren't Lawrence Riddle."

Hank froze. Had he heard her correctly? "You're glad I'm *not* Riddle?"

"Correct. I'm glad you're not. Because you, Thankful Murphy, are marvelous in your own way. You are a man worth keeping, a man I'll love forever."

"You're sure?" Why did uncertainty linger? Still, his heart swelled and flooded him with warmth, to hear her say she loved him, that he was worth keeping...

Why did he doubt?

"Don't fret." She rose on her tippy-toes and gave him the quickest of pecks on the mouth.

"Don't tease."

She chuckled and eased away.

"I love you, Jane. I know I said it already, but you don't understand— I'm not sure I've been in love before now. I mean before you. See, I married Dora quick, after too brief a courtship. We were foolish and naive."

"I don't know that I'll ever tire of hearing you tell me you love me."

"How, in all of God's creation, did I find you?" His heart pounded, and he needed to feel her, to touch her. He pulled off his gloves, stuffed them into his coat pocket, and cupped her face. Her skin, warm and soft, and smooth, and the delicious fragrance of her skin... "How soon can we marry?"

"You haven't asked me yet."

"Marry me."

Despite his earnest heart, she seemed determined to joke, to keep the conversation on light topics. "I don't hear a question mark, Mr. Murphy."

Through her sparkle and teasing, he saw, clear as day, her fear...

Fear of separation—

Fear of loving him too much.

Fear that someday, when death took one of them, she'd be left alone, and this time, she wouldn't muster the strength to survive.

"I'll fight your fear," he whispered, "one day at a time. I'll show you, every day of our lives, that I'm here to stay. I'll remain unmistakably yours—"

Her green eyes grew luminous, filling with tears.

"— until the Lord sees fit to call one of us home."

She pressed her lips into a line, the expression clearly telegraphing the emotion that rose within her. She'd needed to hear these words. She'd needed them... and he'd somehow had the right thing to say.

"Even then, when one of us is gone, I'm banking on a kind and merciful Lord bringing us together again."

Jane nearly leapt into his arms. She pushed off the walk and caught him about the neck with her arms. He held her fast, not caring one bit who might be watching from windows or from a wagon rolling by.

They'd all best get used to it.

Thankful Murphy intended to embrace his bride every chance he got.

For the first time in his life, his given name fit. He'd always been a grateful sort, and today, he honestly added thankful to his list.

"Duchess? You didn't let me finish. Somehow, in all of God's creation, my path crossed yours. I removed my family to Mountain Home for no reason other than the community could support one more grocer. And what do I find? I find my woman. You— the one woman, in all of humanity, that doesn't scare me."

He knew, deep inside. Just like he knew the sky was blue. And the way he knew, without question, that winter was around the corner.

Some things a man didn't have to be told twice. "You, Duchess, are my miracle."

Chapter Twenty-Seven

On Monday morning, Oscar had healed— superficially, at least— such that he resumed wearing his prosthesis. He paused to express gratitude on his way to work, as he walked with ease and without a borrowed crutch.

He'd nearly managed to paste on a pleasant smile when Hank arrived, whistling a merry tune.

Whistling.

Oscar glared. And clenched his jaw.

"Good morning, Oscar." Hank's smile was radiant. Like looking at the sun, Oscar had to squint to so much as look in Hank's direction.

"Are you unwell?" Hank paused, evident concern in his expression. "I see you're on your two feet today. That's good."

"If you count a purchased prosthetic foot as mine, then yes, I am indeed on my own two feet."

"Why are you in a sour disposition?"

"Why are you jovial beyond reason?" He behaved abominably, but he'd been provoked! "Why must you approach a Monday morning by whistling?"

For a moment, Hank held still, his expression flat.

Oscar nearly apologized. One did not criticize a man for a pleasant attitude.

Hank dissolved into laughter. "Whatever has happened to you? You're as sour as three-day old milk."

Oscar clenched his fists. "Perhaps the question should be, whatever has happened to you? Why are you so happy? You make the rest of us downright miserable."

"You know what you need?" Hank grasped Oscar by both shoulders.

Oscar leaned back, itching to knock Hank's too-personal touch away. He wasn't in the mood. "I'm certain you know."

"Yes, I do know. You need to make amends. Miss Ina is the kindest, most forgiving woman I know. She nursed Mrs. Hudson— the first one— for years. No matter how ornery the woman became as her cancer worsened, Ina was as patient and loving as could be."

"Why are you telling me this? Ina and I are no more. She's a princess, and I'm a..." Soldier? Guard? What station was low enough to emphasize the fact he wasn't good enough for her?

"You know Ina's not going to slam the door in your face." Hank lifted his brows, as if to emphasize his statement. "She's a lady. She'll hear you out. I know why you're as miserable as a goat in a corset, because I was that miserable until I accepted the truth."

Oscar glared. He'd had enough of a lecture.

"Do you want," Hank asked, "to be miserable every day of your life? Do you?"

Oscar turned away. He headed for the broom. He couldn't tolerate Hank's smiling face— or his serious face— for one more moment.

"You love that woman," Hank stated, as if it were an absolute truth, a chemical equation that proved true over and over again. "If you're going to spend one happy day in all of your miserable life, you must stop fighting—" he cast about, as if uncertain what foe Oscar faced, "— whatever it is you think is more important than she is."

That statement struck a powerful chord. The harmony echoed well after the keys were struck by a powerful hand.

What is more important than she?

He'd never denied Ina's importance, or her value, or her worth... he'd denied *himself*. He would not burden her with a cripple.

What is more important?

Hadn't she so much as told him, in a hodgepodge of words over their many weeks, that her greatest fear, her greatest pain, was proving invisible to those she loved?

Which meant that with every passing day, with each moment he stayed away, determined to protect her, that he'd struck at her tender underbelly— her most vulnerable spot.

Every— Day—

His conscience burned.

Now he had much more than that morning in his rented room to atone for, when he'd said awful things, intentionally striking where he'd do the most damage.

In that moment, he understood with lightning

clarity, that if he didn't do something to correct his gargantuan faux pas with Miss Ina, that he would live embroiled in misery, until his dying breath.

He nearly doubled over, the pain was so intense.

How could he willfully hurt the woman he loved?

If he didn't make a mighty big change and find a way to beg Ina's forgiveness, and let her decide if she wanted him or not, then he wouldn't deserve a moment's happiness.

He wanted to deserve her more than he wanted to walk without pain, more than he wanted Hank to stop his infernal whistling, and more than he wanted his next breath.

Hank pulled off his grocer's apron and headed for the back door. "I'll be back from the city council meeting as quick as possible. Thanks for covering the counter."

As scheduled, the city council meeting discussed the Harvest Festival.

The mayor had waxed eloquent time and again about the event's many successes.

"Allow me to congratulate Mr. Hank Murphy and Miss Jane Vancoller for restoring the festival to its former glory. Their personal and romantic contributions brought a lucrative week to the city's businesses, as I imagine their own establishments noticed.

"In retrospect, our Harvest Festival achieved what

we set out to achieve."

Applause, cheers, and whistles circulated in the large parlor within the Abbott mansion.

Abbott clasped his hands behind his back and rocked from toe to heel. He nodded, as if accepting the cheers as his due.

Good thing Hank had been in an excellent mood before the meeting began.

"For the minutes," he glanced at the city council secretary, a man who seldom spoke a word but took immaculate notes, "those reasons were, one: to bond the community, two: to prepare our citizens for winter, three: to matchmake where needed, and—"

Hank's blood chilled, and he surged to his feet. "What did you just say?"

"I said, 'to matchmake'."

"You manipulated the contest?" This was ever so much worse than Hank's original assumption, that Abbott adored being the center of attention. "Your whole purpose was to meddle in our lives?"

"Thankful A. Murphy, your assumptions are offensive. You fell in love with her all by yourself. All we did was put you two in the same room to see what would happen."

"Why?" He'd never understand men like Abbott. "Why would you do that?"

"Because—" He sighed as if bored. "You two fought over a bit of real estate that would continue to be a burr under your saddle, causing contention between you two for decades to come. But if you were in love, it wouldn't matter one way or the other who leased the shop. I had every confidence you'd find a way to help one another, to share the place."

"It didn't matter," Hank repeated, "who won."

"No, sir."

Hank battled the dual emotions of anger and fierce protectiveness. "I seated her at the pie contest table, effectively selecting her seat, and thus her pie."

And, ultimately, her winning— and entertaining the audience— instead of risking humiliating her before the entire county.

Now protectiveness trumped all other emotions. "Do you realize that if I'd not determined that a gentleman should sit closest to the platform's edge, that the pies would've been reversed?"

Abbott shrugged. "Murphy, you're overly dramatic, aren't you?"

"Did you want to laugh her to scorn?"

"Is that what happened? Did Jane find herself before a pie as large as her chair? No. She had the ladies' pie and she won the contest."

He had to tell Jane about this. She deserved to know what her friend, Ann Abbott, and landlord, the mayor, had been up to.

He forced himself to breathe. Why was he upset? Because the Abbotts set out to matchmake, or because he'd been blind to their efforts?

"She won the pie contest," Abbott said, "and she won the competition overall. Tell us, Murphy, what does Miss Vancoller intend to do with her prize?"

Did he dare admit he didn't know? No one mentioned what Jane will do with the storage room when they ate dinner together on Sunday, nor during their walk afterward. "I suggest you ask her."

"We've tried. She's been… unavailable."

That made him smile. "She'll discuss it with you when she's ready."

The last person Ina expected to find at Mrs. Vancoller's home in the middle of the day on Monday was Miss Jane Vancoller.

Because Ina had remained at home in the nine long days since Oscar had thrown her out of his room at the boardinghouse, she'd been unaware that Jane hadn't returned to the Tea Room since that same Saturday morning.

All the while she'd been suffering a broken heart, so had Jane.

With her stomach upset and her heart in shreds, Ina set her teacup on its saucer and the pair upon the tray.

Both Mrs. and Miss Vancoller had listened to Ina's dilemma with kindness, patience, and a listening ear. "But what do I *do*?"

"Jane?" Mrs. Vancoller deferred to her daughter.

"You need to talk with him, explain how you feel."

"Oh, no. I couldn't possibly." She twisted her reticule strings, her heart breaking. "I— I can't. He threw me out… and since, he's not spoken to me…"

"Men," elderly Mrs. Vancoller said, "are quite difficult creatures. They tend to be rather stubborn and unwilling to risk their hearts."

Ina could have wept. Yes, Oscar was both difficult

and stubborn. His heart had been barricaded so deep, she could lay siege for the rest of their lives and never capture the prize.

Did she have the strength to continue the fight?

She couldn't make him love her. Not with potions or wishes or her nursing. Oh, why had she appeared at his room, uninvited? Why had she stayed as long as she had? If she'd been more sensitive, more aware... if she'd only gone the first time he'd told her to, why they—"

"Pardon me." Jane rose and hurried to the front door.

From the sound of voices, Mr. Murphy had come to the door. Ina peeked at the watch pinned to her bodice. Five o'clock. Outside, shadows grew long and darkness would fall soon.

Nights were the hardest, which was beyond absurd. She'd been alone in her home, no matter the time of day or night, since her parents passed away. She'd often returned from nursing the first Mrs. Morgan late at night, unlocking a dark and empty house.

To find herself loneliest in the dark of night made no sense.

Hank and Jane walked together into the parlor, their arms linked. From a single glance, she hadn't a moment's difficulty noting the love between them.

A yearning, powerfully strong, swept through Ina until she feared she'd behave poorly. How she wanted Oscar to look at her the way Hank Murphy looked at Jane.

Wanting wouldn't change Oscar's mind. He'd made his wishes well known that Saturday. He'd thrown her out like so much refuse, tossed her desire to help into her face.

"Good evening, Mrs. Vancoller, Miss Dimond." Mr. Murphy, for all his less-than-formal clothing— the man dressed like a miner or a miller, not like a merchant, not like Oscar— did have good manners.

"Good evening." She tried to smile.

Now that he'd come to call, she should be going. Just as soon as she'd exchanged pleasantries, she'd make her excuses.

"Hank," Jane said, sitting beside him in the pair of chairs near the sofa, "we were just discussing Ina's predicament."

"No, Jane. Please." She'd not come to involve Oscar's business partner.

"What is it?" Genuine concern marred the man's features.

"Tell him, Ina," Jane urged. "Perhaps we can help."

She stood, her nerves jangling. "I'll go, and leave you in peace."

"Ina—" This from Mrs. Vancoller, who apparently wasn't in possession of the manners her daughter exhibited, for she launched into a retelling of all Ina had confided. Embarrassment flooded her cheeks with heat, and she knew she must be blushing.

"Just this morning—" Hank had stood simply because Ina stood.

How she wanted a man so attuned to her, so polite and kind. She wanted, she *needed* Oscar.

"— Oscar was in the foulest of moods. He took exception to my happiness."

"What is the matter? Is he in pain? Is it his prosthesis, again?"

Three pair of eyes watched her with pity.

Miss Ina Dimond had seen more than her share of pity in the expressions of men and women, people who assumed they understood why she'd been passed over, neglected, left alone.

So few comprehended why, much less her feelings in the matter.

But she and Mrs. Vancoller had become friends over the past months since Jane had asked her to call on her mother, to check in on her in the middle of Jane's longest days in the Tea Room.

Jane turned to Mr. Murphy. "What is it? Tell us."

"Miss Dimond, I assure my business partner is of sound body. He wore his prosthesis once more, rather than moving about with a crutch. The worst of his injuries seem to have healed.

She let out a stale breath. "That's good."

"It's his heart that's suffering."

"Oh, goodness! Dropsy?"

"No, no. I believe he's miserable without you. He regrets all he said in anger, and hasn't any idea how to seek your forgiveness."

"Well— I can't— He can't— Goodness, I—" The thought of Oscar's ongoing misery, over something so simple, drove her to her feet and her feet to the door.

"I must go. I must."

"Where?" Mrs. Vancoller sounded alarmed.

"I must find Mr. Harris, immediately." She turned the knob, let in a swirl of bitterly cold air, and only then remembered her coat.

Jane must've collected her wrap from the hall tree, for there she stood, holding it for Ina to slip into. She tied her bonnet strings beneath her chin, lest her good hat blow away in the gusts.

"Goodbye." Ina rushed down the walk, resolved to go directly to Oscar's rented room. If all he needed was a bit of encouragement, a sign that she'd forgiven him, he needn't wait long.

Hank watched Ina go, all a flurry, and wondered if he should attend her. Perhaps, now, he understood a bit of what drove Archibald Abbott. Or maybe, it took a man in love to want the rest of the world to find as much contentment, as much happiness.

He looked to Jane as she returned to the seat at his side.

The day had been long without her. How would his life be better, to return at the end of the day with her there?

Her smile gave him a peek into that life.

"You've taken off your locket." He'd noticed, all at once, and the observation had flown the coop. "I'm sorry. I didn't mean to say anything."

Months ago, she'd shared a little about the significance of the locket. He definitely recalled her saying her mother didn't approve, and she'd taken to hiding it beneath her bodice to avoid conflict with her parent.

"My apologies, Jane, Mrs. Vancoller." He needed a

meal and a bath and bed. He needed to go. He rose, but Jane took his hand and tugged him back into his chair.

"Yes, I took it off. I don't need to wear it any longer." The revelation couldn't have surprised him more. Until now, he'd never seen her without it.

He did recall, with clarity, the thought that her disclosure of that story would be an intimacy of depth and meaning, one reserved for a new love.

"The locket contained physical remembrances of Lawrence. His photograph, a lock of his hair, and his engagement ring." She looked to her mother, with something akin to sadness in her eyes and expression. "I discovered I no longer need to wear the tokens."

He swallowed, hard. "Why not?"

She gathered his hand between hers, and despite the fact her mother sat with them, part of the conversation, she said simply, "I don't need things to remember those I loved." She shrugged. "Like the library, as it has outgrown the Tea Room, I find I don't mind if the books are elsewhere."

He squeezed her hand, holding fast and pleasure at her discovery fueling his confidence.

"You, my dear Thankful Murphy, have a heart made of gold."

Another memory, her words more believable this time. How he wanted to be as good as she believed him to be.

"You've opened new doors for me," she whispered. "And with those new doors, I have the confidence to let go of the past. I don't have to hold fast to those emblems, because I have you."

Chapter Twenty-Eight

When Ina left the Vancoller residence, she considered waiting until tomorrow to find Oscar. She could bathe, take care with her appearance, and find him at the store. If she delayed 'til tomorrow, she could recreate their initial meetings, and wear the blue he'd liked so well, despite the fact the frock was made for summer and winter's bitter temperatures had arrived.

But the thought of waiting, of adding one more sleepless night— and worse, delaying setting his mind at ease... she couldn't do it.

The man she'd come to love with all of her lonely heart needed her.

Mr. Murphy had said the Grocery Emporium had closed for the night, and yes, there the building stood, dark inside. Few residents remained on the streets in this weather.

Her cheeks stung with the cold. She quickened her pace and opted next for Mrs. Ihnken's boardinghouse. He might have gone elsewhere to eat, but she saw no sense wasting a moment seeking him at restaurants if he were in the boardinghouse dining room.

She nearly lost her courage, but he'd taught her a thing or two about confidence. She raised her chin, knocked on the door, and waited.

Old Mrs. Ihnken never smiled. She seldom had a kind word for anyone. But the woman stood guard of her home and her residents. "Good evening, Mrs. Ihnken. I've come on an errand, looking for Mr. Harris. It's most urgent."

"I can't afford to heat the outdoors. Come in, quick."

Ina fought a smile as she slipped in and the old woman closed the door. "He's in the dining room."

The aromas of roasted meat, gravy, potatoes, freshly baked yeast rolls... her mouth watered. She'd had a poor appetite for more than a week, gutted as she'd been by the harsh words Oscar had hurled.

Would he send her away, again?

He'd been clear, last she'd seen him. He'd ordered her to go, said hurtful things...

Wasn't a lifetime of happiness, and another chance, worth the risk?

"Don't just stand there," Mrs. Ihnken snapped. "You said it was an emergency."

"Oh, yes. An emergency." As she followed Mrs. Ihnken toward the dining room, a grandfather clock chimed the hour.

Six o'clock.

Before the great clock ceased its music, she found herself standing before a dining table with no fewer than eight residents enjoying their supper.

Oscar paused, a forkful of beef and potato, dripping a rich gravy, halfway to his mouth.

Mrs. Ihnken waited for Ina's emergency announcement, as did the other residents.

Ina panicked. Her heart fluttered against her ribs and a lightheaded spell nearly stole her balance. She opened her mouth, but couldn't find words.

This might well be her last chance.

"Miss Dimond." He set his fork on his plate, dropped his napkin beside the place setting, and stood, all in one smooth movement. "What is it?"

"An emergency. Come quickly." At a loss for any other way to speak to him without a curious audience, she ran for the door.

He followed, his stride sure and careful. His leg!— never again would she cause him the kind of damage and wear that had laid him low and caused them to quarrel.

At the doorway, he searched her face. No doubt, he wanted an explanation before he abandoned his hot supper.

He might be angry with her, so angry he'd never speak to her again.

She'd take her chances.

"Your coat, sir. You'll need your coat and hat."

As if Mrs. Ihnken was as curious an eavesdropper as people said she was, the woman brought his coat and hat. "Trouble at the pharmacy?"

"Oh, yes. A terribly ill patient. Doc Cheney needs the medicine right away."

White lies would easily trip her up. All it would take to lose Mrs. Ihnken's favor was her curiosity and

Dr. Cheney in the same room...

"You have your keys?" Mrs. Ihnken blocked the exit.

"My keys?" Oscar blinked.

"Your keys. To the Emporium. And your medicine cabinets."

He patted his pockets. "My keys. Yes."

"Off you go, then." The woman cracked the door and nearly pushed them both through the opening and shut it faster than anticipated.

Oscar took her arm and walked them toward the store, his pace too quick for his leg's comfort. At the corner, he finally slowed. "Tell me about this emergency."

The moment of truth. Or, more accurately, the fib that had taken him away from his hot supper. The fib that might end their association forever.

"The patient is very ill. Morose and grouchy. Severe trouble sleeping."

"That does sound serious."

She shivered. "It's terribly serious. Between fits of anger and horrors, he needs a cure."

"Only one thing I can think of will cure all that." He drew a little nearer and lamplight from a window glanced off his pale hair.

The man was exceptional.

He'd shown her more kindness— that Saturday morning of the festival aside— than she'd known in years.

"What is it? You have an elixir?"

"I do. I have just the thing."

Thus far, he played along, though they no longer

had an audience. A good sign, indeed. Some things needed saying, and she wasn't in the mood to be rushed. With the temperatures falling fast and dark clouds blocking the light from the moon, neither of them would tolerate remaining out of doors for long.

"Very well," she told him as she took his arm. "This way."

She let him set the pace, and when he walked quickly enough she worried for his flesh where it met his prosthesis, she asked if they might slow. "This cold has bothered my rheumatism. I must slow."

She'd not fooled him, but he didn't argue.

By the time they reached her home, she'd nearly frozen clear through. She fumbled with the key in the lock, at last surrendering the key to him and his nimble fingers.

Once inside, she lit a lamp and he saw to the oil-burning stove in the parlor. She shut the doors into other rooms, to trap the heat.

Then nothing remained but the unvarnished truth. "I'm the patient with the devastating emergency."

"Oh? I thought that was me. I'd hoped you'd come to my rescue."

She chuckled, giving away her nervousness. "Would you come, had you known?"

"Yes, ma'am." He removed his hat, lifted it as if they'd passed on the street. "Tell me true, Miss Dimond. Did my malevolent behavior spoil all chances for your association?"

Real concern lined his handsome face. As if he honestly feared he'd lost her.

He tossed his hat onto the sofa, then set to work

on the buttons of his overcoat. All the while, his eyes remained on hers.

"No, sir. Nothing is spoiled."

"Then listen to what I should've said aloud, long ago. The day I followed you to the park, when you'd told me, and everyone within sound of your voice, that you loved me—"

Oh, no. This? She cringed and covered her face.

His gentle hands settled on hers, easing them away from her face. "I want to see your eyes when I tell you I knew from that moment we sat in the park, side by side, that I love you."

"You did?"

"I did."

"Why didn't you say something?" How their journey would've been different. They'd have wasted far less time. They'd have enjoyed far more laughter and fewer tears.

"If memory serves, we discussed other topics of conversation."

"You told me jealousy was a form of insanity."

"Yes, Ina. You'd have to be insane to choose me."

"Do you believe this, still?" He'd been adamant that terrible Saturday morning.

"It's a difficult belief to change."

He'd finished unbuttoning his coat. He'd removed his gloves and put them in his coat pocket.

Feeling brave, emboldened by his admission, and requiring a method of showing him the truth of her words, she removed her gloves, and stowing them away, slipped her hands inside his coat, and around his middle. She stepped into his embrace, and rested her head against his shoulder.

"Once, at a time of high emotion, I told you I loved you, but the timing and setting left much to be desired. Allow me to repeat the sentiment now. I've thought of little else since that morning when you refused my care—"

One of his hands soothed her shoulders. "I'm sorry, Ina."

"Thank you, but please, let me finish. I love you, Oscar Harris. My affection and love are not temporary."

"I threw a glass bottle."

"You were hurting."

"Don't make excuses for me. You don't intend to run for the hills, do you?"

"Never."

"That's good, because you've become the most important person in my life."

His confessions of love and sweet words of commitment soothed rattled nerves and the sleeplessness she'd not been able to shake. "Say it again."

"You are the most important person in my life." He kissed her forehead.

She straightened, and met him halfway for a kiss that awakened hope and dreams of forever.

"What now? I've never known someone like you."

"I want permission to court you."

She chuckled. "Courtship. Aren't we too old for that?"

"I'm not too old to go courting, and you certainly are not."

"I've never been courted before."

"My reasoning, precisely."

"Jane! There you are." Ann Abbott waved from her favorite table near the window of the Tea Room.

Jane felt like a mouse, cornered by a cat.

She'd safely avoided Ann for the better part of two weeks, since that awful morning when she'd fallen apart at the hitching post.

Somewhere, midst the nightmares in the early hours after pulling the children to safety, Jane had realized that Ann had been beside her in the street asking questions... then Jane ran for the children, and Ann...? Disappeared? Left? Watched from a distance? Wandered off to harass someone else?

The more Jane considered the possibilities, the angrier she had become, until she determined to avoid Ann until she'd mastered her emotions.

"Where have you been?" Ann took advantage of the fact she was the only guest in the Tea Room at the moment. She opened her arms, expecting an embrace.

Setting aside their differences, Jane greeted Ann. "I've been busy."

"But the Tea Room! And you won the contest, and the lease is yours. Aren't you over the moon?"

Actually, no...

"I understand you have a new romance." Ann's cat-in-the-cream smile made her seem even more the predator. "Mayor Abbott and I are delighted you two discovered each other. We knew you'd be perfect together, that you'd be the right fit, and what did I tell you?"

"I don't recall. Did you tell me something?"

Ann's excessive cheer mellowed. "I believe I told you those little boys needed a mother, and that you'd be a stabilizing influence on their busy little bodies."

Jane had no recollection of that conversation. "It's lovely to see you. I must be going— I need to collect the invoices from the kitchen."

"Oh, goodness. You can't go yet! We have the real estate next door to discuss."

Jane's temper ran short where Ann was concerned. The woman's sense of entitlement rubbed Jane's sensibilities raw.

From the moment she'd learned she'd 'won' the dubious honor of paying the overpriced lease, Jane had been less than anxious to make the arrangement permanent. She had a clear idea of what she wanted to have happen with Hank's storage room, and leasing it for herself, moving walls, and extending her Tea Room's offerings weren't part of that plan.

"I've given the arrangement a good deal of thought." Ann set down her fountain pen, upon an array of colorful Thanksgiving greeting cards. Sheaves of wheat, pumpkins, festively dressed maidens and scarecrows decorated the fronts, with harvest wishes and sentiments of gratitude.

Ann wove through the tables and, speaking heavily with her hands, described her plan to expand the Tea Room to best seat large groups, incorporate the library near the front window where it had been situated during the Harvest Festival, and mentioned Hank's storage only in passing.

"He'll remove his storage to a warehouse, naturally, so you might make good use of this quality real estate."

Jane took a moment to gather herself. "Why, Mrs. Abbott, are you so interested in what I do with my business?"

"Why, because I adore your Tea Room. It's so cozy. And an ideal place to meet, now that the weather has turned and gathering outside is no longer an option."

"I'd not planned to address this subject today, but my mind is made up. I will not expand the Tea Room."

"You... what?" Ann gaped, a most unbecoming expression.

"I will not expand the Tea Room."

"But— but you wanted to. Just weeks ago, you agreed that enlarging was necessary, to accommodate the larger clubs."

"I believe, Ann, that that plan was yours all along. You wanted my establishment to be larger."

Ann's eyes narrowed. She fell silent for a long moment, then, assuming her stiffest posture, folded her arms tight against her chest. "Of course, I wanted your place to be large enough. You asked me, as president of several clubs, to meet with you, here, petitioning me to bring the clubs, and our rental fees, to your establishment. Do you not remember that unseasonably hot day in August, when we sat right here?"

"Yes, I do recall."

"What happened?"

"I've done a good deal of thinking. And I've come

to the realization that the Tea Room is best suited, as designed, to meet the needs of small groups. One woman who stops for a rest and refreshment. A pair of women, who meet to pass a pleasant hour together. That is why I established the Tea Room, and that's how I want it to stay."

"But—" Ann opened her mouth and closed it again. "But you need the money the clubs bring, especially the larger ones with a budget for meeting rooms."

"I did. I'm less concerned now."

Ann, who'd never been happy unless at the center of all the newest of topics of conversation, who enjoyed being the one to pass along juicy tidbits, abandoned her angst. "Why? What has happened?"

"I'll tell you what has happened: Hank Murphy has invested a tidy sum of money on bringing necessities into the valley in advance of winter storms. He deserves the privilege of renting the store between us for storage."

"The Abbott Brick Block is not a warehouse at the depot." She sounded incensed. "We are the best of addresses, for the best of businesses. You won the competition, and thus you will have that additional floor space to expand, to increase your income, to make a good deal of positive change for our community. Just think what you'll manage to do for the women of Mountain Home."

Jane pitied Mr. Abbott. The man must never have a moment's peace. Did Ann ever listen to what people had to say, and accept their decisions without her own agenda?

"In the days and weeks I've been away from my business," Jane told Ann, I've had a significant shift in my beliefs. I'd thought, while here every day, that the clubs were all about the people, the members... and now I realize that the clubs don't matter to me nearly as much as the individual people do."

Mrs. Abbott seemed ready to bolt for the door... or perhaps to launch back into her tirade.

Was Jane the first person, ever, to tell Ann no?

"You do realize, don't you," Ann stated in her imperial tone, "that without expansion into the adjacent real estate, you will not only lose the paid accounts of my largest clubs, but you stand to lose the library? Do you not recollect that the library was removed from your premises because of your lack of adequate space?"

"Yes, ma'am. I do recall."

"Do you not remember your hysteria, in this room, when you learned one of the library titles had to be retired, due to damage?"

"My paradigm has shifted."

As if Ann couldn't grasp Jane's reasoning, or if she couldn't find a reason midst the madness, her expression carried disbelief. "Why?"

"I've discovered many new things in recent weeks. I've learned that I value my relationships with individuals more than I'd supposed." She'd also learned that she'd lost many precious opportunities because of her fear of losing those she loved. Change might not come quickly, but she'd already begun. A positive change, for the best of reasons.

"You're certain you won't change your mind?"

"I'm certain." Jane had never been more at peace

about any business decision. The sale of her engagement ring and gold locket— sans the contents, of course— would ensure her business could continue as designed for a few years, if she lived simply.

Now that Mama had become far more interested in spending time with the little Murphy boys, she spent less time in the shops, and less money on black bonnets.

Mrs. Abbott sniffed. "It grieves me to have to do this, but you've left me no choice. The Ladies' Library Association has determined, given our recent growth in membership and quantity of volumes in circulation, that, in the instance of your failure to cooperate—"

Failure? Failure to cooperate? That was rich, indeed.

"— we would lease the moderately sized second-story room at the end of the Abbott's Brick Block. The room is ideal, and the library will be open for several hours each week."

"What a wonderful idea." Jane was sincere in her compliment— but Ann puckered anyway.

"You're not supposed to like our alternatives."

"Please, Mrs. Abbott. Don't make plans based on my likes or dislikes. I'm only a library subscriber."

"Indeed."

To her immense relief, Jane discovered yet one more thing about herself. She'd held on so tightly to the books that represented a physical tie to Law's memory, that she'd spent an unnecessary amount of time in the past. The time had come to live in the present. And happily anticipate the future.

Chapter Twenty-Nine

Jane gathered the invoices and spoke quietly with Harriet in the kitchen. She'd been considering her options, especially now that she knew marriage was coming in her future. Perhaps she and Hank would have time to discuss those thoughts that night when he brought the children and came for supper.

Mama had been baking and roasting all day, planning on Jane's thirtieth birthday supper as a reason to bring her grandchildren-to-be into her home once more.

Jane hugged Harriet, and, opening the back door to the alley, was caught unaware. "Snow."

"What? On October 20?"

Sure enough, snow fell in huge flakes, without a hint of wind. The ground hadn't yet frozen, so the snow didn't stick to the dirt, but it had begun to gather with significance on the dried and frozen grass and other vegetation. Naked tree branches seemed painted white by an artist's brush.

The sky appeared white, though still daylight.

She ducked her head and walked close to the building to Hank's door. She knocked as a formality, and opened the Emporium's back door. Inside the shop smelled like new wood, fresh spices— cinnamon, nutmeg, and cloves— and male voices combined in laughter.

She found Oscar and Hank together, without a single person waiting for service.

Hank pulled her into his arms and squeezed. "I've missed you."

That made her smile. "I missed you, too, though it's been mere hours since I saw you last."

"Happy birthday," he whispered against her temple.

"Thank you."

As they stepped apart, she waved to Oscar, who sat on his stool on the far side of the U-shaped employee/owner side of the counter. "Good afternoon, Mr. Harris."

Broad smiles remained on the men's faces.

"Care to share in your happiness?"

"Indeed, I do." Hank slipped his arm about Jane's waist. "Go ahead, Harris."

"I'm honored to share that Miss Dimond has consented to become my wife." His happiness lit him from within. She'd never seen him so... *happy.*

"When is the blessed day?"

Both men laughed once more— giddy, nearly, and that made no sense.

"It's snowing, fellows. Snowing in late October, and you're laughing."

"Yes." Hank gestured to his business partner. "Moments ago, Mayor Abbott was in, his chest puffed out like a banty rooster, tooting his horn about the efforts he'd made to ensure the town's safety, come a blizzard."

"And you're laughing about this?" If an Abbott usurped her effort, she would be irritated.

"No. I sort of promised Abbott he could take credit as the town hero, if he gave me the storage room." Hank's statement trickled to a halt, as if he realized the subject of the contested real estate— the lease she'd won the right to— remained a source of contention between them.

Perhaps she ought to let him in on her plans.

"Last night, when I asked my bride-to-be to marry me, she agreed instantly, and set about choosing a date in the coming two weeks."

"That is fast." She knew Ina to be a woman of a calm disposition. If she were certain that she wanted to spend her life with Oscar Harris, then Jane had no objection to their happiness.

"Indeed. I told her we couldn't marry until we'd courted. We agreed to delay a few months."

Jane glanced at Hank. He'd been eager to wed her as soon as she'd consented. Had Harris given him ideas about courting her first? Given she'd wed not only a bachelor, but a full-sized family, perhaps courtship would be a grand idea. They'd be so busy with young children and one nearly-grown young man, they'd have next to no time to themselves.

"Now don't go getting any ideas, Miss Vancoller." Hank clasped his hands around her middle, cradling her against his chest.

She could've sighed and snuggled up, but the audience— even if he was Hank's business partner— felt uncomfortable.

"Have you set a date?" she asked Mr. Harris.

"We have. We're planning on Valentine's Day."

"I'm certain Miss Dimond is over the moon."

His chuckle and happiness radiated from him like sunlight and blue skies. "*I'm* over the moon."

"Come to dinner tonight," she invited on impulse. "You and Ina. She and my mother have become good friends, so I know she'll be at ease. The Murphys are joining us tonight too."

Hank cupped a hand about his mouth to stage whisper, "Today is my lovely lady's birthday."

"Happy birthday, Miss Vancoller."

"Thank you. Say you'll come to supper."

"I'll ask Ina, but I imagine she'll be delighted with the idea, storm or no storm."

Jane peered through the window to the snow that now, instead of coming down in silent, enormous flakes swept sideways on the breeze. The falling snow obscured her vision of the buildings on the opposite side of Main.

"I believe I'll scurry home before the weather worsens, and help Mama with dinner preparations. We plan to eat at six-thirty. We'll set a place for each of you."

Jane's thirtieth birthday quickly became one she'd remember forever— for all the best reasons. She'd never enjoyed a crowded dining room so much, nor had she laughed, and loved, and savored the nearness of the most important people in her life.

As she'd left the Emporium hours earlier, she'd remembered to extend an invitation to Harriet, bringing their total to eleven: six Murphys, two Vancollers, Mr. Harris and Miss Dimond, and Harriet McCormick.

She and Mother had extended the dining table as far as possible, brought in every spare chair in the house, and out of necessity, made a picnic spot in the arched doorway between the parlor and dining room for the smallest children.

As the family gathered with friends, they toasted the engagement of Mr. Harris and his bride-to-be, Miss Dimond. They toasted the storm as the inches piled up in haste, as Hank felt vindicated from those who disbelieved his winter warnings. They supped on a feast of well-prepared dishes that the Murphy men, from father down to the two-year-old complimented liberally.

With six adults and one thirteen-year-old (whom Hank allowed to have one watered-down glass) enjoying wine with their meal and laughter, they opened and savored all three bottles Oscar had brought along.

Somehow, in the course of the discussion of weddings, careful use of wintertime fuel and resources, the question arose about whether Hank and his brood would move in with the Vancollers when they married.

"We have ample room," Jane's mama insisted. "Four bedrooms upstairs means all five boys won't have to share."

"Will you be our grandma?" Russell had asked close to one hundred questions, each of which Hank did his best to answer. The little man was a thinker, and numerous worries stuck in his mind until they made sense.

"I do hope so," Mary Vancoller said in response. "Would you like that?"

"We don't have a grandma." Russ seemed to think about that. "Yes. You can be our grandma."

"What will you call me?" Mama took another sip of wine.

"Jimmy can't say Vancoller. I barely learned how to say it right. Austin yelled at me for saying Van Collie instead."

"Grandma Van?" Mama positively glowed under the promise of inheriting four grandchildren plus an extra that might as well be.

As the conversation continued, Jane found herself surprised how pleased Mama was with the promise of a house full of undisciplined children.

Jimmy abandoned his plate and rounded the table, headed for his papa, but upon noting "Grandma Van," he raised his arms and yelled "up!"

"Pick me up, *please.*"

"Up!"

Jane, feeling the cozy and relaxing effects of the wine, laughed with everyone else. They had their work cut out for them. Who'd have guessed she'd be a stepmother? If their father couldn't persuade them to

go to school— and stay there until class was dismissed—
how would she manage?

Nearly all mothers were home, working all day
long with a thousand and one chores and meal
preparation, food preservation, gardening, and sewing
to meet the family's needs.

Before she knew it, the conversation had turned
into a Murphy Family Council, centered around her role
as Hank's wife and the children's new stepmother.

An idea took root and grew amidst the laughter
and good-natured banter. "I've an idea," she told the
gathering, when at last a lull in the conversation
signaled her opportunity. "Harriet— how would you like
to continue as the manager of the Tea Room?"

She flushed and attempted to pass the attention
on by, the others wouldn't allow her to. "I suppose I
could. I've been handling it well enough in your
absence."

"Yes. Indeed." Jane lifted her glass in one more
toast.

"We'd not need to hire another. Our current help,
Jennie, does a splendid job."

Jane had watched the girl earlier that day and
been pleased.

"Don't you want to manage your own business?"
Hank finished the apple dumplings— Mary Vancoller's
prize-winning secret recipe, and upon discovering an
apple dessert had been selected for Jane's birthday
supper, had nearly swooned. "You worked diligently to
bring the business to fruition. Help me understand why
you're ready to leave it so soon."

Though she didn't consider Miss Dimond a

confidant— yet— and her husband-to-be was more connected to Hank than to herself, and the children she'd soon call her own were listening, she decided to answer. "Hear me out on this." She raised her wine glass by way of explanation.

"Before I knew you well, I said things like 'these children need a nanny' and I believed I'd never have children. Now that I'm inheriting several, I imagine I'll fret over their wellbeing, especially if I'm at the Tea Room. The more I consider the possibilities, the more I want to be with them, to tend and to care for them. I want to be their mother."

The commotion quieted, especially among the children. Even young Jimmy turned away from Grandma Van's jet buttons he loved to twist and count, to pay attention.

"Miss Jane," Clyde said into the almost-silence, "is Mama." As if the connection were utterly simple in his mind.

"You promise?" Russell stood, a dinner roll in one hand and a tin soldier in the other. A few minutes ago, he'd built a fort out of the bread basket. "You promise you'll be our mama?"

Promises, especially to children, were a delicate thing. To break a promise of this magnitude would cause troubles far greater than any they'd faced so far.

She wanted to explain that if she wed their father, and when that occurred, then she'd be a mama who'd love them forever. She met Hank's eye, desperate for guidance.

"Promise." Russ demanded. "Pinkie promise, like you did with my bestest knife ever, even though you knew that knife wasn't mine after all but was your best knife and I stole it from you and I'd been a naughty boy and I deserved a spanking and to stand in the corner for a whole hour."

Jane tried hard not to laugh. Between the alcohol and the quirky child, she almost laughed at his explanation. The boy held out his pinkie, ready for the solemn oath handshake.

Not a promise she intended to make lightly. "Hank?"

He nodded, trusting her with a certainty that moved her. This dear man, who'd been so distrustful when they'd met, who'd been full of pain and doubt and memories of a woman who'd not been a good mother.

These little boys made her want to be good, to make up for the years they'd gone without the influence of a mother's love.

The whole family— friends included— watched with solemn respect as she pinkie promised Russell she'd be his mama and love him forever.

"That means you must marry me." Hank kissed her temple, despite their audience.

She rather liked how a little wine increased his affectionate side. "I have every intention of marrying you."

"How 'bout right now? Everyone's here, aren't we?"

"Now?" Jane blinked, startled.

"Sure. Why not?"

"Uh— a marriage license, for one. And a minister." She didn't want a Justice of the Peace.

"Who else would you want present?" Hank seemed

determined.

Why not? He owned her heart, and she loved him with a completeness that felt utterly right. She'd regretted a long engagement with Law, would have preferred to have wed him and been widowed, than to have lost him before the wedding.

She looked around the table at her closest friends. Harriet, who'd been with her from the beginning.

Hank's friend and partner, Oscar.

Ina, who would be Oscar's wife.

And Mother. Her seventy-year-old mother, who would love more than anything to see her daughter wedded.

"You can't mean right now. In a snowstorm?"

He shrugged, confident and serene. "Why not? My preparation for a snowy winter is what brought us together."

"That it did."

"Yay!" Russell jumped up and down on the balls of his feet, shouting in joy. Soon Clyde and Jimmy followed, jumping and shouting "Mama, Mama, Mama!"

Jane shook her head. "Now what? It's terrible out there. I can't imagine Pastor Gilbert wants to come out in this weather."

Hank, in his gentle and kind way, took her face in his hands and kissed one cheek, then the other. "Jane, will you marry me?"

"You're asking, now?" Happy tears filled her eyes. Jane Vancoller did *not* cry!

"I am. How about tonight. We've had a celebration meal. Your mama's here. I'll never be more certain than

I am right now that you're the woman I want to spend every day of my life loving."

"Hank..." She covered his hand with her own. She loved him. Far more than she'd realized.

"Mrs. Vancoller?" Hank turned to her, and Jane watched the silent exchange between the two people she loved most. Mama's happiness was real, vibrant, and palpable.

"You have my permission, and my blessing." Mama hugged Jimmy tight. The little boy had been on and off Grandma Van's lap enough in the last fifteen minutes to make Mama dizzy.

Hank rose. He bent and kissed Jane's forehead. "Looks like we need a marriage license and a minister."

"You're going out in this?"

"Yes, ma'am. I have a hankering to make you my wife."

Chapter Thirty

In some ways, Hank Murphy viewed Thanksgiving Day, eighteen hundred and eighty-seven as his first Thanksgiving.

The past year had brought him to a place where he was ready to embrace Thanksgiving and all it meant. Part of the deal included his readiness to *feel* Thanksgiving. As a man with meager sentimentality, this surprised him.

Perhaps the surprise came along with the blessings that had flooded his life in the past months... and a realization that gratitude went hand in hand with a thankful heart.

Who'd known, when he removed his family to Mountain Home, Colorado, that he'd find more than a home in the mountains; he'd found the woman he loved, and together, they'd provide that home and safety he'd always craved. She'd helped him provide that security for his sons.

Though if she heard him refer to the boys as his,

and not theirs, she'd have a thing or two to say about it. With marriage had come her wholehearted embrace of his family. His much younger half-brother and his four sons had never been so well cared for.

Life was good. Business at T.A. Murphy's Grocery Emporium and O. Harris's Fancy Pharmacy had done a brisk business through the mayor's Harvest Festival and well beyond.

Snow had a way of making people anxious to prepare.

As he'd expected, that first snowstorm, a little over a month ago on his new wife's birthday, 20 October, had brought a rash of folks in from all over the Mountain Home Valley to ensure they had the necessities squirreled away on their homesteads.

Jane, his wife, his partner, the woman he loved with all of his heart, had followed through with her promise to be a mama to their boys. She'd thrived at home— her choice, but so good for the kids. Many pinkie promises had been made and kept, and with each one, the boys found their ability to trust and follow and believe came easier.

Now, on Thanksgiving Day, the wintry weather had remained severe. True to his inkling, true to his speculation, the inches of snow continued to pile higher and deeper. Hank imagined the time would come, before spring, that the railroads through the mountain passes would lose the battle against the wind and snowfall.

The ghosts of his failure had mostly passed, and he had Jane to thank for that.

Sweet Jane, who believed in him, stood by him,

and made him want to be the man with a heart of gold—the fellow she'd seen in him from the beginning.

He joined the ladies in the dining room as they set the table for eight, with a picnic blanket on the floor for the littlest ones. Much like Jane's birthday dinner that first stormy October night, they'd invited the same group of close friends to celebrate Thanksgiving with them.

Even now, Oscar Harris and his bride-to-be, Ina Dimond, had arrived early enough to contribute to the work of the time-consuming meal.

Hank's mother-in-law, elderly Mary Vancoller, descended the stairs in a blue wool gown that emphasized the blue of her eyes.

"Mama!" Jane's voice wasn't a scold, precisely, but neither was it filled with joy. "What is this? Blue? You're wearing blue?"

"Mind your manners, Jane."

"But why? Why did you set aside your weeds?"

"It's time."

That's all she said on the subject, leaving him to wonder what had gone on in the sweet old woman's heart and head.

Hank couldn't help chuckling a bit. He made sure his back was to the ladies. He wasn't dumb.

He finished the job he'd been assigned, to gather the chairs from all over the house, upstairs and down, so everyone over eight could have a place at the table.

It seemed his mother-in-law had set aside her widow's weeds for the grand occasion. Yet one more reason to be thankful. He'd never expected he'd see the day.

By the time their last guest arrived— Miss Harriet McCormick, the unmarried woman, as reliable as could be, who'd taken over as Tea Room manager when Jane Mary Murphy— he did like how well Jane Mary went with Murphy— had determined all on her own that her little boys needed a mama and that meant leaving the work of her previous life to someone else.

He'd never admit it, at least not to Jane, that her decision pleased him deep down inside where his old heartaches used to live. The little boys who'd been scarred by a mother whose affection had been missing, her natural love for her offspring so broken she'd not cared one way or the other about them. But children proved resilient, and this Thanksgiving season, he'd had more than a little bit to be grateful for, and Jane Mary Vancoller Murphy tended to top the list.

Promptly at one o'clock (his wife and mother-in-law were nothing if not uncommonly talented in the kitchen and prompt), family and dear friends were called together from the parlor, the kitchen, and the back steps where the little ones had decided that long icicles needed to come down for a sword fight.

In the past month since he'd married into the family, his mother-in-law had deferred to him, teaching him, he realized, how to be the man of the house.

"Hank," she instructed. "The tradition among the Vancollers is the man of the house does two important things on Thanksgiving Day. He asks the Lord's blessings upon our meal, and he carves the turkey. Are you ready for your responsibilities?"

"Yes, ma'am."

She'd also assigned him the head of the table.

From the night he'd wed Jane in this room, young Pastor Kenneth Gilbert and his wife rustling up a marriage license before joining them for a birthday celebration he'd never forget, that chair had been his. With seamless effort, Jane had taken over the role of Mother, leaving the pleasure of grandmama's role to Mary. He'd never seen the old lady so content and so— *happy*.

Hank did as was expected of him. He led the family in prayer, including their guests, the closest of friends who'd been present to celebrate Jane's birthday and their sudden marriage.

Jane and Mary had taught him that new important truth; a person could choose their family. The ties of friendship and love were often stronger than the ties of blood, and for folks like Oscar and Ina, that blessing proved to be an important one. As for dear Harriet McCormick. Dutiful, kind, long-suffering, and the most loyal of employees— maybe one day the love of her life would surprise her, and sweep her away. In the meanwhile, she rather enjoyed the boys calling her Auntie Harriet.

With everyone seated at the heavily laden table, the dishes hot and fragrant and smelling of abundance and plenty, Hank did as he was told and asked a blessing on the bounty. Once he started thanking God for the blessings his family had benefited from, he discovered the list had grown so long a man's food could grow cold and his sons (at least the two-year-old) could help himself to the bread basket before he said amen.

Hank carved the turkey. Steam rose from the

tender bird, and the meat melted in his mouth (don't tell Mary he snitched; even golden sons-in-law can lose favor for misbehaving at the supper table). Dishes were passed, the children served, and the laughter started.

Hank wasn't one to make much of a man's wife seated at the foot of the table where he could admire her from a distance. He made it clear from the day they wed that she was to sit beside him. If the little ones needed help, why, that's what Grandma Van and Uncle Elias were for. Mama and Papa could help too, but only if they managed to glance away from each other long enough to take care of business before the little fella figured it out on his own.

Oscar brought the wine again to the holiday feast. Four bottles this time, as three hadn't gone quite far enough. He'd poured the first round during dinner, and by the time the dishes were cleared and everyone had taken to visiting and sipping, he poured seconds and thirds. Elias, who'd convinced them all at nearly fourteen he could handle his without a goodly portion of water, tried to wheedle a second glass out of Oscar, but Hank noticed and put an end to that attempt.

"If you want a second piece of pie, Elias, you go right ahead. You'll have one glass of wine on Thanksgiving, and no more."

"'Til when?" The challenge in the boy's voice contained more wistfulness than anything. In such a hurry to grow up.

"'Til I say so."

"My pa said the same thing to me." Granny Van told Elias. "Seems like yesterday."

"My pa also had an expectation that we come to

the Thanksgiving dinner table with an idea in mind of what we were most thankful for. I've been thinking about that, myself, and I'd like to start. Everybody be thinking of what you're thankful for, as it'll be your turn soon enough."

With that, Granny Van (Mama, Mary, and mother-in-law) folded her hands in her lap. "Today," said she, "I am most grateful for lost loved ones. I miss my husband most on days like today, so as my gift to him, I put aside my widow's weeds. I choose happiness and love. I have lots of little boys in this house to love."

Hanks' eyes filled with suspicious moisture, almost as full as his belly.

Mary, the mother-in-law he'd come to love as if she were his own, nudged Elias. For a moment, Hank thought his kid brother would refuse to participate. Most boys his age had a hard time coming up with something to express gratitude for.

"Me?" Elias set down his empty wine glass. "I'm grateful on this Thanksgiving Day for the best sister-in-law ever."

Happy tears wet her cheeks. She hugged her mama and then she hugged Hank, who wasn't ready to let her go.

The little boys gave more predictable answers. Thankful for snow. And a warm coat. Jimmy was thankful for his horse— nothing more than a stick with reins and a head fashioned of fabric and wool stuffed inside, but he'd ridden that horse clear to Texas and back on a cattle drive, and he loved that horse with all of his young heart.

Oscar and Ina, as one might expect, were grateful

for each other and the courtship that they carried on in the months before their wedding. The two were so in love, Hank wondered why Oscar was so determined to wait for Valentine's Day before he married the woman, but some subjects, he'd learned, were too private to go around prying the lid off.

Harriet expressed gratitude for good friends and the end of a season. Sweet elements, thoughtful elements. Like Harriet.

Probably because Mary in her wisdom designed it as such, Hank and Jane were last to speak up and share the gratitude in their hearts.

"Would you like to go first, dear wife? Or me. It's up to you."

She held his gaze with so much tenderness, so much love, it felt like one of the boys had caught him unawares and pounced on his chest, knocking the wind from his lungs.

What a gift. What a blessing! The faithful love of a good woman. A man couldn't ask for anything more... even if that something more was the faithful love of a good mama for his boys. So he said precisely that, sharing with those closest to them the tender truths in his heart. "The faithful love of a good wife has chased the demons from my past and opened new views I hadn't known were there. I love you, Jane Murphy. I love you with all of my heart, and I want to make more memories with you."

Jane sniffed and blotted curious moisture from her eyes with her napkin, because everyone in the household knew that Jane Vancoller Murphy did *not* cry. "Today, on Thanksgiving, and on every other day of the year, I'm thankful for second chances."

She had that look in her eye again, that expression that told him she still believed him to be in possession of a heart of gold, that he could do no wrong, and that his reasons were always pure and as wholesome as a man's could be.

What a lucky man— but no, luck had nothing to do with it.

He took his wife's hand in his own, kissed her knuckles, then kissed her lips, even if a kiss like that made the young ones moan and fuss. "No kissing!"

"Yes," Hank insisted. "We're of a mind that we'll kiss in front of you every single day. You know why? You need to know that your Pa and your Mama love each other (they'd chosen to call her such, starting with Clyde. If they'd wanted to call her Miss Jane or just Jane, she would've gladly accepted their choice, but Mama it was)."

Jane chuckled, that soft sweet sound that reminded him all over again how very blessed he was. God had smiled on his family, had led them out of dark times and pain into a place where they'd found the missing piece of their hearts. Holding Jane's gaze as tenderly as he held her hand, he reminded his children of one important truth. "Parents who love God and love each other will always have room enough in their hearts for all of their children, all of their neighbors, and every friend in need."

"Amen," whispered Granny Van. Hank rather liked that name. She might have started as Grandma Van, back when she'd claimed the boys as her own grandchildren, but Clyde, in his wisdom, had shortened the mouthful to Granny Van.

"Amen," Jane echoed.

Hank's heart, filled to overflowing with love and comfort and warmth, took in each member of his family— including the friends that filled the extra chairs and expanded the size of their family to exactly right. "Thank you," he told them all, including the Lord in that simple prayer. "Thank you for making our home and our family a place filled with laughter and sunlight and safety, in the middle of a storm. I can't think of anywhere else I'd rather be."

Jane squeezed his hand. This time, she leaned nearer to him and kissed his cheek.

"*No kissing.*" Russell had no patience for such things. But one day, he'd be a young man and some lovely young lady would capture his attention and he'd whistle a different tune.

Until then, Hank determined, he'd be the best example of how a man treats a woman, how he showed her respect and patience and gratitude.

For in a family was the best place of all, to learn how to live.

The End

Please *share* this book with a friend.
Lending is enabled on this digital book.

Please *recommend* this book.
*Please share your thoughts on this book
with friends.*

Please post a *review*.
*Reviews from readers make all the difference to
those browsing and buying, as well as to writers.
Please take a moment and leave an honest review— as
few as 20 words will do.*

EASY REVIEW LINK:

www.kristinholt.com/review-unmistakably-yours

*One Quick Click ~ makes it easy to review this title,
anywhere!*
includes *all* eBook stores where this title is sold,
& Goodreads

Dear Reader,

(I've prepared a special website page for you, containing this same information— with the links— so you can locate any of the historical information that interests you: **www.KristinHolt.com/history**

Note: capitals and lower case letters in this web address (url) are irrelevant, but very important to spell Kristin with two i's and no e's; *Kristin is "e-free".*)

I enjoy writing books set in the 1880s—a time where people were pitted against some of the greatest natural weather disasters—and thus able to show their strengths. This title, *Unmistakably Yours*, was a perfect opportunity, as the many authors in this series each wrote a book focused on Thanksgiving Day (and all that this holiday means to Americans) to revisit my favorite fictional city—Mountain Home (and series: *Holidays in Mountain Home*).

Thanksgiving has a special place in my heart. "Thanksgiving", as Americans know it, is unique— though it began as a Christian celebration within a Christian colony in the New World, the United States became a true "melting pot" with immigrants coming from all over the world, and of many different religions. To Americans (United States citizens), Thanksgiving is an opportunity to reflect upon the abundance and gifts of the past year. As a Christian, I see Thanksgiving as an opportunity to express thanksgiving to God for His infinite blessings.

Beyond Thanksgiving, this novel includes a look at Harvest Celebrations/Festivals, and their place in American history. In the Western United States, these small-town festivals included many of the same events and entertainments I've drawn upon, and many more.

As mentioned in the foreword, the nineteenth century definition of "love-making"— including "lovers" was very widely used as a ***G-rated term*** that simply meant those who have a romantic attachment, and those who are falling in love and courting.

Other historical tidbits you may have noticed within this title:
>   Victorian Folding Chairs
>   Speaking Trumpet
>   Running water in the new 1886-1887-built Abbott's Brick Block
>   Screen doors
>   Lemon Ice Recipe
>   Tea Rooms
>   Starter Pistols
>   Coca Wine
>   A Victorian Apple Dumpling Recipe
>   Social Clubs for Women
>   And Social Clubs for Men

I've discovered numerous newspaper clippings that elaborate on the types of clubs women formed, that helped form the Ladies' Library Association that once met in Jane's Tea Room. Watch for an article to be published on my site, that I'll include a link to within my *Unmistakably Yours* page. I'll update this page for everything related to this title, *Unmistakably Yours*. More blog post articles, more historical tidbits, more details that help to set the stage and enrich your reading experience of all titles set at the same time.

Have you discovered online price converters (how expensive was something at the time of your book)? For example, I had to look up how much to have Hank assume the ruined wedding cake was worth in 1887's dollars. Having paid for one daughter's wedding thus far, I know how much cakes can cost. This "inflation calculator" has proved wildly helpful to me as an author and as a reader. Who knew that Hank's $4 in 1887 is comparable to $110.76 today. True, I paid a whole lot more than that for my daughter's cake, but my low-balling, I admit, was part of illustrating that Hank's a clueless man. (How would he know how much wedding cakes cost?)

Please visit my ever-growing cache of articles that help to fill out the setting and historical background for *Unmistakably Yours*. Many blog articles are already cataloged there, and I'll add more as they become available.

Remember you'll find an easy link to everything here: **www.KristinHolt.com/history.**

Kristin

All Stories in the Thanksgiving Books & Blessings Collection
(beginning with earliest time setting)

GONE TO TEXAS by Caryl McAdoo, full length

GATEWAY TO THE WEST by Susette Williams, novella

TRAIL TO CLEAR CREEK by Kit Morgan, full length

HEART AND HOME by P. Creeden, novella

NO TURNING BACK by Lynette Sowell, novella

DAUGHTER OF DEFIANCE by Heather Blanton, novella

UNMISTAKABLY YOURS by Kristin Holt, full length

ESTHER'S TEMPTATION by Lena Nelson Dooley, full length

A Peek at Lena Nelson Dooley's
Esther's Temptation

Please enjoy the first chapter of Lena Nelson Dooley's title in *Thanksgiving Books & Blessings* Collection One: *Esther's Temptation*

Chapter One

August – Deep in the heart of Texas

1896. How could it be 1896? When Jac Andrews started this quest, he figured he'd be married with children by this time in his life. All the years had passed without achieving his goals—both of them.

He sure hoped that was Denton, Texas, up ahead and not a mirage. His head ached from the bright sunlight and long hours. He'd been in the saddle so long he felt as if it were fused to the seat of his pants. Pants he'd worn until they could almost stand up by themselves. Finally, he could have a bath, clean clothes, a shave, a hot meal, and a real bed. In that order.

But the long ride had been worth it. He was bone weary, but he could sense that indefinable excitement he always felt when he was about to catch his prey. Peter Graham and his daughter had to be just ahead. He'd been chasing this gang for too many years— through hard winters, mostly mild summers, and he'd seen a lot of the territory in the United States. But this was the farthest south they'd ventured. Denton, Texas, was the end of the line. For him and for the Grahams— in more ways than one.

As he approached, the haze hovering on the horizon solidified into a nice enough town, but Jac hoped it wouldn't take long to bring the Grahams to justice. He wanted to get on with his life, and he couldn't until he had finished this one thing. Although he was only thirty years old, he felt ancient. He'd seen enough of the seamy side of life to age him beyond his years. Criminals and their evil deeds had hardened him so much he barely knew who he was anymore. Certainly not the idealistic young man who became a Deputy U.S. Marshal all those years ago. He didn't even know where he belonged. Maybe when he finished this final arrest, he could find out. For the first time in over ten years, he could have a life of his own.

But he didn't dare take his mind off his prize. This arrest had to come before anything else. He wouldn't saddle any woman with a man who was hardly ever be home. He would really retire from hunting criminals and maybe find some kind of business he'd enjoy. He had plenty of money stashed away to buy or start one. He didn't use much money while he'd been trying to catch this slippery weasel, who preyed on unsuspecting, upstanding citizens.

Because of his obsession to catch Peter Graham and his daughter, he was no longer a marshal. The U.S. Marshal in Washington, D.C., had given him a choice, give up this quest or turn in his badge. Jac knew his boss thought the ultimatum would make him back down. With great reluctance, he'd removed the star with the circle around it, the badge that made him official. Since then, he'd been on his own as he followed the trail of this *confidence man* and his family.

Good thing he'd saved so much of his pay over the years, and his needs were negligible. A pile of his money remained safe in a bank back East, waiting for him to get to the point where he could start living a real life. He wouldn't have to worry about finances while he established himself. That thought brought a stiff smile to his face.

Sometimes, he'd been so close to catching the Grahams he could almost taste victory. But he always arrived after they left the vicinity. Then it would take him a while to find their trail again. They committed crimes in such a way that no one could prove they did it. Finally, Jac figured out there had to be *two* girls. And they must be identical twins. It was the only way they could've pulled off so many of those seemingly perfect crimes. But Jac knew there was no such thing. This family needed to be brought to justice, and he was the man to do that very thing.

Jac stopped his horse in front of the first hotel he

came to. He looked up at the second-story windows. They even sported curtains. This must be a higher-class establishment than most of the places where he stayed during this long quest. After tying the reins of his mount to the hitching rail, he removed his saddlebags and slung them across his shoulder.

He stepped up on the high wooden sidewalk without bothering to go down to where steps would've made it easier. His legs were long enough, and he was too tired to go even that much farther. The steady cadence of his boots on the boards, and the jingle of his spurs, accompanied him through the door. He wanted to remove his traveling gear and put on clean clothes. His whole body itched, because it had been so long since he'd worn clean garments.

A young man sat behind the hotel's front desk, writing in an open book. His head bent forward, and Jac realized the man didn't even notice anyone was around until he dropped his saddlebags on the counter.

"I'd like a room."

The man looked startled as he slammed the book shut and glanced up. He stood and pulled the hotel register from a shelf under the counter. "Do you want a room that looks out on the street or one in the back where it's quieter?"

Jac wished he could say, *In the back.*

He would enjoy the quiet. He knew how loud some towns became when the cowboys came in to drink and blow off steam.

Of course, this was pretty far South. Maybe most of the people around here were farmers and ranchers, not rowdies wanting to let loose and have what they called fun. He needed to be able to see who came and went. That was the only way he could keep a lookout for any of the Grahams.

"In the front would be fine." Jac reached for his wallet. "Do I need to pay now?"

"How long you staying?" The man smiled up at Jac who stood several inches taller.

"I'm not really sure. How about if I pay you for a week, and we'll see if I need to be here longer?"

The man pushed the register book toward Jac, handed him a pen, and moved the inkwell closer to him. "That would be fine, Mr ..." He watched as Jac wrote his name. "...Andrews. That'll be five dollars for the week." He turned around and retrieved a key from the numbered cubbyhole behind him. "You're in room three."

"Where's the best place to get a bath, a shave, and a meal?"

Esther Brians put the finishing touches on her upswept, Gibson Girl hairstyle when Allen knocked on the door of her apartment. She shoved one last hairpin into her hair to anchor it before she answered the door.

"I'm coming." Thick carpet muffled her footsteps as she crossed the parlor. She opened the door and hugged her brother. "Why didn't you just use your key?"

Allen returned her hug, then stood back. "I only kept the key because you insisted. It's a good idea for me to check on things for you when you're out at the farm, since you're living here alone. But I won't use it for any other reason. You deserve your privacy." He glanced around the room that had been Marie's home before she and Allen married. He had spent a lot of time here visiting with his sister and later courting Marie. "I like what you've done with the place. It really expresses your personality."

"Thank you, kind sir." Esther gave a low curtsey. She and her brother had enjoyed a playful relationship all their lives.

"Are you ready?" Allen picked up her jacket from the claret-colored velvet settee. After helping her into the wrap, he opened the door, and they proceeded down the stairs into the warm, August twilight.

Esther placed her hand in the crook of his arm as they walked across the street to the hotel. "It was really nice of Marie to offer to keep Gerald and Linda's children so we could take them out to dinner for their anniversary."

"She loves those two little ones. And I do, too. They come over to our house a lot, since we live so close."

When they entered the lobby of the hotel, Esther glanced around. She didn't come here often, but she always liked the friendly, yet elegant, atmosphere. The gaslights around the walls gave a warm glow to the plush carpeting and matching wallpaper. Esther liked that they used a lot of potted plants in the decor. It enhanced the sense of opulence ... and freshness. When she came to the hotel, it made her feel that Denton was as cosmopolitan as Chicago or even New York City.

A man descending the wide staircase that

dominated the room drew Esther's attention. He stood taller than any other man she had ever seen. Although his body looked lean, muscles rippled under his shirt and slacks. His dark, clean-shaven face sported a neat mustache. He must have spent a lot of time in the sun, and the tan looked good on him. Much of his forehead appeared lighter than the rest of his face, evidence he wore a Stetson most of the time. The fine lines fanning out from the corner of each eye revealed that he squinted against the blazing sun, and they only enhanced his good looks.

He wasn't dressed like a cowboy, but as he walked down the stairs, he had the bowlegged gait of a man who spent most of his life on the back of a horse. His luxuriously thick, dark hair looked wet. It was slicked back, but separate locks were pulling into strong waves as they dried.

For some unexplainable reason, Esther felt drawn to him. Her fingers tingled with the desire to brush back an errant curl that had drooped over his strong forehead. She had never felt this way about any man.

For a moment, she held her breath in wonder. His most arresting feature, his eyes, shone a clear, icy blue. When his gaze met hers, something passed between them, a feeling both exciting ... and disturbing. As if they were connected somehow. Uncomfortable, Esther quickly looked away.

What in the world is wrong with me? Maybe it was because all her close friends had husbands, and she wanted one, too. Why did some stranger affect her this way? Esther felt relieved when Gerald and Linda arrived at that moment, and the four of them went into the dining room. She tried to dismiss the man from her thoughts as she followed her brothers and sister-in-law to their table.

Jac stopped halfway down the stairs. *What just happened?* Needing something to eat, he was going to the restaurant, minding his own business, when a vision of loveliness entered the hotel. Her beauty almost took his breath away. He had seen those new Gibson Girl calendars. She looked as if she just stepped out of one. Petite with curves in all the right places, her delicate features proclaimed class and character. Her red hair formed into a poufy style that had a cluster of curls nestled in the crown. Curly tendrils brushed her cheeks and neck where he wished he could place his lips. He could just imagine how the silky strands would feel wrapped around his finger. *I have to stop thinking like that!*

When she looked into his eyes, he felt something he'd never experienced before. Something that crackled through the room, almost sucking out all the air, leaving them nothing to breathe. He wondered if anyone else sensed it. He glanced around, but no one paid either of them any attention.

He couldn't seek a relationship yet. If he found one, or one found him, it would have to be a relationship with no strings attached, at least until his mission was over. He wasn't ready to settle down, and that girl had strings dangling off her so long they would really hogtie a man.

Jac almost turned around and went back to his room, but just then his stomach rumbled so loud he was sure everyone within a mile radius could hear it. He had to get something to eat. If only she and her companions hadn't gone into the dining room.

Jac continued toward the open doorway of the restaurant. His attention went immediately to the table where the woman and her friends sat. At least they were on one side of the room. He would just choose a table on the other side, and that would be the end of it.

With that decision made, he looked around the room for an empty table. He hadn't thought this town would have many people staying at a hotel, but in the restaurant most of the tables were occupied. Finally, he spied an empty one on the exact opposite side of the room from where the woman and her party sat. With the large dining area separating them, he could almost forget she was there.

However, when Jac walked across the room and selected a place to sit, he chose a chair that gave him a clear view of the beauty. He couldn't take his eyes off her until the waitress came for his order. He chose pot roast. It had been a long time since he had anything like that to eat. And he could tell from the mingled delicious smells wafting from the kitchen that hot rolls would arrive with his meal. In a place like this, there should be plenty of butter to melt into them. Soft white bread tasted better than the hardtack he carried in his saddlebags. He'd eaten enough hardtack these last few weeks to last a lifetime. His mouth watered just thinking about the meal he'd have tonight.

When the waitress went to get him a cup of coffee, he glanced toward the table where the vision of loveliness sat. Her every move was grace itself. Her dainty hand fluttered like a butterfly on its way to pick up her glass of water. When she turned to speak to the man on her left, she cocked her head toward him, revealing a profile that looked just like his mother's cameo. It was the only piece of jewelry he still owned that had belonged to her, and he valued it. He kept that cameo locked in a safety deposit box of the bank where his savings resided. Someday, he planned to give it to his wife ... if that day ever came.

"Here's your coffee, sir." The waitress set the steaming china cup and its saucer in front of him. He glanced up at her, almost sorry for the interruption, but his stomach gave a louder growl than before.

"I guess it's a good thing your meal is almost ready." The woman gave him a friendly smile.

"Yes." He lifted his cup toward her. "Thank you." At least, he was able to remember his manners.

He took a sip. Jac liked his coffee hot and strong, but not too strong. This coffee tasted wonderful. He set the cup down and looked back across the room.

Why torture himself this way? That woman had an escort. She might be married. But somehow, he didn't think she was. He had spent too many years watching people not to know the signs. Nothing indicated that the couple was married or even romantically involved.

The other couple at the table was another matter. Marriage screamed from every look and touch they shared.

"Are you ready for this?" The waitress set his meal

in front of him.

"Yes, bring it on." Jac smiled up at her.

Steam rose from the plate, bringing with it the pleasant aroma of roast beef. Surrounding the meat, a generous helping of rich brown gravy covered carrots and potatoes. His stomach growled again. This time louder. He hoped the group across the room couldn't hear it.

The waitress giggled as she walked away.

The first bite almost melted in his mouth. *Heavenly!* He chewed slowly, savoring the almost-forgotten flavors that mingled and reminded him of just how much he gave up to bring the Grahams to justice. He hoped that, at last, this was the town where he would arrest the man and his daughter or daughters.

The waitress returned with a dish of butter and a basket of hot yeast rolls. "Don't forget to save room for dessert. Tonight, we have apple pie."

Could life get any better than this? Jac took his time eating. He wanted to enjoy every minute of this good food. But more than that, he decided to just relax and enjoy watching the beautiful woman. Who knew? Someday he would be ready to settle down. Someday maybe he would find a woman much like her to marry.

When they were seated at a table in the dining room, Esther decided to forget what had happened in the hotel lobby and concentrate on her brothers and sister-in-law. "Well, Linda, I guess it's nice for you to go out without the children."

Linda smiled at her. "Oh yes, it's a real treat. It was good of you and Allen to plan this little celebration."

"Actually, it was Marie's idea." Allen picked up his linen napkin and spread it across his lap.

"Why didn't she come with us?" Linda smiled at her.

Esther laughed. "You mean besides the fact that she's keeping your children for you?" Linda nodded. "I offered to keep them at the apartment, but Marie thought it would be special for Gerald's brother and sister to take the two of you out."

Allen picked up his fork and absently turned it over and over in his hands as if checking its weight. "She really likes having Olivia and Stephen at the house." He put the fork down and cleared his throat. "She's hoping we'll have a little one ourselves pretty soon. I told her it has only been a few months since we married, and I enjoy our time together, but I'm eager for our own children, too."

Gerald patted his wife's hand. "Well, we have an announcement to make, and you two are the first to hear it."

Linda blushed and looked down at the table in front of her. "We are going to have another baby."

Esther got up, hurried around the table, and hugged her. "I'm so happy for you." When she passed Gerald on the way back to her chair, she hugged him, too. "And I'm happy for you, big brother."

The waitress came to their table. "What are we all having tonight?"

"This calls for steaks." Allen looked at each of them in turn. "Unless you want something else. We have a lot to celebrate."

When the waitress left, conversation flowed around the table, but Esther's attention was divided.

That cowboy sat across the room. She could see him when she turned to talk to Allen. He seemed to be enjoying his food, but once in a while, she felt his gaze on her. Why did he do that? It made her very uncomfortable. Even though she enjoyed having this time with her relatives, she couldn't forget the man or the impression he made on her when they stood in the lobby.

Esther knew it didn't make any sense. She felt drawn to him, even here in the dining room. She noticed when his coffee arrived. While he ate his roast beef and hot rolls, she looked at him from time to time. He had perfect table manners, not like most of the cowboys she had seen in the past. She didn't want him to catch her watching, so she peeked at him out of the corner of her eyes to make sure it wasn't when he was looking at her.

She was acting like a desperate old maid. Just because everyone else was married, it didn't mean anything was wrong with her life, did it? Her business was successful, and she had a comfortable home, good friends, and a family who loved her.

But they weren't a husband and children. She felt that deep longing she'd harbored since she became an adult. She wanted to be loved by a man the way her father loved her mother. The way Gerald loved Linda. The way Allen loved Marie. The way Marie's brothers

Oliver and Leonard loved their wives. She wanted a home of her own, not just an apartment above a store ... and she wanted children. To feel their arms around her neck. To have them call her, *Mother*.

Oh yes, Esther wanted all those things more than she could tell anyone. But that cowboy across the dining room wasn't the man to give them to her.

The End Sample
of
Lena Nelson Dooley's
Esther's Temptation

Books by Kristin Holt

www.KristinHolt.com

And while you're there, please sign up for my
newsletter:

www.KristinHolt.com/newsletter

*Receive a free novella, exclusively for Newsletter
Subscribers! Be the first to hear about new releases,
sales, and subscriber-only extras.*

Learn more about Kristin Holt's Series:

HOLIDAYS IN MOUNTAIN HOME

SIX BRIDES FOR SIX GIDEONS

THE HUSBAND-MAKER TRILOGY

PROSPERITY'S MAIL-ORDER BRIDES

And **collaborative works**

USA TODAY Bestselling Author

KRISTIN HOLT

Hi! I'm Kristin Holt, *USA Today* bestselling author of Sweet Romances (G- and PG-rated) set in the Victorian American West.

While secular in nature, my titles are "Appropriate for All Audiences" and appeal to selective readers and fans of Christian historical romance.

I write frequent articles (see the link at the top of my home page: www.KristinHolt.com) about the **nineteenth century American west—every subject of possible interest to readers**, amateur historians, authors... as all of these tidbits surfaced

while research
ing for my books. I also blog monthly at Sweet
Americana Sweethearts:
SweetAmericanaSweethearts.Blogspot.com

I love to hear from readers! Please drop me a note:
www.kristinholt.com/contact-kristin

Or find me on Facebook. You're invited to join a
fantastic Facebook group for authors and readers of
Western Historical Romances, Pioneer Hearts. You'll
find links to both of these, along with all of my social
media links, on my website, particularly on the "About
Kristin" page (the link is in the footer of
www.KristinHolt.com), or if you'd like, use this web
address (url): **www.KristinHolt.com/about-
kristin-2** (just remember Kristin is spelled with two i's,
and is "e-free.")

Thank you for reading *Unmistakably Yours*. I'd love to
hear your thoughts about this novel (or any others
you've read).

Warm Regards,

Kristin